THE
OUROBOROS
KEY

PATRICIA LESLIE

ODYSSEY
BOOKS

Published by Odyssey Books in 2014
ISBN 978-1-922200-33-4

www.odysseybooks.com.au

National Library of Australia
Cataloguing-in-Publication entry

Author: Patricia Leslie
Title: The Ouroboros Key / Patricia Leslie
ISBN: 978-1-922200-33-4 (pbk)
ISBN: 978-1-922200-34-1 (ebook)
Dewey Number: A823.4

Cover designed by Elijah Toten

To Craig, Cheyne, Kalin & Toni;
dream big and be prepared for winding roads,
but never ever give up.

PROLOGUE

MESOPOTAMIAN VALLEY—ZAGROS MOUNTAINS
PRE-SUMER, C. 5000 BC

Deep below the earth, in the roots of a mountain, time stills.

Turns.

And begins anew.

Niches gouged out of compacted earthen walls lead down to a rounded wooden door. Plain, aged and cracked, its hinges creak as it opens.

Candles in the niches splutter, fighting for survival. Burning dust and charred wax sour dead air. Light spills down walls to the floor and no further, leaving gaps of blackness until the next candle and the next.

Around the door, crude symbols have been carved; stick figures, two-legged and four, snouted and beaked, dance and kill in a glory of blood, stick animals dying or dead at their feet. Between and beneath the simple pictures swirls and twirls and curls pulsate, living lines stretching outward and upward, snake-like into the primitive world above. Lines that glow red as the first tree roots are reached and then hot as they leech out into open air and space.

Above meets below and the world is changed forever.

The round door leads to a round room. Fire burns in its center, a shallow well dug into the earth to contain it. Even still, flames lick the ceiling and cast out darkness with burnished light. This is the birthing room of creation, the foundry of Life and Law. As a boudoir it is basic in appearance, its walls cloaked not with the rich red of velvet but the living color of fire and blood. Its bed is the earth, its wine the pure water of springs eternal.

Its walls are covered in intricate circular designs, patterned hands, coiled snakes, knotted vines, fish and birds, water and cloud-filled skies. The murals lead to a tree opposite the door with stars for blossoms and a spider's delicate web for its roots.

Leaning against the wall, ends resting on the trunk of the glittering tree, are four wooden branches, long and straight but still with the odd leaf and notch, and a drip or two of sap. The fire throws deep shadows across the neatly cut poles and renders them almost invisible.

Lost in sleep, the two occupants of the room are ignorant of the world above. Their skin glows with the heat from the fire and the sweat of their own exertions. Marks on their flesh that days ago were powerful symbols are now nothing more than ash smears on dirty skin. They have been a week in the cave, creating and building. This is their last day, the day of Sealing and of Beginning.

One of the figures stirs; a soft sigh escapes tired lips. The woman rolls away from her lover and stretches. She stands, sniffs the heady perfume of lovemaking, and slowly begins to walk around the fire. It's already dying, soon will be nothing but embers. A box with carved sides sits neglected nearby, a black and silver cloak thrown over it and a dish on top of that. The dish had been overflowing with fruit on the couple's arrival, now empty it has another purpose to serve. She takes it and returns to the fire, squatting down as close to the flames as she can and starts to sing, the empty dish in the dirt between her feet. With this gift the final steps of their journey are taken.

Words fade on a slow hiss and the man wakes. Joints pop as he stretches. He smiles with pleasure, watching her through slitted eyes as she stands and sways into her lonely dance. Orange light glowers and encircles her thighs, living shadows grasp at her heavy breasts.

The fire has shrunk to reveal a red-gold cauldron decorated in a similar fashion to the tunnel walls. He has not seen the living lines outside the door, will not see them. They began to grow when the door closed on his arrival and will fade when the door reopens for his departure. He gazes at the pot and sees not dreadful beauty but earthly meaning, lines of power and blood.

Somewhere in the world above him the first Ky-in is being born; his child. At the end of this day he would hold the boy in his arms and give him the gift he and the woman had spent a week creating. A gift that has the capacity to bring unity to a people divided, but only through the actions of the Ky-in.

The singing lulls. The woman stands transfixed, a dish glowing in her hands, a haze of sparkling dust rising from the container to shroud her in silver light. Tickles of desire torment him. He sighs, forces the desire down and concentrates instead on the next step in the ceremony.

Starfire … the essence of male and female combined; the ultimate recipe and the final seal on their creation. He stands and joins the woman by the fire.

"It is time." His voice is rough from sleep and sex. She nods, her lips parting to accept the silver light into her body.

He feels a little uncertain now that they are so close to the end. Will their actions be the gift they intend or a burden to his son's blood?

"The burden is of service only," the woman breathes. "An unknown secret locked inside the soul of the Ky-in until needed."

"I know," he apologizes. He'd forgotten that the woman knew his every thought. "I see the millennia ahead, a time when we will be but a shadow of memory, and I worry."

The woman locks her gaze with his. "A shadow is all we ever were, all we need to be. There will always be someone willing to risk the dark to find us, someone with the eyes to look past the glare of the light and there will always be the Ky-in waiting to serve."

"But to serve what? How will he know?" the man persists.

"The Ky-in serves Life as do you and I, and the knowledge will be in every fiber of its being passed down from parent to child until the Ky-in is reborn."

He stares into the woman's eyes, dark pools unmarred by light, deep with knowledge and power. He'd been lost in those eyes since first stepping foot into the room, wading at the edge until venturing into the unseen depths the night before to consummate their creation. Their love was more than his soul could bear; bones ached, head throbbed, lips parched without her to satisfy his thirst. Fingers quivered with the need to touch. Her skin was so soft and cool. O Blessed Mother, how he wanted her.

"Honor there is," she whispers, "in sacrifice and service. The Ky-in requires both to be born and his time is nearly here. We must begin."

"Yes," he agrees, fists clenched. "We must."

The light of the Starfire covers the woman from head to toe. She leans toward the man and kisses him, a dry wing of touch. The dish is between them and he places his hands underneath, his fingertips brushing across her stomach. As their lips meet for the last time, charged with the passion of nine days, the tingle of power washes through him, burning his senses until the pain of his victory and loss threatens to explode his heart. His sobs are loud in the stillness of the cavern. He and his line are charged with the service, she and hers the sacrifice. Both will be united for eternity. He will not see her again.

The couple part and begin to pour the Starfire into the cauldron. The cauldron sizzles as the liquid bubbles, steam billowing and the room is filled with the aroma of the woman's power. He feels faint, dizzy, as the air around him crackles and the room seems to shift. He digs his toes into the dirt floor and locked his knees against the tilt of vertigo, searching for balance as nausea turns his stomach.

Beside him the woman is whispering words that ring bells deep inside him. He closes his eyes to listen and the vertigo leaves him. The room is hot and he feels smothered, enclosed inside the earth, the bells sounding like a song he should know but doesn't. His heart thumps inside his chest in time to the melody and then he realizes that the song, too, is a heartbeat, the sound of the earth as it turns.

"Mother," he calls, and feels himself being embraced, being loved in the strong arms of She who holds and loves all in the earthy palm of Her hand. He will surely miss the grounding of that touch.

He opens his eyes to blue sky, a black bird circling far above, a field of long grass and wild flowers spreading out beneath him. The bird swoops down, landing on the low branches of a tree, its bark splotched and stained, marked forever with the lines of power. Wise raven eyes stare and wait.

The man sits, groggy and tired, but uplifted. He ignores the bird and the tree, and looks down at his fist still clenched. His hand burns and he spreads his fingers. There is a rustling in the grass. He glances up to see that the bird has come closer. It clicks its beak and inclines its head in curiosity.

"This is it," the man tells the raven. The raven lifts its head and opens its powerful beak to crow in triumph.

Nestled in the man's protective grasp is the gift, a circle of metal that changes color as he moves his hand, at once gold and then silver, and then something else he doesn't recognize at all. The band is a serpent's body turned on itself and not quite small enough to fit over his finger. He closes his fingers over the gift.

The bird crows again and spreads out its wings, flapping them through the grass and raising a cloud of springtime dust and flower petals. It raises slowly, the man feeling the beat of wings on his face and in his hair, and then it takes flight, cawing and circling. It sounds like a child's cry and the man knows that his son has been born. He rises to his feet, an elegant figure in the tatters of once fine raiment, and follows the bird as it flies toward the horizon. Bolts of lightning arc between sky and earth joining the two in dazzling lines that remind him of the woman's cauldron. And the woman's keening song.

A bad omen, he worries. A storm on the day of the Ky-in's birth. Then he shrugs the gloom away. He isn't without a certain amount of power himself.

Enki walks on.

This isn't the end, but the beginning.

Deep beneath Enki's feet the round door splinters, cracks and buckles. The stick figures crumble to dust on the tunnel floor. Dank air has turned frigid. The candles are extinguished. Only the fire inside the room offers illumination, its flames dying as the woman had known they would once the man had departed. Her time is nearly finished but her work is far from done. She reaches for one of the wooden poles and holds it over the flames, forging, creating as she had done with the gift. Working quickly, singing the words that will transform the branches into staffs, burning into them the law that will one day unlock the power of the serpent ring, she ignores the changes around her.

Her skin is growing darker, motley in the shimmering light, and thicker. It requires great effort now to move her arms, and her feet have rooted themselves into the earth, her body lengthens; changes shape.

When the last staff is finished and all four sit fastened together to form a cross over the glowing cauldron, the woman smiles with satisfaction. The key is complete.

The fire fades, the door and the tunnel beyond have collapsed. She'd heard the birth cries of Enki's son on the echoing call of the messenger some time before, felt the change as the gift was given and laughed with joy as the Ky-in within the newborn child awakened.

She coils her elongated body around the still-warm cauldron and fills the room with her drowsy girth. She whispers a single, sibilant word and the key flashes with blue light, separates and vanishes. Her eyes close and her tongue flicks across her dry lipless mouth. Her body expands as she breathes in deeply and relaxes. Her work is done. Time to sleep.

Tiamet dreams of children.

1

Footsteps crunched through the patchy undergrowth that covered the prehistoric ruins of Chaco Canyon. Crumbly rock, twigs and leaf litter disintegrated into sand with each step. Lean, moleskin-clad legs mingled with the stands of desert brush, pausing where two bushes intertwined to ease their way through the sharp branches. Woodhens squawked and scrambled across the rocks in a flurry of feathers and dust. Wings raised and beak open, an irate hen bailed up the intruder, alternately protesting and pecking at the scuffed leather boot protruding from the dry grass and bushes.

"Sorry," Dan Tenney said, backing away and taking a dozen steps to the left onto bird-free rocks. The angry protests of the birds quieted only after he squatted down on the rough surface and was still. Dan watched and listened as the noise gave way to peace and the whirring of dragonflies.

"Damn birds," he muttered under his breath, pushing his faded Stetson back. He removed the lens cover from his camera, blew a speck of dust from the shutter release and twisted to aim at the disturbed nest. The hen looked out from the grass, glaring at the suspicious figure, then pulled her head in, fluffed out her feathers and attended to her chicks.

Dan left her in peace and turned the camera back to the horizon and the sunrise he'd come to see. The camera spanned the sky, pale wisps of cloud stretched across its expanse, gray in places where night still touched them, glistening in others where a white sun already streamed light and warmth across the earth. Streaks of indigo and blue, bleached by the dawning sun, backlit the distant hills and Dan thought of his mother. "She'd love this," he said, soft words in the quiet sunrise.

He could almost hear the squeak of the wind vane, old even when he was little, spinning on an angle above the porch back home. He remembered getting ready for a new day's adventure. His mother making sure his bootlaces were tight and using a bandanna to keep hair from his face. Her lips, thin while she worked, broadened into a satisfied smile when she finished and puckered up for a sneak-kiss on his freckled nose.

Together, he and his mother had wandered far from the skinny cows his grandfather ran in the outer paddocks of their New Mexico ranch. They experienced the desert and life in equal measures. Dan had not realized how well her lessons had stuck until a few weeks ago when he had spent a weekend in the city with some old army mates. He'd hated every minute of it. Too crowded, too busy, and too much had changed between the four men. He had a photo on his bureau, buff young soldiers with carefree smiling faces. Kyle was in insurance or the stock market now, Dan wasn't sure which. Mike had shown up harried and with baby spit on his shoulder. Chad was the only one still in the service. He took his duty to country seriously.

Dan didn't fit in and had no desire to. The minute he returned to the ranch, late on the Sunday night, he stalled the engine of his beat-up truck and sat listening to and breathing in the desert. The only other person for miles had been Gran, waiting at the house. He loved the desert, loved not having a steady job, loved the clapboard ranch house and the truck, the hills and the loneliness of living in the middle of nowhere. He had learned a lot that weekend with the others, and the weeks since on his own.

Meg's son to the bone, his grandmother called him whenever he came within reach. She would rake her fingers through his shoulder-length dark hair and smile, lips stretching in a mixture of pride, concern and relief.

Dan raised the camera to his face and peered through the tiny window Meg had often called her little glimpse of the world. He grinned at the image of his mother that materialized. She was such a hippy with her long flowing hair and wild clothes. He was lucky he'd not been named Sky or Free.

She was dead now, missing on one of her adventures not long after Dan left home and the desert to join the army. Dan was given leave to help search, then to attend a memorial service in her honor, and finally, just days before shipping out, to settle her affairs. There was no will. Not that one was needed. Gran owned the ranch outright. All Meg had were her dreams, her vision, her son and the camera.

Dan pressed his finger on the shutter. The camera clicked and whirred, clicked and whirred. The relative quiet of the dawn encouraged the memories to roll on.

There'd been a letter waiting for him at the base posted the day before Meg had taken pack and camera into the wilderness, and vanished. A yellowed piece of paper with the words to an old lullaby scrawled across its fading lines, doodles of sleeping babies and birds filled the margin, a string of hearts crossed the bottom edge. It was signed "Megs" in the romantic loopy letters she used.

He angled the camera to catch the small animals and birds that were beginning to flit across the desert floor below his perch.

In the year since he'd left the army, he'd taken to pulling out Meg's camera and driving the hour or so to reach the Chaco ruins to capture the ancient dawn, their favorite time of day. The pictures would be grainy and probably over-exposed, and end up in the tatty shoebox under his bed, along with the camera when he was finished. But there was a serene enjoyment in hiking out to the monuments. If he went early enough, and he always did, he could sneak out further than the tourist track allowed, searching the sky for the coming sun, and lining up his shot. He heard his mother's voice as he peered through the imaginary "eye" that his two hands made.

"See the picture God has given you, Danny. Map the lines, the perspective, experience the color and the magic."

Dan readjusted his position and his knees creaked.

"Read God's plan, Danny. It's a beauty. The rocks, the sand, the sky … it's all laid out for us, better than any book." Meg Tenney loved nature with a passion. It was the only time she ever got religious with her son.

The camera clicked through half a roll of film, Dan listening and seeing as his mother had shown him, feeling, as his mother had, the earth vibrating with life.

This morning was the second time in the past week Dan had been out to the prehistoric villages. One of the kivas, a partially underground structure left behind by the ancient Puebloans, had caught his attention two days ago. Encircled by worn rocks and small compared to the others, dustier and less interesting to tourists, it sat at the far edge of the ruined village. Sagebrush replaced several of the hand-hewn bricks and the hole in the roof had widened as the walls crumbled and cracked with age. No one but the local wildlife had been inside for years. Dan had leaned over the doorway and stared at the dirt floor below, absent of any booted prints, and not entered. A fleeting memory of having been in this spot some time before sent a chill through him and he'd backed away, not stopping until he'd passed the circle of stones. A raven flew low over his head, shrieked, and landed in the sage. After that, he'd almost run. He hadn't planned on returning.

Black birds and crumbling bricks crowded his dreams that night. So vivid he'd woken with the sure knowledge that during the night some part of him had been sitting by a fire inside the kiva. A pot of water boiled in the flames and smoke streamed from the burning wood. A stranger sat beside him, talking as if they were old friends. The dream ended in laughter.

It was the first time in weeks Dan hadn't woken up shivering with dread. Giving up on sleep, Dan had pulled on his jeans and a tee-shirt, and tip-toed out the back door, boots tucked under one arm and the camera swinging from his neck. The truck started third go, regular as clockwork, lurched to the end of the drive and chugged passed ranches and through desert, and along the historical park's neatly tarred tourist road. The sky was starting to gray out by the time he reached the trail leading up the mesa wall and he decided to put the kiva off a little longer to take pictures of the dawn.

Now the voice in his dreams echoed through his mind. He sighed and prepared to move on. His grandfather had spoken to him only once about the images and voices plaguing his sleep. Gruff and spare, the old man had confided that his own mother had been so gifted.

"Listen. Most times the dreams'll be rubbish. Young boys got lots of big thoughts rollin' 'round their head. But you got to listen always, 'cause sometimes it'll be the spirits an' they get mighty pissed when you don't pay 'em no mind."

Dan didn't like what his grandfather had said and he didn't really believe in it. But he couldn't ignore it. His mother had eased his worries with stories, long walks and lots of hugs, but that wasn't going to happen this time. Dan was all grown up. His mother was long dead. He had to face the dreams alone.

Again the woodhen squawked and Dan lowered his camera to look across at the nest. It was then that Nick Somers stepped into his life. Rocks slid from behind, gravel and dried wood crunched beneath a heavy footfall, and Dan forgot both birds and dreams.

"You a photographer, a hermit or just plain lost?"

Dan nearly dropped the camera. "Shit!"

"Sorry to interrupt."

Dan turned to see a pair of denim legs and earth-stained hiking boots standing behind him. "What?" He struggled to his feet, off-balance with the surprise of finding he had company. "That's not what I meant. Where the hell did you come from?" He squinted up at the man, studying his face for a moment before looking past him. The stranger was alone and Dan relaxed with relief.

The man, his face shaded by a purple Minnesota Vikings cap, grinned and jerked his thumb back toward the main tourist trail. "Down there," he answered. "Figured I'd have the place to myself for a few hours. That your truck in the parking lot?"

Dan slung the camera strap over his shoulder and wiped his hands down his thighs before resting them on his hips. "Yeah, it is. This area's off limits to tourists, y'know. You'll get kicked out if you're caught." He dragged his gaze back to the man's face and noticed the tired lines that creased outward from eyes and mouth. Straw-blond hair poked from beneath the cap and disappeared under the upturned collar of an old college letters jacket. Thin beneath the jacket if the gauntness of the face was anything to go by.

The man's lips shifted into a smile caught somewhere between not quite happy and wryly amused. "You're here."

"I work here."

"Well, I guess I'm caught then. You going to kick me out now?"

Dan thought about it. He'd like to. The man had shattered his morning quiet; only problem was that Dan didn't really work for the park. He was on the books sure enough, but only as a seasonal laborer and guide, and the season had been over for two weeks.

"This time you're off the hook."

They grinned at each other, the stranger's mouth settling into a friendlier shape that altered the hard edges of his face into something more approachable. Dan decided right then that he liked the man and stuck his hand out.

"I'm Dan Tenney."

The man looked from Dan's face down to his hand and back again before he returned the gesture and they shook hands.

"Nick Somers." Nick's gaze stayed on the move, staring past Dan and at the dawn he was now missing.

Dan turned to the horizon and the white sun breeching distant hills. "She's a beauty, isn't she?"

"That she is."

"My mother used to call it 'God's Picture.'" Dan heard Nick shift beside him, felt the man direct his eyes from the landscape to him. He snuck a look. Yep, the guy was staring at him.

"Used to?"

He felt like he was back in boot camp. Somers had the same all-seeing hawkish gaze as his old drill sergeant. His back automatically straightened, chest puffed out a little. He'd lost a lot of weight since his discharge but he was still in pretty good shape.

"She died."

2

The word "died" triggered something in Nick. He felt foolish. The younger man had straightened out of his casual slouch into a tense and wary posture. Ex-military for sure, he noted. If his wife were here, she'd kick his ass and tell him to lighten up. It would be worth a thousand kicks to have her back though. He let go of his officer's face, as Kari had called it, and let through some of the emotion he preferred to keep buried.

"Sorry."

"Was a while back." Dan shrugged and let his shoulders fall naturally.

Nick looked at the camera for the first time. Not a bad set up. "She a photographer too?"

"Yeah. Better than I'll ever be."

Nick slotted the guy into the "tree-hugging cowboy" type. He knew this was someone Kari would like, from the dusty hat to the washed-out tight jeans and worn at the heel boots. Looked okay to him. Clever eyes, he thought. Honest too. Kari's opinion always mattered, even when she wasn't around. He blinked away memories and ghost voices.

Dan watched him, the camera turning circles in his hands. "What are you doing so far off the trail?"

Nick tried not to remember the last time he was here. "This was one of my wife's favorite places." He waved a hand at the vista. "She loved New Mexico, all this … earth." Nick recognized the look in the younger man's eyes, an understanding of loss, and tucked away compassionate in the memory file now tagged "Tenney". "She died a few months ago." He shrugged one shoulder and inclined his head to his backpack. If he kept his movements minimal perhaps the pain wouldn't show. "Wanted me to scatter her ashes in the desert."

"I'm sorry." Dan shifted from one foot to the other, his face half-hidden by the shadow of his hat. "I know a place you might like. It's … well, it's special."

Nick had been putting off dealing with Kari's request for months.

Chaco's Aztec Monuments was just one of the places he'd visited in the last week. But nothing had felt right so far. What would one more hurt? He felt comfortable with the man. Kari would like him. That was enough.

"Okay. Show me."

Dan's answering smile confirmed the decision. A flash of white on the tanned face, it was a smile that reached to his eyes and beyond.

Nick followed him through the bushes and maze of rocky paths. It wasn't far. He figured less than a mile. Hidden by head-high scrub and a scattering of pinon trees, the kiva was overshadowed by a fat finger of rock.

"Found this place just the other day," Dan said. "No one comes here. Not even marked on the map. Think your wife'd like it?"

"Yeah. I think she would." Nick looked at the dry bushes, the earth and crumbling rocks in shades of yellow and rusty red. Kari had painted their house in these same shades, rich and warm. "Can we go in?"

"Doorway's up top. You can get up round the side there." Dan pointed to a jumble of rocks and hand-hewn bricks. Standing only a few feet from the wall, the kiva was hard to distinguish from the landscape surrounding it. "Just be careful. Kiva's been here a long time."

"Thought these things were banned from wandering tourists?" He knew they were and if he were with anyone else he'd make no attempt to go further.

"We're not wandering tourists. We're followin' a path."

Nick searched around. "What path?"

But Dan had already climbed up and was lowering himself inside. Nick followed, leaning over the hole to watch the young photographer drop with a light thud and disappear into the shadows.

A cricket chirped and birds warbled as he sat, feet dangling in the weak shaft of sunshine that lit the way down. He twisted out of his pack, shoved his cap into one of the outer pockets and dropped the lot into the hole. It made no sound and when Nick glanced in to check, only a lone strap could be seen. He gripped the ragged roof of the kiva and followed his gear. Eyes blinking in the gray dust rising around him, Nick held back a sneeze. He waited for his eyes to adjust, and heard the click and whirr of a camera.

"Not enough light for that."

"You're haloed," Dan said. "Just enough."

Light dribbled in through the cracks in the wall but did little to break through the gloom. Nick struck a match and held it high. Walls that had not seen light in an eon appeared out of the darkness, smoke-stained and bare.

The light flickered and died. Nick struck another match and walked around the small space. "Weren't these used for religious purposes?"

"Some were," Dan answered. "This one's a bit small."

There had been a fireplace once. Half-covered now in years of dust and wind-blown debris from the desert outside were rocks that circled the spot waiting for the next fire to be lit. Dan cleared away some of the rubbish, piled the woodier pieces together in the center and tucked a handful of dead leaves and grass into the gaps. "Light this," he said, nudging Nick's leg. "I don't think the spirits will mind."

Nick twisted around, eyebrows raised, then saw Dan's work, shook the match in his hand until it was out and knelt beside him. "Thanks," he said and lit a third match. "Saves my fingers."

He glanced around. "How're you planning on getting us out of here?"

"Well, we could jump, or …" He jerked a thumb to the edge of the firelight's reach. "Pile up a couple of rocks and climb out. The people that lived here would have had a ladder. Don't imagine it'd still be layin' around just for us."

"Don't imagine so," Nick agreed. He reached for his pack and unzipped it. The container holding Kari's ashes was wrapped in her favorite shawl, a soft strip of velvet and silk he'd bought for her on their honeymoon, and nestled in the folds of a thick towel for protection. He pulled aside the toweling and lifted the shawl-covered urn. Inside were the last remains of the woman he loved. He still couldn't quite believe it. She didn't feel gone.

Nick dropped broken twigs into the flame and sighed as if he'd made a momentous decision.

One more stick and Dan started to talk. "My granpa died when I was twelve an' we buried him under his favorite sitting place at our ranch. My mother planted a Palo Verde tree and scattered flowers on his grave. Gran said a cactus would have been better." He took a deep breath and grinned. "Prickly old man he was. Anyway, we each said a few words, sat around for awhile thinkin' about him and how things would be different and such."

His voice lightened as he recalled that day. "Meg, that's my mom, brought a picnic lunch … and then we left, but we never said goodbye. 'He isn't dead,' she'd said. 'He's in the wind and the rain and the stars. He's in every nail and plank of wood in the house that he built, every fence paling he erected, every hole he dug, every rock he shifted.' An' she was right, y'know. I can still hear him grumblin' every time I do something stupid or feel his approval when I get somethin' right. Still with us and always will be … in here." He touched his chest above his heart. "It's hard when they leave."

"What about your mother?" Nick had never wanted to talk about this before, still didn't. But there was something in Dan's story that spoke to him. The slow drawl and husky voice reached in and knocked on doors Nick had been avoiding since Kari was first diagnosed with cancer.

"She went out walkin' one day and never came back." Dan's voice tightened, the words clipped. Nick understood. This loss was harder to deal with. "Had a memorial service in town. Me and Gran went out to the Palo Verde for a picnic, but we never got to bury her. I was in the army then too, things were different."

Nick nodded. "Yeah, they often are."

Dan stood, obviously embarrassed that his mother's death still affected him as much as it did. He cleared his throat and started piling up a few rocks beneath the doorway. "I'll wait outside. Take your time."

Nick listened again as Dan scrabbled his way out of the hole, closing his eyes to the shower of dust that marked his exit. Footfalls faded and he was left with the sound of the birds and crickets. He peeled away the layers of shawl and held it to his face, inhaling Kari's scent and remembering the last time she'd worn it, their last spring. They had a month at the beach to recover from the latest round of chemotherapy and to celebrate remission. The first few days they lay around the holiday cottage. Every day after that they walked along the cool sand, waves washing against them, sometimes talking, mostly not.

They made love in the sea, on the sand, in every room of the cottage, desperate each in their own way to take something of the other with them when they left.

Tears coursed Nick's face. Surely this pain was his heart splintering into a thousand pieces. The shawl muffled his sobs and he kept it to his face long after he'd stopped. He couldn't let go, he wouldn't let go. But he would go on. He knew that much.

The urn stood on the ground, catching the light now the sun was a little higher, and glinting like gold. Nick wrapped the shawl around his neck and reached for the urn.

He spread Kari's ashes at the base of the wall inside the ancient hut, beneath the sagebrush. "I'm not saying goodbye," he whispered.

Dan was sitting cross-legged on one of the standing stones when Nick came out, pulling the shawl from his neck, face solemn, eyes blurry with tears. He folded the shawl and pushed it into his backpack. The sun had risen much higher while he'd been in the kiva. It was going to be a hot day.

"Thanks."

Dan passed across a small paper sack and they shared a paltry breakfast of Trailmix.

"What now?" Nick asked. "What am I supposed to do now?"

"How about lunch at my ranch an' a trip down to the Badlands?"

That sounded good. The Badlands were as stark and dried out as he felt. He took another handful of the Trailmix. "Little early for lunch, isn't it?"

Dan stood and hooked his camera and bag over his shoulder. "Not by the time we get to the ranch it's not."

3

The parking lot was crowded with SUVs, a bus and a couple of over-the-top motor homes. Dan's stomach had started fluttering at the kiva and barely stopped since. He'd recognized Nick's face in the match light, softer in the gentle glow of the tiny flame, the lines deeper. The fringe of his hair, free of the cap, had thrown a shadow across his eyes and as he dipped his head, Dan was taken back to his dream of the night before, the face before him as familiar now as his own reflection.

His throat was dry as he lit the fire, voice scratchy as he started to talk and make the connection he'd seen in the dream. He'd felt like he was interfering in something deeply private but the words flowed regardless. His throat was still dry. His stomach rolled. He'd felt another presence in the dark hut, more than one. He hadn't experienced that since he was a kid. Almost forgotten it. He shuddered, hiding the stab of fear with movement. Open the truck door. Pull out a map. Don't think about childhood mysteries. Don't think about dreams. He spread the map out on the hood of the truck.

"This is where the ranch is." He pointed at a blank spot near a patch of blue. "That's reservation land around there." The finger skirted blue and into green. "And the Badlands are down here." He looked up to see the other man nodding. "This yours?" Nick had sat his pack down on the hood of the dark blue SUV parked next to Dan's truck. "You can leave it at the ranch if you like. My heap might not look like much, sounds like even less, but she'll make it down to Bisti and back. No problems."

Nick didn't look convinced. He frowned and for a minute Dan thought he'd changed his mind. Probably still upset. Maybe he had other plans. It didn't really matter. His dreams were never wrong. He knew they were meant to be friends, whether they went off exploring this afternoon, or not. Nick put his hands on his hips as he inspected the truck.

"Mine'd be more comfortable."

"You got me there," Dan agreed with a grin and a duck of his head.

His truck was no smooth ride.

"Let's do it. Hope you've got something better than Trailmix for lunch." Nick unlocked the SUV and dumped his gear inside.

"Sure," Dan answered. "I got a couple packs of 'Nuts Over Cherries' mix. Tastes great." He laughed at the groaned response and re-folded the map. This was going to be a good day. He could feel his body filling with the lightness of being only a truly good day brings. He crunched the truck into a better start than usual and led the way back to the ranch. His smile stayed beacon-bright all the way home.

Dan didn't have another nightmare for seven years.

4

They're on their way. Get out now!

Sweat beaded on Professor Irene Flemming's chest and trickled between her breasts.

"Holy Hannah!" She caught her bottom lip between her teeth, deleted the email off the system with trembling fingers, and shut down the computer. *Hurry up and close. Hurry up…* Heart racing, stomach churning, she left the machine to its own devices while she gathered what she needed. Personal items had been thrown in the trunk of her car earlier in the day, only last minute things were needed now: a spare notebook and pen, the journal she was part way through, her phone, and a book to read should she need it.

Her overstuffed pack weighed as heavy on her shoulder as her billowing worry did on her psyche. A last look around the study—a booklined sanctuary filled with a lifetime's collection of artifacts, journals, and cabinets jammed with notes—the computer finally off, and she switched off the lights. The most valuable of her possessions, her current research, was already hidden away in the basement. She turned on her heel, backpack swiping the keyboard with a crash, and headed for the garage. The one thing she treasured above every rare book in the library, above the sensitive documents she'd hidden from prying eyes, was packed safely in her old Mercedes Benz 200.

Irene locked the internal garage door behind her, moved to the open trunk of the car and dumped in the pack; not taking the time to close it off properly, a leather-bound and pressed notebook tumbled out, the pages covered in strange symbols and lines of her messy scrawl. She reached to gently push it back into the safety of the bag, but heard tires squealing on the street outside. A fast moving car coming closer, now slowing … Irene swallowed back a healthy lump of rising fear.

"They're here," she whispered with dry lips and reached further into the trunk for a flashlight. Her fingers folded over the aluminum shaft and she pulled it free before closing the trunk with a soft thud. She stepped back to the internal door and the light switch beside it. The garage fell dark as the approaching car slammed on its brakes, tires protesting, right in front of her house.

Ohmygod! She waited in the dark, clutching the flashlight to her chest as her eyes adjusted to the dim light. Three car doors opened and closed, and she hoped that meant only three intruders as she made her way to the waiting auto.

She heard thuds on the front door, deep muffled voices, and the smashing of glass as the men broke into the house.

Irene felt an edgy calm, as if she was the center of a brewing storm. She reached into the back seat and lifted her winter coat to feel underneath for the artifact hidden there. Reassured it hadn't mysteriously vanished, she tucked the coat over it once more and quietly closed the back door. The driver's door was still open and beckoning. She took a quick, deep breath, pushed the fear away, and risked a burst of low light to check her keys and fumble them into the ignition.

"This is ridiculous, just ridiculous," she told her keys as they finally slid into place.

Doors slammed inside the house. Voices shouted to each other in rising urgency. Irene used the light again to find the automatic switch for the garage door, pressed it, prayed for quiet, and turned the key in the ignition. The engine spluttered, caught its beat and grumbled to life.

The garage door was half-open.

Banging on the internal door heralded the arrival of the men and Irene's calm deserted her from one breath to the next. She shoved one foot on the clutch, threw the car into gear and pushed her other foot down on the accelerator.

The car clipped the garage door as it jerked forward, gears crunching. Irene ignored the high-pitched creak of reforming metal and the crash of the internal door finally opening. She heard their voices, deep and alarmed, heavily accented. The Mercedes swerved around the tail end of the car partially blocking the driveway, and left deep grooves in the lawn as she made her escape.

She crunched the gears again. "Please, please, please …" as the car gave a sickening pause, and broke out in fresh sweat as it lurched forward and settled into a faster speed than she'd ever driven before.

The rearview mirror showed four men, not three, running down the drive. Two of them stopped. The others went for their parked car. All of them looked huge, and very pissed off.

"I am so fucked." Irene turned the corner without slowing, her hands clenched tight to the wheel.

The scene in the mirror shifted to houses, night-shadowed trees and white street lamps. Irene saw a glimpse of her terrified face, hair disheveled, eyes wide; she didn't let go of her breath or switch on the headlights until she turned two more corners, and slowing only a little, joined a traffic-laden street.

She didn't start to calm down until she took the exit leading out of Denver and headed deep into the mountains.

5

Nick scribbled a word onto a yellow Post-It notepad. He'd aged in the handful of years since his wife's death. Lines that had been soft wrinkles throughout her illness had deepened with grief. His neck pinched painfully as he stretched and rose from his seat. He looked around his office as he twisted the kinks from his spine.

His business partner, Elliott Byrd, liked to describe the office décor as "shabby chic"—just a little more shabby than chic. But the rooms and secondhand furniture barely qualified for shabby. Décor was not the priority. The desks almost qualified as antique but the computers they held were top of the line. Behind one scuffed office door was the "equipment room" where Elliott stored his growing collection of electronic gadgetry and all the cables, chips, wires and tools to fix, adjust or rebuild whatever passed through his eager hands.

Nick had been in the private investigation business for going on six years, ever since Elliott had tracked him down in Atlanta and dragged his protesting butt halfway across the country to Denver to be his partner in the fledgling enterprise.

He'd allowed himself to be persuaded into joining Elliott's scheme and since that time the pair had built up a steady, if not quite booming, business that employed a handful of freelance staff—a very small handful. Simone Lang was one. British born and unflappable, Simone was a retired surveillance agent; rich enough not to actually need the work and bored enough to be counted on for odd hours and odder requests. Dan Tenney, camera in hand, was the occasional other. Sherrie, the receptionist, was the one and only permanent staff member.

With vertebrae popped neatly into place, Nick pulled the sticky note from the pad and walked out to the reception area of Byrd & Somers Inc. The dull walls had been brightened with a few framed prints and a vase of tall flowers that Sherrie replaced each Monday. An African Violet in a hand-painted terracotta pot sat on a small round table beside an umbrella bucket near the front door. Under the window nearby was a similar pot full of dirt and a stick that occasionally flowered. A frangipani, Sherrie had told him, when he'd asked why they were growing sticks. It had beautiful, creamy white flowers and a yellow center, when it could be coaxed into sharing its delicate beauty. Not often, both Nick and Elliott had noted, but Sherrie insisted the stick was worth the effort and tended it liked the exotic tree it was.

Nick glanced at the violet, thought it might need a little water, and turned his attention away from the office and back to his newest case and the note in his hand. Alisdar Finbar Shaw, known as Finn to his friends, believed the note might be a clue to the strange disappearance of his associate, one Professor Irene Flemming. Byrd & Somers Inc. had taken on the case a few days previously after the Denver P.D. had failed to find any trace of the woman. Finn's friends included Simone Lang.

Elliott, as usual, had commandeered Sherrie to help collect lunches so Simone played receptionist until they came back, taking over Sherrie's highly decorated desk and computer for the interim. One slim hand rested on a bright blue mouse, the other held a pen poised over a notebook. The occasional click of the mouse was the only sound in the open office area as she researched the missing professor's work, trying to find a clue somewhere that might explain why the professor had vanished.

The office was pleasantly quiet. Simone had turned Sherrie's radio off as soon as the receptionist had walked out the front door, a pleasant respite from the usual noise that followed the girl everywhere she went. Nick stood over Simone for a second, watching her work straight-backed and barely moving.

"How can you sit so long at that thing?"

"Hmmm?" The web browser flicked from page to page, slowed to let the cursor glide over a few lines before clicking on another link and moving on.

"Simone?" Nick leaned against the desk, bumping the keyboard to get her attention.

"Nicholas, did you want something?"

"Any calls?"

Simone reached across to the message pad and flicked over the blank top page, shaking her head. "Let's see, Elliott and Sherrie are still out. Dan did call, but didn't say anything I felt should be committed to paper. He's finished filling reports out at the precinct and is on his way to the gallery. He promised to be back here by three."

"He'd better be. I need to get down to Castle Rock by four. Did you finish the report on John Leary's recent activities?"

"As a matter of fact, yes." Simone gave a cool smile and pushed back from the desk to cross her legs, hands slipping from the keyboard to rest on the desk edge. "He and his secretary were quite active after hours. I swear Dan was blushing. That lens he talked you into buying has quite an effective zoom range; not a blurry pixel in sight. He does take a good photo, all the right angles." Her smile warmed as she spoke. "Mrs. Leary isn't going to be at all happy. I imagine this will be one set of family photographs that won't make it to the mantelpiece."

Simone's gaze wandered back to the computer screen, fingers crept back to the keys, but Nick didn't move. "Was there anything else?"

"I was just talking to your Professor Shaw. He's coming over shortly with some of Flemming's journals, wants you to take a look at them." He slapped the Post-It note onto the monitor. "Also mentioned something about the Sangreal. Seemed excited. Know what that is?"

"You know, he really does prefer to be called Finn. Professor sounds so stuffy and he's anything but stuffy." Simone pulled the note from the screen and read the single word. "Sangreal. Sounds familiar. Did he say anything else?"

"Nope."

"Finn would be the one to know. I wonder what he's thinking?"

"Talk that over with the professor … Finn, when he gets here. Meanwhile, see what you can find in here." He tapped the monitor. "I don't see what any of this Albigensi stuff the professor was into could have to do with her vanishing …"

"On the contrary, Nick. This is 'the stuff' where ancient mysteries can be found. Secret societies, historical cover-ups. Who knows what scandals we might unearth, perhaps what Professor Flemming might have come upon?"

Nick rolled his eyes at Simone's enthusiasm for unearthing scandals and returned to his office to call the soon-to-be unhappy wife of Mr. John Leary.

With Nick's departure, Simone returned to her research. She bookmarked the website she had open and typed in the new search request. *Sangreal …* She said it out loud a few times, playing with the syllables, and then whispered, lips moving silently over the vowels and consonants as the screen filled with lists. She clicked on the first one, and smiled.

"Of course!"

6

Dan left the downtown precinct in a fit of disgust. He hated paperwork of any kind and government paperwork the most. His hand and wrist ached from filling out forms. His head ached from trying to figure out what he should and shouldn't commit to paper.

"Stripped half a forest bare with all that paperwork," he grumbled to Simone over the telephone. "Complete waste of time. Next time Elliott needs someone to cover him on a case, he can damn well find someone else."

Simone laughed and commiserated. Then suggested he ask for a bonus. Dan started feeling better right away. He could use some extra money. His first photographic exhibition, co-hosted by two Denver photographers, was eating into his usually low financial needs.

Dan smiled. The big opening was just over twenty-four hours away. He couldn't quite get over the tumble of excitement every time he thought about it. Maybe he could get Elliott to part with some cash tomorrow night as well.

The incident that had Dan tied up at the police station for most of the morning hadn't been a normal occurrence. A simple stake-out of a client's home to catch a suspected stalker had turned into a major bungle.

In his briefing to Byrd & Somers Inc., the client, a Mr. Samuel Jones, had failed to mention that his personality, and business as it turned out, was anything less than stellar. A low-key case had, in the space of a few minutes, turned into a violent and confusing drug bust.

Dan had been caught in the middle. The handcuffs hadn't stayed on long, but he still remembered the coldness of the steel on his skin.

He rubbed his wrists and forced the memory away as he crossed the road to Nick's gray Ford Taurus, gleaming in the early winter sunlight. The SUV had been replaced a few years ago for the more discreet, slightly battered sedan. Nowadays, Dan's truck never went further than the fence line of the ranch back home. He had his eye on a replacement, a much smoother ride with the grunt to go as off-road as he liked. Maybe after the exhibition he'd have the cash to go ahead and buy it.

Dan opened the car door and sunk into the seat. Gran was arriving in the morning, determined to defy age and gravity to fly up and attend her grandson's first opening. He started the engine and joined the flow of traffic. Frowning, he thought about the hotel room he'd booked in her name. Maybe he'd go check it out one more time and have a word with the concierge. He'd wanted her to stay with him at Nick's place; there was plenty of room and Nick didn't mind an extra boarder for a few days. But she was determined to live it up in a hotel and make a real holiday out of the visit. He knew she thought of it as her last chance for an adventure. There was no denying the time.

Dan directed his thoughts back to the exhibition. He planned to spend a couple of hours helping out at the gallery before heading back to the office with Nick's car. Jai and Karl, his co-exhibitors, were already there. Dan rubbed his temples. There was so much to do. Collect the last few pieces from the framers, hanging, checking the catering, lighting, sound system. Damn. He slapped the steering wheel with the palm of his hand in annoyance. They all had to say a few words and he still hadn't written anything down. The only part of the whole event he wasn't looking forward to.

He gripped the steering wheel tighter and prepared to turn left. The gallery, a gutted and re-furbished boutique, was just around the corner. His stomach rumbled and Dan thought about lunch. He hadn't eaten since breakfast and that hadn't been much. A bowl of cereal shoveled down in between uploading digital photographs for Simone. He checked his mirror and noticed a beige Volvo creeping too close to the Taurus's rear end. The same car had been behind him for several blocks. He was sure of it. Traffic cleared and he made the turn, the car followed. He glanced in his side mirror. Suspicion tickled his spine. He looked for a space to park, ignoring the situation for the moment to concentrate on traffic. The street was busier than he expected. A few cars drove around him, their engines revving impatiently. There were no empty spaces. Maybe around the corner. Dan flicked on his indicator and looked over his shoulder for oncoming cars. The Volvo was still there.

When Dan moved out, his shadow came with him. When he turned the corner to drive around the block, it followed. He changed lanes to turn at the upcoming intersection. Traffic lights ahead changed to yellow and Dan gunned the engine, slipping through before they flashed red. The mirror and a blast of angry horns told him that whoever was following had done the same.

"Goddammit!" He fumbled in his pocket for his cellphone, but his jacket was tangled between body and seatbelt. Another quick look over his shoulder and Dan thought he saw the passenger of the car behind reach for a gun. "No way. No fucking way!" He shoved his foot down on the accelerator, turned the steering wheel hard to his left and shot into a narrow street he hoped would at least lead him away from traffic.

"Nick's always tinkering on this thing. Let's see how well she handles." He took another sharp turn and another.

The beige Volvo stayed with him all the way.

Dan sat slumped in the front seat of the Taurus. His head, resting uncomfortably on one shoulder, throbbed with pain. One minute he'd thought he'd lost his pursuers, the next he'd felt a nudge from behind, turned in his seat to see the Volvo, up close and ugly, and then the Taurus had come to an abrupt and painful stop. He had enough time to register the sound of squealing tires and grinding metal before he was thrown forward into the ballooning airbag. A huge lump was already forming just above his left temple where his head had smashed against the window on the last violent turn. His whole head felt like it was caught in a vice and his eyelids flickered until he could control them enough to keep them open, wincing at the fresh pain the effort produced. The side of his face ached and he could taste blood. He wiped his mouth with the back of his hand and stared at the red smear it left.

Blood on my hands. He blinked once and looked through the shattered windscreen, confused. Why did it seem so familiar?

Dan tried to open his door but it was stuck fast in the twisted metal of Nick's car. Fighting the numbness in his head and the pain everywhere else, he pushed out the cracked window and climbed through the space. Shards of glass fell from his clothes as he dragged himself through the small opening. He could hear it falling to the seat and floor and grinding under his boots as he moved.

Once free of the wreck he had to steady himself with one hand on the roof. Head spinning and knees threatening to give way, he tried to think what he should do next. He touched his fingertips to the lump on his head and winced.

Dan didn't hear car doors slamming or running footsteps coming up behind him. He'd forgotten about the Volvo. Rough hands pulled him away from the mangled vehicle. He fell to the ground with a gasp of pain and landed in a stagnant puddle of water on the side of the road. He looked down. Numbness was taking over. In the distance, he could hear their voices, feel them pulling at his clothes.

One of them had his wallet. "This isn't him!"

Dan could see blood on his hands.

"You idiots! Didn't you check to see who was in the fucking car first?"

Bloody fingermarks stained his blue shirt.

"Kill him!"

"Don't be a fool. Leave him …"

Dan had stopped listening. *Holy fuck! Run!* The two thoughts ran into each other as realization hit. His reaction was instant. He threw himself at the men that blocked his way, sending his fist into one face and a foot into another. The first two men went down and stayed down, a third turned in defense. He blocked Dan's next punch and got in one of his own to the injured man's ribs. Dan doubled over in pain, the dizziness in his head surging, ringing in his ears as he continued to act on fear and instinct. He drove his elbow into the other man's stomach. Dan heard the *whoompf!* of expelled air as the man staggered beside him. He brought a fist up to smash into his attacker's jaw, turned and ran.

A bullet burned the air past his head as the men gave chase.

Dan ducked and weaved as best he could, turned a sharp corner and ran into a dark, narrow lane. He stumbled into the shadows. The pain in his head worsened with every jarring step, dizziness threatened to drop him to the ground. He wiped at his eyes. Everything was blurry, pinpricks of light flashed on and off, his eyeballs felt icy cold.

When he heard his pursuers enter the lane he turned and watched them approach. He fumbled again for the phone in his pocket. A blaze of agony hit his shoulder as his fingers wrapped around the phone and pulled it free of his jacket. The phone clattered uselessly to the ground. Dan staggered backward, scanning the buildings around him. Everything was so familiar, unfolding around him like an old dream. He couldn't hear over the hot, heavy throbbing in his head. Dan slumped, no longer able to stay upright or keep his eyes open. And yet, he had the strangest feeling of having been through all this before.

A round face appeared in the basement window in front of him. Tatty hair framed grimy cheeks. Dan reached out thinking perhaps this strange man could help.

But the men from the Volvo had caught up with him at last and spun him around to face them. Dan braced for what he knew would happen next.

Obscenities were hissed. The two men traded insults with each other. Dan didn't care. He couldn't feel his legs any more. The only thing holding him up was one man's tight-fisted grip on his shirt, pushing him up against the building. His head hit the wall with a sickening thud. Tiny flashing lights in his eyes burst into brilliant flares and all went black.

7

Simone walked into Nick's office, high heels clicking on the hard floor, and handed him the photographs from her previous night's stake-out across the desk.

"Leary and his secretary hard at work." She sat down in one of two spare chairs, arched her back in a slight stretch, and watched Nick flick through the pictures, pausing on each one to raise an eyebrow or tighten his lips. "A lesson to be learned there, I'm sure."

Nick whistled at the last photograph, a full color exposé of Leary and his secretary on a desk. He could see why uploading them with Simone standing right next to him would have embarrassed Dan. His own cheeks were growing uncomfortably warm. "A lesson?"

Simone steepled her fingers together and inspected each polished nail. "When copulating with the secretary … always close the blinds." A glint of humor lit her dark eyes. "They always forget the blinds."

"Makes our job so much easier." Nick shuffled through the photos one more time, stopping again at the last, and then put them aside. Mrs. Leary was meeting him at The Grind Café in Castle Rock to see for herself. Perhaps they should have made the appointment more private. He looked at his watch and frowned.

"Dan back yet?"

"No, and before you ask, I haven't heard from him either," Simone answered. "He'll be grouchier than a grizzly with toothache by now."

Nick raised one eyebrow at both Simone's comparison and her perfect imitation of Dan's drawling accent, a stark contrast to her own worldly urbane mannerisms, before allowing the corner of his mouth to turn up in a smile. She was right. Dan hated paperwork.

Elliott sauntered in, a serious look on his face and his shaggy red hair a mess. Lunch had been over for a couple of hours. Sherrie's voice drifted in through the open door as she chatted with whoever happened to be on the other end of the phone. He ran his hand through his hair, scratched his scalp and let the hand fall to his side, taking a deep breath before clearing his throat. "Nick?"

Nick's amused grin faded. For all his brawn and intimidating muscle, Elliott didn't often look serious. He left that to Nick. Simone stilled her hands.

"I've just been talking to Lennard down at the precinct. Dan left there about one. I tried calling his cellphone—no answer. Karl Liebman at the gallery called, squealing about unreliable artists. Seems Dan never showed."

Nick saw concern reflected in the eyes of his friend and business partner. Dan was an easygoing guy, drifting in and out of their lives with the changes of the seasons, but for all his drifter ways, he was as dependable as a rock, especially where the business was concerned. If he was delayed, Dan would have contacted them.

Nick reached for the phone and dialed Dan's cell, not moving until the recorded AT&T voice requested he leave a message at the sound of the tone. "Call in." He disconnected and hit redial, just in case, but the result was the same.

"Perhaps he stopped somewhere," Simone suggested.

But Nick knew he hadn't. Dan was under orders to have the Taurus back by 3:00 pm sharp. Nick looked at his watch again.

3:39

By almost four, Nick had his hand on the telephone to call Dan's cellphone again, and then the police. It rang a strident buzz of warning in the small office and Nick almost knocked the receiver from the phone before he could answer it. He barked his name and waited. It'd better be Dan. It wasn't.

"Ray Lennard here, Nick. Just got an accident report in on your car. You'd better get down to 5th and Oak as soon as you can."

"What about Dan?" Nick asked. The police captain didn't answer straightaway and the extended silence only served to increase Nick's apprehension. He hated waiting for bad news, hated the way his imagination kicked in with images of blood and gore courtesy of CNN and too many bad movies, all rounded off by the memory of the fading life in his wife's eyes.

Lennard's "bad news" sigh was unmistakable. "There's no sign of Tenney."

"What?"

"Witnesses say the car was being chased before it crashed. Detectives Walters and Tingle are down there now. They're expecting you."

Nick ran a hand over his haggard face. "We'll be right there. Thanks, Ray." Kari's white face shimmered before him. He hated this part.

"Holy Mother of God!" Elliott Byrd breathed out in an astonished whisper. He crossed his heart and started muttering a prayer.

The side of Nick's car had been ripped apart. Its metal body was mangled almost beyond recognition, as if it had been used as a chew toy for a giant dog.

Elliott and Nick pushed past the crime scene barriers and walked across to the officers-in-charge leaving Simone behind to look over the faces of the onlookers. She had sharp eyes and often saw beneath the surface of what people presented to the world. But when Nick glanced back, she shook her head and started to follow.

Nick's stomach turned as he came closer to his wrecked car. His eyes locked onto the deformed front end, noticing with sickening detail how tightly it was wrapped around the streetlight. Glass littered both the interior and surrounding roadside. He finally averted his eyes from the wreck to give the detective a perfunctory greeting.

"Tingle, what have you got?"

"Nick. Elliott." Detective Pete Tingle flipped opened his notebook and pulled a pen from behind his ear. The private investigators were on reasonably good terms with the detective. He'd worked a few cases with Elliott back when he was still on the force and had knocked back a few beers in his off-duty hours more than once with Nick.

Elliott stood with his hands on his hips, staring at the wreck. "What the hell happened?"

"Y'know, I was talking fish with Danny just this morning. Thinking about a trip down to the Gunnison next season …" Tingle tapped the notepad with the end of his pen and walked closer to the Taurus. "Tony's still taking statements from witnesses." He jerked his thumb in the direction of the other detective who stood talking to a group of people. "It seems that our Mr. Tenney was involved in a high-speed chase. He came down Oak …" He paused to turn and point at the street behind them, indicating the direction of the chase. "Another vehicle blocked their way and he was forced into this alley. Shots were heard, the car rammed into the pole."

Tingle motioned for the men to follow him as he stepped up to the open passenger door that still hung precariously from its hinges.

"One bullet entered here," he pointed to the side window, "and embedded here." His pen travelled from the window to the blood-stained head rest of the seat.

"Look at all that blood," Elliott muttered. His frown disappeared under a wave of hair.

It hadn't been a flash car since Nick bought it, managing a ding along the side a few days after bringing it home from the car yard. A renegade shopping trolley, Nick had said, and had it fixed without too much concern. There'd be no fixing this.

The driver's seat was bloody. A pool, dark and thick, had collected in the base. It was splattered across the windscreen and side mirror. The limp airbag hung heavy and red from its home in the dashboard. Dan's camera lay on the floor in front of the passenger seat; the lens mount dented, glass cracked. Simone wandered around to the driver's side of the vehicle, looking ill.

"Another shattered the driver's window and went through the front," Tingle continued as Simone as she peered in, staring hard at the neat round hole and the ring of cracked glass around it.

"There's blood on the roof too." She straightened and pointed to a bloody handprint smudged with the residue of the airbags.

"We presume Tenney climbed out of the vehicle under his own power. We'll know for sure once Crime Scene arrive and do their thing. Expect them any second."

Nick listened to the detective and watched, stunned, as the evidence was pointed out and discussed. How could Dan do anything under his own power if he'd lost all that blood? He felt sick. Any minute now he was going to lose his lunch. He shut his eyes and swallowed hard. When he had his churning stomach under control, he opened his eyes and stared at the detective.

"What about these men who were chasing him?"

The notepad was closed with a snap and the pen tucked back behind one ear as Tingle explained what they'd learned so far. He walked a few feet away to a dirty puddle.

"We've been lucky with witnesses on this. We're running some plate numbers now and have good descriptions of a couple of the men. It appears that there were three cars involved in the chase and five or six men. The pursuers exited their vehicles and gathered around the truck. From the descriptions given, Tenney was knocked to the ground about here. He jumped back to his feet and a fight ensued. The fight broke up when the uniforms started converging on the scene. The pursuers ran back to their vehicles leaving two men behind …"

"Do you know who they are yet?" Nick interrupted.

Tingle shook his head. "No, but we've got some good leads. Right now it looks like a mob hit gone wrong."

"Why would the mob go after Dan? He's hardly the type to be involved in that circle," Simone asked.

"They weren't necessarily after him at all," Tingle replied, throwing a wary glance at Nick.

"Nick?" Elliott asked. "You been pissin' folks off and not tellin' me?"

"Did your Samuel Jones make a threat?" Simone hadn't been involved in the mix-up, being hidden away in a luxury Vale condominium with Finn at the time.

"Let's just worry about finding Dan for now," Nick replied, shaking his head. He didn't understand it either. None of their cases, current, past or from his CID days, had any particular links to underground crime. Sam Jones didn't have the money or the connections to organize anything like this. The man wouldn't still be lingering in jail if he did.

"Right." Tingle went back to his report. "All three vehicles made it clear, but like I said, we're chasing down the plates so we should know who they were soon."

"Our officers gave chase to the two men left behind." Tingle turned and pointed up the alley. "But they were too far ahead and disappeared in the lane at the rear of this alley."

"Why would they leave men behind?" Elliott moved away from the car and looked along the dingy alley.

Nick was wondering the same thing and trying to picture what might have happened, what Dan might have done. Fit and good in a fight. He'd give it to them … but faced with guns it'd be run or die …

Simone looked along the roadway for clues, a patch of blood here, scuff marks in the loose gravel over there.

"More blood." Simone inclined her head to indicate the evidence nearby. "There appears to be a trail of it leading further down the alley."

"Dan got away from them," Nick said, relief easing his stomach. "But how far did he get?"

8

"Ya shouldna brought 'im down 'ere, ya fool. He's only gointa die, then what'll we do wid 'im?"

"Don' say that, Jed. He ain't gonna die. He's ma frien'."

"Friend! Ya ain't never set eyes on 'im before. He ain't yer friend."

Dan listened to the two men talk and wondered who they were and if they were talking about him. He didn't see how they could be; he didn't recognize them, but the bickering voices were soothing. Each word spoken dropped through the ringing in his ears and forced its way through the sludge in his head. Sometimes they faded to a soft buzz. Then the high-pitched drone would pierce them into oblivion and the sludge would harden around them so all he could hear was pain.

Smell came to him next. Mold and dirty clothes. Earth and rotting wood. Smoke occasionally, washing over him and bringing with it the flotsam of cooking food: bacon, bread and stewing potatoes.

Vision was like swimming through curtains of dim light. He wasn't sure if his eyes were even open. He tried to see and to speak, but he couldn't fight his way through the pain to answer them, to tell them the words that grated against his teeth. Every time he reached for the words, a searing flash of pain erupted in his mind. He could see the flames consuming him, feel them burning. They flared up whenever he tried to think, to remember—driving him to the brink of forgetting and madness.

In the center of his being a ball of blackness grew. Dan knew that this was where the words were. He reached out. The fire burst into life, flaming out to flick along his legs, burning his hands, consuming him. He turned away and looked out over the abyss. The pain was unbearable. Dan stepped into the void before him and left the images, the words and the pain behind.

9

The three investigators entered the narrow laneway where they hoped to find some sign of Dan. Elliott searched in and around a beat-up dumpster, tentatively lifting the lid and peering inside. Except for the usual garbage, and the stench of rotting food and stale urine that Nick could smell from across the road, there was nothing. The lid clattered closed and Elliott moved to the smaller cans along the sidewalk. The stink remained in the air.

Simone jumped, startled, and sent Elliott a scowl that would rattle the man to the bone if he'd seen it. Nick appreciated the intensity she was bringing to the search. She appeared to be uncaring, but Nick had learned a long time ago that she was a woman of deep feeling. And damn good at hiding it.

Nick diverted his attention from Simone to the wall behind her. Dripping down the dingy brick wall was a slow drying stain. Nick approached it with all the reverence of a holy icon. He touched its edge with one latex-gloved finger. Blood.

"Look at this," he said.

Simone, a breath behind him, had already seen it. "Dan's?"

Nick stared at the smear of blood on his finger. He and Dan had grown close over the years. Almost like brothers. Seeing this blood on the wall brought back fear he hadn't experienced since the weeks before Kari's death.

"Nick, it's not necessarily Dan's blood," Simone tried to reassure him.

"We'll know soon enough. Get Tingle to send forensics around here A.S.A.P. Something sure as hell happened here and I wanna know what." Nick rubbed his thumb and finger together until the bloodstain dried and faded into the latex.

Simone nodded and returned to the alley to talk to Detective Tingle. Nick squatted down as he followed the smear of blood to the ground. A foot or so from the base of the wall the blood veered sharply to the left, indicating the victim may have fallen. He moved aside some of the collected litter but there was no sign of further blood loss in the spot where the victim should have been laying. He checked the grate over the basement window but could see nothing there either. Nick sighed deeply and stood to check on Elliott's progress.

"Anything over there?" he asked.

"A few spent shells." Elliott pointed to where they lay, gleaming on the ground. "But that's all I …"

Elliott stopped speaking and made a sharp exclamation from his position among the trashcans. His foot had kicked against something hard. Nick heard a clank and Elliott crouched down between the cans and pushed aside some old newspapers.

"Got something," he said.

Elliott looked up, a grim expression on his face.

Nick looked down to the place his partner had cleared on the ground—at the cellphone that lay there. The cover, a painting of a rearing bronco, had been a Christmas gift from Nick the year before. Scratched and cracked, it nevertheless still worked. The tiny screen flashed a warning of missed calls and messages left.

"One of a kind," Elliott said.

Nick could only nod in reply.

Simone volunteered to call Mrs. Tenney and the art gallery. Dan's grandmother had insisted on going ahead with her plans to come to Denver for the opening. She would arrive in the morning and would catch a cab to her hotel. When Simone offered to pick her up, she had responded with, "I'm plenty old enough to look out for myself, young lady. You just find my grandson." Simone promised that they would move heaven and earth to do exactly that.

The exhibition opening would also go ahead with or without the third photographer's presence. The gallery owner tried to not sound too annoyed with the turn of events and Simone tried not to sound too exasperated with his apparent lack of compassion. After all, he'd already invested a lot of time and money on relatively unknown artists, and he did assure her he would look after Dan's grandmother when she arrived.

Nick walked into the office as Simone finished her third phone call to the policeman in charge of the investigation: Pete Tingle.

"Detective Tingle has confirmed that there is a high probability that the blood on the wall is Dan's. It matches traces of blood found on the cellphone and on the roof of the car, and it's his blood type. So …"

"And they found hair with the blood on the wall. Dan's too," Elliott said, also coming into the office.

Nick nodded and considered the box of donuts on his desk. Was he hungry or not? The sandwich he'd eaten sometime in the middle of the night had tasted like cardboard and he'd only managed half. He felt gritty and sweaty; his hair was lank and hanging in his eyes. What he needed was a hot shower and a haircut. It was driving him crazy, but he couldn't bring himself to relax long enough to attend to anything other than his most basic needs. Dan had been in a car accident, beaten up and possibly shot. If they didn't find him soon, Dan would be dead.

The coffee was bliss. "Doesn't bring us any closer to knowing where he is though," he said between sips. "It's been over twenty-four hours since the accident, Elliott, and we haven't heard a word."

"Doesn't make sense, does it?" Simone flicked through the pages of the report. "I can't quite decide if whoever took Dan is incredibly stupid or exceedingly smart. They took no particular care with hiding their identities and yet they've managed to vanish into the woodwork."

Simone looked disgusted as she dumped the report on the desk and reached for a donut. It wasn't her usual style to eat so casually, but then she looked more rumpled than Nick had ever seen her. Her blond hair less perfect, face not made up, London accent more noticeable. Weariness oozed from her every movement. She was almost the visual representation of how Nick felt. He shook his head and drank the coffee. Simone would never look that bad.

"Did you hear that?" Elliott glanced at his wristwatch. "It's way too early for Sherrie."

"There's someone at the front door." Simone stood and walked out, coffee in hand.

Nick hadn't heard anything and still couldn't, but he followed the other two out to the reception area. He did hear the dull thud of a trunk slamming closed, followed by a car taking off. Elliott raced to the door, opened it and went no further. Simone and Nick stopped side-by-side. Coffee and donuts were forgotten. At Elliott's feet, hunched against the door jamb, was a body. It toppled over, one hand flopping across Elliott's feet.

Indigestion burned its way from Nick's stomach to his mouth. He looked away, not wanting to see if it was Dan or not. He mentally paced the distance from the front door to the men's room. He could make it. If he left right now, he would make the bathroom and the toilet bowl, and still have a little left over for the sink.

"It's not him." Simone's hand on his elbow refused to allow him to leave.

Damn, Nick thought, *I won't make it now. Lucky if I get to the door.*

"Nick. It's not him." Her fingers pinched hard and Nick looked. He couldn't help it.

The dead man had short, blood-matted blond hair. He wore dark jeans, a buttoned-up polo shirt and leather shoes. His complexion was pale, except for the black and red circle around the bullet hole in his temple.

Simone pulled out her cellphone. "I'll call the police."

10

As far as campsites go, Irene Flemming's was mediocre in appearance. It had been nearly a decade since her last solo trip. As a professor of anthropology at the University of Colorado, she'd been on plenty of field trips, but rarely alone. Alone lately was in libraries or basement archives. But the small saggy tent had held its stand against her rusty skills as an outdoors woman and lasted the night; a fact she was extremely satisfied with. She classed her first cookout a resounding success: charcoaled sausages, reconstituted eggs and brewed tea. Having to wait until breakfast and better light to get the camp stove working didn't worry her. She was too tired to eat the previous night anyway. And now, with her stomach full and a fine day ahead, she was excited to finally be out from between four walls. Doing what she was meant to do. Fulfill her purpose in life.

She'd woken to birds calling and the sun shining. Could things be much better than this? She didn't think so and didn't remember ever waking so easily and ready to be moving as this morning.

She swirled the dregs of her tea around in the cup before emptying it on the ground. She'd turned the little camp stove off as soon as she'd finished cooking breakfast. She rinsed the pan with the remains of the tea water and left it to dry in the sun while she struck down the tent, packing it neatly, coiling ropes in tiny bundles, tucking the pegs into the side pocket of the backpack.

The tighter the bundle the easier it was to carry, she'd been told, and she meant to follow every bit of advice she received to the letter. By the time she was finished the cookware was dry and the stove was cool enough to pack.

"Time to get moving."

She inspected her pack and mentally ticked off the list of things to remember. Water. She shook the water bottles. Enough to last to the safe stream marked on the map. Check. Tent pegs. She'd counted them before erecting the tent and again on taking it down. She looked around the rectangle of flattened grass anyway. None left behind. Check. Cookware packed. Check. Pack secure, walking stick at hand. Check, check and check. She was ready to go.

Irene ran her fingers through her hair and pulled it back into a makeshift bun before covering it with a hat and lifting the pack to her shoulders. Her back cramped in protest. Her lips tightened into a thin, determined line. Since she'd fled home, she'd done many things she normally wouldn't. She could do this too. Ignoring the stiff muscles and creaky joints, she hefted the load onto her back, adjusted the straps and retrieved the walking stick. If she put a little more weight onto the stick than she had the day before and if her steps were less purposeful in their stride, she appeared not to notice. She had a place to be and a task to complete. The stick was strong. Her body would loosen up as she moved.

"Confidence is high." She forced her lips into a grin. Her voice sounded different out here with no other voices collected around and no walls to contain it. She pushed her glasses into position and pulled out a map. More familiar with paper trails than wilderness trails, she nevertheless knew how to read a map. It helped that the trail she was following had been marked in fluorescent yellow. Confirming the route one more time, she nodded, refolded the map and started out.

"One more night and I should be there."

An hour later, Irene approached a thick belt of trees, pausing only to sip some water and crane her neck to the treetops. The canopy was thick and the temperature considerably cooler. Branches crisscrossed and leaves overlapped to form a dense cover deep with shadows. Her toes burned a little in her boots and a rogue muscle between her shoulder blades cramped and relaxed.

Permanently stooped from years of hunching over papers, her shoulders and neck had long been the barometer of her mental state. A low ache equaled general tenseness, a stiff neck came with intensity of thought, and spasms usually indicated nervous excitement. The sun felt so good on her back she considered taking a rest. She checked her watch. She was making good time and felt generally good. No, she decided. Best to tackle it head on. She'd take a break when she physically needed it and not just because childhood fairytales warned her about entering dark woods.

She stopped for an hour before noon, checking her watch to mark her progress, and then roughly for ten minutes every hour after that. Walking university halls and grounds, and to and from her home gave her enough fitness to manage the hike, but only if she didn't overdo it. It was the weight of the pack, the roughness of the track and the altitude she had to be wary of. Regular rests had been slotted into her schedule.

The tree cover grew thicker and she was sure her boots must be shrinking as she walked. Her feet were squashed and starting to throb. She was used to being hemmed in by towering shelves crammed with books, papers and journals. Fairly used to being crowded by masses of students. But the trees had proved more forbidding than expected, as if the mountains weren't bad enough. The feeling of being watched haunted every step.

"It is definitely getting darker." The professor looked up, squinting to catch a glimpse of the sky through the trees. It was even cooler now and, yes, darker. A tiny frisson of nervousness curled tight in her stomach. The trees loomed over head. Her brow wrinkled with concentration. She blinked and shook her head, but it didn't help the slow ache growing behind her tiring eyes. Staring into the gloom wouldn't make it any brighter. The only thing to do was to keep walking.

"Are there any more clearings?" Irene kept her question low, self-conscious. Not a tall woman anyway, she felt like she was shrinking beneath the weight of the trees. Her voice, too, had shrunk. It sounded now like a squeaking mouse instead of the firm teacher's voice she had cultivated throughout her career, a booming voice to make up for her lack of stature. She hadn't seen another person on the trail since leaving the small town of Smiggins' Rest, and while she was glad for that—she didn't want company—it also worried her. The map came out again and she hooked the walking stick into the crook of her arm while she traced the path with one finger.

"I've definitely passed that mark ..." She turned the map to the left and squinted behind her bifocals. "I should be just about there." She stabbed a point on the map and glanced again at the traces of sky above. "Another hour of light, maybe?" Checking the watch was an automatic gesture. A gift from her sister some twenty years ago, the timepiece had seen her get to class and to appointments on time nearly every day since. The second hand wasn't moving. She frowned and shook her wrist. The time was exactly the same as the last time she'd checked. She unclipped it, tapped the face and shook it again.

"Perfect time for twenty years and today it stops?" Her frown deepened. She thought she'd been making excellent progress. But the day was slipping away faster than expected. Faster than her old Timex said it should. The hands were stuck at two o'clock, she was sure she hadn't been walking that long and here it was already getting dark. She counted the rest stops on her fingers. Three o'clock sounded about right. The lack of light didn't. And who knew whether the watch was running on time to start with?

The discrepancy worried her. She hated discrepancies, had worked long and hard to weed them from her studies. Her attention to details and determination to tie up loose ends had finally brought her within hours of the culmination of years of research and opened her eyes to the synchronistic pattern of her life.

Irene adjusted the pack on her back and retrieved her familiar grip on the stick. The stick itself was part of the pattern she'd taken fifty-nine years to recognize. She'd had it rubber-tipped to protect the end and regularly oiled the wood to prevent age and weathering from affecting the fine grain. Another present from her sister, bless her heart. How could she have known? What little whisper in her heart had told her of the importance of the stick? Professor Flemming shook her heard. Synchronicity? Fate? Or something more?

She would need to pitch her tent soon. The people at the camping store had pressed her on that issue. Make camp well before dark, they'd said. Don't wander from the trail. Be careful with fire. One match and half the mountain will burn down before anyone remembers you're up there. She had written it all down in her trusty notebook. Then torn out the page and tucked the list inside the front cover of the wilderness survival guide she had purchased alongside the lightweight tent, sleeping bag and other camping paraphernalia. To the letter, she'd promised.

She looked along the trail. It seemed to disappear into the undergrowth. Only the path itself was reasonably clear and easy to follow. She walked around a sharp bend. Ahead, not too far from the trail, appeared a break in the trees.

Irene clambered over rocks and logs to reach it, forgetting the trail and warnings not to leave it. Another day and she would be at her destination. Another day and she would be closer to learning the truth than at any other time in her life. The anticipation fueled her strength and determination. Turning circles in the sun, eyes closed to feel the last of its warmth on her face, she was surprised at the happiness engulfing her. She couldn't remember ever feeling quite so liberated and felt like cheering loudly, calling and whooping like a wild woman.

According to the map and the guide she'd talked to in the town, she should reach her destination late the next day as long as the weather didn't change and she kept track of what she was doing and where. Professor Flemming stopped spinning. Time to erect the tent.

11

Not too hot, not too cold, Dan thought and then frowned as he tried to remember what it felt like to be too hot or too cold. A dull ache, a bump in the flat terrain of his mind's eye, pushed the thought away. He walked on, forward as he always had, through the gray desolation of the empty void.

A sound echoed around him, a low moan of pain that shook the dead ground beneath his feet and sent a restless wind across the barren landscape. His clothes flapped against him as the wind corkscrewed around his body, picking him up and spinning him crazily into the sky above, clouds heavy with moisture. He glanced down once, suddenly scared, and called out a single word—a name—but it hurt to speak, to think and all the tumbling about the sky made him feel ill. The name slid away from him, lost in the grayness.

The wild wind caught the clouds in its wake and he could feel their moisture on his face. The shock of its coldness brought the spinning to a terrifying halt and he felt himself falling.

He came to with the smell of dampness in his nostrils and on his skin. Someone was wiping his face.

"Ya awake?"

Dan heard the question but couldn't relate it to himself. He was pretty sure his eyes were open this time. He could make out a crumbly ceiling above him. Not his ceiling. Not his room. Water dripped on his lips and his focus the quandary of the ceiling behind to study the face looming beside him.

Shadows danced across it, turning it from a young face to old, from mildly pleasant to ugly and deeply rutted.

"Ya must be gittin' mighty hungry. Ya ain't et in ages. We's just' been givin' ya water. S'all ya would take."

Dan opened his mouth to speak. His throat locked around the sounds and refused to work. Something hard was pressed to his parched lips and water dribbled past them and over his tongue. It tasted sweet and cool. He licked his lips again and croaked a thready, "More."

He felt a hand under his head, lifting it and tried to reach for the cup himself.

"Careful," the stranger warned, even as Dan realized the stupidity of any movement. Hot tears rolled from his eyes and gathered on his top lip.

"Shitshitshitshitshit."

The hand under his head moved to his shoulder and he was taken into an embrace.

"S'okay. S'okay."

The voice soothed and rocked him, or maybe it was the arms. He didn't like it. He didn't want it to stop.

A long, hairless tail swished in front of his face and Dan knew he was awake again. He felt cold and lonely. And scared. Where was Nick? He thought he'd heard his voice earlier, calling out. Maybe he'd dreamt it. He stared absently at the spot where the tail slithered, turned and became a rat. A dark shape hovered over them both and the rat vanished before Dan could blink.

"'Bout time!" A rough male voice floated down to him. Dan felt hands push under his armpits, attempting to lift him into a sitting position. His head rolled painfully back before he could control it.

"Sssshit," he groaned.

"Sorry 'bout that," the voice said.

Dan felt the blackness beckoning, trying to close in on him. Instead his chin was gripped tightly and his head held upright so he could look right into the face.

"Mister, ya gotta wake up now."

The voice called him. It drifted down, coiled around him like a rope and pulled him back to the surface. He blinked and waited for his eyes to focus again. The face was still in front of him. It was old and battered, and totally unfamiliar.

"Who?" he asked. His tongue felt thick and swollen. It stuck to the roof of his mouth. The stranger's face left his field of vision for a moment. Dan's eyelids drooped, not quite closing. He felt something wet on his lips and automatically parted them to drink thirstily. Tepid water spilled from his mouth.

"Slow down there, Mister."

The cup was pulled away.

"More," Dan mumbled.

"Ya can have it all, jus' slow down 'fore ya make yerself sick."

The cup returned and Dan drank as slowly as he could. Probing hands rifled through his clothes and fluttered around his head. Dan finished the water in a gulp and pushed them away. "Stop … Hurts." Pain flared through his shoulder as if to prove his words true.

"Gointa hurt worse in a minute," he was told. Clothes were pulled away and Dan saw a flash of stained bandages before they were removed. The sudden odor of whiskey invaded his senses and he threw his head back in retreat. Liquid fire splashed over his shoulder, lancing through muscle and tissue. He could barely feel the hands that held him down or hear the voices trying to calm him. Fire consumed him, ate him whole as he screamed out his agony.

A hand covered his mouth and he struggled against it. The soft voice came to him, whispering, promising. "S'okay. It's me. Yer safe."

Dan clenched his teeth on further cries as the alcohol burned into his wound. He managed to hold onto consciousness, but only just. He didn't notice the second man, wasn't aware of his presence until the fog began to clear.

"What …?" he protested. The second man knelt beside him and offered him some more water, then started dabbing at his head with a damp cloth. Dan growled at him and the man shrank back. Shakily, he was offered the whiskey bottle instead. Dan wrenched it from the man's hands and drank it as thirstily as the water.

When the pain finally started to recede, Dan let the bottle drop from his numb hands. He looked blearily at the two men staring at him, their shape turning fuzzy and multiplying as his eyes lost their ability to focus. He groaned as the alcohol continued to numb his body against the pain. Fog surrounded him now. Everything turned gray and dull once more as he relaxed and slumped against the rough wall.

"It's the pain," Jed tried to explain to his shocked friend. "Ya better find some more a'that booze. Reckon he's gointa ta need it."

Will nodded, then picked up the cloth and continued to wipe the sweat from the unconscious man's face. When he was satisfied that the injured man was sleeping peacefully, he got up to go hunt down whatever he could find to help the man get better. Will collected strays like some people did shoes. Jed had seen his friend in action before.

Jed felt a lump in his throat as he watched Will care for the stranger. He had such a look of tenderness on his face that the old man felt suddenly unnerved. It didn't pay to care so much about someone—it only hurt in the end. He sighed inwardly. There was nothing he could do about it except be around to pick up the pieces if he could. Will was like an old dog with a bone once he got something into his head, wasn't anything going to make him let it go until he was ready.

Dan felt sick. His stomach churned and tied itself in knots. He'd barely awoken before he was leaning over, retching violently onto the ground. His head thrummed harder with every movement, but he couldn't stop. He felt a cool cloth on the back of his head and heard someone say, "Prob'ly tha booze." There was more talking, but he was heaving again and couldn't concentrate on the words.

As the retching slowed, Jed put a cup of water to Dan's mouth and tipped it up so he could drink. "Slowly," he admonished.

Dan was incapable of doing more than sip anyway. He opened watery eyes to the man in front of him. He felt sicker than he'd ever been before. He was cold and shaking, his lips trembled, and his eyes burned watery and scratchy at the same time. When he was finally able to speak, his voice was slurred and shaky.

"Feel … like … shit." He slowly pulled his legs up underneath him and pushed himself a little further up the wall to sit straighter. The effort cost and new waves of nausea passed over him.

"You oughta not move 'round so much, Mister. Might get sick again," Will told him.

Dan turned his head and cracked his eyes open to look at the second face. He wanted to know what was going on, but he couldn't get his mouth to form any more words, and his head hurt.

One of the men leaned in, peering into Dan's eyes. "Ya still with us?"

The only response Dan could give was a slight change in breathing and a faint sound that could have been a grunt of acknowledgment. He wasn't sure if it was audible outside the thumping in his head.

"Bring over some a'that soup and bread. We gotta get some food into 'im," Jed ordered. The man's eyes were dull, lips slack. He should be in a hospital, but how the hell were they supposed to manage that?

Will filled a battered enamel bowl with the clear broth Jed had made and grabbed a couple of rolls he'd filched that morning from out back of a bakery. He brought them carefully over and passed them to Jed. Jed fished about in his pocket for a spoon, wiped it on the tails of his shirt and slowly began to feed the semi-conscious man.

The liquid seemed to sit in the man's mouth a moment, but he got the first spoonful down and then the next. Jed could hear his stomach rumbling. He paused and waited to see if the soup would stay down. When he could see it would, he had Will crumble the bread into the soup and began again. He was able to get at least half the bowlful in when he noticed the man's eyes grow distant. The next spoonful of broth dribbled back out his mouth.

Will wiped Dan's face with the cloth, concern creasing his brow. "He's out again."

When Dan woke next, he was alone and still confused, unable to tell where he was and no idea how he'd got there. He pushed himself up the wall till he was standing and gasped as a wave of dizziness and pain took his breath away. His knees started to buckle, and he had to push hard against the ground and wall to stay up. Breathing heavily, he put as much strength as he could muster into getting upright, steadying himself with one hand. Weakness was fast overtaking his drive to keep moving. Bile rose in his stomach, a strange humming started in his ears—every movement of his left arm brought stabbing pain to his shoulder. He held his arm tightly across his chest and repeatedly swallowed, willing himself not to faint or vomit.

The humming grew louder, more persistent, but he ignored it and took a step forward. By the time he reached the small fire, not much more than glowing embers in the dull room, he was exhausted. He half-fell, half-sat by the fire and blinked furiously against the rising grayness in his head.

Jed hadn't gone far, waiting at the end of dingy corridor for Will to return from another scavenging trip.

"What tha hell!" he exclaimed when he returned to their hiding place to see the man sitting, staring blankly, by the fire. "Will!" he bellowed into the darkness behind him. He heard Will's shuffling feet and his short gasp of surprise.

"He's up!" Will cried out happily. He sat down beside the silent man and began to open an old, worn satchel. "We got some good stuff for ya," he told him, pulling an oversized sweatshirt from the satchel and placing it on the ground between them. "Look!"

The man turned his head away. His hands rubbed against his knees, fingertips catching on the rough denim of his jeans.

"Mister?" Will reached for the man's chin and turned his head sharply back.

The man hissed in pain, flinching and suddenly very focused it seemed—on getting away. He glanced around for an escape, mumbling incoherent words as he stumbled back from the fire, feet scraping on the dirt floor.

Jed saw the change and knew the man wasn't aware of where he was; a fine sheen of sweat glistened in the poor light and his breathing was ragged. Will had frozen in place.

"Will! Come away, over 'ere," Jed hastily commanded. "Yer scarin' 'im."

"But …" Will began.

The sick man retreated until he could go no further, the cold wall at his back an impenetrable barrier, though he was trying hard to push it over.

Will moved to stand beside Jed.

"It's okay, Mister. We ain't gointa hurt ya," Jed said as softly as he could. "Me an' Will's been lookin' out fer ya. Cleaned ya up some, kept ya hid."

Will looked at Jed worriedly. Jed ignored him and continued to talk in a low voice, edging his way close to the fire and studiously avoiding any movement the confused man might think threatening.

"Will. Come and finish unpacking yer bag, but move slow. He ain't awake proper. We don't wanna scare 'im no more."

Jed got the fire going strong and started with fixings for a meal while Will unpacked the warm clothes he'd found and placed the extra bottle of whiskey and some more bread in their supplies kit. Both men stole secret glances across to the injured man. When his head drooped and his fisted hands relaxed in sleep, Jed carefully stood and made his way over.

"Go an' get those blankets, Will. We'll keep 'im by the fire so's he don't wake up alone agin."

12

"Nick? You in there?" Elliott winced and threw one hand up to shield his eyes as a beam of light shone into his face.

"Right here," Nick replied before moving the light away. They'd left Simone to deal with the police and returned to the alley for a more intense search of the buildings. Something about the barred window bothered Nick, so they'd broken in to see what they could find.

"Anything?"

Nick pointed the light toward the ground a few feet away. Its beam cut through the dark room like a knife, dust swirled in its bright glare. Elliott walked over to the pool of light on the floor and squatted down beside it. He extended his arm and dragged one finger through the dark stain on the floor.

"Looks like blood to me," Elliott confirmed as he inspected the russet-brown discoloration. "Sure is a lot of it here."

Nick's face remained in the shadows behind the flashlight. "But what was he doing down here?"

Elliott shrugged. "Crawled in looking for a place to hide out?"

"How?" Nick shone the light around the small basement room. There was no easy way into the room. He and Elliott had to force their way through the fire escape on the first floor just to get down there. The light moved over to the only other opening in the room—the barred, glassless window. A glint of steel flashed in the light as it crossed the blackened wall.

"What was that?" Elliott asked, jumping up and going over to the window. "Shine that flashlight back here."

The wall flooded with light and both men could clearly see bare metal exposed against the grime of the brick wall. Elliott put out his hands to feel the wall, knocking lightly on the bricks and stopping to smile grimly when he found one loose. He carefully pulled the brick from the wall. Nick shone the light into the hole then reached out to pull down the small lever illuminated by the flashlight. A faint clicking noise sounded from within the wall. Elliott started checking the bricks directly around the lever, but no more were loose.

"What the fuck?" Nick muttered, hitting the window bars with the palm of his hand in irritation. The bars rattled in response.

Elliott shook his head and rested his hands on his hips. "There must be …"

"Shuttup a minute, Elliott," Nick snapped. He grasped the bars with both hands and shook. The entire framework shifted in his grip, and he slowly slid it to one side. It grated slightly as it scraped along a steel runner embedded into the wall.

The two men looked at each other in amazement.

"A secret entry? What the hell is this place?" Elliott growled.

Nick flashed the light around the room once again, this time looking for anything that might be hiding another secret entrance. The walls were lined with rubbish and debris left behind by countless squatters over the years. In one corner an old mattress was propped against a pile of rotten boxes. In the opposite corner were some large crates, broken and splintered, and littered with rusty tins and empty jars.

They each took a corner and began to search.

13

Dan felt trapped. It was hot and hard to breathe. He shifted restlessly and pushed at the thing that was holding him down, wrapping him so tightly he could hardly move. Then whatever had him trapped was gone and he was free. He relaxed a little as his face cooled down. His panicky breathing evened out and Dan opened his eyes.

He was in the same place with the two strangers. One of them put a cloth down and a cup of water appeared. Wavering beside it was a bottle of whiskey.

"Water or whiskey?" he asked, smiling happily.

Dan pulled his face together in what he hoped was a grin. "Whiskey, but ya better give me the water first."

The old guy did as Dan suggested and put the water to his lips. He drank as much as he could before turning away and gingerly lifting one arm to wipe his face. His hand ran along his chin, feeling the stubble, then reached around to the back of his head, searching for the source of the persistent throbbing.

"Ya okay?"

Dan winced as his fingers found the rough bandaging and pushed against the tender wound. "Fine," he replied warily, and began to sit up.

His carer leaned forward to help; even so, the effort tired Dan out. A faint feeling of nausea rolled through him. The humming and dizziness returned in full force and he put his hand to his face again to wipe at the increasing clamminess of his skin. He stayed as still as he could and prayed it would all go away, and gradually it did. The nausea and dizziness eased enough for him to realize his shoulder hurt like hell.

"Whiskey," he mumbled.

The remaining water was emptied from the cup and replaced with whiskey. Dan took it and sipped carefully. The alcohol burned all the way down and he hoped it would stay there long enough to dull some of his pain. The flickering of the flames from the small fire hurt his eyes and left ghostly white images dancing before him. He narrowed his gaze until the flames, and the ghosts, were mere blurs in a distant landscape.

"My name's Will," Dan heard the man closest to him say. "That's Jed, over there." Dan turned his head in the direction of the single grunt that had acknowledged the introduction. The voice continued. Sometimes Dan could understand what he was saying—something about strange men in alleys and safe underground. Other times, the words tripped over each other and were drowned out by the constant humming, buzzing noise in his ears. He sat hunched over and tried to concentrate. What did he say his name was?

"Will?"

The voice stopped.

"More whiskey."

Will obligingly refilled the tin cup then carefully wrapped an arm around the man as he drained its contents and sagged with exhaustion.

"Lay 'im back down, Will. He's tuckered out."

Dan didn't know where he was, but it all seemed familiar: tall buildings, faint glitter of sunlight on glass windows, hundreds of winking eyes. Except they weren't windows, they were bubbles, hovering in the still air, crowding in on each other, on him. Reaching out to one, his hand went right through its wet skin. It looked disjointed, bent at an impossible angle; the color sapped out of his fingers. Past his hand he could see a gray, barren landscape and he strained to see more, stepping into the bubble and starting to panic as the wetness slapped against his face and plopped around him.

There was no retreat, stepping back only caused clouds of dust to rise off the ground. Soft, gray brown sand covered his boots and clung to his jeans, settling on his shirt as he continued to move. He felt dry, like a shrub left too long without water, baking under the desert sun, and knelt down on one knee. His knee sank into the sand—it felt wet. He dug his hand into the soft earth, hoping for water but pulling it free to reveal blood.

It was all over him, dripping from his hair, squelching in his boots. Its rank smell invaded his nostrils and he doubled over in agony to vomit filth onto the rough road beneath his feet. A torn and faded sheet of newspaper blew against his leg on its meandering way down the alley, finally coming to rest against the wheel of a smashed car. *Oh, God! Oh, God!* Horror filled every cell in his body, his hands trembled, his mouth opened in frozen terror. The screeching of tires echoed through the buildings. He looked wildly around him.

Blinding headlights shone in his face and he was frozen—caught like a wild animal in their glare. The tires came to a shuddering halt beside him and he lost his footing with its impact. The crashing reverberation replayed in his head again and again—glass smashing, tortured metal twisting, a scream that vibrated through him, rattled his ribcage, ripped through his throat. He scrambled to his feet determined to run and going nowhere, held in place by the strong grip of hands. Hands at his shoulders, on his arms, pinning him to the wall while he twisted and turned until finally the fright and the panic overtook him. *It's a dreamadreamadream*, he mumbled. *Wakeupwakeup!* He knew when his heart stopped, when the last breath left his lungs. His eyes rolled back in his head and he became a boneless rag doll in the grip of the nightmare that held him.

14

Nick Somers was a worried man. The mystery of Dan's disappearance had been torturing him for nearly a week. The lack of his quiet brotherly presence was a painful hole he was determined to fill. And the mystery had just deepened with the twin discoveries of blood Nick knew was Dan's on the floor of the barred basement, and a secret entry into said basement.

He almost missed seeing the slight indentation in the wall caused by a too hastily closed door. As it was, he only noticed it when he felt the tickle of a draft on the back of his hand.

"Elliott," his voice came out as a throaty whisper. He cleared it and tried again. "Elliott! Found it!"

Elliott hurried over. Nick pushed against one section of the grimy wall. It moved slowly, grinding on rusty hinges, but it did open. Nick and Elliott peered into the darkness.

"Where's your car parked?"

"Round the corner," Elliott replied.

"Bring it round to the window. Get your first aid kit and another flashlight."

Elliott nodded and took off out through the window. Nick flicked on his flashlight and carefully stepped into the secret passage.

Will heard the outer door open; sounds echoed in the quiet of the underground passages. At first, he could only hear the soft tread of wary footsteps. Will didn't think it sounded like one of the other homeless people that knew about the underground sanctuary. The steps were too deliberate, then they stopped altogether. The door sounded again and another set of footsteps and whispered calls came down the passage.

"Nick? Nick?"

"Shhhhhh, I'm right here."

Will jumped at the sound of the second voice—it was so close. In the next instant, two beams of light travelled down the wall toward him.

"Holy mackerel," he breathed, and bolted.

Nick and Elliott both heard the movement and brought their flashlights up just as Will made his escape. The light caught the flapping edge of his coat as it disappeared around a bend.

"Stop!" they yelled, chasing after the running figure as fast as they could without tripping on the rough ground underfoot.

Jed leaned over the injured man, trying to calm him down and ease him out of the violent nightmare he was embroiled in. The man thrashed about, mumbling something unintelligible. His eyes snapped open as Will came running in.

"Jed! Jed!" Will puffed, his face pallid in the dim light.

"C'mere and help me with yer friend. He's having a real bad dream," Jed said without looking up.

Will knelt down beside him and rested a hand on the restless man's shoulder. "We gotta hide, Jed. Someone's comin' from outside."

"NO!" Caught in the trap of his nightmare, Dan yelled and pushed the men away from him. Jed and Will fell back, astonished at the other man's sudden strength. Will's coat tails fell into the fire and went up in a swoosh of flames.

"Jed!" he screamed.

Jed grabbed a blanket and began hitting the flames on his friend's back. Dan looked about, wild, startled at the screams bouncing off the walls.

"Nononononononono."

Nick heard the screams and ran down the passage, bursting into the room as the flailing Will kicked the half-full bottle of whiskey into the fire.

"Dan!" Elliott called out as he ran in, almost knocking Nick over. His voice was drowned out by the explosion of the glass bottle. Dan's head whipped round, his eyes fixed on the twin orbs of the flashlights. The look of horror that passed over his face had Nick rooted to the spot.

"My God! Dan?" Nick's voice was rough with concern over the condition of his friend. Dan was still in the clothes Nick had last seen him in. Over the top he wore a stained, baggy sweater and an old army overcoat. His hair was unwashed and hung like ragged string; a dirty cloth bound his head. He stood, mesmerized, staring into the beams of light.

Groans from one of the strangers broke the spell. The flashlights lowered and Dan spun on his heels in an apparent desperate bid to flee his friends.

"Dan! Stop!" Elliott called. Nick had already started after him; both were swallowed by the darkness with only the jolting flashlight to mark their trail.

Nick sighed with relief when the passage Dan was racing down ended with a solid brick wall, but it caught in his throat as Dan threw himself against the wall before turning to face his danger.

"Dan? It's okay. It's me, Nick," he called softly. Nick heard Elliott coming up behind him. Dan's head jerked, his eyes—open wide but not seeing—darted around. His breath came in harsh, ragged sobs as he pushed himself up against the wall, his feet slipping in the soft dirt beneath him.

"Dan, it's okay."

Dan dived forward, but was caught by the two men and held firm. They pushed him back to the wall, calling him, assuring him over and over, trying to bring him back from where he was. Dan struggled to escape, fought his captors with all his waning strength, his breath coming faster, harsher, through muttering lips until he could take no more. His eyes rolled back in his head and he went limp in their grip.

Nick pulled an unconscious Dan into his embrace, gently pushing the dirty hair from his closed eyes and whispered, "It's okay. It's okay. We've got you. The nightmare's over." He looked across at Elliott; the uneven light of the flashlights threw haggard shadows across his face.

Elliott rested one hand on Dan's back and nodded. "The nightmare's over," he agreed.

Nick could only hope that it was.

15

The nightmare wasn't over and Nick was beginning to wonder if it ever would be. He reached across the hospital bed and rested his hand on Dan's troubled face. The murmuring from the otherwise still form continued; next would come thrashing followed by cries of terror and pain, and then, finally, a period of almost wakefulness. Nick had sat through the entire sequence numerous times over the last few days. It had only taken the first occurrence for him to decide the almost wakefulness was the worst part.

Though, at least they'd been able to get nourishment into him at these times. It was like feeding a zombie. The waking dead. His mind wandered morbidly to all the horror movies he'd seen over the years. Dan just seemed to have no recollection of who or where he was. He answered questions in word groupings of one, and the answer would be so slow in arriving you'd think he hadn't heard. When it finally came, it made no sense. His eyes were dull, his face expressionless until he eventually just slipped back into unconsciousness. They may have the body of Dan Tenney back, but his mind was still locked away from the world.

The doctor was on the verge of ordering heavy sedation to enforce the rest his patient needed.

The murmuring faded away, and Nick could see sweat forming on his friend's brow. His mouth was a tight grimace of anguish. Nick used his free hand to clasp Dan's.

"You're safe, Dan. Wake up," he whispered to the man trapped in a world where he was anything but.

16

"But I like my ol' coat. I don't wanna new one," Will grumbled.

"Will," Finn Shaw began, "your old coat has, frankly, seen better days m'boy. Come winter it just ain't gonna do for you."

Will stared at him suspiciously. Finn threw his hands up in the air and turned away, shaking his head and muttering about the stubbornness of mules. Simone had roped him into bringing Will and Jed down to the army disposal store to replace Will's burnt coat and stock the two men up for the coming winter. Simone, he reminded himself once more, had too much power in that little finger of hers.

The whole story of Dan's disappearance had finally come out soon after Nick and Elliott had fought Will off when their mutual friend had collapsed in their arms. An equally worried Jed had struggled to pull Will away, sternly taking them all to task for the trouble they were causing. By the time an ambulance had arrived, Elliott had most of the details, including a sketchy description of the men who had shot Dan. After Will had been treated for minor burns at the E.R. and released, Elliott had persisted with cautious questioning, but when Nick and Simone had arrived, Will had been overwhelmed by their intensity and clammed up, refusing to say another word. Steely glares from Jed prevented further attempts at interrogation.

So, they tried a different tact. Elliott and Simone would go with the information they already had and continue the investigation into the mysterious attack.

Finn "volunteered" to take the two homeless men under his wing and, as a thank you for their care of Dan, see to it that they lacked for nothing, at the same time prying as much information from them as he could.

Nick would stay with Dan and do what he could on their current caseload. Simone, assisted by Finn, had made some inroads into the missing professor case over the past week and a half. Nick had a thick file to go through and several phone calls to make.

"What's wrong with this coat, Will?" Finn asked.

Will's voice was petulant. "It's too tight and there ain't enough pockets. My ol' coat has lotsa pockets. Can stash all kindsa things in 'em."

Finn raised his eyebrows. "Yeah, I bet you can at that."

Jed returned from another part of the over-stocked store. "Stop yer bitchin', Will. Ya sound like a kid."

Will began to pout and Finn had to hide his smile behind his hand at the interplay between the two friends.

"An' don't get ta sulkin' neither," Jed continued gruffly. He shoved a bundle of thick cloth at his friend. "Try this."

Will shook the bundle out to reveal a heavy coat, almost exactly the same as his old one. His face beamed, and he hurriedly took off the rejected coat to try on the new one. He admired himself in the full-length mirror and shoved his hands in the deep side pockets. His smile grew wider as he inspected the garment all over. It had the required number of pockets, including some hidden ones, and Will let out a harrumph of joy. He turned to Jed and wrapped his arms around him then shuffled over to where his old coat lay and quickly began to shift his belongings to their new home, his hand hesitating over Dan's wallet. His smile faltered, but his fingers wrapped around the wallet and held it securely before transporting it to an inside pocket of his new coat. He turned back to Jed, smile returning.

"Thanks, Jed."

Jed cleared his throat and looked a touch embarrassed. "Don't thank me," he said, jerking his thumb toward Finn. "Thank him. He's payin' fer it."

17

"Do you see anything yet, Elliott?" Pete Tingle asked.

Pete had been assigned to the Tenney case and ordered, in Elliott's hearing, to make sure everything stayed within the boundaries of the law. So far it had, but judging by the continual shifting and stomach rumbles, Pete was hungry and uncomfortable. The truck, Elliott freely admitted, smelled of stale food and a mix of other scents that even he didn't want to think about. He kept all his equipment in perfect working order but the truck had become an oversized trashcan.

Elliott's grip on the binoculars tightened as he drawled a sarcastic reply. "A house, some trees, couple of cars … same ole, same ole." He couldn't remember Pete being this annoying in the old days.

A disgusted sounding grunt came from the passenger seat as Pete returned to fiddling with the camera. Of all the various and different aspects of police work, Elliott knew from experience that sitting around waiting for something to happen was the worst.

"Wait," Elliott said. "Here comes Simone."

The investigators had finally tracked down their suspects: men whom they hoped were currently inside the run-down house they had staked out. They'd had a major breakthrough that morning with the confirmed identity of the second man responsible for Dan Tenney's current condition. The description of the other man at the scene had matched that of the deceased Terence Smith, dumped outside their office a few days ago. They had traced the second suspect to this house. One of the cars parked out front of the rather ordinary looking house matched one of the chase cars that had run Dan into the telegraph pole.

They came up with a plan to "ascertain the identity and number of occupants of the hovel," as Simone had so eloquently informed Nick Somers during her last check-in call, and put it into immediate practice.

The identified man was one Roger de Laurac. A mystery man, it seemed. There was no rap sheet, no suspicions or rumors. A name mentioned in passing by an informant who confirmed the descriptions given earlier by Will. A complete stranger, whose name set warning bells ringing in Simone's head. She couldn't put her finger on it, but there was something about that name she thought she should know.

On the way to the house, they passed a treeless reserve with a great tent erected in the middle. "Revival!" banners boldly declared. "Tent Mission" a nearby bus claimed. Simone smiled at the suited ushers and the line of cars looking for nearby parking and decided on just how she was going to get inside. Elliott let her out of the car around the corner then continued on to pull up in a narrow lane just down from the marked house.

"No problem," she mumbled to herself as she strolled up the sidewalk a short fifteen minutes later. Her usual designer clothes had been exchanged for an off-the-rack skirt and printed tee-shirt, and a brown bob cut wig covered her blond hair.

The plan meant stopping at a couple of houses on the way, but it couldn't be helped. It had to appear that she wasn't targeting the one particular house. As she'd learned over the years, details were everything.

She pushed open the rusty front gate and walked up the path, pausing to straighten her blouse before knocking loudly on the weathered front door. *Who would have thought*, she mused, *that I would spend my retirement working for a two-bit detective agency?*

"What is she doing?" Pete asked, watching Simone visit two other houses before approaching the target.

"Spreadin' the word of the Lord," Elliott replied, smiling and listening to the woman's spiel via the tiny transmitter in her earring.

"What?" Pete hissed.

"Spreading the word …"

"I heard you the first time," Pete interrupted, grabbing the earphones from Elliott's head. "Does your mother know where you are?"

Elliott ignored the jibe and smiled back. "She's very good at it. Simone, that is."

Pete listened for a moment before shoving the earphones back at Elliott and reaching for his camera to zoom in on Simone as she swung open the gate.

The house was a double-story brick and faux-wood log reminiscent of the 1970s or 1980s—Elliott wasn't too sure. He was sure that it was fairly ugly and in need of a serious amount of tender loving care.

Elliott continued to watch through the binoculars. There was a time when he'd hoped to get a little closer to Simone than their current working relationship; he'd suspected that she and Nick had once been a couple … of sorts, but that impression had faded once he'd seen how devoted she was to Finn Shaw. The wistful thoughts vanished as the front door opened.

"Okay," he whispered. "Here we go!"

18

His boots were gone, noticed that right off. Standing in a pool of stagnant water, feet sinking in soft, slimy mud—it slid between his toes and oozed over the top. Dim light filtered down from somewhere up high and he strained his eyes to see; he thought about climbing up to the light, but the walls, when he touched them, were slick with dripping moss. A slight scurrying sound caught his attention. A few feet away a rat was gnawing on … *my boots?* The boots were charred and smoldering.

Dan was curious about that, but it was the rat that held his attention. Its glassy eyes stared warily. Its paws held tight to the ruined leather as its tail flicked around its body. Dan stepped away, filled with dread, his back coming into contact with the wet wall. Something slithered across his foot, and he started moving, stumbling to get away from the horror rising up behind him. Not again! He slipped and fell flat on his face in the brackish water, its eerie color stained his skin a sickly green. The mud was drawing him in, sucking him down. The slithery thing brushed by him again, touching his feet, his hands. He could see it moving in the water, a dark shape undulating around him.

Dan knew somehow it wasn't real. That he'd wake up and it would all be gone. It sure felt real though, and he was running before he made it to his feet. In a tunnel littered with things he didn't want to look at. He barely noticed the slimy mud turn into hard road. Something soft and rotten tripped him up and a foul odor filled the air. He lay in a heap on the road, gagging and retching.

The click of claws on the cobbled lane filled him with new fear. Rats squeaked their approach. They were coming for him—he could hear them laughing. Coming for him, and he was trapped. A resounding crack came from further up the alley, followed by the sound of bricks crashing to the ground and tumbling down. Stairs? Dan was back on his feet, running and slipping, the rats screeched behind him, bricks crashed ahead.

The dim light faded until Dan was forced to feel his way forward along the wall. His hands searched frantically along the old bricks for some sign of the staircase he knew was just ahead. His feet searched out safe places to step. The soft touch of a hairless tail had him flat against the wall. Cold bricks numbed his back, the coldness spreading through him. His foot came down on something soft and hairy. The sound of his scream mingled with the scream of the rat. He squeezed his eyes shut and clenched his lips between his teeth, desperately trying to hold the screams in.

Silence descended onto the alley like a blanket, deadening the sound of the clammering rats, smothering the echoes of his screams. The rats were still there; he could feel them glaring at him. He cracked one eye open. Glowering, hate filled eyes stared back at him. He stumbled over loose rocks that made no sound as they rolled across the cracked sidewalk and disappeared into the gaping blackness before him. His hair flew in a gust of wind that blew him faster along the path. A whispered voice called out to him as he finally reached the stairs. The path heaved threatening to throw him into a gaping maw. He glanced backward—far below were the desolate sands and bleak cliffs, and for a moment, he yearned for the short-lived peace he'd felt there.

The whispers grew more persistent—urgent, the wind stronger. He turned his back on the scene and continued on his way, climbing upward without stopping, leaving it all behind.

The wall that stretched out before him was rotten and crumbling. A large crack rent the bricks and a sliver of light shone through. Dan put a hand up to protect his eyes and stumbled back at the brightness. Soft voices called him and he turned back to the wall, unable to look away. A hand reached through the crack, beckoning him closer. He stumbled in his rush to reach the hand, pushed against the wall, pulled away broken masonry. Light gushed in. His fingers wrapped around a hot, pulsing ball of energy; skin burned and he smelled the searing of flesh, heard it shrink back from bones that fused together in the immense heat. He threw his head back and screamed his agony, trying to let go but only succeeding in dragging the ball back through the wall.

Energy vibrated through his body and into the crumbling staircase and decaying walls. It flashed brightly then dimmed to reveal a dark sphere. His eyes fixed onto the shape—he could see figures running, people milling around a crouched figure, a small fire and two old men, a lone man standing on the edge of a vast abyss.

The wall tumbled down and the hand reached back in. The whisper had become a voice, a voice he knew and trusted, calling his name over and over. The sphere grew in his hands till it overtook him with a cool, wet, gentle slap against his skin. He was standing inside the sphere, eyes closed. It was so peaceful here, safe. A woman sang a lullaby, feathers brushed across his face. The voice was clear now; it grabbed hold of him and refused to let go.

"It's okay," the voice said. "You're safe."

He opened his eyes. The wall was gone, the dark alley and the laughing, screeching rats gone with it.

Nick was prepared for the onslaught of the night terrors that followed on the heels of the mumbling and thrashing about. He pressed the call button and within minutes two nurses entered the room. They took note of Dan's vital signs and slipped soft restraints around his wrists to prevent him hurting himself or knocking the I.V. from his hand. The thrashing had started quickly. Nick looked at the nurses, sensing a change, but the nurses kept their faces professionally blank.

Sweat poured from Dan's body, his teeth clenched against a howl of pain and what Nick recognized as pure terror. This man lying in bed was so far from the friend he knew—a man of quiet, deep thinking and well-timed wit. He'd thought Dan had no demons to haunt him, no skeletons kept hidden, and yet here he was grappling with the demon from hell, and all inside his own mind.

Dan's head rocked from side to side and he arched his back. His eyes remained tightly closed.

Here it comes. Here. It. Comes.

Nick held both of Dan's shoulders in a vain attempt to bring the man out of his nightmare by touch alone.

The nurses gripped Dan's struggling legs and held him down as best they could. His heels dug into the bed, his arms strained against their bonds and his neck grew rigid as he fought nameless terrors. The nurses looked worried. This had to be the worst episode yet.

"Mr. Somers," one of the nurses spoke, "come down here and hold onto his legs. Right here." She motioned where he should stand with her head. "We need to get the doctor in here."

Nick hesitated as he looked at his friend's tormented face then moved down to the end of the bed. The nurse nodded and rushed from the room. The door had barely finished swinging behind her when Dan's teeth unclenched and he let out an almighty scream. Nick let go of the leg and raced back up to clasp Dan's shoulders.

"Dan? Dan? It's okay. Wake up for Christ's sake. Wake up!"

The scream faded away and the thrashing lessened as the terror began to recede. Nick grabbed the damp cloth he'd been using earlier to wipe Dan's face and methodically began the routine over. Trails of desperation hung in his voice as he continued to speak to his friend trying to placate him, to bring him back.

"It's okay. Just wake up."

Dan gave a long, shuddering breath and his eyelids struggled to open. Nick saw the dazed eyes and his heart sank. "Please, God?" he whispered.

Dan frowned, his hands shifting, trying to move up to his face. His eyes cleared as he stared at the man leaning over him. He swallowed deeply and in a hoarse whisper uttered the one word that told his friend he was back.

"Nick?"

19

Simone climbed into the front seat of Elliott's pick-up and pulled the faux pearl clip-ons from her ears. She pushed her "sensible" shoes off her feet and let them drop to the floor, opened her purse and dug out a pack of cigarettes and a gold inlaid lighter.

"Well?" Elliott asked. Simone wasn't the sort to fidget, always cool and collected. The visit to the suspects' house had gone smoothly, as far as he had heard, and they'd managed at least two faces on camera, but Simone was obviously bothered by something.

"I think we've found our connection," she said, pausing to light a cigarette and draw smoke deeply into her lungs. "There's at least a half dozen men. Two French, southern by their accents, and one American that I heard. I doubt if any of them are Mafioso."

"Then who are they?" Pete said from the back seat. He packed the camera away and clipped down the lid of its silver case.

Simone stubbed the cigarette out in the ashtray. Smoking helped her focus, let her gather stray thoughts. This time all it did was get up her nose and give her a sick headache. "Religious fanatics, murderers, and quite possibly kidnappers."

Elliott took the earrings from Simone and tucked them into his shirt pocket for safekeeping. The tiny transmitters had taken hours to build and he didn't have another pair. He turned the key in the ignition and gunned the engine. "Let's go tell Nick."

"Yes, let's." Simone put her head back against the seat and closed her eyes. The wig itched, but she would leave it on until they were clear of the mark. Frown lines creased her forehead and she lifted her hands to massage her temples. A sick, sick headache.

Nick was beaming with relief. Simone didn't think she'd ever seen him look so happy and open as he looked right there in the drab hospital corridor. The look suited him, she decided, suddenly wishing he'd shared it with her on the few occasions they'd dated. Simone pushed the thought away. She hadn't wanted love and romance back then anyway, and now … well, now she had Finn. The man was fifteen years older than her, but the quiet place in her heart she'd always kept fiercely protected from hurt was filled with devotion. And she knew, without a doubt, Finn felt the same way about her.

"Does that look on your face mean good news?" Simone asked.

Nick glanced at her, then to Elliott, no doubt reading from their expressions that they had news of their own to share. Elliott was chewing his bottom lip. Nick focused on that for a full second.

"What's happened? What did you find out today?" she urged.

"Quite a bit," Elliott said quietly. "But nothing that won't keep a bit longer. How's Dan?"

Nick nodded and the smile on his face widened. "He's back."

Simone watched as the strain of past days vanished under a new lightness of being and returning color in Nick's face. Nick rocked on his heels, seemingly lost for any more words than those two.

"Nick?" she gently prodded. "Tell us what happened."

"He was having another one of those nightmares—the worst one yet—but this time he came right out of it at the end."

"I wouldn't have thought him to be the type plagued by bad dreams. I'm glad he's beaten them back," Finn stated solemnly. He stood behind Simone; hands firmly buried in his pants pockets as usual.

"He's still pretty confused and he's got the world's worst headache," Nick added, then grinned again. "When I left, he was grumbling about jackhammers and herds of stampeding cows."

"When can we see him?" Simone sagged as the built-up tension drained away.

"Maybe tomorrow. Give him a chance to sort through what happened first, okay?"

Simone leaned against Finn, relaxed and happy.

Nick shook his head and hitched the belt of his jeans up. With his hands on his hips, he studied the faces around him. "Now," he started, unable to keep the weariness from his voice, or the smile, "tell me what you found out."

Simone cleared her throat before speaking. "Perhaps we should move to a more private location?"

"Good idea," agreed Elliott.

"The doc won't let me back in to see Dan until he's finished all his testing, so let's go back to the office."

The visitors all nodded but hesitated before leaving.

"I'll just stick my head in and let Dan know I'll be back soon. Meet you all there," Nick added. "And, Elliott, pick up some take-out on the way, will you? I'm starving."

"Sure thing, Nick," Elliott answered.

"Simone?" Finn held his hand out. She took the offered hand and followed him down the corridor. She looked back once, just in time to see Nick disappear behind the door. A faint grin appeared on her lips—a grin that developed into a full-blown smile. Finn squeezed her hand and gave her a gentle tug. Simone hadn't realized the depth of concern she'd felt for Dan, but Finn had known. Finn always knew.

"We can call his grandmother with the news on the way." Like Dan, the old lady had grown on her and she knew that she'd be keen to get back to the hospital for a proper visit now her grandson was awake.

"What?!"

The remains of the Chinese meal Elliott had picked up sat in the middle of Nick's desk, ignored. The office was small and chairs had to be filched from other desks but they all managed to squeeze in. Simone didn't flinch as she continued with the day's discoveries.

"It appears that Roger de Laurac may belong to a group calling themselves 'The Brotherhood', also known as the 'Brotherhood of the Grail'."

Nick groaned. "And how did you find this out?"

"I visited their home, hideout, call it what you will, this morning, undercover. The name we received earlier already struck a chord with me, but while I was there, I saw certain objects that indicate the occupants were connected to some sort of group."

"A gang?"

"Not exactly," Simone said, glancing at Finn.

"The objects that Simone described," Finn began, tapping the files on the desk before opening them and passing some pictures of similar objects across to Nick, "point to a quasi-religious group."

Nick looked perplexed. He flicked through the photos, stopping at one that showed an ornate seal of a cross on a shield surrounded by fire. Other photos showed crosses with vines, fancy goblets and ornately texted manuscripts.

Finn went on. "Apparently, we've managed to upset an offshoot group that styles themselves on the medieval Templar Knights, of all things."

"You're kidding! How the hell did we do that?" Nick was glad there was no mafia connection, but just as concerned now about religious fanatics.

"It seems that these type of groups are coming out of the wood-work. We think the professor might have upset them too and 'cause we're looking for her …" Elliott trailed off. He stood and turned to the office window, one hand running through his thick hair in anger and frustration.

"How is the professor involved?" Nick asked, though he already suspected the answer. Simone's words of almost two weeks ago came back to him: "Secret societies, historical cover-ups—who knows what scandals we might unearth?"

"Her research," Elliott answered. He pushed a thick book across the table. "I haven't read this yet, but Finn and Simone believe that the professor made a few discoveries of her own alluded to in this book."

Nick looked at the book's cover. *Catholics, Cathars and the Code*, by Professor Irene Flemming. He flipped it over and read the blurb on the back then looked back up in disbelief. "This is all over some mythical cup? Hasn't that subject been done to death?"

"It's a little more complicated than that, Nick," Finn assured him seriously.

"It's the Sangreal," Simone added in a soft voice. "The bloodline of the Messiah."

20

Professor Flemming forgot all about her sore feet and aching back. The field of flowers she walked through surrounded her with glorious scent. The township of Smiggins' Rest had been surrounded by trees getting ready for winter, but here it was like eternal spring had covered the land. Snow-capped mountains were all around, yet the earth was warm and wild flowers bloomed. Impossible and wonderful!

A soft breeze rustled through the grass bringing with it gentle music and the professor noticed a small group of people at the far edge of the field near where her path would re-enter the woods. One of them was playing pipes of some kind, another clapped along. The rest watched her approach.

As she reached them, she could see they were all smiling. Two men and a woman stepped forward to welcome her. Each was carrying a walking stick similar to her own.

"We have been waiting for you," the woman said, holding out her hand. "Your journey is nearly over."

The men stepped up to her side and together the four rejoined the group and then walked into the woods, pipe music trailing behind them.

21

Dan walked down the alley. All signs of Nick's crashed Taurus had been cleared away. He pressed his thumb and forefinger into his forehead in a vain effort to ease the constant ache behind his shaded eyes; then, pulling his baseball cap down a little lower and adjusting his sunglasses, turned his head toward the end of the alley. His nightmares were more vivid to him from this point than actual events. He remembered fighting and running and feeling helpless. Being shot fit in there somewhere, but it was all jumbled in with his dreams and a strong feeling of being cut adrift. His dreams had eased, but he always awoke with the thought that there was something he hadn't done, some connection he had failed to make, and until he made it he was still drifting.

He grasped the body of his mother's old camera in his hand and gently squeezed the shutter release, capturing the dirty, graffiti-covered wall on film. A few photos here and there, and time in the darkroom later, might help him make sense of whatever was happening.

Boot heels crunched over loose gravel as he made his way to the far end of the narrow street, leaving patterned imprints in the muddy remains of a puddle in the cracked road surface.

Elliott had told him about finding his phone under the trash. The unit was locked away in Nick's office awaiting a new cover, all traces of blood cleaned away. The trash, too, was gone, though the cans and dumpster would soon be overflowing once more with the discards of modern life. He looked around, kicking at the odd bit of paper, a forgotten can, avoiding the real reason he'd come back until it couldn't be avoided any longer. He turned to stare at the barred basement window. It'd been boarded up.

He was lifting the camera to his eye when shuffling from behind caused him to twist around, wincing as he did—the fast movement jarring the ache in his head to a slow throb. It didn't do much for his nerves either. He was scared shitless and didn't know why.

"They closed it off, but ya can still get in. If ya wanna, ya can," Will told him.

Dan nodded at the old man appearing from the shadows. Will had visited him in hospital, and after, a couple of times, but Dan really had little memory of him other than that. He had the feeling though that he should. The homeless old man had something to do with the strange disconnectedness he was experiencing.

"Not so sure I wanna go in," Dan answered.

"I can show ya the way," Will continued. "It's jus' a room, nuthin' to be scared of."

Dan licked his lips. *Scared. That's my problem. Just plain scared of wakin' up and still being in that tunnel.* He snapped himself out of it with a mental shake. Scared, but he'd been scared before and come through it. He nodded to the man again.

"Show me the way."

22

Simone and Finn sat in Professor Flemming's study, poring over the journals and various piles of paper they'd found in the basement. Elliott sat at the computer in the corner doing the same with the woman's electronic mail, bookmarks and files. Everything had been gone through several times before, by the police and by the investigators. And no doubt by the Brotherhood.

"Guys? I think I've got something here," Elliott's voice broke the relative silence of the room.

Finn and Simone looked up, Finn a little dazed from the amount of reading and information gathering he'd become so engrossed in.

"Come and take a look."

The couple joined him by the computer, looking over his shoulder and peering at the screen.

"It's one of her bookmarks—a book shop in New Orleans. I did a search of its database and came up with this." Elliott tapped the keyboard and the screen flicked to a list of books all referring to ancient bloodlines and obscure research studies.

"She sent them a pile of emails about this book here." Elliott pointed to one of the titles that simply read, *Desposyni*. No further details, no price or mention of author, just the single word title.

"One of her journals mentions New Orleans too," Finn added, going back to the pile of notebooks he'd put aside for further reading. He searched through the pile and pulled out the one he wanted, flicking through the pages till he found the needed information.

"Here it is. Old Tomes Bookstore, New Orleans." He looked up with a pleased expression. "She flew down there a few months ago to view that book. There's a pile of notes here about it." He skimmed through the pages, tracing the lines with one finger and stopping as he came to a name. "It seems she viewed the book once, but when she went back the next day it was gone. There was a note in its place from a woman, but she doesn't say what it said." Finn flicked through the rest of the notebook but found nothing further.

"Did she think to include the woman's name?" Simone asked.

"Isabel McTavish," Elliott breathed quietly.

"Yeah, that's it," Finn agreed. "How'd you know?"

"It's here." Elliott hit the print icon and the printer beside him came to life. When the page was complete, he passed it to Simone. "An email from Isabel. It mentions the book, but I don't get the rest of it."

Simone read it through quickly, then again more slowly, shook her head and passed the page on to Finn who read the email out loud. Hearing it didn't make it any easier to understand.

"Blind man, see the light. You will find it amongst the children, the many awaits you. Look for the Raven and the Dove, and the Fisher will find you. *Desposyni* is only one beam."

Finn looked perplexed for a moment, turned back to the notebook and then looked up at his colleagues. "The email was sent before she went to New Orleans."

"Print out all those emails, Elliott, and see what else you can find out on Ms. McTavish," said Simone.

"Already on their way to the printer," Elliott said with a nod toward the laser printer in the corner of the room. The machine obediently started whirring and churning out sheets of white paper. "What about that message, Prof? Code, isn't it?"

Finn nodded. "Definitely, and I'd guess that it refers to parables in some way, which means …"

"Catholics, Cathars and Code," Simone provided.

"Exactly."

23

Will and Dan stood in the middle of the basement room, staring at a dark stain on the floor.

"This is where I dragged ya first and bandaged ya up. Ya sure bled a lot. We wanted to get ya to a doc, but there was all those strangers outside," Will offered.

Dan remained silent, rubbing his healing shoulder and trying to remember something—anything—but it was all a blur. He turned to Will and shrugged.

"You were out cold." His smile faded as he watched his friend look blankly around the room—he still had the wallet. He'd wanted to give it back, but the few times he'd seen him there'd been others around. Dan's friends made him nervous and the chance to return it had slipped away on each visit. Will had just about decided that it'd been so long he might as well keep the wallet. Why stir up trouble now that things were getting back to normal? *Yep, I'll jus' keep it now*, he'd told himself outside in the alley and then he'd forgotten about it. His next words came as much as a surprise to him as they did to Dan.

"I've got yer wallet." His hand appeared from inside his great coat with the troublesome object.

Dan stared at it a moment, then reached for it, flipping it open to make sure it was indeed his. His ID photograph stared back at him. *God, that's an awful photo.* "Thought the bad guys took it."

Will shuffled his feet and shoved one hand in his pocket. The other came up to play with a chain around his neck. "I found it after. Was mindin' it for ya, and then I couldn't find the right time to give it back."

"Reckon you just did, Will. Thanks." Dan's relaxed smile helped, but something else hovered, waiting to be done.

"Didn't mean to keep it so long …" Will's voice trailed off. The chain around his neck irritated his skin; the circle pendant it held was growing hot and it burned him. He'd been wearing the darn thing for years. Found it in this very room when he first moved into the area—he didn't remember where he'd lived before then.

His thoughts, as fuzzy as they were, wandered back to that day. It had also been about the same time he'd met up with Jed. Now *that* he remembered, easy as pie. Had to be about the best day ever. Jed was as grumpy as usual, but never seemed to mind having Will for a friend, looked out for him real good. In fact, Will remembered with a rare burst of clarity, it was Jed who had given him the chain to keep his treasure safe. The ring wasn't really a ring—too big—and Jed was worried it would get lost if he kept it in one of his pockets. Jed had given him the chain and warned him never to show it to anyone.

Will hadn't thought about it since, until recently. Over the past few weeks, the ring had been bothering him constantly, making his skin feel itchy and shivery. The last couple of days he'd fidgeted with it non-stop. Every now and then he imagined he could feel the little snake nipping his chest, getting ready to sink its fangs in. Jed had caught him tugging at it just that morning.

"It's time to let it go," the older man told him in a soft voice. Hadn't sounded much like Jed. Will had been worried he'd done something wrong, but as soon as his words came back to him, Will knew that Jed was right—it was time.

"Will? You okay?" Dan asked.

Dan sounded just like Jed, soft and worried. Will didn't know anyone else who spoke to him as nice as Jed and Dan. He could feel a slow flush in his cheeks, had to get the chain off now, couldn't stand it on his skin a second longer. Now.

"I got something else to give ya," Will said. A feeling of peace swept through him as he reached up to unclasp the chain from his neck.

Nick waited in his shiny new red SUV for Dan to return from the alley. His stomach started twisting about the same time Dan had disappeared around the corner. He'd gone to open his door several times already; the only thing keeping him in the truck so far was Dan's need to revisit the alley, by himself.

"Dammit!" he muttered, throwing the door open and climbing down from the cab. He slammed the door closed again and walked around to the sidewalk, glaring up the alley. *Damn fool should still be in hospital …*

With his hands on his hips, Nick turned his back. There was a deli-catessen across the road. Pushing through the streamered doorway, he ordered two coffees from the woman behind the glassed-in counter.

"How about a sandwich ta go with tha coffee?" the woman asked. "Ye could do with some fattenin' up, ye could. We got all sorts of salads and breads, chicken, fish, raven, dove. An' a mighty fine selection o' mustards an' relishes—some of 'em hot enough ta bring light ta tha blind."

"What?" *Did she say …?* He looked down at her hands. A tattooed snake appeared from beneath her long sleeves. For a second he could have sworn its tongue flicked out at him. She pulled a pair of latex gloves on with a snap, and the snake was gone.

"I said: we've got all sorts of salads and breads with chicken, fish or mixed seafood, and a wide selection of imported mustards and rel-ishes. What would be ye fancy?"

The woman looked at him with sharp, glittering eyes. Nick thought he could hear the snake whisper to him. He shook his head and rubbed his wrist. Weird.

"Just the coffee," he replied. Handing over some money, he took the coffees and walked out to see Dan leaning against the truck, fiddling with his camera, waiting for him.

Nick walked right up to him and handed him one of the Styrofoam mugs. He felt a little unnerved by the woman in the deli, but he pushed it away to concentrate on Dan. The younger man hadn't been quite the same since the accident and Nick had brought up his opinion on early release from hospital several times. Dan had been adamant that he would be fine and the doctor agreed so long as he kept to his medica-tion and someone kept an eye on him.

Still, Nick wasn't too sure it was a good idea. He couldn't put his finger on it exactly, just a feeling he had that something was off. Until now, Nick had thought it was the effects of the head injuries, like the headaches, or perhaps the constant pain, certainly enough to put any-one off their game.

Now, as Nick held out the coffee, he thought something else entirely, and maybe it was the weirdness in the deli that brought it to mind, but Dan looked as if he was seeing something far different to the dingy street in which they stood. Traces of a smile lit his face and his eyes held a faraway expression. He didn't blink.

"You okay?" Nick asked.

It took a few seconds, but Dan finally came back to the here and now with a pained shake of his head as he realized Nick was standing in front of him.

"You okay?" Nick repeated, pushing the cup into Dan's hand.

Dan sipped the coffee then pulled his sunglasses from his shirt pocket and put them on. Grabbing his cap from where it lay on the hood of the truck, he shoved it back on his head and nodded. When he moved to get back in the truck, Nick held him back with one hand.

"You sure? You looked like you were off with the fairies there for a minute."

"Just fillin' in time waitin' around for you," he joked, pulling free.

The men got in the truck and Nick turned the key in the ignition. The engine roared. He glanced sideways at Dan as he leaned forward to place his coffee in the cup holder attached to the dashboard. A chain gleamed from beneath the other man's shirt. He frowned. Dan didn't wear a chain.

"What's that around your neck?"

Dan pulled the chain free and dangled a round metallic pendant of some kind in front of his face, staring at it intently. Nick felt strange again, like he had in the deli, and he thought he heard Dan say something about being homeward bound. But when he frowned and concentrated hard, Dan was talking about Will and a gift.

Nick shook his head to clear the fog around his mind—*I'm losin' it*—and put the truck into gear. "Let's get outta here," he mumbled, putting his foot down on the accelerator and jerking the steering wheel around. "This place gives me the creeps."

Dan shrugged and let go of the chain. He gazed out the side window, smiling at the figure at the far end of the alley. *Seeya, Will.* He sipped again at his coffee and sank down into the seat with satisfaction, the ring pendant and his daydreams forgotten, for now.

The multi-colored streamers that hung in the doorway of the delicatessen burst outward in a sudden gust of wind. The sharp-eyed woman stepped onto the street. She waited for the shadowy figure from the alley to join her and, together, they watched the truck turn off and disappear into the city traffic.

"It's on its way," the shadow murmured.

"It's time for things to be put right." The woman nodded. She held out her hand to the mysterious figure; a small black snake curled around her wrist. It hissed at the gnarled hand that joined with the woman's but was ignored. The wind blew along the street, eddies of dirt and dust rose into the air around the pair. The bent figure of a homeless man straightened inside the old coat he wore, until he stood tall once more. Age and hardship still lined his face as he spoke again.

"Not all those who wander are lost," Jed quoted. "Even though they've been wandering for generations." Nodding once, he turned to the woman. "You're right. It's time, but first I have a friend to look out for."

24

Finn sat hunched over an old manuscript, absently rubbing his head. The document was yellowed with age, its pages fragile and thin. He turned them as if he were reading the most valuable book in the world. He sat there for hours, not noticing the time or his aching neck and eyes as he read on, engrossed in the history of the Templar Knights as written by one A. Gabran. It wasn't his regular area of study though; of course, he'd heard of them, who hadn't? Still, Finn was amazed to learn of the power the Knights had held and their subsequent persecution under the Catholic Holy Offices of the Middle Ages. He was even more fascinated to learn of their links with the royal families of Europe and the hints of the secrets they guarded. He could hardly believe his eyes, yet every word made perfect sense; every fact coincided with events recorded in history. The manuscript presented a viable alternative to history as he knew it—or had known it. No wonder this stuff was all the rage in literary and filmmaking circles, it was fascinating.

Daylight was fading fast when he finally closed the manuscript and sat back with a sigh. Irene was certainly in deep. This was turning into the most complex research briefing he'd ever worked on and it appeared that, for Irene at least, it was a lifelong obsession. He stretched his arms above his head and smiled with pleasure as the vertebrae in his back popped into place. Too long sitting down. He turned tired, gritty eyes to the window. Simone had left an hour ago, Elliott much earlier, and the sky had since turned a darkening yellow as the sun slipped away. Dark clouds crossed its expanse like shadows of a future storm. He could see them swirling around on themselves, the faint glimmer of the yellowed sky shining through like a sunbeam, bringing light back into the darkness.

"Lighting the path to the truth," he fancied, then turned to look at the other book awaiting his attention. He'd barely started decoding the unusual message Irene had received via email when this manuscript had completely distracted him. He knew who the blind was, or were; the manuscript had mentioned several times who the

Desposyni were, and Elliott had found several references to them on the Internet. Had he just stumbled across the meaning of "the light"? He returned his gaze to the night sky. It was almost completely overrun by darkness. *Yes,* he thought. *That's it!* Finn was amazed at the simplicity of it all.

He stood, filled with renewed energy, and pushed the manuscript and book into his leather satchel. A smile played on his face. Flicking the switch on the desk lamp, the room descended into darkness as well. He flicked it back on and the edges of the overfilled bookshelves came into view. So much knowledge. He touched the switch again and made his way out of Professor Flemming's house.

As he pulled the front door closed behind him, he had the feeling that he was standing on the edge of something of such great importance it could change the world. A secret, at once so great and so simple, that the past and future would be altered forever. His smile widened as he walked down the path to his old sedan; he looked forward to stepping into the light.

"Yesirree, I do indeed!"

A silent figure watched from the shadows, waiting for Finn to leave before slipping into the house. The window blinds were pulled closed, and the switch on the lamp was touched once more to light the room with a dim glow. The stranger walked around the room, touching the books, stepping over the piles of journals and obscure papers, finally stopping at the computer. With deft movements the computer was switched on, and within minutes the whirr of the modem filled the room. The keyboard was tapped quickly, a short message sent, and then all files, messages and bookmarks were deleted from the memory. A few more taps and the rest of the files stored in the machine were also gone.

The stranger stood and returned to the center of the room—head raised, arms hanging straight down, palms outward. Lips moved in a soft murmuring incantation. Dark shadows flew around the figure. A gusty breeze shifted loose papers; the fluttering sounds of wings on flight filled the silences between the whispered words. A slow roar built up and the room spun on an impossible axis. The stranger's words halted, head lowered, hands relaxed as the room continued to spin crazily. Books and journals caught in the maelstrom flapped ungainly to its center and disappeared into an unseen void.

Finally, the spinning slowed, the roaring dulled and the stranger left the room, and the house, disappearing once more into the darkness outside. Inside, the desk lamp glowed, somewhat crookedly, from its perch on the professor's desk. Its small light bathed the surface, barely touching the empty bookshelves and quiet computer. A single feather floated down to land at its base, the light reflecting in the blue-back glints in its soft shafts.

All was still and quiet, as if the giddy whirlwind of only moments ago had never been.

25

"Damn, it's hot!" Elliott said, pulling a bandanna from his back pocket to wipe the sweat from his face. He was tempted to remove his shirt but for the memory of last summer's sunburn. The legacy of pale Irish skin was one of the few his migrant grandparents had passed down to him. He dragged the cloth under his chin and down his throat, then, holding opposite corners of the square, pulled it tight and flicked it around until it resembled a rope and tied it around his neck. Running a sweaty hand through his hair, he picked up his discarded garden rake and resumed his morning's duty of watching the house across the road. His disguise was perfect; he looked exactly like a man raking his front yard.

Byrd & Somers Inc. had rented the house the day after Dan had finally woken from his nightmare. Elliott had moved in the same day, Finn and Simone helping with the removal of the company's household furniture from its store of props and equipment used in the various undercover operations the company undertook. Elliott had bought the furniture years before and it had been used, collectively and individually, a number of times for similar stake-outs and temporary changes of address for family and friends. It wasn't much, some cheap pieces he'd picked up at thrift shops—enough to make a place looked lived in and provide some comfort to whoever was on watch.

Since moving in, Elliott had regularly been seen out front attending to yard work. The garden had never looked better; a load of chicken manure had been lavishly shoveled onto the beds, neglected bushes had been pruned and a variety of perennial color planted along the garden path.

Finn and Simone had visited several times; Simone displaying a vast collection of hats and scarves. Pete Tingle arrived on his motorbike the day after the move, looking more like a criminal than a policeman, and spent the afternoon tossing around a football with Elliott. Yesterday, Elliott had produced a couple of rickety lawn chairs and the two men had greeted the sunset with a few beers.

Elliott's plan was to be as open as possible with the neighbors so that members of the Brotherhood holed up across the road would become used to regular comings and goings. The plan was working. The stake-out targets were relaxed and when Elliott had given them a boisterous greeting the day before, one of the men had replied with a quick wave. Even better, Mrs. Robeson from next door had brought in a plate of double choc-chip home-baked muffins for the boys to eat and a pitcher of lemonade to slake their thirst, studiously avoiding the empty beer bottles and rough outward demeanor of Pete Tingle.

Inside the house, Pete kept an eye on the cameras set up at each window and an ear on the listening devices they'd installed around the target house. Elliott and Simone had snuck around the first night and set up surveillance points at the living room and kitchen windows, as well as tapping the telephone line. Internal access had proved impossible. The house was always occupied by at least two members of the little gang. What they had was enough though. Since the surveillance was set up the small group of investigators had learned the names of all the regular visitors to the house and caught their faces on film. The Brotherhood of the Grail had been tagged and identified, but still a firm connection between the group and the disappearance of Professor Flemming had yet to be discovered.

A small red light on one of the devices flashed. Pete picked up the headphones to listen to the telephone conversation from across the road. A few minutes later he removed the headset and picked up his cellphone to punch in a number he now knew by heart.

"Nick? It's Pete. Looks like we've got some action at last."

Elliott finished raking all the leaves into one small pile in the corner of the garden just as a black van pulled into the driveway of the Brotherhood's hideout. He strolled over to the garden hose, turned on the tap and stood watering the garden, watching the new activity.

Three men hustled out of the van and into the house. A fourth opened the side door and stepped out. He glanced suspiciously at the man watering the garden before discounting the nosy neighbor and concentrating his attention up and down the street.

The anxious man started pacing the length of the van, his hands moving from his chest to his pockets to his hips to run through his short brown hair and back to his hips. He jumped, but looked relieved, when the garage door opened and a fifth man came out and spoke to him. With a mutual slapping of backs, the agitated man climbed into the driver's seat and gunned the engine briefly before driving the van into the garage.

Elliott turned the water off as the door slid closed and the van disappeared. He spent a few more minutes coiling the hose into a tidy pile under the tap and watching for any more signs of activity. When nothing else occurred, he made his way down the side passage, entered the rented house through the rear door and practically ran up the stairs to the bedroom where the recording equipment was arranged.

"What've you got?"

Pete looked up as Elliott burst into the room.

"They're moving out," the detective replied, concentrating on the muffled sounds of conversation coming from the bugged kitchen.

"You call Nick?"

Pete nodded. "On his way. Quiet a minute, Byrd, and listen to this."

Elliott sat down next to the equipment as Pete disconnected the headset and increased the volume. The voices were muffled but understandable in the quiet room.

The two men stared at each other as they realized what the disembodied voices were discussing.

26

Dan had been quiet ever since they'd left the alley. Nick looked across at him and saw he was asleep. He tired easily and should still be in bed instead of out and about, but there was no keeping the man down.

At least I know where he is and can keep an eye on him.

He pulled the truck to a stop at a red light and took the opportunity to look at Dan more closely. His usually tanned face was pale. His pain-tightened lips were relaxed in sleep, head resting against the open window of the truck. Nick's gaze travelled down to Dan's chest and froze as he waited to see it rise and fall on a breath. When no such movement came, Nick's stomach tightened with irrational fear. He recalled the times when he'd gone to check on his sick wife asleep in bed and felt the same anxiety. Without thinking, Nick reached across and touched Dan's face, then moved down to lightly touch his hand to the still chest. Dan's heartbeat was steady, his breathing deep and slow. Nick relaxed. The knot of fear released.

Horns blaring behind him brought his attention back to the present, and he put the truck into gear and sped off. Dan stirred, sighed and shifted position as the truck wound its way through the city streets. But he didn't wake. Nor did he appear to hear the buzz of Nick's cellphone or the brief conversation that ensued. He stayed that way until the truck came to a halt inside the garage of the rented house and his door was wrenched open.

Dan woke with a start, the beginnings of a dream keeping him a moment longer from full consciousness. His brow furrowed in concentration as he tried to hold on to the threads of the dream; recapture the fading voice. Something about Ouroboros, whatever the hell that is, and finding the way. The voice had been familiar—gruff and clipped with a mixed accent. If he could just remember what it was saying.

"Dan?" Elliott shook his shoulder.

The voice was gone, words lost. Dan scowled at Elliott and climbed out of the truck. He started to share his frustration at the broken chain of thought when he felt his legs sag. The world seemed to shift beneath his feet, vision narrowed to a pin-hole. Any second now he was going to throw up.

"Whoa there, pard! That must have been some dream you were having," Elliott commented, catching Dan's arm and holding him up.

Dan leaned against the truck, his lips tight as he fought to control the bout of dizziness. The driver's door slammed closed and Nick came around the front of the truck.

"You okay?"

Dan lifted a shaky hand to remove his hat and sunglasses and blinked a little dazedly at the two men watching him. "I'm fine. Jus' moved too quick," he replied.

"You should be in bed," Nick grumbled.

Dan's mind returned to the lost dream. There was something he needed to know. Maybe he could still find out. He nodded slowly, his head throbbing. "You're probably right."

Elliott and Nick flashed concerned glances at each other and back at Dan, then, with Elliott still supporting him, guided him into the house. The constant need for rest irritated Dan immensely and he fought it as much as he could. To have him admit he needed it, without an argument first, only worried his two friends all the more.

"Sofa?" Elliott asked Nick, who nodded and eased past the pair to make sure it was clear.

"I can walk y'know," Dan complained, pulling his arm free and sinking on to the garishly floral sofa with a groan. "This must be the ugliest stick of furniture I've ever seen," he mumbled, laying down and closing his eyes.

"Ugly but comfortable," Elliott added with a laugh. "Spent many a night recuperating on this little beauty."

"Yeah, I bet." Dan's voice was husky and soft, sleep already catching him in its grip.

Nick snorted at Elliott's comment but kept his eyes on the now sleeping man. Dan looked ill, had lost weight and Nick wondered, not for the first time, if letting him stay in Denver instead of taking him home to New Mexico was the best idea. Would he even go though? Nick knew he wouldn't. His grandmother was still healthy and fit, but too old to be looking after an invalid, whether he would admit to needing it or not. Dan could be a stubborn cuss when he wanted.

"Where's Pete?" he asked Elliott quietly.

Elliott jerked his thumb toward the staircase. "Upstairs."

Nick nodded, reached out to brush Dan's shoulder with his fingertips, then turned and headed for the stairs. Elliott shook his head and returned to the kitchen to finish the sandwiches he'd been making when the two men arrived. Nick had a tendency to worry and a deep ability for caring that surprised most people. He didn't look like a caring person and most of the time, he didn't act like one, but Elliott knew better. And it wasn't just from witnessing firsthand the devotion given to Kari. There'd been a time or two when Elliott had been on the receiving end of Nick's concern.

Elliott scraped mayonnaise across several slices of bread, left the knife in the jar and grabbed a handful of lettuce. His last two years with the Denver P.D. had been spent in the bomb squad. Retirement from the service had come at the hands of an unpredictable bomber and a fuse too short to allow Elliott and his colleague time to run to adequate safety. Protection gear had saved his life; his partner had not been so lucky. Doctors had repaired the broken bones and lacerations. Nick had kept the rest of him together through the long days of guilt-ridden recuperation.

"Missed his calling," he told the tomato he was about to cut into thick slices and layer over the lettuce. "Would have made a great dad."

The bedroom door opened with a muted swish. Nick paused a moment before stepping in. Pete was busy, scribbling in a small note pad. A woman's voice, hard, cold and disturbingly familiar to the blonde investigator, crackled in the air.

"Ye get no favors from me, Roger. Ye were warned of the dangerous path ye chose."

A man's desperate voice replied, "I punished the one responsible, Isa—"

"The one! Yer arrogance is overwhelming. The judgment has been made and further discussion is pointless."

"I didn't know. I swear it on my oath, on the sacred cross of …"

"Tsssh! Ignorance is not a blanket to pull over yer head when the weather turns foul. Ye be a leper, Roger de Laurac. Seek me out no more!"

Nick jumped when the room filled with the sound of dial tone as the woman disconnected the line. The scratching of pen on paper continued another minute before Pete finally stopped and leaned back in his chair with a sigh.

"That was it. Enough for an arrest warrant. The woman accused him of the attempted murder of Tenney and he admitted his involvement as well as the murder of Terence Smith. So that lets you off the hook for that one."

"Was there any doubt?" There had been hours of questions when they'd reported the arrival of the dead Mr. Smith to the police.

Pete laughed. "Lots of it. You're not known for your gentle nature …"

Elliott walked in with sandwiches and a pot of coffee. "Lunch is served," he announced with a wide grin, putting the tray down on a bare patch of table.

"It's after two," Nick said. He took the coffeepot and a mug from the tray.

"Well, late lunch anyway. Dig in."

"Speaking of obstinate drifters, where'd you leave him?" Pete asked Nick. He reached for a sandwich and began picking at the filling.

"Sleeping on the sofa," Nick answered. "What's the word on the Brotherhood of the Grail?"

"They've been ordered to disband by some governing body they apparently operate under."

"Who?"

Pete shook his head. "I don't know, but whoever it is, they've got these guys scared."

Nick raised his eyebrows. In all the time they'd been watching the group, the main thing they'd learned was that the men seemed to operate on a level that made no allowances for things like individual thought and opinion, compassion or fear. They followed Roger de Laurac without question.

Their duty and loyalty to him and the vows of the Brotherhood were all consuming. What does it take to scare these guys? Nick wasn't really sure he wanted to find out, but they had made a commitment to find the professor. It had already cost them so much. They would see it through to the end if only to exact a little more retribution for Dan's pain and suffering.

Pete took a bite of his sandwich and glanced at Elliott. "There's more."

"Oh?" Nick said around a mouthful of bread and salad.

"Pete's got them on tape discussing their failed attempt on Dan. Seems like that's why they're in the shit with their bosses." Elliott had already wolfed down one sandwich and was reaching for another.

"Because they failed," Nick stated.

"No," Pete countered, "because they did it in the first place. Stepped out of bounds, so to speak."

"They ain't happy about it though and whether they'll be good little boys and go home is totally up in the air." Elliott's expression suggested that he was hoping the group would be anything other than good. Nick silently agreed. A little retribution would certainly assuage some anger over the whole situation.

"The woman?" Nick asked.

"I'll play it back," Pete said.

When the tape ended, Elliott spoke up. "Did you hear that? He almost said her name." He turned to Pete. "Wanna bet it's the same woman?"

"What woman?" Nick couldn't quite place the voice.

"I was over at Professor Flemming's house this morning with Finn and Simone. We found another possible lead. Apparently our professor's been in contact with one Isabel McTavish about some book. She sent Professor Flemming a coded message, who then made a trip to New Orleans not long before disappearing," Elliott said.

"De Laurac called Isabel to plead his case …"

"And failed," Nick interrupted. "Description?"

"Nothing physical, though that's a Scottish accent. I'm sure of it," Pete replied.

The room was quiet as the men ate, drank their coffee and thought about the day's revelations. Nick could feel how close they were to solving the case yet, with every new discovery more mystery was unraveled.

"We've got enough to get them charged," Elliott suggested, "but no connection to the professor."

"Until now," added Nick. "This woman is the connection."

"We'll know more once Simone gets here." Elliott looked at his watch then glanced at Nick over his coffee mug. The two had been friends a long time, and Elliott could tell something else was bothering the man. He also knew Nick wouldn't speak about it until he was ready. Which means probably never. He stared into the bottom of his empty mug and waited.

"I wonder what it is," Pete thought out loud.

Nick looked at him sharply. "What?"

The detective met the look and continued with his train of thought. "What it is that Roger de Laurac didn't know."

The sleek black Jaguar pulled up in front of the newly rented house across the road.

"Roger, that fancy car you like so much is back," the dark haired man called from the front room. He stood a moment watching as the car door opened and a woman got out. The woman patted her coil of hair, hidden under the muted blue shades of a silk scarf, and glanced casually over, nodding to him as he watched through the window. The man, Michel Sicarius, stared hard at the woman, not returning the faint greeting but not turning away either. His hands stayed clasped behind his back; his posture remained intense and brooding. She was a beautiful woman with expensive tastes— the car and tailored pantsuit she wore proved that. But none of that interested him.

"I see you, Questor," Sicarius breathed, "and soon I will know you."

28

Simone closed her car door and touched the remote alarm on her key ring. The skin on her back crawled and she looked across the road at the house the team currently had under surveillance, bringing her hand up to smooth down any stray strands of hair. Something inside her quailed at the sight of the man standing behind the picture window of the living room, staring at her. The man radiated danger, his glare reducing the distance between them to zero.

Her glance took in the whole of the man and she mentally listed the description the team had of Michel Sicarius: six-foot tall, wavy black hair that curled beneath his ears, olive skin, heavy French accent. Sicarius was one of the more shadowy of the mysterious Brotherhood. Other than his name and the fact that he was regularly seen in the company of de Laurac, nothing much was known about the man.

She nodded in his direction before adjusting her jacket and walking around the car to the sidewalk. She walked up the garden path and entered the temporary offices and home-away-from-home by the front door. The tingling at the base of her skull didn't cease until the door closed behind her with a defiant click.

Sicarius gave her the creeps. She'd watched over hundreds of people in her less than illustrious career: criminals, betrayers, the just plain sneaky. All of them had been easy to read, had their little tells and habits that shone like beacons. Open books to her well-trained eyes. All except the brooding Frenchman. He kept the doors to his personality and intentions closed tighter than a bank vault.

It had the dual effect of making her intensely curious and a little scared, as if this single man embodied all the childhood "boogieman" stories she thought long forgotten. A tendril of fear, that perhaps the stories were true after all, threatened to betray her resilience to such old wives' tales.

Soft snores came from the sofa. Simone shrugged her morbid thoughts aside and crossed the room to crouch beside Dan, wondering, not for the first time, when things would return to normal. She missed his wry sense of humor and keen observations. Both still there, but dulled by persistent headaches and need for medication. Concussion was a tricky thing and Dan's had been severe.

A whisper-soft touch on her shoulder alerted her to Elliott's presence.

"He'll be fine," he said in a low voice.

"I suppose sleep's the best thing. If only it were more peaceful."

Dan's snores were halfway between sleep-filled and pain. A light sheen of sweat covered his face.

"Some rest is better than none at all. Nick and Pete are upstairs. Come on up. They've got good news to share."

"Mmm … I have some interesting information as well." Simone wasn't convinced on the quantity versus quality of sleep statement, but what could she do? Absolutely nothing. The helplessness affected them all. She pulled the rug at Dan's feet up and over his prone body and left him to his rest.

"So what exactly is the Desposyni?" Elliott asked as soon as Simone had settled into the remaining chair in the room. Simone squirmed uncomfortably on the hard wood and removed her jacket. It was stuffy in the room. The weather outside not much better, hot even for this time of year, and she longed for the cool autumn days of England.

"Literally, the word means 'heirs to the Lord' and refers to those families that are part of the messianic bloodline. The messianic bloodline, of course, includes Jesus Christ." Finn had been brimming with excitement when he'd filled her in on everything he'd discovered in the professor's notes.

"The family of J.C.?" Elliott asked incredulously. "I didn't think any of that was real."

Simone nodded. "Though J.C., as you call him, was just one member of an already established bloodline. Albeit, one of the most well known …"

"And this book Elliott mentioned?" Nick prompted. "Find anything more on it or the woman?"

Simone pulled a single sheaf of paper from her file of notes and passed it across the small table. "This is some basic information we found on the Internet. It's fairly vague. Judging from the professor's notes the book is much more detailed and mentions a number of surprisingly familiar names as well as assorted chivalric societies. We have found no mention of our neighbors; though the place has obviously been searched more than once." Simone inclined her head in the direction of the house opposite them. "Finn had more insight into Professor Flemming's hiding places than others would have. Apparently she was quite the wily old bird."

"Chivalric societies? Knights on white horses and troubadours?" Pete queried.

"Yes, actually. Though it's a little more involved than that. What we know is only the surface of traditions that go further back and far deeper into human history than general stories allow," Simone confirmed, passing yet more papers around the table.

"Order of the Realm of Sion, Knight Protectors of the Sacred Sepulchre, the Order of the Sangreal? Fancy names. All sounds … lofty," Nick commented.

"But we're not in England or Europe," Elliot began. Surely these societies would have no real power here."

"Haven't you seen *Conspiracy Theory*?" asked Pete. "It's a classic. Mel Gibson had this theory where he proved …"

Nick cleared his throat. "This isn't a movie, Tingle."

"I know, but …"

"Gentlemen, please." Simone held up her hand before continuing with her summary. "These societies, and others like them, certainly do exist here and they always have, at least since the arrival of Europeans."

Pete nodded as if he'd known all along—conspiracy.

"George Washington, Benjamin Franklin, Thomas Jefferson and Elliott Adams were all connected to the Rosicrucians or Freemasons, and the Great Seal is directly related to alchemical traditions."

"Alchemy?" Nick sounded disbelieving.

Simone rested her hands over the manila folder of notes on the table in front of her and continued. "Traditions of these societies are alchemical but it's not mad scientists looking for formulas to turn lead into gold. It's the secret esoteric knowledge in which the societies have their roots. The symbols on the seal are occult in origin."

"So there is a conspiracy, isn't there?" Pete asked enthusiastically. Simone's answering sniff was noncommittal.

"And the connection with the professor?" Nick asked before the detective could expound further on any wild theories.

"This information isn't enough to warrant her being kidnapped. Seems like anyone can pick up a book or go online and find it out for themselves," Pete said.

Simone looked at each of her fellow investigators. "Neither Finn nor I believe she was kidnapped."

Dan stood in an open field of bright blue cornflowers. A cool breeze swept through and the carpet of flowers bent and shifted in its wake. A shadow flickered over him, growing larger, and he tilted his face to the sky. A giant raven flew overhead, circling the field and the lone man, descending slowly as it gently curved its way through the air. It finally landed before him, a blue-black giant of a bird that stared at him through cold, hard eyes. The raven fluffed its feathers out, shook its head and began to change.

"You?" Dan asked, astounded. The man that now stood hunched before him, his old face as lined and weather-beaten as ever, pulled his worn coat tightly around him and nodded once.

"Me."

The three men stayed quiet as they stared at Simone, waiting for her to continue. She stood and walked to the window to gaze at the house across the road. Her hands found their way into her pockets as she leaned against the wall and watched a small group of children running down the street. Without breaking her gaze, she began to speak again.

"All this is common enough information if you know where to look. Though I'm fairly sure that book would be an exception. The professor was quite excited about finding it. She flew down to Louisiana for the sole purpose of viewing it." She turned back to the center of the room. "We believe that she discovered some hidden knowledge in the book, perhaps something else connected to it, and that she went off chasing it down. And that's where the Brotherhood and the mysterious Ms. McTavish come into the picture. I called the store on the way over here.

They don't know an Isabel McTavish, haven't heard of the *Desposyni*, and would be quite happy to take a copy off my hands if I should happen to come across it."

Pete beamed. No doubt every word Simone said only added to his conspiracy theory. She was almost convincing herself and had to admit that the case was getting more interesting by the minute, especially without the worry of a missing friend.

"As Elliott found, the professor emailed some businesses in a town called Smiggins' Rest when she got back," she added. "It's a little village up in the mountains. The businesses she contacted were The Rest Motel, High and Wild Wilderness Supplies, and Olde Things—an antique store."

"Is the McTavish woman connected with any of these people?" Nick continued with his questions.

"Not that we know of. However, and rather obviously, we do believe there might be some relationship between Old Tomes Bookstore and Olde Things Antiques. The bookstore has heard of the antique shop, but we haven't contacted any of the Smiggins' Rest businesses for reciprocation of contact."

"But we think she went there?"

"The professor booked accommodation for one week at the motel and asked the wilderness store a bunch of questions about equipment rental and maps," Elliott said, passing across print-outs of all the emails from Professor Flemming's computer.

Nick frowned and threw a quick glare at Pete. "Why didn't the police find all this?"

"The messages had been deleted. I ran my latest FDE upgrade through her computer and found them," said Elliott.

"FDE?" Nick asked.

"Forensic Data Examination," Elliott explained, his eyes lighting up. "It's a new program I've have been working on that can search through a hard drive for lost and/or corrupted data. It's faster and more accurate than any other on the market, and ..."

"Elliott," Nick interrupted. They all recognized the light in Elliott's eyes and knew they were in for a complete description of one of the man's pet projects if he wasn't shut down quickly. Simone hid a grin and waited for Nick to gain control of the man's information steam train.

"… it can easily recover data from crashed drives too. The scope is …"

"Elliott!"

Excitement still touched his features as Elliott finally realized Nick was speaking and looked up.

"The abridged version is fine. We want to find the professor this century."

"Find anything else?" Pete asked, appearing a little dazed at the speed and direction the conversation was taking.

"Only one other thing: a reply to Isabel McTavish's message." Simone moved back to the table and opened her notebook. "The coded message was, and I quote, 'Blind man see the light. You will find it amongst the children, the many awaits you. Look for the Raven and Dove, and the Fisher will find you. Desposyni is only one beam', end quote." She looked up from her notes to see Elliott nodding and Pete looking even more baffled.

Nick's expression had grown pensive. "And the reply?" he asked softly.

"Something once lost, then found. Now …"

"On its way homeward bound," Nick finished. The pensiveness had turned to intense concentration.

"Why, yes. I take it you've heard the phrase before? It's from a quite well-known novel."

"Part of it, yes, but not in a book. Dan said it earlier today," Nick replied, turning his face to the woman by his side.

"Dan?"

Nick nodded. "And the woman in the delicatessen where I bought coffee talked about ravens and doves … and the blind seeing the light. We were at the alley."

Simone sat down.

Elliott stared at Nick. "That was her on the tape. Wasn't it?"

Nick dropped the pen he'd been holding onto the table and watched it roll toward the recording equipment.

"Yes."

29

"It will be dark soon, Michel. Time to go," Roger de Laurac spoke softly to the dark-haired man. The two had known each other most of their lives. Their home villages in the French countryside were only a day's walk from each other. Both villages were too small to host their own schools and the boys had attended lessons at a much larger town. They'd met on the bus. The sandy-haired youngster half-sitting on the seat in front had been involved in a heated discussion with a youth two years his senior, and this had fascinated Michel Sicarius. Roger was everything he was not—tall for his age where Michel was short; he was thin compared with Michel's chubbiness, and the boy was articulate and very intelligent.

Fascinated with the skinny boy's impassioned words and fierce gesticulating, Michel had stood scowling when the argument appeared to be taking a more physical turn. And though he'd grown out of the awkward shyness of his youth and left the chubbiness behind with the short pants, he had been a dark force supporting the wordy and sometimes brash Roger ever since.

Michel turned to his old friend. The two had been working together for a few years now—comrades, brothers-in-arms in defense of the truth and its progeny. Michel's loyalty to the Code was unquestionable. He, as did his whole family, lived and would die to protect the Sangreal. Roger's was not. In the last few months things had been slowly changing between them. At least, Michel thought so.

Roger's words no longer had the same pull as they'd once had. A purist in his beliefs, Michel had suspected the words Roger now espoused suited the man more than the cause and framed an ideal more mercurial than Michel was prepared to accept. Roger had changed and the change had been noticed by more than his childhood friend.

"Everything is different now, Roger. It is time for things to be put right."

Roger grasped the hand that his friend held out. "Our time will come again, old friend."

Michel answered in a faintly melancholic tone that belied the passionate intensity and the conflict in his heart.

"Our time is now."

30

Waking up was slower the second time round—a natural progression from dream state to reality instead of Elliott's bolt from the blue. As such, the dream words floated around in his memory a little longer and when Dan finally opened his eyes it was with the certainty that there was a whole lot more going on than one missing professor.

He looked around the room. The curtain had been drawn and it was dark and stuffy with the day's heat. "How long have I been asleep?" he muttered, pulling himself into a sitting position. He rubbed the last of the sleep from his eyes and pushed unruly hair back from his face. His wandering eyes fell on a small coffee table that had been pulled up to the sofa. It held a bottle of water. Dan grinned and reached for it, unscrewed the lid and drank. Feeling partly refreshed he decided to go in search of food and headed into the kitchen. On the bench was a note telling him to look in the refrigerator. Within minutes he was sitting down at the breakfast bar consuming the last of Elliott's sandwiches. Outside the kitchen window the sun still shone, though less brightly than earlier. He felt like he'd slept for days instead of just a few short hours.

When his hunger was satisfied he placed his plate in the sink and leaned back against the bar, slowly sipping the water and thinking about his dreams. He couldn't remember them being quite as intense as these last few, nor so real as the one from which he'd just woken. The scent of wildflowers tickled his nostrils and his skin still felt sunshine warm—almost as if he hadn't been dreaming at all. But it had to be a dream, didn't it? Birds didn't turn into cranky old men. Fields of wildflowers didn't just appear out of nowhere.

That was the stuff of books and movies, not even the type he usually paid attention to. Give him a good old B-grade Audie Murphy western anytime, an action story with karate and life or death situations. It had to be imagination playing tricks on him, and yet the man in his dream had spoken with his grandfather's voice.

The ring he wore on the chain around his neck rested heavily on his chest. It felt warm and he reached up to touch it. The metal vibrated as his fingers ran around the circle. A strange sensation and a little spooky. Dan pulled the chain over his head to inspect the ring closer. Too large to be worn on the finger really, even for Elliott or Professor Shaw, both big men, and too small to fit over his hand. Dan wondered about its purpose. Will hadn't known.

It appeared to be made of five separate bands of metal though he couldn't tell of what type—not quite steel, not silver. He spat onto the ring and rubbed away some of the grime that coated it, then polished it on his shirt. The small patch of cleaned metal glowed under the fluorescent globes of the kitchen. He held the chain high and let the ring swing in wide arcs, the light catching it and shooting tiny beams of brilliance around the room. His eyes widened and he caught the ring with his other hand, studying it even harder.

He closed his eyes for a moment in thought, gripped the ring tightly, then turned and walked out of the small kitchen to the stairs. Words from his dream echoed in his head.

"What else can you tell us about her?" Simone asked.

Nick closed his eyes to think and the image of the woman behind the counter grew in his mind. "Black hair, long and tied back, green eyes, fair skin but tanned."

He opened his eyes and drew a small circle on the back of one wrist with his finger. "She had a tattoo of a snake on her wrist. I ordered coffee while I was waiting for Dan. She asked me if I wanted a sandwich. Said they had all sorts—chicken, fish, raven and dove, and relishes hot enough to bring light to the blind."

"Raven sandwiches?" Elliott screwed his face in disgust.

Nick's mouth turned up in a lop-sided smile. "Yeah. Well, I said no to the sandwich."

"And Dan?" Simone continued.

Nick ran his hands roughly through his short hair and kept his eyes averted from the others. He dropped his hands to the table edge. "It was weird. When I came out he was leaning against the truck, staring into space, real faraway look in his eyes."

"He's done that a lot lately," Pete put in. "It's the after effects of the concussion and drugs he's taking. I had the same thing for days a few years ago. Had a head-on with a metal pipe. Not fun."

Nick shook his head. "No. This was different somehow. We were in the truck when I noticed he had a chain around his neck. I asked him about it and he showed it to me. Said he got it from Will." He paused again and looked up. "That's the weird part because I heard him say that rhyme, exactly the same, but when I looked at him he told me about Will."

Simone frowned. "What does it all mean? We've got some woman from Scotland sending coded messages to a professor who's gone missing while searching for something she may have read about in a book. The same mysterious woman holds some position of power over the Brotherhood and is contacting Mr. Somers here in a highly unusual manner. And now, it seems that Mr. Tenney is involved in the …" she searched her vast vocabulary for a suitable word, "… weirdness!"

"Maybe Flemming found out whatever it is that de Laurac didn't know and, whatever it is, is also about Dan," Pete suggested. "Sounds like she wanted Finn to know. Wants you to know too."

"You're right, Pete. She's playing us all," Nick agreed in a low voice. "But why, and what does Dan have to do with it?"

The door to the hallway swung open to reveal the man in question, his face unreadable as he turned something in his hands. He finally looked directly at the people around the table, took in their curious gazes and held the object aloft.

"I have these dreams," he said. "Since I was a kid. Don't always pay them a lot of attention, but sometimes they don't give me much choice. They're kinda mixed up and strange, but the damn things don't go away until I've made some kind of connection."

Dan stared at the pendant, seeming to find strength in the unusual circlet to speak out when he never could before. "They tell the future and they're always right."

Nick pushed back his chair and started to stand. Dan's expression was moving from unreadable to faraway and he wasn't sure he wanted to hear any more about dreams or codes or mysterious people. Not if it made Dan as strange as everyone else involved in this case.

The pendant dangled on the end of the chain looped around Dan's fingers, patterning a circle through the air. His voice was low and oddly accented as he spoke:

"Ouroboros is the Lore of the Graal
In the Land of Elphane it belongs
The path begins with the Rest
Seek the Light and ye shall find the Way."

31

A wooden cross, intricately carved and polished to a high sheen, stood sentinel in one corner of the living room. Marks on the carpet, a power point and antenna outlet identified the area as the usual place for a television and assorted accessories. But the low table, covered with a plain white cloth, protected the sacred cross from touching the ordinary brown-shag carpet that graced the majority of rooms. Not a single television resided in the house. An equally well-carved vine circled around the base of the cross, each leaf fine and delicate with spidery veins and perpetual drops of dew. Books, icons and other fetishes belonging to the men had been packed away. The cross and the vine, always the first to be displayed were also the last to be removed.

The six remaining members of the Brotherhood of the Grail gathered in the room to make final plans. They'd been delayed long enough and now that they had lost support from their patrons, staying in Denver was a waste of time. They were forbidden from any more searching, even though the professor was obviously not returning and even more obviously not leaving behind any substantial clues. Roger de Laurac, leader of the group, spoke in quiet but insistent tones, pressing home the importance of his words to his brothers.

"Our benefactors have betrayed us. We were promised the Key and now we are being denied."

"We should have left weeks ago, de Laurac. Hanging around waiting has been a waste of time." Ben Grady was a newer recruit to the Brotherhood and hated the forced and boring inaction of the group's time in Denver, making no bones about sharing his opinions. His career as a thug in the north of England had not prepared him for the intricacies of religious conspiracies.

Roger ignored him. Action would come soon enough and the decisive execution of Terry Smith, Grady's former partner, was fresh enough in everyone's mind to prevent any more than a few disgruntled words.

"We will leave one hour after dark. Joseph will come with me in the Mercedes. Ben, Nigel and Rayce: take the van. You know what to do?"

The three men nodded. Ending a mission was always the same: dump the vehicles, clean them out and strip them down so they resembled shells with no link back to the Brotherhood.

Nigel Fields had been working with Roger nearly as long as Michel. He knew the routine and had planned the Brotherhood's exit from Denver within a day of their arrival. Roger knew he could rely on the man's attention to detail. He would have made a great travel planner.

"Gonna dump 'em south of town by the old rail yard. There's a run-down hotel on the corner nearby. The Rail Splitter's Retreat."

Roger nodded. "This is fine. We will meet you there at midnight. Michel will sweep the house after we have left."

"Here are the travel packets," Nigel announced, handing each of the four men a small package containing a passport, travel tickets and further instructions. He ignored the brooding Frenchman in the corner. Michel had made his own arrangements. "This time tomorrow we will each be far from here on our way out of the country. Make no attempt to contact each other, or to continue with our plans. Roger will be in touch when it is once again safe."

"Any questions?" Roger asked. The men all shook their heads.

Michel stepped forward from the shadows holding out a bottle of rare French red wine. Roger smiled grimly, took the uncorked bottle and poured its contents into six pewter goblets lining the mantelpiece. The dark liquid swirled inside the goblets, reflecting warmly in the dulled metal, a whirlpool of deep red fire. Each of the men took a goblet and then formed a circle in the middle of the room. They held their cups towards its center in a solemn toast.

"To the Brotherhood of the Grail—friends to the last, we will not be vanquished." Roger's voice was deep with the romantic accent of his French origins.

"To the chalice and the Vine," they chorused in traditional response to their leader's words.

Only Michel stayed silent, watching the other men as he sipped the bitter liquid. His eyes locked with Roger and for that second in time they were as strangers.

"Shimti," Michel murmured, and then a little louder, "comme si-dessus, ainsi ci-dessous."

32

"Now yer scarin' us," Elliott said, breaking the silence caused by Dan's strange recitation.

"The Brotherhood is unimportant," Dan said.

His friends looked at him askance. Dan knew he didn't sound normal. The words felt different in his mouth, clipped and pronounced in a way he'd never spoken before. He felt different too, as if there were two voices speaking, one of which only he could hear. It should have unnerved him, but the dual voice comforted him, rocked him in its gentle grasp. Nick had crossed the room without him noticing and placed a hand under his elbow, drawing him into the circle the others made. The action was just as comforting as the echo in his head.

"What're you talking about, Dan?" Nick looked worried. Dan didn't blame him. He probably should be.

"How can ya say they're not important when we finally got all the proof we need to put them away?" Elliott dropped the sheaf of paper he'd been holding onto the table.

Dan looked at each of them again, then brought himself together. A shudder went through his body, the echo faded. "The Brotherhood are bein' handled by their own people, right?" he asked, glancing across to Simone.

"Apparently so, but justice will not be served until they have been brought before our people."

"Reckon we should leave it to them and get back to the real job."

"We can't just forget about what they did," Pete said. "They've committed real crimes here. You could have died because of them. Very nearly did die."

"Ain't forgettin' anythin'," Dan assured him, shaking his head. "They made the mistake and they'll pay. I'm jus' sayin' that we need to get on with other things."

Nick cut through the confusion like a knife. "What does the rhyme mean, Dan?"

"It's what we have to do. I think it's also where the professor is."

"Where'd you hear it?"

Dan held the circle of metal inside his clenched fist. Its edges, both rough and smooth, bit into his flesh. "A friend told it to me in a dream."

"Who?"

Their eyes met across the table, grave and resolute. Dan shrugged, awkward about sharing the strange imaginings of his dream world. "The Raven." He wished his grandfather was here.

Pete Tingle whispered, "Too weird, too weird," over and over to himself. Elliott wiped his face roughly, looking alternately at Dan and Nick, disbelief evident on his face. Simone stayed in her seat, face pale yet not particularly surprised.

A staccato beeping emitted from the listening equipment. The group, startled, simultaneously turned toward the machine.

"That's the motion sensor on the bug I installed," Elliott said a little loudly, rushing to the device and tweaking knobs erratically.

Simone reached over and turned the volume up on the machine just as voices began to speak and the tape began to roll.

Nick waited till the last voice faded away before issuing his orders. "Pete, call your boss and update him. He might want to hear the tapes before he moves in. Tell him to come on down if he does, maybe bring a little support."

Nick had sprung into action. Dan had seen it many a time over the past seven years. The man's mind worked like a spring-loaded trap, one in which he caught his prey by all means possible. The Brotherhood had no chance.

"I'll see if I can clean that last piece up and get a transcription. There was something at the end I didn't quite get," Elliott said, fiddling with the equipment with more surety now. He pulled a headset over his ears and replayed the tape, filtering the recording through the laptop he'd connected to the tape machine.

"Simone, call Finn. I want him back here to talk to these people if we can."

Simone retrieved her cellphone from her jacket pocket and left the room to prevent interference with Elliott's computer.

"Dan? You up to a stroll through the neighborhood?"

"If you insist." Dan grinned.

Nick nodded and gripped his friend's uninjured shoulder. "Simone and Elliott, you cover us. Dan, Pete and I'll go over and see what they're up to. We'll take the radios …"

"Wouldn't Dan be better to wait here?" Simone questioned. Dan did look better after his rest, but not that great that he should be running around with a gun.

"We're only going for a little look-see. I'll be fine." He turned a grimace of discomfort into a scowl and took a step toward the doorway, ready to dart out and down the stairs before anyone could tell him to stay behind.

"This is light duties stuff, Simone. Dan will be watching our backs while we do all the work." Nick passed him a handgun, the H&K he usually used when being armed was necessary, and gave him a short nod of reassurance.

"I got it!" Elliott broke in. He stared at the flashing computer screen. A jagged line travelled across the display, pulsing and dipping to the tones of the recorded voices. "It's not English though, sounds French. Hang on," he added and pulled the headset plug from the CPU. The voices of the gathered Brotherhood filled the room again as they toasted their friendship and their cause. Finally, a single voice could be heard softly speaking.

"I'm not certain about the first word, but the rest is definitely French," Simone said. She stilled noticeably as the voice was recognized. A distinct chill permeated the room. "Sicarius."

"What's he saying?" Elliott asked impatiently.

"Shimti," Simone repeated the unknown word first then continued in English. "As above, so below."

"More riddles," Nick said, his voice laced with disgust. "We'll figure it out later. It's almost dark." He patted Elliott on the shoulder. "Leave it. Let's go."

Dan followed them out, *Shimti* ringing in his ears. Had he heard that before? The echo of a voice in his head rose once more. Yet this time it wasn't his grandfather or even a male voice that he heard. Its sibilant feminine tone, strange and deeply fearful, caused him to grip the gun tighter as he moved down the stairs. He hoped he could do this.

Five minutes later Nick, Dan and Pete had snuck out of the house and disappeared down the street to show up in the yard next door to the Brotherhood's hideout. They scaled the run-down boundary fence and crawled to the garage door.

Simone watched them from a protected corner by the front stoop of the rented house. "All clear from here," she whispered into the radio headset she now wore.

Dan's hand moved to acknowledge the message and Nick ran, hunched over, to the center of the door. He stood listening a moment for sounds on the other side, then whispered into his own radio, "Can you tell where they are?"

Elliott slipped behind Simone, a remote listening device in his ear. Simone covered the microphone and leaned back till her head was close to Elliott's. "Tell me what you hear."

"The three Americans are still in the living room and two of the French men have gone into the kitchen. The sixth is unknown."

Simone nodded and relayed the information to the waiting agents. She saw Nick look to Dan and begin to count with his fingers. Dan nodded and, as Nick reached three and opened the door, moved into a covering position pointing his H&K into the darkened opening. Nick squatted down behind the van, gun unholstered as he slowly moved around the side of the vehicle.

When they were certain they were alone, Dan waved Pete forward and held cover while the two men planted magnetic tracking devices to the tail shafts of both the van and the Mercedes. They activated the devices and waited for Simone to confirm they were online. On Simone's confirmation, Nick dragged himself out from under the car. He paused, watching Dan. He appeared tense, facing the internal door to the house, and on the verge of moving in.

"Simone," Nick whispered fiercely into his radio. "Dan's heard something."

Simone turned to Elliott, one eyebrow arched. Elliott slowly turned a dial on his headset and listened intently for a few seconds, then nodded to Simone. "The same. Sixth man's still wandering free."

"It may be the sixth man. We can't pick him up on the monitors. Watch your backs," Simone said into her mic. She saw the okay signal from Nick and continued with her vigilant observance of the house, her hand held tightly to the butt of a .38 special.

Nick alerted Dan that the job was done. He and Pete back-stepped out of the garage. Dan remained in position outside the door, half-hidden by bushes and shadows.

Simone heard Elliott swearing behind her and then an urgent, "Get 'em out. Now!"

"Move! Move!" she hissed into the radio to the two men still inside the garage.

A second later, Nick appeared, stretched up to the door and quickly closed it, Pete ducking out just before it reached the ground and clicked shut. All three men faded back into the bushes and over the fence. A few minutes later they were walking in through the rear door of the rented house.

Elliott beamed with relief. "Guillaime sent Grady, Fields and Limousin out to clean sweep the garage. You got out just in time. Sounds like he and de Laurac are working on the inside."

"They hear anything?" Nick asked.

"Not a peep," Elliott assured him.

Dan dropped onto the sofa and rested his head on its high back. He was breathing heavily.

"Gettin' old, pard?" Nick joked.

Sweat-damp hair clung to Dan's skin and Simone gave a lady-like grunt. Dan's pallid complexion was enough, as far as she was concerned, to prove his unfitness for physical duty. *Men! Never listen, worse than children.*

"Been outta action too long. Feel a hundred years old," said Dan.

Elliott hissed from the front door to attract their attention.

"What is it?" Nick asked.

"They're moving out," Elliott informed him, tapping the headset he still wore to indicate he could hear them talking again. Simone nodded in agreement.

"Damn! Any word from Lennard?" Nick joined Simone and Pete at the window.

Pete pulled out his cellphone to check in at the precinct and tell his colleagues to hurry up.

"Even if Lennard's on his way, they can't get here in time," Elliott said.

"Simone, you take the car and I'll get the van," Nick directed. "You'd better wait here for the captain, Elliott, and catch up with us later. Have you got the bumper beepers ready to go?"

"Two more minutes." Elliott walked over to the breakfast bar and picked up first one then another hand-held receiver. They were already switched on so he checked the frequencies, configurations and signal reception, then passed one each to Nick and Simone. Next he picked up four squat magnetic aerial devices.

"Stick these on your dashboard. It's an old 180 system with a few modifications, should work fine. Use the headsets, keep the sensitivity low and you should have no problem picking up the signal. If the multi-path fades, tweak the dials till you can hear it again. Don't forget to turn into the needle and you won't lose them. Got it?"

"Got it," all three confirmed.

Dan remained by the window. "And?" he asked, almost dangerously.

Nick glanced out the window and across the road. The room they were in was dark so there was no chance of them being seen. He turned his face part way toward Dan.

"And what?"

"Me and Elliott jus' s'posed to sit here and shoot the breeze?"

Nick sighed and Simone felt a momentary pang of pity. She knew what was coming.

"I want you two to wait for the cavalry to arrive. Wait for Finn and the police. Let them know what's going down."

"Will do," Elliott said quickly.

Simone waited for the protest to come and Dan didn't disappoint her. The man's temper was slow to burn but when ignited flashed white hot. Being mentally and physically exhausted couldn't possibly be helping.

"No way! I ain't sittin' around here doin' nothin' while you chase all over the city. What if you need help? They might pull the same stunt as before. I'll be damned if I'll jus' sit here and wait for y'all to get yourselves killed and I'm damned sick a'bein' treated like I'm gonna break if someone so much as sneezes in my direction!" Frustration dripped from every word as he stood, hands on hips facing his friend and occasionally emphasizing his anger with a belligerent jab of his finger into the other man's chest.

Nick gaped for a second at the over the top reaction to his perfectly viable suggestion. Simone's pity dried up as Nick's own temper, no doubt tainted with guilt, took hold.

"You'll damn well stay where I tell you to stay," he growled. "We need someone to stay here to meet the cops and keep watch on the house."

"Elliott an' Pete can do that, don't need no one holdin' their hands," Dan persisted.

"Maybe not, but you do dammit! Look at you. You look like crap! You ain't fit enough to be going out. This is more than light duties."

Hallelujah! Simone concentrated on the receiver in her hand to avoid giving away the smirk she could feel stretching across her mouth.

"Well, that's just fuckin' great!" Dan sneered, turning on his heel and striding out of the room toward the kitchen. "I ain't no fucking baby ya gotta coddle and watch out fer all the time."

"Someone's gotta do it. You seem incapable!" Nick threw at Dan's retreating back.

"Fuck you!"

Dan's last comment was accompanied by the sound of the kitchen cupboards being wrenched open and slammed closed. Nick moved to follow him into the kitchen, but Simone put a hand against his chest and stopped him.

"Mr. Tenney no doubt is feeling the restrictions of his slow return to health. I suggest we leave him to his own devices and get on with ours." She wiggled the tracking device in her hand. "We have bumper beepers to follow."

"I'll keep an eye on him," Elliott added.

Pete had obviously decided to keep a respectable distance between himself and the feuding friends and was already halfway out the front door.

"Damn, I wish this was over." Nick grabbed his jacket from the coffee table and walked to the door that connected the house to the garage. "I'll go now and wait in the next block for them to leave. Let me know if anything comes up," he called over his shoulder.

The door closed behind him and those left inside waited for the sound of the truck's rumbling engine before they felt the tension ease. Grumbling from the kitchen prevented Simone and Elliott relaxing too much. They exchanged futile expressions and returned to monitoring the house across the way.

Simone radioed Nick when the garage door opposite them opened and the black van drove out. It was half an hour before the Mercedes followed it, easing its way down the drive with a purr. She waited another five minutes, watching the receiver to trace the direction of the vehicle before walking out to her Jag.

The chase was on at last.

33

No further movement or sound came from the empty house, so Elliott turned away from the window and went to find Dan.

Dan was sitting on the kitchen counter, leaning comfortably against the wall with his legs stretched out along the bench and crossed at the ankles. He was calmly finishing off a carton of banana fudge ice cream. Elliott blinked in amazement. All signs of temper had disappeared.

"You're not mad anymore?" he asked, a little bewildered. He and Simone had listened to the grumbling the whole time they were waiting for the Mercedes to move out and had discussed, at some length, the increased moodiness of their fellow investigator.

"Nope."

Elliott leaned back against the bench opposite Dan. "You okay?"

"Yep." Dan spooned the last mouthful of ice cream from the carton. His face was placid, his body relaxed.

It dawned on Elliott that he'd probably never be able to figure Dan Tenney out. Every time he thought he had him pigeon-holed, he'd peel back another layer and find something new beneath the veneer the quiet man showed the world.

"You weren't mad at all, were you?" Elliott asked.

"I was a little pissed. Gettin' kinda tired of all this," Dan answered, vaguely pointing the spoon toward his shoulder and head.

"Why'd you play it up so much?"

Dan shrugged. "Nick was sportin' his guilty look. Didn't want to worry him, and when he's pissed at me, he ain't worrying. Truth is I couldn't fight my way out of a wet paper bag an' I know it. I ain't no use to Nick and Simone, only slow them down."

Flashing lights lit up the interior of the house like a crazy lightning show and the conversation ended abruptly as Elliott and Dan walked outside to talk to the police.

Captain Lennard, Pete Tingle, a police photographer and several uniformed officers approached the Brotherhood's house. Pete had talked fast into his captain's ear, pointing at both houses, the garage and the direction the offenders' vehicles had taken. Dan and Elliott stayed quiet, preferring not to attract too much attention.

The captain nodded and spoke into his radio before ushering the group along the path. He knocked at the door, identified himself and, getting no answer, let himself in.

Elliott needed to go back to his tracking equipment. He left Dan with a warning to be careful and "not do anything too damn stupid" as he walked back in to the rented house.

Dan kitted up with a flashlight and gloves and made to join in on a walk-through of the house looking for evidence, wary that there still might be someone inside. The whole block was in the process of being cordoned off and curious neighbors were already gathering along the bright yellow police tape.

Finn arrived and Dan waved him over as the group entered the dark and forbidding house. The men flicked on their flashlights. They would not turn on any lights until they had completed a walk-through. Lennard went first, directing the beam of his flashlight across the hard wood floor, side lighting it briefly to check for any evidence before walking in. Though they didn't suspect a crime to have been committed on the site, they weren't sure and had decided to err on the side of caution rather than walk in blindly and possibly ruin any trace evidence.

As the men walked further in, beams of light flicked around the walls searching out any signs of booby traps and, then, any signs at all. The group split up. Finn and Pete started with the living room, Captain Lennard and the photographer headed toward the kitchen. Dan decided to check out the inky black hallway leading to the rear of the house.

"Was there any indication that they might leave nasty surprises behind?" Finn asked Pete in a low voice.

"Not specifically, but everything about this case is so unusual," Pete replied as he trailed light across the floor, up the wall and along the ceiling in a steady circle.

Finn copied him, shining his light in an oblique fashion over the sparse furniture, being careful not to touch anything. "Did something happen today?" he asked.

"Riddles." Pete had yet to fill his captain in on the level of mystery surrounding the case and the surprising connections back to Dan Tenney. "The biggest one is Dan."

"Dan?" Surprise made Finn's voice sound higher than usual.

Pete nodded and then realized Finn probably couldn't see him. "Yeah, we got most of them on tape, some written down. We'll go over it all later." He gave a short laugh. "I hear you'll be in your element. Any luck with the code words?"

The internal door to the garage was bathed in light as Finn and Pete worked their way toward it.

"A little," the older man admitted gruffly. "Found some things out about the Templars—the real ones. Make these guys look like petty hoods."

Pete stopped moving to look at the professor, whose body was backlit by the outside lights shining through the window. "They were virtually disowned by whoever controls them today. De Laurac was called a leper. Know what that means?"

Finn turned to face the detective in the dark, one hand on the knob of the garage door. He kept his flashlight pointed to the door's base.

"Excommunication," he said, pushing the door ajar.

Captain Lennard and the photographer had found nothing of any note in the dark and were ready to start turning on lights, but a brilliant flash of light that tore through the front of the house stopped them in their tracks. The heavy thud and urgent voice that followed had them moving again, with as much speed as they dared, into the living room.

Dan was in the bathroom, attracted there by the plumes of steam escaping around the door. He touched his outspread hand to the middle of the door and shone the flashlight all around it. The door moved under his light touch and he pushed a little harder. It swung open and steam enveloped him, reflecting the light of his flashlight as he guided it around the tiled room. Finding no sign of a trap, he stepped into a plain room with dull tiled floor, dripping showerhead, and a chipped and stained bathtub full to the brim with hot water. Steam lifted off it in clouds.

As the steam escaped and the room cleared, Dan noticed the fogged mirror of the medicine cabinet. Words had been scrawled across it. Beads of condensation were only just beginning to form at the edges of the letters. The person responsible must have only just left. He dashed back out of the room and down the hallway, pulling out his gun and checking behind the half-open doors.

The final door opened out into what looked like a huge sunroom filled with potted plants. The walls and the ceiling were mostly glass, and moonlight lit the whole area. Dan scanned the room; the door leading out to the yard was wide open. He was just about to follow when he heard Pete's horrified voice echoing through the house.

The unexpected sound of one object striking against another was so quick that neither Finn nor Pete had time to react. Pete had turned his back to the door on hearing the footsteps and mutterings of the captain and photographer in the next room, so he missed most of the blinding light that filled the room from behind him.

Finn's strangled cry of pain as he grabbed his face came milliseconds after he caught the force of the brilliant light in his eyes. His eyes burned, his skin seared, pain lanced through his head and he fell to the floor shaking and curling himself into a ball.

"Professor!" Pete yelled, dropping to his knees beside the stricken man. Within minutes the room was flooded with overhead light as the captain flicked all the switches on and rushed inside. The photographer started taking pictures of the room, of Finn rocking from side to side on the floor, of the doorway and the switch that had lit the fuse to the flash of light.

Pete grabbed Finn's shoulders and held him still. "Professor Shaw? I need to look at your face. You gotta let go. Professor?"

Finn didn't or couldn't hear him. "My eyes, my eyes." Pete pried Finn's fingers away and assessed the damage. Skin shiny, red and blistering, eyes squeezed tightly closed. Not good. Not good at all. He clicked his tongue on the roof of his mouth and glanced up at the captain.

"Get an ambulance here right away and I need some clean water to wash his eyes out."

Lennard had already ordered the uniformed officers that had

rushed to the house to radio for an ambulance so he went into the kitchen for the water. Dan ran into the room, pushed the photographer away and dropped beside the fallen man's head.

"What the hell happened?"

"Booby-trap in the doorway. Flash of light, like a welding flash, went off. No explosion, but the professor was pretty much looking straight at it. He's in shock. We need to get his head and shoulders raised."

Dan placed his hands under the big man's shoulders and started to pull him up into his lap.

"Professor?" Pete said. "You need to stop rubbing your eyes so I can clean them out. Dan's just raising you into his lap. You'll be okay, but you have to stay calm and still. Are you hearing me, Professor?"

There was no reply other than more groans, but when Pete went to move the hands away again, Finn let him. Lennard came back carrying a bowl of water and some clean cloths, and Pete began the job of cleaning, very gently, around Finn's eyes. The cool water must have helped soothe some of the pain as Finn calmed enough to talk.

"What the hell was that?" he demanded through clenched teeth.

"You'll be okay," Pete tried to assure him. "An ambulance is on the way. You've got what I hope will only be like a welding flash in your eyes. They'll hurt like hell for awhile, but you should be okay. They'll fix you up properly at the hospital."

"I can't see," Finn whispered, fear evident in his voice.

Pete and Dan looked at each other over Finn's head. Dan looked as concerned as Pete felt.

"Don't even try, Finn. Keep your eyes closed," Dan told him.

"I'm blind." A pained grin formed on his lips and he started to laugh. "I was blind and saw the light, and now I really am blind."

His laughter sent chills through Pete and the men gathered around him. Dan laid one hand on Finn's shoulder and the other across his forehead as Pete finished washing out the eyes and laid a wet cloth over them to keep them cool and still. He held Finn's hand and looked back up into Dan's pale face. "Do you know what's going on?"

Dan shook his head. "I don't understand. I don't understand any of it."

Using the tracking device had allowed Nick to follow the van without being seen by its occupants. As they neared the rendezvous, he took a shortcut in an effort to get to the rail yard first. They wouldn't know he was following them at all if he was already there when they arrived. The signal started to break up as he came closer—too many reflections bouncing off the warehouses in the area. He pulled his truck up near the Rail Splitter's Retreat, just outside the sphere of the streetlights, checked his gun and got out. Keeping to the shadows, he ran over to the yards and positioned himself behind a pile of rusting steel girders. He made it just in time; the van arrived as he hid behind the discarded remains of track work.

The men climbed out of the vehicle, their figures shadowy in the poor light filtering across the yard from the street. Their movements were furtive as they began their task of stripping and vandalizing the van. Nick eased his cellphone off his belt to call Simone. No signal.

"Damn," he muttered, shoving the phone in his jacket pocket. He eased himself around the pile of girders to watch the men and look for a closer position only to see the red and blue flashing lights of squad cars. "Goddammit! They were supposed to stay back," he whispered. He glanced back toward the hotel and along the street but there was no sign of the black Mercedes or Simone.

The men from the van were startled by the unexpected arrival but quickly turned to get back in the van. A squad car came to a screeching halt blocking their escape and sending rocks and dirt flying into the air. Two officers jumped out with guns trained on the driver and his passenger. The van's engine roared and the driver wrenched the gear stick into reverse. The police issue pistol that poked its way in through his open window and the cold voice that followed halted his intentions.

"Cut the engine. Now!"

The two men did exactly that. The third man attempted an escape from the rear, easing the doors open and jumping from the van to run off into the night. Nick immediately moved to cut the runner off before he could lose himself among the empty workshops of the rail yard.

A wire fence loomed before the man as he fled the scene. He gave it a perfunctory glance before leaping onto it and climbing to the top. He appeared cool and calm, relatively speaking, as he pulled himself higher up the wire. It wasn't until he reached the top that coolness under fire altered.

"One more inch and I'm gonna blow your balls through your brains."

The menacing intent in Nick's voice was unmistakable, yet Grady—and Nick was fairly sure that's who it was up the fence—didn't appear to be the kind of two-bit hood that gave in easily. He ignored Nick and his very real ultimatum and kept climbing. Near the top, the criminal tensed to push himself up and over the barbed-wire.

But there was no ignoring the press of hard steel into his groin and the dangerous growl that followed it, Nick made sure of it. "Maybe I'll go metric and make it a centimeter."

Grady froze. Nick's threat at last seemed to have the desired effect. "All right. Lemme down."

Nick pressed the barrel of the gun harder. "I've changed my mind. I'm gonna shoot you anyway." He shoved the gun hard into the man's balls. "Just for the hell of it," he hissed. Then he reached up to grab a fistful of the man's leather jacket. With one violent jerk of his arm, he pulled the man from the fence and threw him to the ground.

Grady grunted with pain. Nick changed his mind again; shooting was too good for the fanatic. As far as he could see, the man needed far more than that, and Nick needed to exact some revenge. He picked Grady up by his shirt collar and threw him through the air to land with a thud on the rocky ground. The air in his lungs was forced out with the impact and he groped blindly for a handhold. He stopped moving when he opened his eyes and saw that Nick now pointed the gun at his head. A dark shadow of fear spread over his face. His lips moved in mumbled prayer.

All hell broke loose as the police caught up to the two men and brandished their weapons.

Nick gave one more intimidating hiss before pulling back, hands in the air, gun pointed to the sky.

"Damn!" Nick Somers hit the steering wheel of his truck in frustration as he watched only three of the fleeing Brotherhood members be handcuffed and pushed into separate squad cards. The Mercedes had not arrived—or it had and left before they were seen. He tugged his cellphone from his belt and punched in Simone's number again.

The squad cars that held the three members of the Brotherhood were pulling out. The remaining officers were securing the scene. Nick had explained who he was when the police had surrounded him and Grady, and the officers had released him almost straightaway. After answering a few questions, positively identifying the prisoners and giving the van a quick check over, he had returned to his truck to contact Simone. The signal on his phone was strong and clear, as long as he didn't move around too much, but Simone's phone was either turned off or out of area.

Simone couldn't be out of area so why turn her phone off? A seed of worry began to grow in his gut. He buried it with the thought that perhaps poor signals were the cause and tried Elliott's number instead, relieved to hear his friend's voice answer on the second ring.

"Elliott, the uniforms have got Limousin, Grady and Fields. There's no sign of the Mercedes. How quick can you and Pete get here?"

Elliott's voice crackled, faded out, then became clear. "Hang on a minute, Nick ..."

He nearly dropped the phone as the piercing siren of an ambulance stabbed at his eardrum. "Elliott! What's going on?"

"Sorry, Nick ..." Elliott was interrupted by muffled voices, but he continued before Nick could ask again. "Finn Shaw's been hurt. Booby trap. Ambulance just took him away ..."

"How bad?"

"Not sure. It's his eyes mostly. Pete gave him first aid, says it's not life-threatening ... but his eyes ..."

Nick cut in. "Was anyone else hurt?"

"No ... no ... Finn was closest ... no blast, just a flash of light. Pete was right behind him but looking away. Wasn't even singed. Dan was in a different part of the house. I think he found something."

Nick relaxed, marginally. Another injury and Simone currently missing. "Can you get away? I need you and Pete here. The Mercedes didn't show up at the rail yard and I've lost contact with Simone."

"Okay. Yeah, sure. I'll let Dan know and grab some gear. Should be able to pick the Merc up from my end. Pete's around here someplace."

"You okay?"

"Fine. Lennard's got a Crime Scene squad going over the house. Dan found something, did I tell you that?"

Elliott was puffing now and Nick visualized him jogging back to the house to get the portable tracking equipment.

"Give me twenty minutes," Elliott said without a hitch.

"I'll be waiting."

Nick disconnected and climbed out of the truck to peer up and down the street leading into the rail yard. "Dammit! Where the hell is Simone and the Merc?"

Less than ten minutes later, Nick answered his cellphone before the first high-pitched chirp could complete a single note.

"Five minutes on the E.T.A., Nick. What's the word from Simone?"

"No word, still can't get through to her."

"Can you pick her up on the bumper beeper?" Elliott asked. "Oh, shit! Hang on."

Nick pulled his phone from his ear as a series of crashes and thuds came over the line followed by a muffled string of curses and the distant screeching of brakes.

"What the hell?"

Elliott's pick-up came skidding around the corner. He pulled in ahead of Nick, and Nick could hear Pete through the phone loudly abusing the man for his wild driving. Nick climbed out of his truck and walked up to the new arrivals. When he reached the pick-up and peered inside, he saw the men slouched over and shuffling in their seats.

"What the hell are you two doing?" Nick demanded, causing them both to jump.

Pete banged his head on the dash as he sat up. "Aw, hell!" he said, rubbing the back of his head. "Elliott dropped the cellphone swerving to avoid a pedestrian two corners back."

"Now, Pete," came Elliott's muffled rebuttal. "I missed that old lady by a good three feet. Ha! Got it!" He straightened up triumphantly waving the phone in the air. "Guess I can disconnect now, seeing how you're here," he said with a grin.

They'd made it in record time and Nick was well acquainted with Elliott's tendency to exaggerate a wild story or two.

"No word from Simone, huh?" Elliott began the phone conversation again.

Nick leaned back against the truck and folded his arms. Shaking his head briefly, he replied, "Not since she first started tailing the Merc. They were thirty minutes behind me. Should be here by now."

"Thought the cops were gonna stay back?" Elliott asked. "Where's your beeper?"

Nick inclined his head back to his truck and Elliott went back to get it. "They didn't."

"Cowboys!" Pete muttered.

Elliott came back with the tracking device, punching in a series of numbers and letters on its touchpad.

"Can you pick the Merc up on that one?" Pete asked.

Elliott nodded. "A faint signal, it's a little hard to place it though, too much local interference. I'll hook up to the portable unit. That'll give it a boost."

"Okay, let's try backtracking a ways. We might be able to get an accurate reading away from here."

"Right," Pete agreed. "I'll follow in Elliott's truck." He held out his hand for the keys and climbed in behind the steering wheel. "Don't let Elliott drive yours though, Nick. I don't think the insurance will replace your vehicle again so soon."

Elliott reached in through the open window and gave the detective a quick flick to the head. "Look who's talking!"

Pete nodded and turned the ignition on. He did a U-turn with a squeal that left the other two men glaring after him. "Let's go then." He smirked out the window. "Haven't got all night."

"That guy ..." Elliott began.

"Drives just like you," Nick finished for him. "Let's go."

35

Simone checked the tracking device again then reached across to the glove compartment for a street map to check against the direction of the signal. The dark Mercedes was, indeed, heading in the general direction of the rail yard. She placed the headset back in her ears and continued through the city. The black Jag glided along the streets, in and out of traffic, stopping at lights, moving steadily forward.

When the monitor needle dipped to the left, Simone turned the Jag at the next left-hand turn. When the beeping signal disappeared, she dropped one hand from the steering wheel to adjust the dials slightly. The beeping came back stronger and louder than before so she fiddled with the dials until it was once again at a weaker reception. Then the needle jumped to the right and stayed far to the side. Simone checked her map, perplexed.

"Odd," she thought out loud. "That's the opposite direction to the rail yard." Nevertheless, she prepared to turn off at the next right bend and continued to follow the signal diligently—turning into the needle every time until the indicator returned to the center of the gauge and stayed there.

Simone pulled over to the curb. She'd followed the Mercedes into the backstreets of the industrial area of the city and traffic was light. She looked up and down the street. Traffic was more than light: it was virtually non-existent. Simone picked the monitor up for a closer look; the needle hadn't budged.

She shrugged and pulled back onto the street. Judging by the increased frequency of the beeps, she guessed the Mercedes had stopped somewhere just ahead and was proved correct after travelling through the next intersection and passing the parked car. She didn't slow down, but did risk a glance inside as she went past. It was empty. She swore under her breath and continued down the street, turning at the next corner before once again pulling over to the curb.

Looking into the rearview mirror, she switched the engine off, pulled the headset away from her ears and got out of the car. She reached back in to collect her kit vest, then closed the car door softly and pressed the lock/alarm button on the key ring. The car instantly locked and the red parking lights flashed once to indicate the alarm was set. Simone didn't like taking chances with the Jaguar.

Patting the holster under her arm to ensure the gun was exactly where she put it was a force of habit she'd tried to break many times. However, she didn't even think about the action as she walked briskly to the corner and peered around to observe the silent Mercedes. She contemplated calling Nick to tell him of this unexpected change in plans, even retrieved the phone from her pocket, but instead she switched it off. She'd call when she had something more to report. In the meantime, it would be better if the cellphone didn't ring, or vibrate, while she was trying to be stealthy. She put it back in her vest pocket, patted the gun again and darted across the road and down to the parked Mercedes, a gleaming sentinel in the deserted street.

Captain Lennard put a hand to Dan's chest preventing his attempt to gain entry to the house. "You're to stay out of there, Tenney! That's an order. Crime Scene's not finished."

"Fine. I'll stay out but I need to check out back. The guy who did this might still be there, waiting for everything to quiet down."

"It's more likely that he's in that crowd over there with his hands in his pockets," Lennard replied, jerking his head toward the people. "Look at them. Bunch of ghouls," he scoffed.

Dan dragged his fingers savagely through his hair in obvious frustration. Captain Lennard knew him well enough to recognize the narrowed glare in Dan's eyes; he was cooking up a plan to get back in the house.

Lennard had worked with the team of private investigators many times over the years. They didn't always see eye to eye, but the team were dedicated and they got results. Hell, he'd partnered with Byrd when they were both still street cops working the roughest beat in the city. He knew Dan wasn't ready to give up so he decided to get his opinion in first.

"Professor Shaw is the third man to be taken out by this gang. Who's next? One of my officers? 'Cause you know damn well you won't be going in alone." He let that thought sink in a moment. "I'd have Byrd and Somers chewin' on my ass if I let you go in too soon."

Dan was furious. He wanted to find the bastard that set them up and give a little back, but Lennard could see he was listening. This time the captain spoke with more reassurance, in a voice offering support not hindrance.

"We've got three of them in custody now. We'll get them all but we have to play it smart. You need to get them where they belong. You'll find the way to the rest just as long as you keep your head and follow the right path."

Lennard stopped speaking then, glancing into the other man's eyes to see if more persuasion was needed.

It wasn't.

Dan had listened to every word and echo of what the captain had just said. He was fairly sure Lennard didn't even realize the words he'd spoken. He nodded and met his worried eyes. "Keep us updated. I want to know every single thing your people find. I want to know everythin' they don't find too—a full analysis."

"I'll send you a copy of the report as soon as it hits my desk," Lennard agreed. The police captain clapped Dan on the arm in an extra gesture of support and turned away, radioing Walters down at the rail yard for a report on the arrest.

"I've gotta call Nick. Elliott's already gone, the bastard." Dan crossed the road, wondering how the hell he could catch up to Elliott and, in turn, Nick and Simone. Then his eyes fell on Pete Tingle's Harley and he smiled. But first, he would call Nick.

Elliott and Nick drove in silence. Elliott was concentrating on the conflicting signals the tracking device was giving him. Nick had given a rundown on what had transpired prior to his arrival at the Rail Splitter's Retreat, and Elliott had reported the discussion with Lennard regarding the tape and the crime scene. Since then, other than to announce or comment on directions, the conversation had lapsed.

"I don't know, Nick," Elliott finally spoke again. "I don't think this thing is working. I feel like we're going round in circles. We're nowhere near the house or the rail yard."

Nick shook his head. "They must have made one hell of a side trip." He stopped at a red light and searched up and down the streets. "This is the edge of the industrial estate. The place is a maze. What's the signal like now?"

"Erratic. If they're not moving, that might explain it." Elliott pulled off the headset and handed it to Nick, then searched under his seat muttering about a street directory.

Nick put one of the earphones to his ear, hoping that the signal would suddenly come true. He threw a quick look at Elliott as he opened up the directory. Elliott shrugged. "I've tweaked. I've coaxed. I've cussed it out. That's the best I can get."

Nick snorted in disgust and dropped the headset into the console between the seats. "This is stupid. We're driving blind here. Call Dan. See if he's heard anything."

The light changed to green and he steadily moved forward. Going straight was as good as any other direction right now.

Elliott grabbed his cellphone and was just about to make the call when Nick's phone began to buzz. He raised one eyebrow at the timing and put his phone back on his belt. Nick pulled his free and held it to his face.

"Somers," he said expectantly. "Elliott told me. Is he okay?"

"What is it, Nick?" Elliott whispered. "Dan?"

Nick ignored him to concentrate on the caller's voice.

"Have you heard from Simone?"

"Is it Finn? Is he worse?" Elliott persisted.

"No," Nick said into the phone, "and the signal's intermittent. We're out near the factories but we can't tell where it's coming from … No, you stay there. We need someone at base … Yes, I absobloodylutely insist! … I'll keep you in the loop, don't worry. Check the equipment and stay wary. Who knows what the hell's gonna happen next … Yeah, right … Bye." Nick dropped the phone into his shirt pocket.

"Nick! For Chrissake!" Elliott hissed.

"Dan's fine, hasn't heard from Simone." Nick stopped speaking and chewed on his bottom lip, thinking. They were driving past an all-night diner. He swerved the truck into the parking lot. "I need some coffee," he said and waved to Pete to pull over.

Elliott managed to wait until they were all sitting down at one of the cheap tables in the diner, coffee in hand, before he questioned Nick some more.

"What else did Dan say?"

Nick grimaced as he took a mouthful of the strong brew. "He thinks it was Sicarius that set them up; he left a message. Apparently, they just missed him."

"Not another one," Pete groaned. "How does he know it was Sicarius? He sign his name?"

"Sort of. The message was similar to what we heard over the wire, but in English."

"That was convenient, seeing our resident translator is currently missing. What did it say?" Pete waved to the waitress and mouthed "cream", pointing to the mug in front of him.

"The blind will lead the blind, and dark will be the path. As above, so below."

"That's just great. Anything else?" Elliott frowned at the amount of cream and sugar Pete added to his coffee. "You know that's heart attack material, right there in one cup?" He turned away to meet Nick's unflinching stare.

Nick repeated Dan's instructions. "He said to hurry up and find Simone. We have a trip to get ready for."

36

Simone crept up to the lone automobile, cupped her hands around her face and peered inside. The car was empty, not one scrap of paper or used coffee cup. She looked at the surrounding buildings. Most of them were dark, any workers having left for home long ago. One or two had a light showing through the occasional window, including the building adjacent to where the car was parked.

Simone walked up to the front door. She pulled a pen light from one of her many vest pockets and checked the entry for security alarms. Finding none, she tested the door. As expected, it was locked. She stepped back to look for another way in. The building was built flush against its neighbors, no way to get to the rear from the front, and all the lower windows were barred.

The front door it is then.

She moved back to the door, her hand fishing around in a pocket until it landed on a small box—her keys to anywhere. She popped the pen light between her teeth, flipped the box lid open and pulled out the skeleton key nestled inside to unlock the door. Simone put her equipment away and removed the pen light from her mouth, listening for any awareness of her presence.

Hearing only her own steady breathing, she pointed the pen light around the doorframe then pushed the door open just enough to let a slim person through. Following the passageway past empty offices, creeping warily up a short staircase, she finally arrived at the lit office she'd seen from the street. The door was open.

"This is taking too long, Isabel. Is all this subterfuge necessary?" Roshen Duvernoy asked the woman by his side. She was shorter than him, but not by much. They could easily be mistaken for brother and sister, and in a way they were, with bonds so strong not even death could truly break them.

"Aye, Roshen. It is. If we came right out and told them, they'd not believe, and we still have some time," she replied confidently.

"Why so many? We only need the one. It would be much easier," he asked.

"The one is made from the many. That is where his strength lies." Isabel smiled in the darkness. "Ye worry for no good cause. Aiden and his friend have already passed through the Rest. The One is, even now, preparing for his journey. As soon as his companions come back together, they will begin. After tonight, they will have the knowledge they need to start, and they will believe."

"And the Leper?"

Isabel's eyes glittered, and Roshen could hear the sibilant whisper that boded ill for the man who had dared to betray the Lore. This woman was perhaps the strongest of them all, even Aiden, though he was the eldest left living.

"His ignorance of the Truth was a shock. How could he come so far yet not truly believe? He will be dealt with accordingly for the betrayer and murderer that he is."

"He's not the only one."

The woman did not reply straightaway. Along the quiet passageways above them, a door clicked open, footsteps on the stairs, muffled voices. The voices raised and a solid thud sounded. The voices stopped.

Roshen and Isabel waited, listening to the sounds of the remaining person shuffling around. Doors banged, drawers slid noisily out from their cabinets. Finally, the person left and there was silence.

"He is now," she whispered.

Simone pressed her back against the wall, gun drawn, listening for sounds through the open doorway. Silence. She was beginning to think she had the wrong building after all when she felt an ice cold breath on the back of her neck. She swiveled around to see who had managed to sneak up on her, her spine tingling, but discovered she was alone. A dull roar began, like the sound of the ocean heard through a seashell, and the cold breath grew into a definite movement of air through the corridors. There was still no sound from the office so she risked a quick look in. The office was empty—almost.

Stark modern furniture filled a sterile bland room. Papers were scattered over the floor and open file drawers. Probably not part of the usual appearance of the office, Simone surmised and moved in closer. She stopped and looked at the floor. An instance of vertigo seized and she struggled to keep her balance.

"Oh, my God …" she started to say. *Weird! So I definitely have the right place.* She looked back at the furniture and scattered papers. The dull roaring increased and for a moment the room seemed to shimmer and shift. Simone squeezed her eyes closed against the assault to her senses. When she opened them, the room had stopped moving, and she carefully took another step in.

As she neared the desk and started to move around it, her foot brushed on something unyielding on the floor. She crouched down and pushed aside some papers. Underneath, bloodied and clawed in death, lay a hand.

Simone's quick intake of air was inaudible over the echoes emanating throughout the building. She quashed her surprise and moved further behind the desk. A chair had been upturned. A dark pool of blood stained the pale gray carpet. Joseph Guillaime, his expensively cut suit stiff with coagulating blood, white shirt stained crimson, lay where he had fallen, an ornately hilted knife wedged between his ribs. Simone checked for a pulse, though she knew there'd be none. Not too many people survived being pierced through the heart with a knife the size of this one.

She tugged her cellphone out of her pocket and switched it back on. It was time to call in.

Roshen and Isabel stood facing each other in the large sub-basement storeroom, their heads raised, arms hanging straight down. Their outfacing palms gradually levitated together, and they leveled their gazes toward each other's face, drawing close in a passionate kiss. A silver cloud formed on their shared breath and they broke apart.

"Shimti?" the man asked, an amused grin lighting his face.

"Aye, for strength," Isabel answered.

The silvery cloud joined them, a life-connecting thread that spread outward until they were engulfed in its shimmering form. Their hands still joined, they stretched their arms outward and flung their heads back to speak the words that would bring the Raven. Dark shadows encircled them and an eerie fluttering of wings brushed past their heads.

The boxes and crates stored in the room started to move. Some broke open, spilling their contents to the floor where they gleamed, a rainbow of color in the darkness, until they were caught up in a whirl-wind of air beneath strong wings and disappeared, forever. An intri-cately carved urn tipped over but was taken before it could be dented on the hard floor. A white shield adorned with a bright red cross, a plain earthenware bowl—all were taken into the vortex.

Simone shoved the phone in its hidey-hole—there was no signal—and did a quick search of the room. It looked innocuous enough: shipping orders, freight consignment forms, invoices and inventory listings—all ordinary stuff. She looked back at Guillaime. The man's other hand held a fistful of consignment orders. She pulled them free and started to read through them.

At the fifth note in the bundle, Simone stopped. It was a note for a crate of books to be freighted from New Orleans to Northern Col-orado. Smiggins' Rest to be precise. She removed the paper from the bundle, rifled through the rest and then tucked them back into Guil-laime's death grip. Pushing the paper into her pocket, she knelt down to give the knife a closer inspection, took a photo with her phone and memorized some of the design for later identification, then quickly left the office.

Leaving the dead man behind, Simone made her way down the stairs, searching for some sign of de Laurac. She had the feeling the man had already left, but if Simone Lang was anything, it was thor-ough.

As she descended to the lower levels of the building, the breeze grew fiercer, pulling on her clothes and pushing against her body. She struggled to keep her footing against it as she pushed on, determined to discover what was going on. When she reached the basement stairs, she nearly fell down. The whole building felt like it was shifting. Ver-tigo attacked again and she grabbed at the railing for support.

Voices floated up to her, the words unrecognizable. She crept down further. The door to the bottom-most level banged wildly on its hinges and Simone could see objects flying past, caught in a silvery maelstrom of wind. A dark shape blocked her vision for a moment and the wind whirled around her feet, then the shape moved and the wind grew stronger, knocking her down the last few steps to land in an undignified heap by the door.

She could feel herself being sucked into the wild currents and reached desperately for a handhold, but the wind was too strong and she lost her grip. Torn from the rail she'd been clinging to, she was dragged across the floor and drawn into the twisting tempest.

Simone was falling and screaming one minute; safe and protected the next. There was too much dust and dirt flying around for her to see what was stopping her from being crushed to death in the twister, so she held on and prayed to see another day. Whatever the thing was though, it felt soft and smooth under her fingers, even warm in places. She put her head down to guard her face and waited for it all to be over.

She thought then that she must have fallen asleep because in the next instant she was sitting on the floor, struggling to open her eyes.

"God," Simone moaned. "Tell me it was just a dream."

A woman's laughter brought her to full wakefulness and she turned bleary eyes in her direction.

"It wasn't a dream?" she asked.

"And what's the difference between dreaming and awake? They're just two ways of lookin' at the same reality."

Simone frowned. She recognized the voice straightaway.

"Don't tell me. You're the one who makes up all the riddles."

The woman laughed again.

"Not I, Questor. Aiden is the riddle master, though you wouldn't know it to look at him. My talents lie in other directions."

"You're Isabel," Simone stated, daring her to deny it.

"I am."

"What happened? What is happening?"

"We caught a Questor in our web, which is well and good for I have a message for you."

"Not another riddle?"

"I speak not in riddles," she said, sounding a touch annoyed.

"Well, I apologize. Please forgive an ignorant fool ..."

Isabel held her hand in the air to cut off Simone's words. "The Bearer of Ouroboros knows the Raven, now you must find the door. The Dove will be your guide." She stood and looked over Simone's shoulder.

"The Dove? Is that the same one you told Professor Flemming about? Can't you be a little more specific?" Simone noticed Isabel looking past her with a loving smile and realized they weren't alone. "Who?" she started to ask, whipping around to see a dark man standing over her. For a moment, Simone thought she was in danger, but the man ignored her completely, staring intently at Isabel.

"The Web is woven, Arwium. It's time to return to Elphane."

The woman nodded. "The quest will go on. Sicarius will take care of the Leper."

"And the Dragonslayer?" Roshen asked sadly.

"His time too is nigh."

As the couple spoke they moved away and joined hands. The woman the Byrd & Somers team knew as Isabel McTavish looked down at Simone. Isabel reached for a leather thong around her neck and pulled a small flask from beneath her blouse. Pulling it up over her head, she offered it to Simone.

"What is it?" Simone asked.

"Starfire. For your friend."

Simone took it, confused. "Which one?"

But the pair no longer paid her heed; they were engulfed by what Simone could only describe as vibrating air and were fading from view.

"Wait!" she called, too late.

A flash of light forced her to look away, and when she turned back, Isabel and Roshen were gone. She stared, amazed, at the space where they had stood then gazed around the basement. She was completely alone in the dark.

37

"Simone! Simone! Wake up!"

"Wha … What? Elliott?"

"Is she okay?" Nick asked as he entered the room, now lit by Elliott's flashlight. Simone tried to sit up, uneven light casting strange shadows across her face.

"Can't see any damage," Elliott answered. "Looked like she was just taking a nap."

"There's no one else around," Pete added, trotting down the stairs, his flashlight bobbing. "Place is empty."

Simone looked around again, dazed. "I wasn't dreaming. It was real."

"What was real, Simone?" Elliott asked. He'd walked down to the sub-basement room only minutes before, following the sound of Simone's cellphone ringing. Nick, who had gone upstairs with Pete to search for their missing colleague, had come down on Elliott's loud call.

Elliott had discovered the location of the Mercedes just a few blocks from the diner where they sat drinking bitter coffee. They'd found the Jag around the corner and proceeded to search the darkened buildings, starting with the one closest to the car—an international shipping company. The front door had unlocked as easily for them as it had Simone and they'd walked in. Pete deliberately ignored several laws about breaking and entering. After all, the door was open, almost.

When they'd reached the stairs, Elliott signaled for Pete to go up and with a nod of assent, Pete had darted up to the next level.

Nick had entered the room closest to the front door. It appeared to be a showroom, though for what he would never know. The only thing on display in the room was dust. He'd crossed its length to check on another door and found a small, white bathroom, also empty. Not even a cake of soap or a roll of toilet paper.

Elliott had left him to it and took the basement stairs with caution. It was black as pitch down there. He'd flicked the switch of his flashlight and the stairs came into view. Halfway down, the light flashed on something metallic against the wall—Simone's penlight. Elliott had reached the base of the stairs when a phone started ringing. He'd eased over to the last doorway and peeked in, gun and flashlight first. The room was empty except for the lone woman who lay in the center of the floor.

"Simone," Elliott had whispered, recognizing the prone body immediately. He'd turned his head back up to the stairs and called for Nick, his voice booming in the cavernous emptiness of the basement.

The cellphone was still ringing. Elliott searched through Simone's pockets till he found it and answered the call. It was Dan. While Elliott assured the younger man that they'd found their missing friend and she seemed okay, Nick moved closer to see for himself.

A bemused Simone was looking around the room. "Did you see anyone else?" she asked.

"No, the place is empty. Tell us what happened, Simone," Nick said softly.

Simone's face was pale, shock still evident in her wide eyes and skittish movements. "You won't believe it. I'm not sure I do now and it seemed so real."

Elliott had finished talking to Dan and was quietly listening. "Tell us, Simone."

Simone nodded, sitting up and patting down her hair and clothes. "I followed the Mercedes here. De Laurac and Guillaime had already left the vehicle when I drove past. I'm sure there was only the two of them in the car. I let myself in—the security system was switched off— and went upstairs looking for the office with lights on."

Elliott glanced across at Nick. Simone continued on unaware of the look.

"The room had been ransacked, papers everywhere. I found Guillaime's body. He'd been stabbed in the heart."

"You sure about that, Simone?" Pete asked. "I've just come from the top level and there were no ransacked offices or body. They're all empty."

"I'm sure," Simone frowned and then reached into her pocket to pull out the consignment note. "I found this in his hand. You'll note the speckles of blood."

Nick took the paper and read it in silence before passing it to Elliott. It was their first piece of tangible evidence—no mysterious messages or strange references to birds; just a simple note that connected one known fact with a suspected one. His eyes flicked to the date. It coincided with Professor Flemming's visit and fit in with a jotting in his notebook, that the book she'd gone to inspect had disappeared.

"Well, he's not there now and neither are the papers. If what you say is right, then the whole building's been cleaned out.

"I certainly didn't imagine that, at least," came Simone's indignant reply.

"So what did you imagine?" Elliott asked. "This place sure is creepy, and right now I'd believe almost anything."

"Isabel McTavish was here, and a man. I don't know who he was," said Simone.

"Did they kill Guillaime?" Nick asked.

"No, actually I think that was de Laurac. Isabel called him a betrayer and a murderer. There was something else too. I can't quite remember. I was caught in a strong wind and someone caught me then I woke up and she was there. We talked. The man paid no attention to me at all. She gave me something called 'Starfire', and then they left. Vanished into thin air right before my eyes." Simone drew herself back out of her memories with a slight shudder and looked into the faces staring at her. "Maybe it was a dream after all. Ha! Isabel said something about dreams too." She shrugged and started to get to her feet when something dropped from the folds of her clothes. It fell to the floor with a soft thud: a small silver flask. Tangled in its leather strap was the black feather of a raven.

38

White hot blades of pain pierced his eyes and filled his head. He cried out, a deep agonized sound that echoed around him … vibrated through him. Strong arms gripped him as he thrashed. Concerned voices offered soothing words, and in the background he could hear the slow steady flap of strong wings.

The field of blue flowers bloomed brightly in the warm sunshine. The burly man could feel the summer sun on his back, warming his bones and easing the pain that engulfed him. He reached out and pulled a handful of flowers from the ground, lifting them to his face to breathe deeply of their sweet offerings. Closing his eyes, he laid back. The flowers formed a soft mattress beneath him, and he all but disappeared in their thick growth.

Keeping his eyes closed against the light, he listened peacefully to the breeze as it blew through the flowers. After a while, other sounds came to him—the fluttering of wings overhead, the call of birds in the distance and the soft, raspy scrape of something slithering toward him. His eyes opened and he turned his face toward the sound in dread.

The flapping wings brushed passed his face, their tips grazing his skin with the lightest of touches. Surprised, he sat up, forgetting his fear, and came face-to-face with a huge black bird. The bird tipped its head to glare at him with one beady eye, its beak clacking as if in speech. He was mystified and confused. The sight of the bird reminded him of something, but he couldn't quite get a handle on it.

"Beautiful mornin'. Ain't it, Finn?" a familiar voice greeted him.

Finn stared closer at the giant raven, his face reflecting his amazement. The soft laugh that came then wrapped around him and he turned to look in its direction.

"What're you doin' here?" he asked the familiar figure seated a short distance away.

Dan shrugged. "It's your dream, Finn."

Finn stood and looked around. The field lay in the cup of a narrow valley. A winding river cut its way along its length. Tall trees grew, like guardians, along the riverbanks, and moss-covered rocks jutted out from the fast flowing water. The mountains that bordered the valley were tall and imposing, almost menacing in their massive size. Snow covered their tops and huge outcrops of rock adorned their sides like primitive jewelry. Finn could hear, and feel, the groan of their great weight upon the earth.

"Is that all it is? Just a dream?" he asked, awe of his surroundings palpable in his voice.

"As much as any dream's ever just a dream."

The great bird flapped its wings against its body and eyed the other man. Finn's dream visitor spoke again, "You need to see past the light before y'can even glimpse at the truth."

"The light being a certain type of knowledge?" Finn asked. "I thought the light was the truth."

"Reckon it is, just not all of it."

"Where are we?"

"On the edge of Elphane."

Finn turned back, his eyebrows arched in further question, but Dan shook his head, held his hand up to prevent more questions and laughed his soft laugh. Then he stood, tucked his thumbs into his belt and strolled over.

"This valley's the doorway to the Forest of Stars." When he reached Finn's side, he stopped moving and speaking to take in the view.

"It surely is a beautiful place, but why are we here?"

"You need to meet someone."

Finn glanced at the bird.

"Maybe two someone's," dream-Dan offered.

"And you?"

"Beats me." He shrugged and pulled his hands free from his belt. Placing one on Finn's shoulder, the other pointed across the field.

The scraping sound of earlier came back and Finn could see the flowers parting beneath the gliding passage of a giant snake. Finn felt his skin crawl and his hands tremble with the irrational fear of a preacher's son who'd grown up on stories of brimstone and hellfire and snakes—the evil messengers of Satan. He gulped for air and licked suddenly dry lips.

"S'okay, Finn. She's here to guide you through the light."

The sun glistened on the serpent's back, its scaly skin a rainbow of riotous color gleaming brilliantly as it glided toward the man. Her forked tongue flicked out to taste the air as it moved. The sweet aroma of flowers, the crystal clarity of mountain air, the ancient earth beneath her equally ancient body, the fear and wonderment of the man before her—they all mixed together to fill her senses and her heart.

She came closer, her cold, slitted eyes sizing up Finn. It starts at last. The thought slipped into Finn's head, and she began to raise her head high above the ground.

Finn held himself steady, trying to control his fear. Just a dream. Just a dream. His breathing came hard and fast. His head felt light and dizziness sent the ground beneath his feet reeling. Sharp stabbing in his shoulder and a sudden weight forced him to turn away from the approaching serpent to stare at a raven perched close to his head.

The bird's beak opened and Finn was surprised to hear Dan's familiar drawl. "This is the land of Elphane where the Albi rule."

Finn forgot his fear yet again to stare incredulously at his transformed friend. The bird stared back, unblinking. "Ain't nothin' to be scared of. It's only a dream. Ain't it?"

The bird's head tilted to the side, then stretched its wings out and lifted into the sky with a whoop of pure exhilarance. Finn watched him join up with the larger bird, already high in the sky, and fly away, dipping and looping through the air.

When he turned back, the snake had risen until its black head was level with his own. He froze in shock. His heart pounded. The serpent hissed, slowly and deliberately. Her long tongue flicked out to brush lightly against Finn's face. He almost stopped breathing as she raised herself higher and then lowered her head to his shoulder and started to wind herself around his body. She hissed in his ear, and this time Finn heard words in the whispering.

"Welcome, Questor. We have been waiting for ye."

Her tongue scraped along his skin and her head nudged his jaw. The weight of the giant reptile was immense and his knees buckled, but he girded his will against her and stood tall.

The serpent hissed again in a jagged reptilian laugh. "Look into the light, Questor, and feel the fire of the stars between your lips."

She slithered around and brought her head back up level with Finn's. Her cold, lipless mouth pressed against his, and Finn's lips tingled, his mouth and throat burned, and he realized he could see—not the shuttered, everyday reality he'd lived with all his life but the secret, hidden dimensions that overlaid everything else. From his lips, a small silvery cloud drifted and began to fan out. Around him, standing among the flowers, along the river and scattered through the trees stood people where before there had been none. He recognized some of the faces. One in particular, no longer in the form of a bird, winked at him. The old man standing beside Dan stared straight ahead, his expression sad but his body subtly changed.

Finn stared harder, trying to ascertain the difference from when he'd last seen the stooped figure, but the weight on his shoulders, shifting and then disappearing, distracted his attention. He turned to see a woman standing before him. Her black hair moved slightly in the breeze, her green eyes glimmered like emeralds on fire. The silver cloud stretched from his lips to hers, glinting in the sunshine before fading away.

"Are they the Elbe?" Finn asked, inclining his head to the people spread out through the valley.

"Aye," the woman answered.

Finn ran his hand through his short hair and ducked his head.

"And who are you?"

The woman's gaze was hard and unwavering. "My name is Arwium." As she spoke, she brought her closed hand up from her side. The movement was slow and strangely serpent-like in its gracefulness. A small black snake was wrapped around her arm—its head raised above her fist, its eyes fixed on the man. "And it's time for ye to look into the light." Her fingers unfurled to reveal a spinning globe of light that hovered above her open palm.

Finn's eyes fixed on the strange object. It hummed and buzzed and spun in mid-air, then exploded in a blaze of light that burned his eyes and seared a path through his body. Finn clapped his hands to his face and fell backward, away from the serpent-woman, away from the valley and dream-Dan, but not away from the light.

39

Simone stood over the hospital bed, leather flask gripped in her fist. Finn lay in drugged sleep, his bulky form outlined beneath the crisp hospital sheets and his eyes tightly bandaged. Nick had driven Simone straight from the deserted freight company to the hospital. She was still a little dazed from her experience in the sub-basement storeroom. Elliott had followed in Nick's truck. Pete took Elliott's car and returned to the house to make his latest report to Captain Lennard.

They'd met a nurse in the hallway, stretching her legs and sipping half-cold coffee. She was on her break, but filled them in on Finn's condition. Then they'd gone in to see for themselves. He was sleeping, and his three visitors had wondered at the sight of seeing him so weakened.

Professor Finn Shaw had a strength that was more than physical. He encompassed an intellectual and emotional potency that few could hope to reach. To see him laid low brought the realization of their vulnerability to the fore. Simone cried and ran to him, but the man was deeply asleep and could not hear her heart-rendered sobs.

Nick and Elliott stayed for a short time before the nurse from the hallway came in and ushered them out.

Simone refused point blank to leave. Her sobbing had subsided only minutes after it started but her face showed the strain she was under. "I would prefer to stay here and watch Finn snoring than go home and stare at my ceiling for the remainder of the night. I won't disturb him or any staff."

After some discussion, and further assurances on Simone's part, the nurse agreed and left Simone to Finn's snores. Simone sighed with relief as the elevator doors swished to a close behind Nick and Elliott, walked over to the public telephone, dropped a coin in the slot and called one of her favorite restaurants to deliver a meal up to Finn's room. It had been many hours since she'd eaten Elliott's sandwiches and she was famished.

By the time she walked back to Finn's side she felt much more in control. She dragged a chair closer to the bed, sat down and rested her head on the blankets beside Finn's limp hand. Dinner would be forty minutes. That gave her plenty of time to think. She had discarded the multi-pocketed vest on returning to her car with Nick, replacing it with a light-weight cropped jacket. She pulled the small leather flask from its pocket and inspected it in the dim light of the bedside lamp.

The flask was round, an almost flat circle, and the leather was fashioned with unusual designs that meandered around it. She ran her finger along its smooth edge and turned it over. The stopper had markings on it that she could feel but not see. She stood up and moved closer to the light. The leather was almost black with age and use, and she could see that the edge was patterned in a separate design that circled the others. She turned it to see the marks on the stopper. It was the head of a snake, its tail filling its open mouth. She stopped moving, squinting at the flask as she tried to remember where she'd seen this before and what it might mean.

Finn moved his head and moaned softly, pulling Simone from her thoughts.

"Finn?" she whispered, not wanting to disturb him, yet sure he would rest easier knowing he wasn't alone.

Simone turned her gaze back to the flask when he failed to respond and noticed that the simple design on its sides actually formed an X shape. She turned the flask over; the other side was similar.

She shook her head and returned to the seat. Absently rubbing the flask with her thumb, she thought back to her conversation with Isabel McTavish. The words she spoke, both to Simone and then the stranger, came back to her. Simone closed her eyes on the utterings and drifted into sleep.

The hospital room was quiet and still, both Finn and Simone were fast asleep in the witching hours of midnight. Nurses walked past the room on rounds, their rubber-soled shoes making a low squelch on the hard floors, their voices murmuring as they discussed patients, recent weather changes, who was seeing who, the vagaries of living with teenagers. Doors opened and closed as they saw to patients who couldn't sleep and issued medication—a routine shift for the night nurses. Occasionally, the elevator doors could be heard opening to deliver a doctor, or more nurses, and then hushed consultations would soon follow.

The elevator doors opened again, but this time no lowered voices followed, no rubber-soled tread hurrying down the corridor. Finn and Simone slept on, heedless of all sounds that passed them by, unknowing of any break to the routine of night noise.

A dark figure exited the lift, his arms laden with paper sacks. His boots, though heavy, made no sound as he walked down the corridor. He paused outside a closed door, checked the number then rested his hand against it, ready to push it open.

Inside the room, Simone opened her eyes—jolted from sleep and instantly alert. Her hand closed tightly around the small leather container it held, the other gripped the armrest of her chair. She kept her head lowered on the bed, not yet sure of the disturbance. Her eyes fixed on the door as it moved inward. In the dim light of the room, the figure that stepped in appeared dark and shadowy. Simone let out the breath she'd been holding only when the figure stepped into the light to place packages on the small table at the end of the bed.

"Simone, you owe me $45.00, and I sure hope yer in the mood for sharin', 'cause I'm hungry."

"Mr. Tenney! You shouldn't sneak around. How did you know it was mine?"

"Intercepted the delivery guy in the foyer. Who else would order take-out from the best Thai restaurant in town to be delivered here so late at night?" Dan shook his head in a mixture of feigned disgust at the woman's apparent self-indulgence and true appreciation of her taste in restaurants. The food truly smelled delicious and Simone could hear his stomach rumbling from across the room.

"How's Finn?" Dan asked, coming around the bed to look at the man's bandaged head.

"Nurses say he'll sleep for a few more hours. We'll find out the true seriousness of his injuries then," Simone told him, beginning to unpack the mini-banquet. She paused to take in the delightful aroma of the various spiced dishes, then quickly finished and prepared to eat.

"There's plenty of food, Mr. Tenney, but, alas, only one set of eating utensils." Simone didn't sound nearly as sorry as her words professed.

Dan walked over to the table, dropped Pete's helmet on a chair and dug his hand into his jacket pocket to pull out a spare set of utensils.

"Courtesy of the delivery guy," he said with a smile. "You gave him a big tip."

"Yes, well, let's eat and you can tell me how you managed to sneak away from your minder," Simone replied.

Dan shrugged and grinned conspiratorially. "I left before Nick got back. Pete's Harley is a nice ride."

Simone smirked at the image of Nick Somers walking into the house and finding Dan had snuck away. She stole a glance at the still grinning man who'd had them all worried over the last few weeks. He seemed a little different in his manner tonight, almost back to his old self, and Simone wondered what had caused the change. Right now, though, she had a stomach to fill. She put aside thoughts of Dan Tenney to concentrate on her immediate priority: assuaging her hunger.

There was no more speaking until the meal was finished and it was Dan who broke eventually the silence.

"Heard you had some fun tonight, Simone," he casually inquired.

Simone dropped her chopsticks into the dish and wiped her mouth with his napkin. "It was eventful," she agreed. "I lost de Laurac, found Guillaime—dead—then lost his body, had a quick lesson in flying without the aid of an airplane, was caught in a web, and talked with the most unusual woman I've ever met."

Dan raised his eyebrows at the last.

"Isabel McTavish," Simone added. "She gave me yet another mysterious message and a gift. At first, I thought the gift was for you but that was before I found out about Finn's adventures tonight."

"What's the gift?" Dan asked. His voice took on a husky quality that made Simone feel that he already knew her answer.

Her eyes darted to the man's face but it was guileless and, as usual, unreadable. She'd dropped the flask into her pocket when Dan first walked in and now she pulled it out again to hold it up between them.

Dan stretched his hand across the table to take it for a closer look. Simone had the urge not to relinquish her hold, her fingers tightened involuntarily around it.

Dan's eyes narrowed for an instant then his voice came, smooth and reassuring. "I jus' want to look, Simone. I won't interfere."

Simone relaxed and Dan pulled the flask from her grip.

"It has a snake design around its edge, see the stopper? And a cross, almost hidden, among those other designs in the middle," said Simone.

Dan looked carefully at the flask, running his fingers along the body of the circled snake, and Simone could plainly see that he recognized it.

"Dan? Tell me, what is it?"

Dan drew a chain from beneath his shirt, hesitating a moment as Simone had done when parting with the flask, before pulling it over his head. He held the two objects in his hands, rubbing them both with his thumbs before clearing a space on the table with his arm and laying them side by side.

The pendant, clean and polished until it beamed with aged magnificence was a perfect circle with notches cut all the way around it. The same type of notches that had almost worn off the outer edge of the flask. Simone tentatively reached to touch the glowing ring. It was a snake, its mouth wide open and filled with its own tail. The facial features of the snake had long ago worn away from the flask, but on the ring they gleamed with cunning and, Simone decided as she picked it up, a certain amount of reptilian self-satisfaction.

Simone stared hard at the ring. "Ouroboros," she whispered. Recalling Isabel's words, she turned back to Dan, taking in the mystified expression she was sure must mirror her own—mystification bordering on understanding. "You're the Bearer of Ouroboros."

Dan nodded. "You need to give Finn the gift now," he said. "It will help to open his eyes."

Simone handed the ring back, picked up the flask and moved closer to the bed. Finn's face, what could be seen of it, was pale, the bandages covering completely any redness around his damaged eyes. His lips were pressed together in a thin line of pain. His hands spasmed and, for a moment, Simone thought him awake.

"Finn? I was told to give you this," she whispered.

Finn began to toss and turn.

"He's dreaming," Dan said. "It's okay, Simone ..."

Simone pulled the stopper from the flask. It was almost as if the snake was opening its mouth even wider. She put the opening to Finn's mouth and watched, incredulous, as a silvery mist eked out to soothe the pain-tight lips. Finn's mouth opened to receive the offering.

"All of it," Dan encouraged.

Simone tipped the flask up until it was empty. "She called it Starfire," she said, replacing the stopper.

Finn gasped as the Starfire worked its way through his body. He sighed, and smiled, then fell into a deep, natural sleep.

Dan and Simone spent the next hour discussing events. Dan filled Simone in on what had happened during the search of the house, and Simone, in turn, spoke about everything she could remember of her meeting with the woman, including the terrifying moments beforehand. She solemnly showed Dan the black feather that had been with the flask.

"She said you knew the Raven."

Dan took the feather and twirled it between his fingers. "His name is Aiden," he volunteered.

"And who is Isabel?" Simone asked, certain he would know the answer.

Before Dan could reply, Finn became restless once more. Sweat poured from his skin as he gritted his teeth against some unseen force. His hands came up to guard his face, and he let loose with a blood-curdling cry. Simone and Dan both jumped to their feet, instantly by his side in an effort to control his struggling body.

Simone reached for the call button only to have her arm held in a vice-like grip.

"No," Dan warned. "He needs to go through this."

"Remove your hand from my arm, Mr. Tenney. I will not allow Finn to suffer this pain unnecessarily," Simone hissed in return.

Dan shook his head. "No, Simone. This is very necessary."

"A little bird tell you that, Dan?" Simone asked scornfully. "We can't let him go through this alone. I won't let him go through it alone."

Dan's grip did not lessen. "He's not alone."

The two stared at each other for a moment, Dan willing Simone to understand. Simone nodded and Dan relaxed his hold. Simone shook her arm free then took Finn's clawed hands firmly in her own and pulled them away from his face, talking to him soothingly, kissing each finger, gently letting him know that she was by his side.

When the rest of the investigating team marched into Finn's room later that morning, burdened with assorted files, a laptop and the essentials for breakfast, it was to find Simone and Dan sound asleep. Simone was in her chair, her head once again using the bed as her pillow, and Dan was on the floor in the far corner of the room, one arm resting on bent knee the other folded across his lap. Both were softly snoring.

Finn, on the other hand, was wide-awake and sitting up, sipping water from a plastic mug. His head was already turned expectantly toward the door when the men walked in.

"Finn! How're you doin'?"

"Oh, I'm fine … Elliott?"

"Yeah, it's me. Has the doctor been in to see you this morning?"

"Not yet," Finn replied, his smile widening.

"You wear these two out, Finn?" Nick asked, amazed the two in question had yet to waken. He paced over to Dan in the corner and stared down at him, shaking his head.

"Young'uns these days, just can't handle the pace," Elliott said as he crept over to Simone and gently pushed her slack jaw closed. The touch disturbed the woman where the voices had not and she sputtered awake.

Nick was less gentle. Hooking one booted foot under the sleeping man's bent leg he yanked it straight out. Dan was awake and standing in one abrupt movement, blinking with confusion. Exhaustion lined his pale face and he put his hand against the wall to steady himself against a bout of dizziness. Nick pushed aside a niggling feeling of guilt, still annoyed that the younger man had not stayed at the house as he was told.

"Bastard," Dan muttered in disgust.

Nick laughed and threw an arm casually around the other man's shoulders. Dan shrugged the arm away, but not before Nick felt a tremble run through his friend's body. Nick's eyes narrowed as Dan stepped away, still scowling, and stumbled toward the chairs and the tray of coffees Elliott had left on the side-table.

"Better let him at the coffee before he bites your head off," Elliott said, grinning. He passed one of the cups to Simone and pulled another one free for Finn. "Got one for you too, Professor." Elliott took the water from the other man's hand and carefully replaced it with the hot coffee.

"Elliott, you are heaven sent," Finn replied as the aroma of the coffee filled the room.

The group sat around drinking coffee and munching on bagels and donuts, the conversation intentionally kept light. It was nearly an hour before Nick pulled the case file out.

"A lot's happened in the last twenty-four hours," Nick began, "and we haven't heard any of what Finn found yesterday." He stopped and looked across at the man in the bed. "You up to it, Finn? I didn't actually expect to find you awake …"

"That and more, my friend. I feel amazingly well," the big man grinned. "I made some headway on the coded message and found some … interesting … information on the Templars."

"Anything specifically related to the Brotherhood?" Nick asked.

"No," Finn answered, lowering his chin to his chest, what could be seen of his brow furrowed in thought. "Leastways, nothing I can see yet. The real Templars, from the Middle Ages, fought wars to protect their Truth, the Sangreal." He settled back into his pillow. "They were hounded and most killed during the Inquisition along with a group called the Cathars, and several others. Religious persecution is a blight on human nature," he added sorrowfully.

"And the Sangreal, the Holy Grail, isn't a cup or chalice; it's a person or persons," Elliott thought out loud. "But who are they? Christ wasn't even married, was he?"

"Why do you think that, Elliott?" Finn asked him.

"Well, wouldn't we have learned about that at school? I took a Bible studies class in high school and the teacher didn't mention anything about a Mrs. Christ or kids."

"There are many things that we don't get told in school. The Bible you studied was not even the complete works. Many Gospels were left out on purpose, the ones we know of edited to hide certain knowledge from the public. The original Gospel of Mark, for instance, told that

Jesus and Mary Magdalene were husband and wife, but it is unlikely you will read that in any store bought Bible." Finn paused to get himself comfortable again, then went on. "The Templar Knights guarded his line as well as the line of his brothers and sisters, and numerous objects connected to them and their ancestors."

"Such as?" Nick queried.

"The Ark of the Covenant, the Sacred Sepulcher, and numerous tablets that told the history of the Great Kings."

"Who are the Great Kings?" Elliott asked.

"I don't know that yet, but I have a feeling we'll find out soon enough."

"Really?" Elliott began, fascinated with the possibility.

Before Elliott could continue, Nick spoke again. "Weren't the Cathars from Albigens in the south of France?" he asked, looking at Simone.

"Yes, they were," Simone replied, her face lighting up, "and they were speaking in French again last night."

"Who did?" asked Finn.

"Isabel and an unknown man were in the building where I trailed Roger de Laurac to."

"Ah, the Leper," interrupted Finn.

"That's right. They talked about him too." Simone dipped her head trying to remember their words. "The man said something like, 'The web of the words has been woven. Time to return to Elphane', and Isabel said, 'Sicarius will take care of the Leper', then there was something about dragon slayers."

"Dragon slayers?" Elliott repeated. "You've gotta be kidding! Is this for real?"

"They don't mean real dragons, Elliott. The dragons were the holy line of kings in France and England during the Middle Ages and earlier. King Arthur was said to be a dragon king. The kings were killed or deposed, their lands confiscated."

"As were the Templars," Simone added.

Elliott slouched against the wall nursing his coffee cup. "And the dragon slayers would be?"

"The Inquisition was the common name for the Holy Offices of the Catholic church ..." Finn began to explain.

"Their time too is nigh," Simone quoted, frowning at the memory.

"What about the code, Finn?" Nick asked.

"The more we get into this the clearer it becomes. The blind are those without knowledge. The knowledge is the light; therefore, until you know and understand the knowledge or the Way you are as blind. '*Desposyni* is only one beam' means the book is only one piece of the puzzle. The Raven, Dove and Fisher are probably specific people. Jesus was known as the Fisher. The dove is often seen as a messenger or guide. The raven too, in some cultures, is seen as a messenger from the other side."

"Isabel told me, 'The Bearer of Ouroboros knows the Raven, now you must find the door. The Dove will be your guide,'" said Simone.

There were a few minutes of silence as they digested the information they were being given and then Finn's head came up again. "What were the riddles you mentioned, Elliott?"

"Well, the McTavish woman basically repeated part of the first message to Nick 'bout ravens and doves. Then Dan said to Nick, 'Something once lost now found, on its way homeward bound.'"

Dan had remained silent and brooding during the whole exchange, but at Elliott's words he straightened in his chair. "When did I say that?"

"In the truck just after Will gave you that chain and pendant," Nick told him.

"What pendant? Do you know what it means?" Finn asked Dan. He had a sudden flash of memory, an object that shone with power held on a chain around his friend's neck.

"Ouroboros ..." Dan began.

"... is the Lore of the Graal. The light!" Elliott burst out. "The Lore is the knowledge!"

"Elliott?" Finn asked, confused.

"Ouroboros is the Lore of the Graal, in the Land of Elphane it belongs," Elliott quoted. "Dan again," he told Finn. "But where's Elphane?"

"What was the next line?" Nick asked. "The path begins with the Rest? The professor went to Smiggins' Rest. And the last line was, 'Seek the light and ye shall find the way' ..."

"Well, gentlemen—and woman," Finn said, patting Simone's hand. "I think you've done exactly that."

"Who's the Raven, Dan?" said Nick.

Dan looked down at his hands. His head hurt and his eyes felt cold. "His name is Aiden."

Finn turned abruptly to Dan. "Is he an older man?"

"Yes."

"You meet the bird too, Finn?" Elliott asked him.

"In a way. Has there been anything about snakes?"

"Isabel has a tattoo of a snake on her wrist," Nick provided.

Simone nodded. "I saw that too."

Finn sat straighter. They nearly had it. "What does she look like?"

Nick described the woman from the delicatessen. "Caucasian, black hair, green eyes."

"And the man she was with called her Arwium," Simone said, using the French pronunciation of the name.

"Ha! Isabel is Arwium and Arwium is the serpent," Finn stated triumphantly, recalling the details of his dream during the night.

"She's a snake?" Elliott asked doubtfully.

"No more than Aiden is a bird or the medieval kings were really dragons. The serpent is a symbol of ancient knowledge," said Finn.

Dan got to his feet and stepped over to the bed. Standing by Finn's side, he pulled the chain over his head and held the ring thoughtfully, then reaching down for Finn's hand, he placed the ring on his open palm. "Ouroboros is also the serpent," he said quietly.

The big man rubbed the metal circle in his hand, nodding. "Of course, it's all beginning to fit."

"This started before we got the case, before I was run off the road. I was havin' dreams. I saw … well, I knew something was starting," Dan continued. "But why am I its bearer?"

The group went quiet as they thought on why Dan had been chosen, but that answer was still to be found. Finally, Elliott broke the silence.

"So, what de Laurac didn't know was that Dan is the Bearer of the Ouroboros and he nearly killed him. No wonder they excommunicated him. Do you think Professor Flemming might have been a bearer of something too?"

Finn started to sit up and swing his legs out of the bed.

"What the hell do you think you're doing?" Simone demanded.

"It's simple. I've done enough lying about. We have a Dove to find and a door to open. Time to hit the road."

"What?"

"We've been all but ordered to Elphane. I believe Elliott's right. The professor was the bearer of another sacred object. She has quite the collection of artifacts in her home and in her office at the university. The Brotherhood are unimportant, a fly in the ointment, so to speak. They've been dealt with and Sicarius will take care of de Laurac."

"And the professor?" Elliott asked.

"I would say that she has already entered the Forest of Stars. Elphane, my friend, is just a step through the door."

Dan grasped Finn's hand in his and held it tightly. "And the blind shall lead the blind."

"That's right." Finn's face beamed beneath the bandages, his customary grin split his face. He held the pendant out for Dan to retrieve. "We have ancient treasure to deliver."

40

SMIGGINS' REST, COLORADO: NOVEMBER 2006

The village of Smiggins' Rest was approximately, depending entirely on the weather conditions of the day, a two-hour drive north-east of Steamboat Lake and roughly ten hours from Denver. The entire drive, once the suburbia of the city was left behind, was a mosaic of small towns and ranches, interspersed with forests of aspen and lodge pole pine and valleys overshadowed by snow-capped mountains. The township was often cut off from civilization during the winter months and had developed a high level of self-sufficiency and an identity that made it unique to the area.

The road in, and out, was narrow, winding and unsealed. Once the turn-off from the highway had been made there were few places to turn around or stop. The road almost disappeared in the thick forest, the looming trees rendering it invisible from bend to bend. It joined up with Little Snake River at the bottom of a series of hair-pin turns that descended like a ladder down the mountainside. It was not an easy drive, but there was beauty in its harshness, a sense of rugged determination no mere chunk of rock—no matter how large—could dissuade, a shifting of reality from the dead streets of towns and cities to the living, breathing reality of the wild.

A covered bridge, in much better condition than it appeared, loomed behind one bend, and the road crossed the river, swallowed by the bridge that continued into a dark tunnel cut through the mountain on the other side. The tunnel opened out onto a road overhung with trees that turned off to the right, back to the river and into the town of Smiggins' Rest.

The town lined one side of the road and was built on the slope of the mountain. Homes, built small to accommodate need rather than display, disappeared into the tree line. The commercial part of town stood, almost as a barricade, between the private residences and the visitors that still seemed to flock here in the warmer months, despite the rigorous drive. The first building was The Rest Hotel. It greeted visitors with old world charm, its dark wood façade beckoning travelers with warm hospitality. Adjacent to the hotel and separated by a shared courtyard was the town's second restaurant—the first being on the other side of the courtyard and operated by the hotel itself.

A supermarket-cum-post office was next. It sold some of everything a person could need while in town. The proprietors were an old couple that had lived in Smiggins' Rest all their married lives, the wife even longer, having been born in one of the residences hidden up the mountain. The same home her mother had been born in and her mother before that. She had met her husband one blustery day some fifty years ago when he'd come into the mountains for a weekend of hiking. The young woman had shown him the trail out to the Big Creek Lakes, quite some distance. They'd walked through a field of flowers to get there, camped out under the stars that night, and had hardly been apart since. One of their sons ran the gas station located behind the store. The woman's sister owned the antique store down the street.

A narrow avenue divided the store from a large bakery that stood on the corner opposite. The bakery differed from the other buildings in that its façade appeared carved out of mountain granite. Walking through the doorway was like entering an Aladdin's cave of baked treasures. Pastries, cakes, pies and breads filled the wire racks that stretched along the walls. The exotic aroma of the baker's special bread hung in the air. Heavy but sweet, the bread tantalized the senses with the smell of dates and wild barley. The pies, thick with unusual fruits and sprinkled with palm sugar, were so delicious that it was almost obligatory to close one's eyes when eating in order to truly appreciate the taste sensation.

The baker had learned his art while travelling the world in his youth and guarded the recipes for his creations as closely as he guarded the secrecy of their source. Only a select few knew the secrets and intricate methods of preparation, and those people all lived further into the mountains. Natives of the village, the baker and his wife shared the deceptively small-boned, almost frail appearance of many of the villagers—an appearance that hid the true hardiness and strength of a people that had been bred to the mountains. The baker had also inherited the dark olive skin of his mother, a fiery-tempered woman from a similarly small village in the Zagros Mountains of Iran. That village too was situated deep in the ranges above the banks of a twisting river. It was from her family that the secret recipes had been learned.

Further along the main street was an assortment of small businesses—a cafe managed and staffed by the baker's family, an art gallery/handcrafts store and, almost at the end, High and Wild Wilderness Supplies. This store appeared hewn from the side of the mountain, and its rear wall was indeed the natural granite the village rested upon. The front of the store was filled with racks of mountain gear, from coats to triple thickness socks, hand-knitted hats to ropes, packs and carabiners. Shelves of maps and books crossed one wall showing the best trails to take to reach the slopes of various mountains and the most picturesque routes to Big Creek Lake. Mounted photographs adorned the walls, the most striking given pride of place behind the antique service counter and old fashioned cash register. A valley cut through by a wild river, white spray flying through the air from the force of water on forever-wet rocks. A field of flowers—blue columbines, lilac irises with yellow hearts contrasted by clumps of vivid Parry primrose—spread out from the river to the tree line, melding in a brilliant array of color beneath the ancient mountain range and the clear blue sky.

Neither of the women who ran the store were from the village. They were some of the very few newcomers welcomed to reside in the area without having married a villager. Both were dark-haired. The older—a friendly, outgoing sort now approaching her fifties—wore her hair in a long, thick braid down the center of her back. She had moved to Smiggins' Rest twenty years before. A lost soul at the time, she had been taken in by the villagers, given a home and a place to work, and stayed.

The younger woman wore her hair short, saved from complete severity by a natural wave that turned the ends up around her ears; she was far more reserved, almost sullen at times. The older woman had seen something of herself in the wary eyes that had met hers two years ago during a trek along the river.

The serious young woman had been hiking with her sister. The other woman had just been enjoying a pleasant day off. They chatted, shared some of the fine bread from the bakery and later ended up back in town. The sisters stayed the night as guests of their new friend and left for home the next day. A month later they were back, and this time, they stayed.

All the photographs that adorned the walls were taken by the sister, a painfully quiet woman who stayed well in the background of social life in the village. The three women spent every spare moment hiking together in the mountains, finding new places to photograph and explore, and learning many of its secrets in the process. The villagers didn't mind. They recognized their own even when they came from far afield.

The last building in town was the antique store. Set at the end of the river road, it fronted one of the oldest homes in the township. Completely built from local timber, hand-hewn by early pioneers, the home overlooked a deep pool in the river where the water was still and black. On cloudless nights the glassy surface reflected the moon and the stars as clear as any mirror, as magically as any scrying bowl.

The people from the village would gather by the pool to hear tales of long ago. Stories of their ancestors and the long journey to find this place, of the secrets they guarded and still did, in the Forests of Elphane, hidden deep in the forbidding mountain range behind them.

The store owner, who collected and sold antiques and other items from around the world, knew all the stories. They were passed down from her father, to him from his mother and so on back to the families that first trekked through the mountains searching for Elphane. She knew the stories and the prophecies of old, knew that a time of change was once again upon them.

On the same night that, back in Denver, five men and one woman were realizing their quest, the old woman looked at the near full moon and saw the faint shimmer that skirted it at such times. She pulled her old woolen cloak tightly around her shoulders and knelt down at the edge of the pond. It was time for the telling, and she was getting much too old for storytelling. Her bones creaked as she leaned out over the pond and upended a tiny leather flask. A single drop spilled into the water and ripples went out in ever-widening circles. The woman held out her hands and whispered a single word, a plea, then went still, waiting for the dark waters to show her what was to come.

41

He wasn't asleep. He was sure of it—just as he was sure that the sky was blue, the grass was usually green and the shuffling noise he could hear in the next room was Nick Somers sitting guard to make sure he was resting. Dan thought about complaining about the cotton wool treatment he was getting, then decided to let it slide. He knew his friend had sensed something wasn't right back in Finn's hospital room. In their usual way, they hadn't really talked about it. Maybe they should.

Even when he'd spent several hours holed up with Finn, who had also sensed something amiss, Dan had said only what was necessary. They talked about his dreams, but not all of them—never all of them— and when Finn had asked how he was, how he felt, Dan had given him his stock answer of late, "I'm fine."

I feel like shit. My head hurts. My shoulder hurts. My eyes feel like cold hard rocks in their sockets. Skin feels clammy and tingly all at the same time. I feel like the world's shifting and I'm left to flounder like a fish on the beach, gasping for air, brain addled from lack of oxygen. If only I could breathe ... but sometimes all that goes away and I feel clear, strong—fine.

"Damn!" he muttered. The world was turning again, spinning wildly. He stared at the ceiling. It appeared to buckle, become fluid. He rolled to the edge of the bed and tried to stand, but the floor tipped violently and he was forced to his hands and knees, face burning. His vision blurred and everything seemed to zoom out. He stared down at his hand, leaning back on his haunches. He lifted it closer to his face— fingers spread wide. It was right in front of him. He could feel his own ragged breath on his palm, yet it looked so small, so distant, like he was looking through the wrong end of a telescope. He closed his eyes. His eyeballs burned against his lids.

"Wake up. Wake up. I'm not asleep. I'm not. I'm awake and Nick is outside. I'm awake!"

He crawled to the window and pulled himself upright. His legs felt like dead weights. Leaning heavily against the windowsill, he looked out with relief. The sky was still blue, he could hear Nick in the next room and the grass was … Dan froze. The tenements of the city were gone; in their place, a field of wildflowers and a twisting river. Something huge and long moved through the field, an unearthly whisper called up to him. His head rolled against the windowpane, his hand reached up to press against the cold glass.

"Oh, God!" he muttered again. His eyes closed against hot tears and he sagged to the floor. The pain ebbed, the world stopped tilting, his confusion eased—he was asleep.

The group arrived in Smiggins' Rest late in the afternoon, two days after Dan Tenney had first held the Ouroboros ring aloft and recited the message he'd been given by the mysterious Aiden, ten hours after departing the city for their trip north.

Nick had pulled in at a diner in Steamboat Springs, ostensibly to take a leak, which he did in fact do, but mainly to have a quiet chat with Elliott about Dan. The younger man had been silent the entire three hour drive. At first, he'd been dozing but he'd jerked awake, his lips pressed tight together, his hands reaching out to catch himself from falling even though he was buckled firmly into his seat and had nowhere to go.

Nick had questioned him, offering to pull over, but all he'd got was, "I'm fine—awake now, keep going." Then he'd sat up straight, neck stiff, one hand gripping the armrest of the door, the other pressed against his chest pinning the chain and ring in place. Nick had darted worried glances at the man, tried to engage him in small talk, chatted about anything and everything he could think of, but was met with silence.

At first Nick thought he was being ignored and grew annoyed, but then realized that Dan seemed to be staring at something just outside his window. His head was angled so he could see the sky, his lips were parted and his face wore the same far-away expression he'd seen back in the alley a few days ago. By the time they reached the approach to Steamboat, Nick had realized that Dan wasn't ignoring him. He simply wasn't hearing him, wasn't there with him at all.

"Did he take his meds this morning?" Elliott asked as he and Nick stood washing their hands in the men's room.

Nick turned the faucet off. "I don't know."

"How'd he sleep last night?"

"Went to bed in the afternoon and didn't come out till this morning. Checked in on him a couple of times and he was sleepin' like a baby, hardly moved all night."

"Has he said anything?"

"Hardly ever does."

Elliott shrugged. "It's probably the medication. All we can do is keep an eye on him. This case isn't helping. He could do without the pressure right now. Damn fool should be back in New Mexico letting his granma look after him or, even better, laying on a beach somewhere being served cocktails by sun-kissed waitresses, not traipsing about the mountains on some mad quest."

Nick grunted. "We should all be on that beach."

They'd stopped near Steamboat Lake for an early lunch. Dan had remained quiet but was, at least, with them and listening. Finn had pulled his bandages off, unable to put up with their irritating presence anymore, and donned dark, wraparound sunglasses. His face was red and still a little puffy underneath the glasses, but he was talking and eating like the accident had never happened.

Pete had asked him what it was like only being able to see the dark.

"But there's more in the dark to see." Finn's answer had been enigmatic enough to warrant a "huh?" from the detective.

"The dark isn't a dead place. It's alive and everything else has more meaning. Sound, taste …" He plucked a French fry from the plate in front of him and held it up. "You wouldn't believe how much better these taste when you can't see them."

Simone snorted in disbelief and Finn's laugh boomed in the small café.

"What's it alive with?" Pete asked.

"Questions, puzzles, riddles … and if I look real hard, I can see through the dark to the answers."

"To the light," Dan added.

Finn turned his head to the quiet voice, as if waiting for Dan to say something else. "Through the dark to the light," he repeated to the silence.

The final leg of the journey was completed without stopping.

42

"After a day spent in the cramped confines of Simone's extremely smooth ride, I find myself in need of a drink," Finn announced with a grin, his still sightless eyes staring at the space above Simone's head.

Simone stepped forward, rubbing her hands together with an almost wicked leer. "I wholeheartedly agree, Professor Shaw." She looked around at the men. It had been a long day. A bit of relaxation over some fine malt whiskey was just what they all needed.

"Anybody else?"

"I'm in," Pete answered straightaway. "Elliott?" he asked the man beside him with a backhanded slap to the chest.

"Wholeheartedly!" Elliott laughed, returning the slap with a rough dig to Pete's ribs.

The group had checked into the Rest Hotel en masse and then separated to dump gear. Pete and Elliott, not having that much to unpack, had finished first. They were now lounging about Finn and Simone's room idly discussing the drive up.

Pete flopped on the bed. Elliott sat beside him, his back resting on the headboard and his hands clasped behind his head as he talked.

Finn was sitting in an antique chair by the window, staring into the strange mix of dark and light that only he could see, when Simone brushed past him to reach the mini-bar. Finn knew her scent anywhere and could follow it around the room without any effort.

"Probably be more comfortable down at the bar than up here with this bunch using up all the air," Simone said, without any particular emphasis.

Just then the door opened and Dan walked in, followed closely by Nick. He nodded at his friends in greeting, gave Finn a more verbal hello and moved over to the window.

"Little crowded in here," Nick commented.

"I was just about to suggest moving to a more spacious location," Simone informed him. The miniature bottles of booze clinked as she inspected their labels with practiced ease. She must have found one she liked because the next sound Finn heard was a bottle opening.

"And that location would be?" Nick asked.

"The bar!" Elliott and Pete answered in unison.

The group spent the evening discussing tactics and going over leads while they ate and drank. It was still well before midnight when Nick reminded them all of the need to allow their bodies to adjust to the higher altitude and thinner air.

"Bed a'bye time," he told them in no uncertain terms.

Simone, leading Finn, was the first to depart. She thought about going back down after depositing the tired man in his room, but a sudden weariness hit her as she quietly closed the door. That and Finn's low voice beckoning her closer.

"They'll probably demand an early rise tomorrow," she muttered to herself as she switched off the lights and slipped across the room to join Finn in bed.

"It's too early to go to bed," Pete said. "I've been cooped up all day, don't need to rest from that."

"Come on then," Elliott said, standing up. "Let's go for a walk. Check out the nightlife."

Pete was up and ready to go instantly. He'd used up his quota of sitting still hours ago. "Nick, Dan, you comin'?"

Dan shook his head slightly. "I'll sit here a little longer."

"You two go on," Nick said. "See you in the morning."

Elliott and Pete walked out, jostling each other all the way, their loud voices not fading away till the outside door closed behind them.

"You okay, Dan?"

Dan stared at his drink—a club soda; he was surprised Nick had waited so long. "Yeah, fine." Dan caught the disbelieving look aimed at him, and the corner of his mouth turned up in a bitter grin. "Well, maybe not fine, but nothin' to worry about. You can go on up if ya want."

Nick must have decided to ignore the not so subtle hint. "Is it the medication?"

Dan's brow wrinkled in thought. "The meds? Haven't taken any for the past couple of days. All they do is make me sleep."

"The doc says you need to stay on the medication for as long as you're getting headaches."

Dan sipped his drink and said nothing.

Nick continued. "Sleep is the best thing, it's what you need. For chrissake, Dan …"

"NO!" Dan had had enough. He slammed his glass down on the table—ice cubes clinked and club soda spilled over the side. "I won't sleep unless I can't keep my eyes open anymore, and I won't take anything that brings it on faster."

"But …"

"There ain't no buts about it, Nick." Dan stared hard at the puddle of soda spreading across the table.

Nick held his tongue as he watched his friend wrestle with anger. The man was running on a short fuse, but Nick was taken aback by how brittle he appeared and he wondered if the first cracks weren't starting to appear.

Dan breathed in deeply, his fingers clenched around the glass as he began to speak. "Everytime I close my eyes I'm dreamin'. Hell," he glanced up at Nick with that same small grin on his face, "don't even have to do that much half the time. It's gettin' so I can't tell if I'm awake or asleep." He drew the glass up to his lips and finished his drink.

The soda collected at the edge of the table and dripped silently to the floor.

"It's like I'm standing on the edge of a cliff. Below me is one reality, behind me's another and I can't tell which is the one I belong in. I think I'm s'posed to step out, but I'm scared as hell of fallin' into another nightmare." He stopped to look around a little self-consciously.

"Go on," Nick encouraged. "What are the dreams about?"

Dan shrugged. "Most of them I can't make heads or tails of. Always end up in the same place though. That part ain't so bad, it's the gettin' there that's tearing me up."

"Is that where you were in the truck this morning? Lost in this daydream?"

Dan nodded and gave a soft grunt. "Puts daydreamin' on a whole new level."

"Is it to do with this … quest we've landed in?" Nick asked. Dan had told them about some of his dreams, but Nick hadn't realized their intensity and the effect they were having on the younger man.

"Most of it. It started about six months ago, but I didn't think nothin' of it. Always dreamed a lot, since I was a kid, they weren't so bad then. Mostly went away when I was in the army, too busy tryin' to stay I alive, I guess. You remember Chaco Canyon that time?"

Nick nodded and Dan dipped his face, hiding behind a partial curtain of hair.

"I was there because of dreams, kinda knew I was goin' to meet up with you … well, maybe with someone anyway, nothin' definite."

Dan paused to twirl his glass around in his hand and push his hair roughly away. When he spoke again his voice was so low Nick almost didn't hear him.

"I dreamed about bein' shot in that alley before it happened. The whole thing, smashed car and all, right up to the part where I saw Will at that basement window. Up until then it was like I was followin' a straight path. After I got hurt, the path was twisted and rocky. It still ends at the same place but it's hell gettin' there."

"Tell me."

Dan squirmed in his seat and looked toward the door that led outside. Nick could see his friend was uncomfortable talking about it—he rested his hand on his arm for support. Dan looked back and began again.

"Hard to put it into words. It's all so … unreal. Like one of those paintings you see of staircases that go nowhere, pictures within pictures. The only time it makes sense is when I get to where I'm goin'."

"Where does the path end, Dan?"

Dan leaned back in his chair and stared into the distance. "It's a valley, with a river and wildflowers everywhere. Once I get there I feel safe. But Nick, it's not real, or I didn't think it was, but now it feels more real than sitting here in this bar, and that scares me more than anything. If dreams become real, where does that leave the rest of it? How do I know what's real and what's not?"

"I don't know, Dan. Maybe it's all real somehow. You still need to get some rest though." Nick stood and waited for Dan to do the same.

Dan nodded. "You go, I'm gonna get some fresh air first." He stared down at his empty glass then pushed it to the middle of the table and stood. "See ya in the morning, Nick." He took his coat from the back of his chair, then turned and walked to the same exit Pete and Elliott had used.

Nick watched him go, debating whether he should follow, knowing Dan would be pissed off if he did. When the door clanged shut, Nick turned in the opposite direction and headed to his room.

Nick lay in bed for hours, a fitful doze was all he could manage even though he was bone-tired. He heard Elliott and Pete return, doing their best to keep quiet and failing miserably. Every loose board under their tiptoeing feet creaked noisily. He heard the snoring of more than one of the men and the faint mumbles of troubled sleep through the walls. He dozed again only to wake a short time later still waiting for sounds that didn't come.

It was almost dawn when he woke again to the realization that the sounds he hadn't heard were those of Dan returning to his room next door.

43

The cold air was bracing, invigorating after the close atmosphere of the bar. Dan pulled his heavy coat on as he stepped out into the night. He looked around for Elliott and Pete, but there was no sign of the pair. So, zipping his coat, he tucked his hands into its deep pockets and crossed the road to the river.

The water flowed almost silently past the town, occasionally lapping at rocks and under tree roots—it was as black as ink under the moonlit sky. Dan looked up at the full moon. It glowed a hazy silver. So far away, but Dan felt if he just stretched his hand out a little, he'd be able to touch it. His hand was almost out of his pocket before he caught himself with an embarrassed laugh.

"Keep it together, Dan. Let's not lose it now," he berated himself. But still he stared at the moon. It seemed haloed by a pulsing ribbon of energy. A shudder racked his body and he forced his eyes away from the silent orb, back down to the ground.

A narrow track ran the length of the river, and without exactly deciding on it, he began to follow. He paid no attention to the darkened buildings he passed or to the river gurgling along beside him. The water began to surge as the bank grew rockier and then jutted out into the center of the river. The sudden narrowness caused the water to foam and spray as it forced its way through the gap.

On the bank, the track petered out at the base of a huge boulder and Dan was forced to stop. He looked around for a new path and was rewarded with a faint clearing in the thicket of bushes that encircled the rock. He stepped through it and climbed up and around the boulder, pausing a moment to unzip his coat before taking the final steps that would bring him to the top.

The boulder overlooked a deep pond, protected by the bar of rocks that so narrowed the river. On the far bank, Dan could see the water rushing by. Part of the surge swept into the pond to be swallowed up by the utter stillness of the deep waters. Dan stepped out to the very edge of the flat-topped boulder and looked into the pond.

The moon was eerily reflected on the glass-like surface, causing the far side to take on a silvery, mirrored effect. Directly below him, the water showed no reflections. It was a dark nothingness, a black hole that swallowed all light. He leaned over, his eyes growing wider, his breath pluming between his lips in a cloud of frosty air. A soft scraping from behind brought him back from the edge as he whipped around to face whatever, or whoever, had made its presence known.

Braida Sinclair sat on the back porch of the antique store. She'd closed the doors to her store hours already and now waited, wrapped in a thick hand-woven blanket. Her eyes were closed as she remembered her long years in the valley—the steady change of seasons, the rise and fall of many moons, the flow of the river. She sighed and let her eyes open once more to the moon. Its call reverberated through her body, still setting her blood on fire after all these years. She sighed again and, in one fluid movement, stood and moved to the edge of the porch. The blanket fell to the wicker seat, and she pulled her cloak tight to ward off the chill before making her way off the porch and down to the river, to the meeting she'd been waiting for all her life.

The narrow path that led to the top of the boulder was smoother than the climb on the other side, and Braida walked it easily, reaching the summit with barely a quickening of breath. But still, she could feel the tumble of anticipation inside her and her heart quickened anyway. She forced herself to calm then stood in the deep shadows—waiting.

The scrabble of loose pebbles falling as someone climbed up to the ledge came only seconds later. She held her breath. There was a moment of silence before the approaching figure topped the ledge. The man, his heavy coat unzipped and his bare hands by his side, stood at the edge of the rock to look out over the water. His confusion and pain washed over her in waves and she shook her head. It wasn't supposed to be like this.

Her foot moved carefully forward, scraping on the granite beneath her, and the man turned around, surprised by her presence.

"Who are you?" he asked, his voice a breathless whisper.

The woman stepped closer to him and pushed back the hood of her cape.

"I'm the old woman who lives in the shoe," she told him with a smile. "She had so many children she didn't know what to do." She lifted a hand to his face and cupped his jaw, gently placing her thumb over his lips when he started to speak again. "Come, child. My name is Braida. I will make you feel better," she said in her age-softened voice. Her other hand took one of his icy cold hands and she moved backwards. When he willingly followed, she dropped her hand from his face and turned to lead him back down to the edge of the water.

"You shouldn't have to suffer so," the woman told him. "You don't need this at all."

Dan was stunned. This old woman, her hair white with age, her skin like delicate alabaster—almost translucent under the light of the moon—was setting off a reaction deep within him that he hadn't known was possible. As her finger moved along his face and into his hair, pushing it back and caressing it as a mother to a child, he could feel a well-spring of emotion building up. At that moment, he knew what it was to have someone care for him without condition, for no other reason than because he was him.

Even his granma couldn't compete with this, her love splintered by the deaths of daughter and husband.

His throat grew thick and ached, his eyes were hot. He hadn't felt such simple love since he was a kid—never so loved and, at the same time, never so lonely.

"Shhhh," the woman murmured, her hands dropping to push off his coat.

He tugged his arms from the sleeves and began to pull his sweater off, instinctively knowing her intention. The woman unclasped her cloak and let it drop to the ground. She wore only a light cotton shift gathered loosely at the waist with a twisted length of the same cloth.

Unbuttoning his shirt, she whispered, "Continue," then slipped into the water, leaving him to do just that. He quickly removed the rest of his clothing, barely hesitating over the idea of stripping naked in such a manner. The woman had stopped at thigh depth, her back to the young man on the shore.

Dan stepped into the cold water and approached the woman. "Are you the Dove?" he asked her in a guarded whisper.

Braida half-turned her head, her eyes lowered. "No, my child. I am not."

She reached out for his hand, gently encouraging him closer, deeper, then stepping further in herself and sinking to her knees, completing her turn at the same time so that she faced him completely.

"Come," she said, swirling the water with her hands.

He moved forward until he was within a few steps of her, then he too sank to his knees, gasping as the cold water engulfed his body. "Damn, it's cold!"

Her throaty laugh rang out. "It's absolutely freezing." She pulled the cloth belt from her waist and let it unwind. Her shift hung loose over her gaunt frame as she swept the cloth through the water then brought it up to Dan's face. Icy cold droplets ran down his chest and he gasped again.

"Be still," she murmured, softly pushing the cloth across his face and around his eyes.

Dan's eyes flickered but remained open and staring at the woman's intense expression.

"Why?" he asked her.

She dragged the cloth down to his shoulders and along his arms. "You already know why."

"Will it end soon?"

Braida hooked the cloth around his neck and, holding both ends, pulled Dan toward her to whisper in his ear. "There is no end. There was no beginning. Time is like the ripples in this pond." She nodded toward the ripples that circled around them. "Past, present and future are together, always moving."

She began to slowly move into deeper water, pulling on the cloth to lead the young man with her.

"But it doesn't have to be so confusing for you. Unfortunately, once the obstruction was put in the middle of your particular ripple, changes were made that had to be played out."

The old woman let go of the cloth to tap at the water's surface. A ring of ripples formed around her fingers. She pulled her hand out then placed it in the path of the moving water, changing the pattern of the original design.

"A ripple within a ripple?"

Braida's answering smile sent shivers up his spine as he caught a glimpse of what the woman must have looked like in her youth, her strength—even now in her twilight years—and the power that simmered just beneath her calm surface. He reached out to take her in his arms, the well-spring bubbling once more.

"You must find your quiet," she told him. Putting her hands on his shoulders, she sank underwater, taking him with her. When they came back up, Dan became anxious as he realized what she meant for him to do.

"Will you come?" he asked, his eyes imploring her to stay with him.

"Part of the way," she nodded. "After that you must continue on your own."

Dan shivered in the cold air.

"Put aside the cold as you must put aside your Self, and then you will find it," she assured him.

He nodded, took a deep breath and sank once more, waiting till he was completely submerged before twisting around and kicking out toward the riverbed. He turned his head once to see the ghostly shape of the woman by his side then turned it back—not to look again.

The river's deep. Dan could hear his heart beating like a timpani drum in the silence that surrounded him and tried not to panic. It occurred to him that he should be running out of air anytime now, but then a blanket of calm settled over him and the panic drained away. He closed his eyes, he couldn't see anyway, and stopped swimming. Suspended in the cold depths of the river he could feel a change in the water. Pressure building below. He remained motionless against it, felt it pushing him till he was floating on his back. The bubbles of air that had been streaming from his mouth as he swam now ceased.

Behind closed eyes he saw again the cliff edge overlooking the plains he'd been so afraid of falling into. Now, he saw verdant fields, waist-high grasses and a sky that was the bluest he'd ever seen. He felt an alteration around him, a ripple in reality, and suddenly he was looking in the opposite direction and the valley of wildflowers stretched out before him. A figure strode up and Dan could see the shape of a dove superimposed over the familiar form. He looked harder and saw more familiar shapes moving toward him. Pure joy infused him. He had found his quiet. Fears and anxiety were banished.

Dan faced the plains again, stretched his arms out wide and leapt from the cliff.

In the river, the pressure that had been steadily building below enveloped him in a headlong rush to the surface where the old woman waited. As his limp body broke free of the water, hands pulled him back to the shore and cold lips breathed warm air back into his body.

"This was too much," Braida grumbled aloud.

"It was necessary for him to get past his fear," a man's voice answered from the shadows.

Braida nodded but her anger had not abated. Her hidden companion placed a cool hand on her arm. "You go and get dried off now. I'll take care of him from here. He'll get some rest at last and be ready to continue the journey."

She looked up. "Are you sure? I don't like to leave him. He was so lost."

"I'm sure," the companion replied. "A very wise man once told me that a friend helps his friends or he's not a friend at all. This man is more than a friend though I didn't recognize it at first. I'll see to him. Go!"

Braida trailed her hand around the unconscious man's face. "He is more than that to us all, Aiden." Her pale eyes looked up into the old man's face. "As are you," she continued, leaning forward to gently kiss his cheek. She bent down again to do the same to the man lying supinely between them and then stood to leave.

After she had gone, Aiden carefully pushed his arms under Dan's body and lifted him into his lap. He gathered the discarded clothing of earlier, piled it on top of the young man and stood. With his face to the moon, he whispered short words that drew the moonlight down to him in a flashing display of eldritch light that reflected like stars across the water.

When the light faded and darkness returned, the riverbank lay empty. The water gently lapped against the rocks and swirled around deadfall and tree roots as it flowed out from the protected cove to rejoin the surge downstream.

44

Dan didn't come back.

Nick jumped out of bed as soon as the thought hit him and roughly pulled jeans on over his boxer shorts.

Dan's door was adjacent to his own and he was sure he would have heard the other man come in. The floorboards were too squeaky and his sleep too light to have missed him. He knocked softly. When no reply could be heard, he turned the knob and pushed it open.

"Dan?" he called, stepping right into the room. His stomach was already tying itself in knots of self-recrimination when he stopped in his tracks. On the bed, sprawled on his naked stomach and with only a sheet covering him from the waist down, Dan was sound asleep.

Nick moved closer to make sure his friend was okay and almost tripped over the pile of clothes Dan had been wearing the night before. He squatted down to sort through them, shaking his head grimly at the sticky mud on the bottom of the boots. Twisting around, he expected to see muddy tracks on the carpet and was surprised to find none. He stood, picking up the clothes to hang over the back of a chair. The boots he took into the bathroom.

Coming back into the room, he padded over to the bed. Dan's snores told him that the younger man was indeed okay and sleeping peacefully after all. He took note of the damp hair before walking over to the window to close the blinds against the coming dawn. Dan stirred then, turning his head, and Nick could see a slight smile forming on the sleeping man's face.

Leaving his friend to his much-needed rest, Nick left the room to get dressed for the day. He could probably do with a walk himself.

It was noticeably colder outside in the early dawn than it had been the day before in Denver and Nick had to stomp his feet and blow hot breath onto his hands to warm up as he walked along the town's main street. The stores were still closed, but as he neared the corner, he caught a whiff of baking bread. He crossed the road, suddenly hungry, and peered in the window of the bakery. The baker and his assistants were busy preparing for the new day. Their actions were strategically regimented with long practice and the knowledge of who did exactly what and where, at the same time keeping up a constant stream of friendly chatter. It was like a well-choreographed performance.

One of the bakers, an older man, happened to look up and see the audience of one at the window and waved for Nick to come in. The tall man looked up and down the street before walking around to the door, his stomach rumbling.

The aroma of fresh-baked pastries and muffins reached Elliott in the depths of a soul-satisfying dream.

"Mmm," he moaned as he was brought from sleep by hunger. "Damn! That smells good."

His sleep-gritty eyes opened to see Nick Somers sitting opposite his bed, booted feet crossed at the ankles and propped on the small table, a newspaper spread across his lap. In one hand he held a mug of hot coffee, in the other a steaming muffin.

Nick didn't take his eyes away from the newspaper as he greeted the sleepy-eyed man. "So, Elliott, how was the nightlife?"

Elliott sat up and ran his fingers through his tousled hair. "You planning on sharing that food?"

Nick nodded and inclined his head to the large bag of delicacies on the table near his feet. "Help yourself, courtesy of the local baker."

"Well," Elliott said, getting up. "I don't mind if I do." The sheet slipped from his body as he moved, revealing his usual sleeping attire—absolutely nothing—and he padded over to the table to sit down in the only other chair. He reached for the bag and then relaxed back in the chair, bringing his feet up to rest beside Nick's.

Nick glanced up as Elliott began rummaging in the bag, trying to decide what he was going to eat first. "Cold enough to freeze the balls off a brass monkey outside," he commented.

Elliott tilted his head back and laughed. "Lucky this old barn's heated then, ain't it? This botherin' you?"

"No need to get dressed on my account, Elliott, but people might talk."

Elliott waved his half-eaten pastry in the air. "What people?"

Just then, the door swung open and Pete walked in. "Hey, Elliott!" He stopped when he noticed the frozen expression on the older man's face and his lack of clothing. Glancing across at Nick, he caught an amused grin and a raised eyebrow.

"You were saying, Elliott?" Nick smirked.

"Ah, have a muffin, Pete?" Elliott spluttered before gaining control of his surprise.

"Sure, thanks. Mornin', Nick." Pete grabbed the bag from Elliott and pulled out the first muffin he laid his hand on, ignoring Elliott's commando state.

Simone and Finn walked in. "Good morning, gentlemen. Pre-breakfast meeting?" Simone surveyed the three men, eyes widening at Elliott. "Or pre-breakfast exhibitionism?" She averted her gaze to Nick. "Dan doing better today?"

"Still sleeping. He came in late from a walk last night."

"Yeah?" Pete interjected. "We walked all over the place. Didn't see him."

"At a guess, I'd say he went down to the river. You know what he's like. Needs time alone occasionally ..." Nick trailed off.

"You talk to him?" Elliott asked. He passed the bag of baked goods along to Simone.

Nick turned his face to the window. Dan's words from the night before were still going around in his mind. "Yeah, we talked."

Everyone waited for Nick to continue, but he remained tight-lipped.

"You sure about the river?" Finn asked solemnly.

"His boots were wet and muddy," Nick told him. "Figured he that's where he went." Nick could see the professor was turning something over in his mind too. "Finn?" he prodded.

Finn looked toward Nick's voice. "I dreamt about the river last night."

"Another one of those vision-dreams?" Pete asked.

"Maybe, I'm not sure. There was a raven, a snake and a fish."

"What's it mean?" Elliott asked.

Finn shrugged. "Not entirely sure. The snake and the fish were swimming in a pool of water protected from the currents. The raven was watching from a tree. It looked right at me and said, 'Welcome.'"

"Said?" Pete sounded skeptical.

"It was a dream."

"Whatever!" Elliott interrupted. "I'd like to remind you all that this is my room. Could you please go discuss dreams and talking birds some other place and give a man a chance to get dressed?"

Nick laughed, folded his newspaper and dropped his feet to the floor. Being naked in general had never bothered Elliott, being the only one naked was another story. "Let's continue this down in the breakfast room," he advised. "Give Elliott here a chance to recover his modesty."

Nick clapped his hand on Finn's shoulder as they started to file out. "Finn, I want to talk to you before you go down."

Finn nodded and stood still, waiting to be guided from the room. He heard Nick mumble a few words to Elliott, and Elliott's, "Will do, Nick," in reply and then Nick was back by his side.

"How're the eyes this morning, Finn? Seeing anything on this plane of reality yet?" Nick asked as he placed his hand firmly on the man's elbow and led him from the room.

Finn's laugh trailed behind and Elliott shook his head as the two men left and he was alone again. He stood, stretched his arms above his head then leaned across the table to take the last muffin from the bag. Munching on the soft, cake-like texture, he moved over to the window and looked down at the river opposite the hotel. Popping the last piece of the muffin into his mouth he turned toward the bathroom. He'd shower, get dressed and then head down to the breakfast room to interrogate the waitress. He smiled suddenly and rubbed his hands together. He loved this job.

45

The hotel corridor ended in an old-fashioned sitting room with floor to ceiling windows that afforded an excellent view of the river. Tall aspens growing close to that side of the hotel framed the window, and the overall effect was like a picture lifted straight from a coffee-table book.

"You have to try talking to Dan again, Finn. This morning, soon as he wakes up," Nick said.

"Has something else happened?"

"He told me about his dreams last night, talked about twisted paths and hidden valleys. He stopped taking the pills because they make him sleep …"

"And to sleep is to dream?"

"That's right, only now he says it's happening while he's awake too."

"Simone and I talked about it yesterday on the drive up. The medication, even the effects of the injury, may have masked or changed the dreams in some way. Having all three to contend with must be putting an immense strain on him."

"And it's starting to show. I can see it in his face, even the way he stands, bowed over, waiting for something else to happen."

Finn bowed his head in thought. "I can talk to him, but will he talk to me?"

Nick pushed himself back into the chair with a ragged sigh. "I don't know. I think he will. He said something about two realities and stepping from one to the other, pictures within pictures."

"It's a common enough thread of thought," Finn told him.

"Your dream last night, Finn … you said you thought Dan was in it but you weren't sure. Why is that? Either he was or he wasn't." Nick could feel a bubble of understanding growing inside him. He was on the verge of breaking through.

"I could feel his presence but I didn't actually see him," Finn began. "There were only the three animal forms. I'm fairly sure the raven was the man Dan called Aiden. I've sort of met him before and it felt the same …"

"Who is this Aiden exactly?" Nick interrupted. "Is he a real person or just a figment of your dream?"

"I believe he's as real as you and me, but who he is exactly, I can't tell you."

Nick noticed the other man's fingers clench around the armrest of the antique chair. *He's hiding something,* he realized and looked at Finn sharply. *What?*

Finn's face remained impassive and he continued on, unaware of Nick's close scrutiny. "I have previously seen the serpent as Arwium but that wasn't the case this time."

"Somebody else?"

"The forms don't seem restricted to one person." Finn paused a moment, thinking.

"Go on."

"I've seen Dan as a raven," Finn finally said.

"And last night?"

"I saw Dan as a fish. A salmon to be precise."

Nick leaned forward. "A fish swimming in the river with a snake?"

"Yes."

"The snake is the symbol of wisdom and the raven is a messenger." So, so close.

"Yes, again. What are you thinking?"

"I'm thinking that you dreamt of Dan swimming in the river and when I checked on Dan earlier, he was wet. Something happened last night, and you need to talk with him as soon as possible. We need to go find this hidden valley. We'll set out first thing tomorrow. That gives us one day to learn as much as we can."

Finn began to stand. "Then we'd better get to it."

Nick stood with him. One more question in mind. "What does the salmon symbolize?" Finn looked directly into his eyes and, for a moment, Nick thought the professor's vision had returned.

Finn's deep voice was amazingly soft as he answered the last question. "The receiving of mystical and prophetic knowledge."

Nick walked into the breakfast room just as the rest of the team finished up. He stopped the waitress as she walked past and ordered trays to be sent up to Finn and Dan before continuing on to join his colleagues.

"You made it," Simone greeted him, lifting a cup to her lips. "Finn not joining us?"

"I left him up in Dan's room. They need to talk. So do we. How's the coffee?" Nick replied, dragging another chair over to the table. Other guests were beginning to filter in, but it was still early and the room barely half full.

"I wouldn't know, I'm drinking tea," Simone answered, taking another sip.

Nick gestured for the waitress to bring over some coffee. "You find out anything, Elliott?" he asked as he turned back to the table.

Elliott flashed a toothy grin. "She's got two sisters, a cousin and a widowed aunt and doesn't recall the professor's stay. But, she said if Flemming went hiking, she would've had to have gone to the wilderness store to gain the necessary permits and latest weather reports. Seems they act as the unofficial ranger station for the area."

Nick raised his eyebrows. "Anything else?"

Pete snickered and Elliott's smile widened.

"Three phone numbers, a party invitation and a walk in the woods."

"And breakfast isn't even over yet," Pete added, shaking his head.

Nick's laugh was short but genuine. "Mountain air agrees with you, Elliott."

Elliott nodded and winked then held his mug up for the hovering waitress to refill with coffee as soon as she was finished with Nick.

"Yes," Simone agreed. "He's quite unbearable already."

"Aw! You're only mad 'cause you got outta bed before noon," Elliott retorted.

Simone scoffed and sipped her tea.

Nick chuckled quietly and then grew serious. "We need to start out tomorrow, first thing. Elliott, I want you and Pete to go over to this wilderness store. Get as many maps and as much information as you can from them about the surrounding area and the professor's visit. Find out what equipment we might need and whether we can hire it. Simone, you go down to the antique store. Find out if they've received this book. Get a look at it if you can. Keep your eyes and ears open for anything else. The smallest detail could be important in this case. We're close and in a town this small, somebody will know or say something we can use. I'll stay here. See if I can get a look at the hotel's registration books and talk to the manager. I'll also check in on Finn and Dan. Meet back in my room by twelve. I want us at the wilderness store this afternoon to get kitted out for an early start in the morning. Pete can you put a call in to Captain Lennard this afternoon? Let him know what we found and what our plan is. I want someone on the outside knowing where we are." Nick paused to look around the table. "Anybody got anything to add?"

"Why yes, now that you mention it," Simone spoke up. "I recommend the scrambled eggs for breakfast with some of that bappir bread. It really is quite delicious, the best I've ever tasted."

"I thought the steak and eggs were pretty good," Pete added.

Elliott raised his hands in the air. "The waitress looks pretty good to me …"

46

Rose, the owner of the wilderness store, was in the back of the store sorting through a pile of ropes, checking them for wear and tear, running them through her callused hands. Her younger partner, Eliana, strode in from the back room with a box of new stock for the store.

"Here are the supplies I picked up in Steamboat yesterday," she said. "Frank's preparing for a big freeze."

"You saw the moon last night?" Rose asked, not looking up from her task.

Placing the box carefully on the floor, Eliana walked over to her friend and knelt down in front of her. When the older woman still didn't look up, she placed her hand over the frantically busy ones, her soft touch immediately halting all movement.

"Rose?"

Rose swept a wisp of graying hair from her face and looked up.

"I saw it. I would have come back last night but ..."

"It was late. I know," Rose said quietly. "You're back now." She paused to look at their still joined hands, tentatively holding on to Eliana's reddened fingers. *Forgot her gloves again.* Taking a deep breath, Rose continued. "I saw the old woman this morning. She looked tired, used up. Tomorrow, she said. We must be ready."

"We are."

Rose shook her head stubbornly, releasing her hold on the other woman's hand to continue working with the rope. "I want you to stay here, Eli. Be safe. There's no need for both of us to go." She frowned deeply at the quavering she could hear in her voice. *When did I get old?*

"I have to go. I want to see Serena ..."

"You might not," Rose interrupted.

"I want to go, I must. We go together, that's what we were told. It's what I want."

"I don't like it at all. Why must we?" *Now I sound like a petulant child,* Rose told herself. But she couldn't help it. She could feel trouble ahead like a bubble near bursting point within her.

Eliana squeezed Rose's knee. "It's who we are. That's why we came here …" Any more words she had were abruptly cut off as the bell at the front door jangled its warning of customers entering. Two men walked in, sharing some joke as they stepped across the threshold. Rose's heart weighed heavier in her breast with every second that passed.

"They're here," Eliana said on a soft exhalation of breath and stood to greet them. She composed her face to something, not exactly happy and cheerful, but less wrought with emotion than it had been bare moments ago. She walked toward the two men. They had one day. One day to get ready, one day to say goodbye.

"Morning!" Elliott enthusiastically greeted the woman who appeared by his side as he flicked through a rack of Gore-tex jackets.

Pete chimed in from the other side of the rack with his own good morning and the woman nodded in return, quietly waiting for them to continue. Elliott's smile beamed as he aimed all his charm in the woman's direction.

"We need some maps and maybe some help to find a trail a friend recently told us about. Maybe you remember her? Older woman, name's Irene Flemming, came up a few weeks ago."

The woman shrugged non-committedly. "A lot of people come through here. I'd have to check our records. Did she get a permit?"

"We're not sure, but she would have had to come here before trekking out into the woods, wouldn't she?" Elliott replied.

"That's right. Weather conditions are very changeable at the best of times and a lot of the trails are difficult." The woman turned and headed back to the counter.

Elliott and Pete glanced at each other, shrugged and followed along behind.

"Musta used up all your charm on the waitress," Pete muttered, just loud enough for Elliott to hear.

"Watch and learn," Elliott muttered back, putting on a big smile when he saw the woman had stopped moving and was now watching them from behind a flat screen computer monitor.

Ignoring Elliott's smile, she continued on. "Did she tell you anything about the trail she took?"

"Mentioned a valley with lots of flowers," Pete told her.

The woman reached under the counter for a large laminated map that detailed all the trails in the Smiggins' Rest region. She laid it on the counter for the men to see.

"All the trails go through valleys with flowers. See if you can find anything familiar on this map. I'll check the computer for permit records." She keyed the name into the search program of the store's database. When a "name not found" result came up, she began a search through the permit lists. "When was she here?" she asked Pete.

"September/October," he replied, watching the monitor display flick to that time period and begin to scroll down the long list of names.

Eliana knew the name wouldn't be there. The trail Irene Flemming took was not listed in the computer or shown on the maps. No permits were ever issued for its use. The trail was strictly invitation only, and those invitations, not written on any card or fancy paper, were rarely sent outside of the small township.

"Not there," she finally told them, unconcerned.

"She should be there though, right? If everyone needs a permit, she should be on this list."

"No, everyone that was issued a permit is on this list. Perhaps the trail she took didn't require one, there are a few easy trails along the river that don't, or maybe she just went off without one. Happens all the time and we don't keep records of people who just inquire about the weather."

"Oh."

Elliott had been poring over the laminated map. He found nothing helpful, but then he didn't really know what he was looking for. There was certainly no valley labeled "Elphane". He looked up and smiled at the woman again.

"Well, darlin', maybe you could take a look at a picture of our friend for us, jog your memory." He glanced at Pete and the detective pulled a photograph from his shirt pocket.

"I wasn't in town for most of September and October." She quickly ran her eyes over the picture, then looked up at Elliott sharply. "Hang on and I'll ask Rose. She was here."

The woman walked to the rear of the store. Elliott stepped back to watch from around a display case of various hiking and rock climbing accessories to see her lean over and mumble something to another, older woman. The second woman took the photograph, glanced at it then stood to meet the men. When they returned to the counter, she handed the photograph back.

"My name's Rose, this is Eliana. I run the store. We were fairly busy in September, not so in October, spell of bad weather, but I do recall this woman. Sold her some gear and a few maps. She didn't need a permit so I didn't issue one."

"Could you show me some more maps?" Pete asked Eliana.

Elliott turned to the older woman, touching her on the shoulder to guide her away. "Rose," he began. "Irene's about sixty or so, not that fit. Where could a woman like that go around here and see a valley full of wildflowers?"

Rose's answer was muffled as the two walked back to the rear of the store. Eliana hid a smile. Turning to Pete, she said in a low voice, "Your friend's quite a charmer, isn't he?"

"He thinks so," Pete smirked.

"I bet plenty of women do too. How many hearts has he captured around here?"

Pete laughed. "Quite a few. It's not working on you though."

"Not my type. Not Rose's either but she'll play along to get what she wants."

Pete turned to the woman. Her face was completely unreadable as she concentrated on pulling out an assortment of laminated maps from behind the counter.

"What do you mean?" he asked.

She looked up at him. Her eyes were dark and deep and Pete felt a single cold shudder go down his spine.

"Do you know who Smiggins was?"

Pete blinked, confused. "Who?"

"Smiggins as in Smiggins' Rest? He was an old guy from the Langue d'oc in France. His real name was Gabran. He and his family came here about two hundred years ago to escape persecution in their home country. Everybody here is descended from that family in some way or another. Everyone is connected here. There are no secrets."

Pete tried to keep his face blank. *No secrets.*

"Why're you telling me this? Does it have something to do with us?"

"It might." Her answer was vague, but it was the first positive sign they'd received since the whole mess began.

"You can borrow these if you like," she said, handing him the maps.

"Will they help?"

"They'll give you an idea of the general area around Smiggins' Rest."

"But not the trail we want?"

"No."

Pete looked over the maps curiously. They covered the mountain range from

Hahn's Peak to the west, Mt. Zirkel to the south, Big Creek Lakes in the east to well north of the Colorado/Wyoming border.

"How will we find where we want to go?" he asked.

"Nine is the sacred number," she told him before turning away to search out the other two people mumbling in the background. When she turned back, Pete could do nothing but stare. "Bring your friend back with you, bring them all. There's a lot for you to do and only today to do it in."

"How come you're doing this? Everyone else seems to talk in riddles."

Eliana leaned close to whisper in his ear. "I'm one of the Nine. It's my task to help you."

"What do you mean, one of ..." The woman cut off Pete's question by pushing a small token into his hand. It was a hardened, unfired piece of clay with an X circled by a snake consuming itself stamped into it.

"You recognize it?" she asked him, almost harshly.

Pete nodded, turning it over in his hand. The clay was rough around the edges like someone had pulled it straight from the earth and stamped the design into it. There was no refinement, no smooth edges. He could almost feel the warmth of the sun that had baked it on the palm of his hand. It was a replica of the design on Simone's flask.

"It's the Mark of Cain. It identifies those chosen to take on the quest. Something of a blessing." She held her hand out and Pete returned it to her, his lips parting to let loose another string of questions.

"Later," she told him. "Take these maps and study them. There's important information on the back—conditions, warnings—it will be helpful if you know what to expect out there. Mystic riddles won't save you from Mother Nature."

The mumbling at the rear of the store petered out as Elliott and Rose returned. The two women gave each other a knowing look. Elliott winked at Pete and began to move toward the door.

"We'll be seeing you later, ladies. You can finish the rest of your story, Rosie. I'll bring the wine and blanket."

Rose gave the tall man an enchanted smile and the two left. As they reached the door, Elliott whispered down to Pete, "Used up, indeed. I just charmed that lady into telling me all about a whole heap of stuff. Got her wrapped around my little finger."

The bell jangled again as the door opened and closed. "Uh huh," Pete agreed. He looked back through the glass door to see the two women standing side by side. Elliott's conquest had her arm wrapped about the younger woman's waist.

Pete could see Rose's lips moving as she said something and wished he could hear what it was. The younger woman's hand lifted up to caress the other's face and Pete thought that maybe he didn't need to hear their words after all. He finished his turn and followed after Elliott. "Uh huh," he muttered again, "completely wrapped around your finger."

Shaking his head, he jogged to catch up. He didn't know how in hell he was going to explain any of this to the captain, let alone get his go ahead to stay on the case. He only knew that he wasn't leaving now.

"Elliott! Wait up! Let's stop at the bakery. I'm starved."

47

Dan understood the reason for his visit as soon as he heard Finn enter his room. He shared a silent look and a nod with Nick; both to assure him of his own wellbeing and acknowledge his need to talk with Finn. As soon as the door had clicked to a close behind Nick, Finn began.

"I had a most unusual dream last night, Dan …" and he proceeded to tell the young man every detail he could recall.

Dan sat on the bed, listening quietly until Finn stopped speaking and then turned his face in the general direction of the window.

"Are the curtains drawn?" Finn asked. He stared hard at the approximate location of the window.

"Yeah," Dan said. "You can tell that?" He got up and padded over to the window to let the sunlight in, watching Finn's face as he pulled the thick material back. Finn smiled as soon as the light appeared.

"It seems my sight may be returning. I can definitely tell the light from the dark," Finn told him.

Dan stepped into the light. "Can ya see me?"

Finn frowned and squinted in Dan's direction. "Maybe a faint shape, a shadow, but that's all."

Dan walked slowly and silently toward the seated man, watching his face for any sign of recognition and not getting any until he completely blocked the light.

"Dan? Did you close the curtains again?"

Instead of replying he moved to the side, watching again for a response and pleased to see a faint grimace cross Finn's face.

Finn closed his eyes and left them that way. Listening, Dan guessed. Birds were in the trees right outside the window, a truck rumbled along the road and … Finn turned toward him with a smile, face uplifting. Apparently he could hear Dan beside him, breath steady and slow, and probably smell him too. The weight of his fear of not being able to see lifted as he realized he wasn't as cut off from the real world as he thought. Witnessing Finn's revelation of restored senses, Dan felt immeasurably happy. It gave him hope that he too would soon be restored.

Dan squatted down in front of Finn and watched comprehension filter across the older man's face a half-second longer. "It will come back," he assured. "Until then, you already know there's more to life than sight. Use what you've got."

"How'd you know?" Finn asked.

"Know what?"

Finn kept his eyes closed, listening, smelling, feeling the air around him. "That I was scared of being blind permanently. I thought I hid it pretty well."

Dan shrugged. "Maybe you did, I don't know. I'm pretty sure you haven't fooled Simone though."

He stood up and walked over to the dresser to get some clothes. "I'm gonna have a shower," he announced and disappeared into the bathroom.

Finn's blind eyes followed him all the way.

Breakfast arrived with a diffident tap at the door while Dan was still in the shower, and Finn called out to come in. The door swung open and a waitress, accompanied by the hotel manager, walked in pushing a room service cart laden with food. The manager smiled a good morning at the man seated by the small table and then verbalized it when she realized this was the blind one of the group before directing the waitress to set the morning's repast on the table.

While the table was being set, the manager turned to the man to explain what and where everything was.

"Mr. Somers ordered a full breakfast for two very hungry men, so I've taken the liberty to include cereal, a large traditional breakfast of sausages, poached egg, grilled tomato and bacon, toast, some freshly baked bappir bread from our local bakery, tea and coffee as well as some juice. Is there anything else I can get you?"

"I think that'll just about cover it, ma'am," Finn replied, savoring the aroma of the sumptuous breakfast.

"Good. You have a mug of coffee to your right, your plate is directly in front of you with a glass of orange juice behind it and the basket of bread is just to your left. Enjoy, sir!"

With that, the waitress and manager wheeled the cart out of the room and closed the door. A few minutes later, Finn heard the shower turn off and Dan moving around in the bathroom drying off and getting dressed. The low whine of the hairdryer came on as Finn reached for a slice of the bread and began to eat. It hadn't been that long since the muffin in Elliott's room, but he found himself hungry all over again.

The hairdryer switched off and Dan walked out, stomach rumbling loudly. "I'm starving," he said as he sat down opposite Finn and poured coffee.

There was no more talk until all the food had been eaten and the men sat back, appetites satisfied. They mutually agreed on the desire to get out of the small room and find somewhere more comfortable to sit and talk.

A sitting room at the end of the corridor held a small breakfast bar, its doors now open to reveal a percolator gurgling away, a stainless steel electric kettle, a dozen or so handcrafted mugs, sugar, cream and an assortment of herbal teas. It seemed they were the only guests in this part of the hotel so there was no concern about anyone being able to listen in or catch them unaware. The squeaky floorboards would alert them to any arrival.

Dan guided Finn to a chair and headed for the coffeepot and more of the strong brew.

Their voices murmured continually for well over an hour, Dan sharing information that confirmed what Finn had found in his research. Finn, in turn, spoke in hushed tones of what he could only describe as grief at the gradual loss of his childish faith in the church he'd grown up with, the church his father had espoused and had pushed at him since his birth.

"*When I was a child, I understood as a child, but when I became a man, I put away childish things ...*" Finn said. "I suppose it takes more than age to make a person grow up. This was my time to put away childish things, to finally let go of beliefs based on half-truths. My faith has been directing away from that for quite some time ..."

"Perception is like a window, a pane of glass," Dan whispered urgently. "We've been looking through clouded glass, smeared with lies and half-truths but the grime's bein' wiped away, bit by bit. Last night I saw through a clean window for the first time."

"Wh ... What did you see?" Finn struggled to get out.

"It's different for everyone, Finn. No one shares the exact same reality. You see things differently yourself ..."

Finn snorted. "I see nothing. I'm a blind old fool."

Dan leaned forward, his mug cradled in his hands. "No, that's not true. You're in the dark for a reason, to learn how to see through a clean window."

Finn didn't seem convinced.

"Not everythin' we're taught is wrong," Dan told him. "We just weren't taught everythin', and how could we be, when it's all shrouded in mysteries an' riddles?"

The conversation turned to the people each had seen in their dreams both as physical beings and spiritual symbols.

"It's almost like all the old fairytales we used to hear as kids have turned out to be true," Dan said as the floorboards squeaked their warning. "It wouldn't surprise me if we happened upon a bunch of fairies and elves living in the woods just outside a'town."

Nick and Simone arrived and slipped into vacant seats to listen.

Finn grinned and gave a half-hearted laugh but his face still wore a ravaged expression.

Nick noticed that their demeanors seemed reversed. Dan was calm and relaxed and Finn was tense. Dan caught his eyes and smiled faintly before tilting his head in the direction of the coffeepot. Nick strode over, filled two mugs with the black liquid and returned to hand one to Simone. He decided to leave Finn to her and moved over to the bookshelf-lined walls. His eyes ran idly over the titles; they seemed to be mostly poetry. Some names he recognized, others he didn't—William Blake, Ted Hughes, Kenneth Slessor, Robyn Morgan, an odd mix and a whole shelf full of them.

"The westerns and murder mysteries are on the other side," Dan said as he slipped up beside him.

Nick looked down at him and then back at Finn, apparently engrossed in a conversation with Simone.

A soft laugh came from Dan then. "Simone really ain't happy unless she's got someone to worry about."

"She should be the most deliriously happy woman in the world at the moment then," Nick replied dryly.

Dan leaned one shoulder against the old wood of the bookshelf and watched the couple across the room.

"You find the professor yet?" Dan asked.

"Oh, yeah. She stayed here a week at the end of September, according to the hotel manager's husband—who spends most of his time sitting downstairs guarding a 'tankard of fine ale, m'boy'." Nick imitated the husband's Irish brogue for the last few words much to Dan's amusement. "The good professor walked around town a lot and spent hours by the river, reading."

Dan looked at him, sensing the undercurrent to Nick's words.

"Books from this library," Nick continued, pointing casually at the shelf with his mug before taking another sip. "Her room was the last one along here." He nodded toward the room in question.

"Anythin' else?" Dan's eyes narrowed slightly.

"Well, no midnight swims in the river or otherwise strange behavior," Nick said, the corner of his mouth lifting in a wry grin.

"You callin' me strange?"

"If the scales fit," Nick replied, lifting his mug to his mouth and finishing his coffee.

Dan returned the grin. "Don't worry. It's a no fishing zone."

The two men smiled at each other, both relieved that, for now at least, things seemed to be back on an even keel once more. Nick didn't need to ask to see that the younger man was at ease. The brittle air of the evening before had faded. He only hoped that this time it would last.

Dan straightened. "More coffee?" he asked, holding his hand out for Nick's empty mug.

"Thanks," Nick replied. "If I don't get my daily gallon of the stuff I disintegrate into quivering jelly."

Dan walked over to the breakfast bar, laughing. Nick returned to his perusal of the books. He put his hand up to slide one from the shelf. *Slessor. Might as well try something different.* He tucked the slim volume in his jacket pocket to read later and went back to sit down with Finn and Simone, to drink coffee and wait for the rest of the team.

48

Simone knocked on the door of the antique store and jiggled the brass doorknob. There was no sound from within. She put a hand up to cut the glare of light on glass windows and peered in, narrowing her eyes in an effort to see through the lace curtains. The store was deserted. She stepped back, hands on hips—she could hardly break in like she had at the Freight Company. What excuse could she use?

Yes, ma'am, the store was closed. I was so desperate to get in and purchase a turn-of-the-century lace doily, I just picked the lock. How about, *I'm not really a thief, just here investigating mystical books that send old professors traipsing around the country looking for the Holy Grail. By the way, have you seen any birds that are really people or people that are really snakes, and what's the fishing like in Little Snake River?*

Really! *Oh, God! Now I sound like Pete.*

Simone shook her head to clear the bizarre thoughts and Pete's speech patterns from her mind. A little walk around the old house would be agreeable. She turned and trotted down the stairs, swung a left at the edge of the garden and began a tour of the grounds.

Toward the rear of the home, the garden turned from bush and vine to a thick mat of brilliantly colored flowers—pink, yellow, blue, white—a riot of color in what would otherwise be a dark and gloomy haven beneath the trees. Simone blinked, surely it was unusual for such springtime display this late in the season. Her thick coat was buttoned right up to her chin, and though she was head-bare, she wore no less than two pairs of gloves to ward off the cold. One pair of silk-lined kid-leather gloves had cost a small fortune a few years ago, but had been worth every penny for the chilblains they had saved her from. The other was a pair of tightly knitted woolen gloves that Finn had given her last winter. Simone did not enjoy the cold weather at all and still wondered daily why she'd moved from cold old England to equally cold Denver. She should be in California.

She paused by the edge of the mini-field of flowers and let her eyes follow it from the riverbank below right up to the porch of the house itself. Her gaze fixed on the porch and on the woman who sat there wrapped in an old-fashioned quilt. *No doubt, hand-made,* the part of her that noticed such things whispered. The woman was as still and pale as a marble statue and, for a fraction of a moment, Simone wondered if she was exactly that or an illusion of some kind.

Visions of indoor tornadoes and vanishing people flashed through her mind and she knew a flash of dread as well. The woman inclined her head and Simone banished the wild thoughts to the same place she'd sent the bizarre ones of earlier.

And then, as it often did in times of stress and, if you asked her friends, as it did at all other times as well, her mouth took over.

"Good morning, madam, would you be the owner of the antique store out front?"

"I would," was the simple reply. "The store isn't open for business yet."

She smiled up at the woman's serene face. "I was hoping to browse through your store this morning, but thought a look at your beautiful home would suffice until the store opened."

The woman stared at her without saying a word.

"What time you will be open for business?"

"There's not a lot of call for antiques this time of day. I usually open about mid-morning, sometimes noon," the woman said. "Is there something in particular you wished to see?" The tone of her voice sharpened as she spoke and Simone saw an intensity in her face that looked familiar and strange at the same time.

"My main interest is books, especially scholarly works. I understand that you might have a collection of interesting items on your shelves?"

"I did have," she replied. "Most of them have moved on now. Did you have a particular title in mind?"

The woman had still not moved, except to speak. Simone gravitated toward her. She had a foot on the bottom-most porch step and a hand on the rail.

"*Desposyni,*" she replied.

The old woman shook her head. "That book is not here."

"But it was?"

"Yes. It was a special search for a private customer."

The woman swung bare feet to the wooden slats of the porch and stood. Keeping the quilt wrapped around her thin body, she came down the stairs until she was at eye level with Simone.

Simone swallowed nervously as the woman drew closer and in a rough voice asked, "Might you tell me that person's name?"

"Aiden Gabran."

"And where might I find Mr. Gabran?"

The woman let go her grip of the blanket and it slipped back on her white shoulders to reveal a thin, white shift. A pendant hung from her neck; Simone recognized the design of an X inside a circled snake. She'd lifted her hand to touch the charm before she realized she'd even moved and caught herself with an embarrassed flush.

The woman didn't seem to be aware of her intention as she raised one bare arm to point to an almost overgrown trail on the other side of the bank of flowers.

"He lives in the mountains. That way."

Simone turned to look in the direction the old woman pointed. The trail curved and twisted into the trees. When she looked back to speak to the woman again, she had already ascended the stairs.

"Ma'am?"

She turned and smiled—gently, wistfully.

"The path is not easy. I wish you well." Her voice was strained with fatigue, face drawn tight in the cold morning air. She pulled the blanket tighter around her shoulders and walked away.

Back at the hotel sitting room, Simone filled a mug with strong black coffee, added a few more spoonfuls of sugar than she would have on any other day, and gulped half of it down with a gasp before sitting down with Finn.

"I just met the most extraordinary woman …"

49

"Good morning, boys. Welcome to Smiggins' Rest. How are you finding it so far? Will you be staying long? Oh, no, I guess you won't, what with the moon and all last night. We don't get a lot of visitors this time of the season you know. Sure glad to see you're all finally here …"

Elliott couldn't believe his ears. He and Pete had just walked into the corner store on their way back to the hotel to pick up some assorted snacks and sodas. The woman behind the glass-top counter had greeted them with a sunny smile and had hardly stopped talking since. They stood by the counter, pinned to the spot by her beaming countenance and more than ample physical presence. She bustled around with a soft cloth, swiping at imaginary dust particles, rearranging jars and boxes that were already perfectly aligned and talking so fast she barely stopped for a breath.

"Ah, ma'am," Pete tried to break in to the flow of words.

"… and you're all such strapping young men. Why, I'm sure you've got the local girls in quite a tizzy. And that woman, so beautiful, almost had my husband's heart aflutter when he saw her in the hotel last night. Lucky I'm not the jealous type, and he's not one to stray. Such a pity you're off again so soon …"

"Ma'am," Pete tried again before sending a flustered look to a chuckling Elliott.

Elliott stepped forward and leant his elbows on the spotless counter; his hands came to rest on one of the woman's as it darted past with the cloth. The woman stopped moving and looked up into his eyes, cheeks blushing. *Not just the young ones either,* he guessed.

"Is there anything I can do for you boys?"

"This sure is a pretty town, ma'am, and we've been enjoyin' all the sights." Elliott gave her a slight leer and raised his eyebrow suggestively, to which she caught her breath, flushed a beet red and giggled like a girl.

"Oh, stop," she protested, her hand staying firmly tucked under Elliott's.

"A friend of ours came up about a month ago. She told us how friendly all the folk are up here and she sure was right. Maybe you remember her? About sixty, grayish hair, and glasses. She's a professor down in Denver."

The woman's face was blank for a moment and then recognition of Professor Flemming's description flooded her face.

"Oh, of course. You mean the Staff Bearer. She kept to herself, a quiet woman really. Always had her nose buried in a book."

"The Staff Bearer?" Pete interrupted.

"Well, yes," she looked from one man to the other. "You didn't know? Oh, maybe I've said too much." Her plump hand went to her face in consternation and worry marred her brow for a fleeting moment before another smile wiped it away. Her hand dropped back down to pat Elliott's affectionately. "Braida would never have told us the story if it wasn't all right to talk about it a little."

"Braida?" Elliott asked.

"My sister. She owns the antique store. You haven't been down that way yet? It's right at the end of the street, last building before the forest takes over. Some say it's the farthermost point of the Star Forest. No one else can get flowers to bloom quite so well as Braida."

She glanced up and appeared to notice that both men appeared confused as they listened to her continual chatter.

"But listen to me ramble. Keeping you boys from your business. I'm such a chatterbox. You ask anyone. Who talks the most in Smiggins' Rest? They'll all answer—why that'd be Alais O'day, sure enough."

"Did your sister tell you where the Staff Bearer went?" Elliott asked her gently.

"Same place as you boys are going, of course," Alais clucked. "Into the Forest of the Stars."

"Elphane?"

Alais nodded and opened her mouth to say more when the shorter of the two men beat her to it. "What else did the story say?"

She adjusted a small display of sour liquorices at the end of the counter and glanced up to see another, older woman standing on the other side of the glass door. Alais immediately recognized the white hair and slight form of her sister and paused in her movements long enough to see her place a single finger over her lips, then reach out as if to do the same to Alais. The talkative woman felt her lips go cold and knew she'd said enough. She pursed them together against the chill. The older woman outside dropped her hand to her side and smiled before vanishing into the thin mountain air.

Pete had followed the woman's gaze out the window when she failed to respond, but could see nothing but a smudge in the glass. The chill in the air was unmistakable though and he shivered inside his winter coat.

"Mrs. O'day? Can you tell us the rest of the story?"

The woman turned a pale, closed face to the men, her happy-go-lucky expression of just a few moments ago gone.

"Are you going to buy the candy, son?"

Elliott and Pete shared a confused glance at the abrupt change in the woman's behavior.

"We'd sure like to hear it, ma'am," Elliott encouraged, straightening his stance and pushing his hands into his pockets.

"Maybe another time, boys. I'm afraid I have other work to be getting on with and I really must attend to it before the lunchtime rush." Alais pointedly looked at the thin watch wrapped around her wrist. The fountain of information had just dried up.

Pete placed the candy bars he'd been collecting as the woman talked on the counter while Elliott went back to the refrigerator to get an armful of sodas. Alais placed all the purchases in a box and quietly accepted the money the men offered her.

As they were walking out the door, they heard her mutter, "You are the story."

Finn closed his eyes. *All the better to listen with.* Elliott and Pete seemed unable to relate their morning's experiences separately, their words tumbling over the other, confirming, clarifying, correcting what each had to say. For a policeman and an ex-policeman they sure had a jumbled and disconcerting way of sharing a story.

"… and I managed to get Rose to tell me that two more people would be joining us in the morning, and we definitely all had to come back to the store today. Only one day …"

"To get things done," Pete interrupted. "Eliana told me the same thing, even without your charm, Elliott. Rose intended to tell you all that anyway. And they are the two extra people. 'We are of the Nine.' That's what Eliana said."

"Well," Elliott continued, ignoring Pete's reference to his charms. "She also said the path was hard and there were still trials to come."

"What trials?" Finn asked, thinking they'd been through enough.

"She either didn't know or wasn't saying. She was most concerned with the fact that we had to be ready for tomorrow, something about the moon."

A sliver of dream came back to Finn then and he saw again the black waters bathed in moonlight. Sitting, surrounded by his colleagues, he could plainly see the reflection of the full moon on the glass like surface of the river.

"It was a full moon last night," his voice, quiet until now, brought the men to temporary silence.

"A shimmering moon," Dan added.

"How's that important?" Nick asked.

"I'm not sure, but it is. Things happen on the full moon."

"Wolves howling and all that?" Elliott said in mock sincerity.

"You know, the woman down at the general store knew that we were coming and why we were here. She even knew about the professor and that she'd gone to Elphane. Said that's where we were going too, as if it were common knowledge."

"Maybe to these people, it is," Simone said.

"Braida had told of a story," Elliott added. "But what's that got to do with the moon?"

"Omens come to pass and magic is strongest on the full moon. Perhaps that's what the story was about," Finn told them.

Nick stood up to refill his coffee mug yet again. "Who's Braida?"

"The old lady who owns the antique store."

Simone nodded and squeezed Finn's hand. "I spoke with her this morning. I could well believe she dabbled in magic. There was a certain mystical air about her."

"What did she say?" Nick asked.

Simone leaned back in her chair and brought Finn's hand to rest in her lap. "She had the *Desposyni* book in her store. Had, being the operative word. It was a special order for a client. A person we seem to be vaguely familiar with, who goes by the name of Aiden Gabran."

"The same Aiden who flies around dressed as a raven?" Nick inquired.

"That wasn't specified," Simone replied.

"Gabran's the name of the guy who first settled this area. He changed his name to Smiggins, and apparently, everyone in town is descended from his family." Simone settled into her chair and tucked her feet beneath her.

"All of a sudden, everyone's clamoring to tell us stuff," said Nick. "What else do we know about this Braida?"

"Mrs. O'day said the Star Forest starts in her garden," Pete supplied.

"She certainly has a beautiful garden," Simone confirmed. "When I asked her where we might find this Gabran fellow, she said the path to his home starts in her garden—it was not an easy path and she wished us well." She paused for a moment. "You know, she wore a pendant very similar to the flask that Isabel McTavish gave me, an X inside an Ouroboros symbol."

"Eliana had one too but it was a clay token, not a pendant. She called it the Mark of Cain, said it identified those on a quest. I thought the Mark of Cain was a bad thing." Pete scratched his head, trying to figure it all out.

"Who told you it was a bad thing?" Finn asked.

"School, I guess … Is that like what you were saying about parts of the Bible deliberately left out?"

"It is common for conquerors to take over a conquered people's stories and beliefs and change them or reverse their meaning," Finn explained. "It has happened many times in history, still happens to this very day."

"The lady I met this morning is far too old to be gallivanting around the mountain range," Simone said. "She can't be a Questor."

"What did she look like?" Finn asked her.

"About five feet, six inches, long white hair, pale skin, quite thin and frail in appearance. She wore a light shift dress and was sitting on her porch wrapped in a quilt. I believe she was waiting for me to arrive."

Finn heard a soft intake of breath from Dan's direction.

Nick must have noticed as well. "What is it?"

Finn leaned forward into the casual circle the group had formed as they talked. *This is what it's like to wait with bated breath. The quickening when a person realizes that something of real importance is about to be revealed.*

"I met her last night by the river," Dan admitted. "She's the other serpent."

"I don't like how this is panning out. I feel like we're being led around like a pack of hounds. They give us a scent here, a scent there and we go off baying into the wilderness." Nick stood and strode over to the window, glancing out before turning to face the group. "And just who the hell are 'they' anyway?"

Pete had been scribbling notes in his pad. He skimmed through the pages until he found the particular jotting he wanted and read out loud. "Isabel McTavish and Aiden the Raven, with possibly the unknown guy Simone saw with Isabel and this Braida woman—all four have some sort of magic powers or appearance of same." He looked up when he finished and asked, "Do you really think Aiden Gabran, Aiden the Raven and Smiggins could all be the same person?"

"That's impossible, Pete. When did you say Smiggins came here? Two hundred years ago?" Elliott answered.

Pete shrugged. "Yeah, but if he's magic … I mean, how can a person be a raven?"

"Let's just stick with what we know," Nick interrupted.

"We should start with the reason we're here then," said Simone. "Professor Irene Flemming was reported missing by Finn. In actual fact, she was designated a Staff Bearer and took off to fulfill her required task of taking said staff to Elphane. Presumably, she was successful and, hopefully, is still in that mysterious place. We can presume this based on the fact that no one around here seems overly concerned for her welfare as well as the fact that we haven't heard from the Brotherhood in two days."

"Captain Lennard's going to think we're all off our rockers and have us committed," Pete observed.

"Not necessarily. Judging from various artifacts in her study and notebooks, this sort of side journey is fully within the professor's character. She travelled to the Iranian Mountains a few years ago just to chase up some obscure lead concerning the dating of residue in the bottom of a pre-Bronze Age storage jar; before that a year in Tolosa, France, chasing tales of lost treasure. The learned professor was always flitting off. Perhaps not quite to such wild areas as these, but flitting nevertheless. What we're coming up with fits neatly into what the professor was studying."

"Where was the original Gabran from?" Nick asked Pete, picking up on what Simone had just said.

"Langue d'oc region, Southern France."

"Tolosa is a Langue d'oc name," Simone added.

"What is Langue d'oc?" asked Elliott.

"A region in Southern France that included Albigensia—strong Cathar supporters," Simone began, only to be interrupted by Pete.

"That's where Gabran and his family were from."

"Then they were probably Cathars or descendants of. Most of them were wiped out hundreds of years ago," said Finn.

Pete looked around the group thoughtfully. "Do you think that's another connection?"

"It's possible," Nick conceded. "But whether or not it's relevant to us is another matter. Unless ...?" Nick paused to look at Dan.

Dan felt his gaze and looked up, surprised. "What?"

"Have you ever been to Southern France?"

"Yeah, actually I have, but not for sightseeing and I don't know nothin' about this Langue place."

Nick left his place at the window and came back to where the group sat. "Where and when?"

"Toulouse and thereabouts, around eight or nine years ago. Was there a few nights on an army exercise. We did our stuff and then got out." Dan kept his face purposefully blank. Nick knew that he didn't enjoy talking about his army days.

"The professor was in France at that time also." Nick caught Dan's eye, then continued. "Tolosa and Toulouse are the same place."

"I knew there had to be some other connection!" Elliott exclaimed. "They must have been marked and chosen back then for this. But why wait nine years?"

"Nine is the sacred number," Pete said. "Nine years, nine Questors. It's a pattern."

"But the professor was only one," Elliott replied.

"We don't know that, not for sure. Maybe she had eight people helping her or maybe one is a sacred number too."

"Perhaps she is counted as part of our group? Even with these women from the wilderness store, we're only eight," Finn pulled his hand free from Simone's grip and rubbed his chin.

"That's all well and good," Nick said, "and we should keep note of that connection, but it doesn't really help us now. It's background stuff. Simone?"

"As we already know, Dan is the Bearer of Ouroboros. I believe we all play a role in this, not just as mere decoration, but possibly something more important. Perhaps as protectors or guardians and in Finn's case some sort of guide." Simone paused to look at Finn. "Maybe some other more obscure role. We really don't know who McTavish and Aiden are or what their true agenda is. We also do not know the purpose of this ring and the staff. What will happen when we get to Elphane?"

"The more we learn the less we know," Finn mumbled into his hands. He tilted his face up and lowered his hands, spreading them out before him. "What of this ring? It seems overly large to fit a finger yet too small to slip over a hand. What could be its purpose?" *If not to be worn, then what?*

"I did a search on that symbol before we left Denver," Pete said. "The oldest known reference to it is in Ancient Sumer. It was known as the Ring of Unity and was a gift from the god Enki to a woman named Hawah on the birth of her first son. Then it pops up all over the world as a symbol of different religions, particularly in Celtic culture where it was considered a symbol of wholeness and wisdom." He looked up from his notebook. Finn was briefly ecstatic that he could see that small movement. "It wouldn't be the same ring though. Would it? It's just a symbol."

Finn rested his chin back in his hands, thinking, trying to see. He hadn't actually seen the ring, though it had been described to him, but something in what Pete had just said rang a bell. *The ring was a gift on the birth of a son—on the continuation of a bloodline.*

"What was the name of Hawah's son?"

"Q-A-Y-I-N, pronounced …" Pete looked at Finn, "… Cain."

"The Mark of Cain is Sumerian?" Nick asked.

"Apparently so," Finn answered. "Apparently so."

Braida watched from the shadowy windows of her home as the eight travelers passed by to begin the final leg of their journey. She recognized, and was saddened for, the women who led them. Neither would be returning to Smiggins' Rest.

The old woman held a deep breath, a sob against knowledge of the inevitable. She would soon be leaving her home as well. Her things were already in order. Her sister's son and his wife, a talented young couple, would be taking over when she left. Releasing the breath, her eyes slid over each member of the group, lingering longest on those who would be irrevocably changed and on the one whose death she had foreseen just moments ago in her scrying bowl.

Tears ran down her tired face. Pain and grief filled her heart. She bolstered her old body against her emotions and stood straight and tall until the very last Questor had faded into the dark forest. Morning birdcalls stilled, the early breeze dropped. The only sound came from the eternal river—the snake that wound its way through the mountains from one world to another.

Braida hung her head low, her chin resting on her heaving chest. She could no longer keep her grief inside. As she sank to her knees, a wild, moaning keen escaped her lips and reverberated around the room.

The residents of the small town, those who were awake at this early hour, stopped their morning chores and turned pale faces to the far end of town. Some dropped to their knees, arms clutching themselves as if in pain; others crossed themselves fervently and prayed, those still asleep turned restlessly in their beds. The baker, a wise old man who kept his mouth shut and his mind open, muttered a quiet prayer for departing souls.

"May your path be smooth and may you be well met," he finished, bowing his head in simple grief.

The call of the banshee wailed on.

Simone followed with Finn behind Nick and Dan as they left the store early on the first day of their trek into the wilderness. She'd marked it in the journal she'd brought along for the sole purpose of recording the journey. *Day One—Got up at a truly ungodly hour, enjoyed a filling, but rushed breakfast and started out.*

Not an overly elegant or particularly descriptive beginning. I can dress it up later. Maybe add a few words about the bleary countenance of my compadres. Perhaps mention the rising of the sun. She peered up at the still dark sky. *When it does rise, that is.*

Simone's rambling thoughts broke off when she recognized the home of the antique dealer. In front of her, Dan had slowed and was looking down to the river. Simone followed his gaze to see the calm waters of the protected cove and noted the well-worn trail that cut through the long grass and flowerbeds.

She turned her attention back to the house, expecting a last glimpse of the mysterious woman and was disappointed when she didn't appear.

Is she there, watching? Simone shifted the pack on her back, but it didn't ease the pinpricks of awareness that spread along her skin. She narrowed her eyes and stared harder for some sign of life in the pre-dawn dimness of the house. There was nothing. Not a curtain flickered, not a shadow moved.

The trail was wide enough to allow the group to travel in pairs. Simone hooked a hand under her lover's arm, unobtrusively guiding him over and around any obstructions, though surprisingly, she noticed, the path was relatively clear.

"There's a tree root sticking out to your right, Finn," she said just loud enough for him to hear. "How're you holding up?"

"This is almost like a stroll in the park. I only wish I could see more than just shadows."

"Well, there's not much more to see anyway," Simone told him. "The sun's only just up and the trees are blocking most of the light. Shadows are about all any of us can see."

They fell silent and Simone's mind wandered back to the previous afternoon when she'd expressed her concern for Finn's ability to go hiking through the mountains. The younger of the two women, Eliana, had taken Finn's hands and led him over to the back of the store where a climbing wall had been set up.

"The trail we'll be taking will involve some free climbing but nothing as steep as this wall. Why don't you try it?" she had suggested to the blind man.

"You can't be serious?" Simone had fumed. "He can't climb that!"

Eliana had kept her expression mild and pointedly aimed her reply at Finn. "Of course he can. How much do you think you can see when you climb anyway? Field of vision is narrowed down to six inches, sometimes less. All you can see is a slab of rock right in front of your face. You don't see your way up, you feel it. Finn?" As she'd spoken she'd taken his hands again and placed them, fingers outstretched, on the wall.

"I'll try anything once," he'd answered with a grin.

Eliana had put him into a harness, checked the connections to the attached rope and turned to Simone, the other end of the rope in her hand. "Keep the slack off, but not too tight or you'll pull him off the wall. Hold the rope straight down if he comes away and he won't fall. Got it?"

Simone had nodded. "I got it. Are you absolutely sure about this, Finn?"

"Piece of cake."

Rose had been watching the interplay and now Eliana flicked her a nod to signal she should take over the belay. Eliana had then returned to Finn's side.

"You'll be fine, Finn. I've done this before and I'll stay with you all the way," she'd told him and did exactly that, talking him up the wall the whole time.

Their voices drifted back down to the rest of the group watching below.

"Feel the surface, its unevenness. Let your fingers find the holds. Left hand eleven o'clock. Right foot—two," she instructed. "Push yourself up with your legs. Your hands are for finding holds and hanging on, not pulling yourself up." She'd nudged his right hand to the next handhold. "Ten o'clock. That's it."

Instructions were mixed with laughter; Finn's voice and the woman's soft tones had made comments that produced yet more laughter; and then, at the top: "Time to fly."

Rose had made sure Simone knew how to ease Finn down and then called up to the pair clinging to the top of the wall. "Ready!"

"Comin' down!" Eliana had turned to Finn. "Let go of the wall."

Finn did and slowly dropped to the floor. Simone let go of the rope as soon as he was back down, running to him in an uncharacteristic display of emotion. "You okay?"

"I think I prefer it this way. Can't see how high up I am. You ought to try it yourself," Finn replied, beaming.

"I've done it before," Simone said. "I prefer to keep my feet on flat ground wherever possible."

Eliana had pushed off from the wall and was down in one flying leap, a huge smile transforming her serious face.

"Don't worry, Simone. I'll walk him along any rough bits the same way. We'll get him there in one piece, I promise."

That only served to make Simone feel worse. Eliana's words sounded like a solemn vow and rang with a foreboding presentiment. Her smile had faltered as she shook her hand, the vow sealed. She wondered what it was she was feeling, not liking it one little bit.

Simone thought about it again now as she watched Eliana's dark figure moving ahead of them. The woman had been serious again this morning; determination to get a job done overshadowing any enjoyment there might be in hiking through the woods on what was promising to be a beautiful day.

"Low branch, Finn. Duck … now!"

53

Deep shadows held the rustle of unseen wildlife—branches above and bushes below stirring, whispering with movement. Tall, aged trees loomed over the trail, branches like arms reaching out to ensnare the unaware. The sound of the eight people walking underneath echoed through the barricade of trees. Alarmed animals flitted away from the danger of their presence. Birds delayed their early morning calls, remaining hushed till the danger of humanity had passed.

The voices of the eight grew still as they travelled. The quiet of the woods and the dim morning light cast a heavy blanket over any need for conversation. As the day grew, sunlight began to dapple their path. Breaks in the thick canopy allowed the light to stream in and trees that had looked threatening with their shadowed twisted presence began to take on a more normal appearance.

The river had been left behind as the path angled through the forest, its roar of passage a distant echo. Then suddenly it was back, a wild torrent of white water rushing through a deep cut in the mountain rock. A small clearing beside huge boulders afforded them a place to stop and rest before tackling the next part of the trail.

Rose, taking point, announced her intention to halt by simply stopping and dropping her pack against a rock. She was worried about the effects of increased altitude on the two injured men. They would need plenty of short breaks if they were to make it through the first day of steady climbing.

Dan winced as he eased his pack from his shoulders. The muscles of his injured shoulder were still tender and any undue movement or pressure caused a fair amount of pain. Nick stepped up to help him out of the straps and take the weight of the pack from his friend.

"Thanks," Dan muttered, leaning his back against one of the boulders and resting his head against the cold granite. His head was giving him hell too.

Nick left his pack beside Dan's and wandered over to the edge of the embankment to wait for the remainder of the strung out group to catch up. Rose stood in front of Dan and bluntly asked him if he was okay.

"I'm fine," he replied. "Really. Besides, Nick's watchin' me like a hawk. Can't even let the spiders bark without him checkin' me over like I sprung a leak."

Rose chuckled at the trace of disgust evident in Dan's voice. "Nevertheless, if the pack bothers you too much or the altitude's getting to you, I need to know. The path gets rougher and steeper from here on in."

Dan nodded and pushed himself away from the boulder to join Nick by the water's edge. Pulling his canteen from his belt, he unscrewed the lid, took a sip then offered it to his friend.

"She's right," Nick said, handing the canteen back.

"I know." Dan sat down on a rock, feet dangling over the edge, and watched the river surge by.

Simone had been right behind them, separated from Finn by the narrowing of the trail and the need for the more experienced Eliana to guide him along. She stood, waiting by the side of the path with legs astride, hands on hips and eyes grazing the back trail. "I felt like Red Riding Hood in there, on her way to grandmother's house and about to be eaten by the big bad wolf." Her smile was wide, too wide, uneasiness hidden in its breadth.

Rose wasn't fooled. The woods were not something to be taken for granted, and in the handful of times she'd made this particular trip, she had never gotten used to its eerie atmosphere.

"Take a load off and have a drink. We need to keep our fluids up," she said, making her way back to where Eliana was breaking through the tree line, with Elliott, Finn and Pete right behind her.

"How's it going?" Rose asked her friend.

"Stroll in the park. Right, Finn?" Eliana replied with a strained grin.

"My words exactly," Finn confirmed.

"Well, the park's about to get a little hillier. I want you two to rope up."

Eliana nodded. They had been through it the day before. She was experienced in leading cold beginners and the less than fully-abled and would take the lead end of the rope, with Pete on the lower end to "play catch", as Finn had put it with a laugh. Elliott and Nick had argued that one of the men would be better able to stop the big man from falling down a slope.

"No," Eliana had argued back. "If he falls, the force of his weight on the rope will increase so much that it won't matter who's on the lead end. We need to prevent the fall in the first place and that takes experience not brute strength."

Elliott and Nick had continued to argue until Dan spoke up in his characteristic drawl. "Reckon she knows what she's talkin' about."

"All right," Nick said reluctantly. "We'll do it your way, but I want Elliott to back you up and Pete to take the rear to back up Finn."

Eliana and Rose nodded their agreement, but although the argument was now settled, Simone still didn't look too happy.

Standing by the riverbank, looking down on the water below, Simone felt uneasy. Something was wrong.

The trail climbed steadily upward, some parts rough and hardgoing, others less so. Numerous breaks were taken—a cold lunch with hot coffee still steaming from the thermoses just before noon. An hour or so after that an extra ten minutes were earned while Rose scouted past an eroded section of trail, returning with a firm determination to lead the party higher up and around the rubble. Dusk came early at this time of year and by the time they reached their overnight stop, long shadows had already fallen across the path and the temperatures had started to drop.

"I don't s'pose there's a cosy little resort up here with a nice warm bar to relax by?" Elliott grumbled to Eliana. He had stopped to make sure she and Finn were navigating the rocky path without too much difficulty.

The woman's answer came out in a derisive snort and a cloud of frosted air. "A bar? Give me a hot tub over a bar anytime."

Finn's usually wide grin barely made it past the lip-curling stage as he paused to catch his breath. "I'm sure Elliott would be into that."

Elliott wriggled his eyebrows and placed his hand over his heart. "A bottle of champagne, a tub of hot bubbly water and thou."

It was the first time they'd heard Eliana laugh out loud, her serious composure gone in the face of Elliott's hilarity. And it was then that Elliott noticed the woman's face glowed.

He was a little taken aback and not quite sure what it was he was seeing for the first time—a different woman from the contained person he'd met the day before. This one was relaxed and happy. There was something else about her he couldn't quite pick up on, and he realized, standing two thirds the way up a mountain, that he'd glimpsed it when she'd made the flying leap from the top of the climbing wall yesterday and again that morning. Loaded up and ready to start the trek, he'd watched as she'd greeted the day with an upturned face and a slow smile of something he couldn't quite recognize, though the memory of it stayed with him. It hadn't mattered that the sun wasn't yet up, that clouds of freezing breath hung suspended before her. She was truly happy to be out and heading into the mountains.

Elliott looked at the trees and bushes around them, the jagged icy rocks and slick ground. It was cold and getting colder. There was no awe-inspiring scenery to take a person's mind off the exhaustion—his legs ached, his lungs felt seared from gulping in the thin mountain air. Under all that though, he had to admit he felt truly uplifted—as if at this given point in his life, he was exactly where he was supposed to be. He wondered if this wasn't what Eliana was feeling as well.

As she came up level with Elliott, pulling off the slack of the rope that linked her to Finn, she flashed him a highly amused smile. "Bring along a box of expensive chocolates and you've got a date," she said. Then, leaning in close, she added, "I'll even bring a friend. We'll have a party. Just the three of us." She chuckled to herself at his surprised expression and moved away to help Finn around yet another rock.

Elliott adjusted the knitted cap on his head. "Woman, this ole mountain man can sure show you how to party."

Eliana gave a sharp laugh as she led Finn past the tall man. "Soon as you find that hot tub, you just let me know."

"Me too," Finn added, his mock serious face staring directly at the other man.

Pete came up behind Finn, a tired smile on his face as well. "Make sure you leave room for the rest of us." He stopped beside Elliott, then turned to look back down the trail into the darkening woods below. A shadow, discernible only because it was moving, parted from one tree and darted behind another. He frowned to see it, the hairs on the back of his neck rising, but when the tree swayed in the growing breeze, he discounted his paranoia as a product of the falling night, the woods and his own imagination.

Relieved, he grinned mischievously. "Oh, Elliott? I like the soft-centered candies and my champagne icy cold."

The log cabin was small and old. Its rough-hewn walls were covered with a blanket of alpine lichen in varying shades of browns and greens. The last rays of sunlight beamed on the lighter patches, and glinted on a cracked pane of glass, creating a weird effect that illuminated the chimney inside.

As the group approached, Nick felt a tremble of trepidation start somewhere inside him. The cabin was plain eerie and he briefly wondered what ghosts haunted it and whether the .38 special he had stashed in his pocket would be any real defense against the supernatural world they seemed to be enmeshed in.

He walked past Rose and up to the cabin door, searching for signs of danger and finding none. The cabin didn't get used often, but it wasn't derelict. The front stoop was covered in a layer of dead leaves and the narrow, covered porch was patterned with animal footprints. Other than that, the cabin looked like it was merely waiting for its owner to return. Nick pushed the door open, one hand in the pocket that held the gun, his instincts telling him to remain alert.

Sharp eyes investigated every corner of the single room from the doorway. A huge fireplace that doubled as a stove was positioned against the back wall, dividing the kitchen end of the cabin from the sleeping area. Cupboards lined the wall to his right, a rough table and chairs were in the center of the room in front of him, and a pile of firewood and row of bunks, head to head, were in the far corner to his left.

Stepping right in, he started at a shuffling sound behind him and had nearly pulled out his gun before he realized who it was.

"Easy, Nick," Dan's soft voice warned. "Ain't nothin' here but us and the critters."

"I don't like it," Nick muttered.

"What's not to like?" the younger man quipped, moving past him to dump his pack on one of the beds and flop down beside it.

Nick managed to refrain from asking Dan if he was okay. Even in the dim interior of the cabin he could see that he wasn't.

A bright light flooded the room and Nick squinted. Rose walked in holding a flashlight.

"There're lamps in the end cupboard," she informed whoever cared to listen. "Let's get settled and get a fire going before we freeze our buns off."

The rest of the group crowded in, lamps were retrieved and lit, and the fire started. Dan and Finn were left to rest while the others spread out bed rolls, got some food cooking and a pot of coffee on the boil. When the coffee was ready, Nick took two mugs over to the resting men.

"You two still alive over here?" he asked with a grin, sitting on the edge of Finn's bunk.

"Just barely," Finn answered. "But nothing coffee wouldn't fix right now." He'd smelled the coffee brewing and his mouth was watering. "Is it dark outside?" he asked, his fingers wrapping around the mug Nick was pushing into his hands.

"Dark and cold. Might snow," Nick said.

Finn sagged back against the wall and sipped his coffee. "This was about the hardest day of my life," he admitted, exhaustion clear in his voice. The flickering light from the fire made his face appear haggard and old.

"You okay, Finn?" Nick was concerned at the air of dejection settling around the older man.

"Just tired. Tired, old and blind."

Nick clasped Finn's knee to show his understanding. "We're all that, Finn. One way or the other."

He then approached Dan's bed quietly, thinking he might be asleep. He'd hardly moved and his eyes were firmly closed.

"Dan?" he whispered. "You awake?"

"Yeah," Dan replied. "Unless this is another nightmare and when I open my eyes, I'll be at home instead of on some mountain with my head about to explode." He cracked his eyes open, closing them again when the light hit them. "Damn, that hurts."

"You're not dreaming. This is as real as it gets."

"Hell!" Dan pushed himself into an upright position and allowed his eyes to open again.

Nick offered him the coffee and he took it, resting the steaming mug on his bent knee.

"Got any of those little white pills on you?" Nick suggested.

"Yeah, in my pack here." Dan fumbled with the side pockets, trying to ignore his throbbing shoulder and not spill the hot liquid everywhere.

Nick pushed his hand away and searched the pockets till he found the packet of over-the-counter painkillers. He popped out two of the white pills and dropped them into Dan's hand.

Dan turned a strained face to the older man. "Thanks."

"Get some rest. I'll let you know when it's time to eat."

54

It was dark and warm. *It should be cold.* Mountains. Icy edge of winter. Wind howling all around. He could hear it. It pulled at his clothes, whipped his hair across his face, cut through him like a knife. *It should be cold. I should be cold.*

Warm, fetid air assaulted his nostrils. He wanted to gag, turn his face away from the rank atmosphere, but it was everywhere, soaking into his skin and hair, saturating his coat. He tried to move his legs and run away from the terror he could feel creeping behind him, a quagmire of mud and sludge held him fast, pulling him down. His legs were already encased to his knees.

Scratching sounds echoed through the tunnel—the patter of clawed feet on rock walls, the sucking of movement through the swampy ooze—closer and closer. Terror grew inside him now. Screams ripped through his head, strangling his throat and electrifying his body. *Not again! Not again!*

The screams never left his body. He kept them in, held onto them as if denial of their release could save his sanity. To scream would be to give in, to lose control, to accept fear—and insanity.

He pulled the threads of reason together in his mind and fought desperately to free himself. The scorching glare of evil pierced his back, *ohgod, ohgod,* and he tugged hard on his legs. The slow squelching as his legs began to move in the thick mire of mud came too late. *Too slow.*

He bent over, burying his hands in the muck to pull his legs free with his hands and glanced back between them to see eyes staring at him. He half-turned and crouched to face the danger just as the monster catapulted itself toward him.

The quiver of spidery whiskers brushed his face, the stink of warm rotten breath expelled over him. He could do nothing except throw his arms up in a pathetic attempt to defend himself ...

Hands touched cool skin and soft hair. The stench was gone. He opened his eyes to see someone standing before him—the shadow of a person, vaguely familiar in some way, yet hidden from him. *Eyes, large and dark; luminescent in their depth, lit from within with burning purpose.*

The monster retreated. Screeching its anger and frustration as it disappeared down the alley that they now were in, its long white tail struck the broken road and lashed at the moss-covered walls.

His body shuddered as he recognized the alley and the same staircase he'd climbed before. His feet were free, standing on solid ground, and he took a step toward the stairs. A soft whisper had him turning back to the figure who had saved him. The shadows swirled and for a split second he glimpsed a face before the dancing shadows blocked his vision. When he looked again, all he could see was a pile of bones scattered on the street below.

Grief replaced his terror and he folded his arms across his body as the physical pain of it hit him.

Noooooooooo!

The dull glow of embers and the feeble light of a solitary candle lit the cabin when Dan awoke to a cool touch on his face.

"What …?" he began, only to feel the touch move to his lips.

A shadow moved across him and he felt the bed shift as a soft voice and a warm breath spoke close to his ear. "Shhhhh. Everyone's asleep."

Dan looked around the dark cabin, at the unmoving lumps that were his friends occupying the other bunks. "Did I sleep through dinner?"

The shadow moved away and a quiet laugh drifted down to him. "You sure did," the voice whispered. "We figured you needed the rest more than dinner so we saved you some. Come over to the table and I'll get it ready for you."

The shadow moved further away, into the light, and became Eliana. Dan pushed back the sleeping bag someone had thrown over him and got to his feet. He looked again at the others, checking who slept where. Their combined heavy breathing and occasional snores were a comforting backdrop against the growing howl of the wind outside. He walked over to the table where Eliana was pouring the contents of a thermos jug into a bowl and sat down to a meal of piping hot stew;

his stomach rumbled its discontent at having been ignored so long.

The woman stoked the fire, adding another couple of logs, and the room filled with light and warmth.

"Bad dreams?" she asked, returning to the table and reaching for another flask. She opened it and poured cocoa into two mugs. "Want to talk about it?"

"Not sure if I even remember it now I'm awake," Dan told her. His gaze drifted to the candle that burned in the center of the table, fixing on its yellow glare. He felt her hand on his and the corner of his mouth turned up in a self-mocking smile. "A giant rat was following me," he admitted, tearing his gaze away from the candle to continue eating.

"Did it catch you?" she asked, solemnly.

"Nearly," he replied with a sheepish recollection of his fear.

Her face was concerned as she watched him eat, and Dan found himself remembering when he met her, just the day before, but somehow now a lifetime ago.

The group had walked into the wilderness store the previous afternoon. Dan and Nick had followed Elliott and Pete straight down the back. Neither of the women were there, though their voices could be heard from another room.

Dan had stopped to look at the rack of maps near the glass-top counter. They'd all examined the ones Elliott and Pete had been given, but he liked to see what else there was. When he'd heard Simone comment on the photographs displayed around the walls, he'd looked up to see the large print hanging behind the counter.

Finn had heard the faint gasp that left Dan's lips as he stared at the scene in the photograph. "What is it, Dan?" he'd asked quietly, sensing trouble.

Dan didn't reply; instead he'd taken a step closer to the counter then moved quickly around it to extend a tentative hand to the picture.

The rest of the group approached the counter. "Talk to us, Dan," said Nick.

"This is it." Dan's voice was barely a breath. "This is it exactly." His fingers traced the line of a river cutting through a field of flowers. "This is the river, the flowers, the trees. I sat here ..." His fingers stopped on a rock jutting up from the river bank. "I walked through here …" His hand found a path through the trees. "I stopped here and turned around to look back." His fingers closed into his hand and he turned to face his friends behind him.

"What did you see when you looked back?" Simone asked.

"You. All of you." His eyes rested on the two women who had silently joined them. "You were in the trees, weren't you?" he said to Rose, not waiting for her to answer before speaking to her friend just behind her. "You were there," he said to Eliana. "I saw you standing there, waiting." He paused, his hand finding its way to the ring dangling hotly against his chest. "Only it wasn't you at all."

He'd turned back to the picture, amazed to see actual proof of the existence of his dream.

"Who took the photograph?" Nick had asked the store owners.

"My sister," Eliana replied.

"Can we meet her?"

"She's there," she said, nodding at the valley in the picture. "The Forest of the Stars."

Dan's hand had moved gently across the trees, as if touching them might take him straight there. "It was her I saw. She's the ninth member of the group, isn't she?"

Eliana nodded once and walked away.

The spoon scraped along the bottom of the empty bowl.

"Want some more? There's bread here too." Eliana got up and refilled the bowl and passed Dan a wrapped package of bread.

"Thanks." He opened the packaging and pulled out a small loaf of barley bread. Ripping a piece off, he dunked it into his stew before biting into it. When he swallowed, he turned Eliana. "Sorry if I woke you."

"You didn't. Already awake," she told him, putting her mug down on the table. "Couldn't sleep."

"You have bad dreams too?"

"Not exactly."

He stuffed another piece of bread in his mouth, smiling around it as he chewed. "Wanna talk about it?"

Eliana smiled back. "I was flying."

<h1 align="center">55</h1>

The group woke early in the morning to a world turned white and filled with the clamor of a furious wind.

"You don't appear in the least surprised," Simone said to Rose.

They had taken a look out the door at the cries of dismay from the men before returning to the task of preparing breakfast and refilling flasks with coffee and hot water.

"We expected a change. That's why we had to reach this cabin by nightfall."

"How could you know when the change would come?" Pete asked them.

"The moon," Rose replied shortly.

"Just what is it about this moon that is so important?" Simone asked.

"Last night, Dan said it shimmered," said Pete.

Dan ducked his head, embarrassed to have everyone's attention aimed solely at him yet again.

"It's known as the haloed moon," Rose explained. "Three days after it appears there's a major change in the weather, usually for the worse. It's a recognized fact by the local weather stations."

"Will we have to sit it out?" Pete asked.

"No, won't affect us at all. We go under the mountain from here."

"Underground?" Dan blurted. His face lost color and he swayed where he stood. He suddenly felt like the cabin was closing in on him, the close atmosphere stifling. Not waiting for confirmation, he turned on his heel and stumbled out into the snow and wind.

"We've got less than an hour before this'll set in," Rose told the astounded group. "Then we'll be snowed in for the winter, lucky if we get two feet from the cabin, let alone down to the tunnels. You'd better get him back here."

Nick was already out the door.

"I can't do it, I won't. They can't make me," Dan muttered over and over. "I won't go back down."

Nick watched him pace across the clearing outside the cabin, clapping his hands together and then rubbing them against his arms to keep warm. Frosty air plumed from his mouth as he continuously mumbled to himself. Dan saw the other man coming and went to turn away, drawing in a sharp breath of pain as Nick grabbed his injured shoulder to stop him.

"What's going on?" Nick demanded.

Even though it must have hurt more, Dan wrenched his shoulder free and took two steps away, his expression somewhere between fury and total panic.

"No way, Nick," he hissed, bare fists clenched. "Ain't doin' it." He released his hands and turned again, unable to keep still in his agitation. "I've been shot, had my head busted, been lost and so mixed up I thought about …" He flicked a desperate look at his friend kneading his forearms with tense fingers. "About … Hell! I still feel like crap. Gotta force myself to get up and keep going every fucking day! I can't go back underground, Nick. Don't make me."

"We have no choice, Dan. This weather is about to get serious. We can only go forward and that means underground."

"No, there's another way. There has to be."

"It's too late to find another trail. We've got to go. Now."

Dan just shook his head and stepped away, a silent "No" hanging in the space between them.

Nick didn't move. The younger man was so on edge he was liable to do anything.

"Dan," he started. "We were told we'd be going underground. It was in one of those cute little messages we were given. I thought you knew, understood better than any of us."

"I did. I do, but it's different now. I can't and if I don't …" Dan's voice trailed off as he looked down the path they had travelled the day before. He hunkered down in the snow, resting his elbows on his knees and allowing his fingers to drag in the white powder.

The wind continued to whip through the trees, sending flurries of snow into the air and over the two men. Nick took the opportunity to move closer, squatting down beside his tortured friend.

"I … something's gonna happen, Nick. Something bad, I can feel it.

Figure if we don't go into the caves we'll be safe."

"I don't think so, Dan," Nick said. "If something's going to happen, then whatever it is will probably happen no matter what we do. No one cheats fate."

"Damned if I do and damned if I don't?"

Nick gave him a slow smile, his eyes showing the depth of friendship and support he had to offer. "That about sums it up."

Dan's head dropped on a desperate sob of decision. "You can't make me do it."

"I know."

Rose's prediction was wrong. It was a good ten minutes past the hour when the weather hit. They were halfway down the cut in the mountain leading from the cabin to the caves—scrabbling over rocks slick with icy sludge, warm breath freezing on their lips as they gasped to breathe in the thin, cold atmosphere of early morning in the Continental Divide. The wind dropped and the echoes of a forest slowly freezing suddenly sounded too loud.

"Damn!" Rose muttered, understanding the abrupt ebb of the wind. "We've got to hurry. Things are about to get much worse."

"What is it?" Elliott asked. He'd been relieved at the loss of the wind. After only a short time of exposure he'd begun to feel its bite cutting through his layer of clothes. He glanced across at Simone who had been gritting her teeth against the hated cold only moments ago. Now, she gazed in astonishment at the winter wonderland that surrounded them. Elliott felt a pang of dread as the look on the woman's face changed to shocked alarm. He looked around the group, only the women and Dan—and Finn too he noted—seemed aware of a change in the atmosphere. Then Nick and Pete noticed and lifted their heads to … hear? *Hear what?* Elliott strained his ears, but all he could hear was a low moan moving through the valley below.

And as the moan escalated to an appalling howl, Elliott understood that this was what Rose had meant. Serious was about to hit with a vengeance.

Rose knotted a rope, the other end already tied to a sturdy tree at the top, to the simple harnesses they'd all donned before setting down the defile—a just-in-case measure that could now be all that stopped them falling from their slippery, exposed perch. She issued instructions in a business-like voice—flat with an edge of urgency to underscore the importance of doing exactly as she said.

The temperature plummeted and the blizzard hit in a fury of wind and sleet. They huddled together for protection and one by one descended the treacherous path. Rose held onto the rope as Nick and Dan, followed by Simone went down first.

"Eliana, you and Elliott help get Finn down. I'll follow behind with Pete. We'll leave the rope," Rose yelled hoarsely, her words whipped away by the wind as soon as they were uttered.

"No!" Eliana yelled back. "Bring the rope!"

Sleet was freezing hard on their coats, the rope was becoming slick and heavy with ice, and the wind threatened to blow them away. Rose shook her head, though the movement, like her words, was almost lost to the other woman. "It's not worth it. We'll pick it up on the way back!" She tried to pull away, but Eliana's grip held firm.

"No!" she yelled again. "Bring it or cut it, but do not leave it!"

Rose detected the intensity of Eliana's gaze even though the hood of her jacket half covered her face and she nodded in acknowledgment. She wasn't sure why the rope was so important, but she trusted the other woman's instincts.

Eliana moved to the edge of the large rock they'd stopped on, balancing for a moment in seeming defiance of the buffeting wind before dropping over to help Finn down behind her. Elliott was already below, his arms reaching up to support first her then the big man whose grim, tight-lipped visage showed them all how nerve-racking it was to be caught out in a blizzard, blind. When the three moved further downward, Pete prepared to slip over the edge, the guide rope gripped tightly in his gloved hands.

Rose turned to him and cupped her hands over her mouth to speak close to his ear. "We need to go back up for the rope. Come on!" She removed the rope from his harness and headed back up the rocky cut.

Flurries of snow followed the group down into the cave, piling up on the debris that had once formed the roof, shortening its length by at least thirty feet. At one stage, its opening had been nearer the site where the cabin now stood, but that had been so long ago that no one on this side of the mountain knew or remembered it.

The opening of the cave was nothing more than a wide fissure in the bedrock. Back when it was just another part of the tunnel, a good degree of squeezing would have been required to fit through the gap and a hands-and-knees crawl of ten feet before the tunnel widened out again. With the collapse of that part of the cave, more space had been provided—by natural means and human encouragement—and the jagged outline formed an effective frame for the view back up to the cabin.

Nick, a step ahead of Dan, slid on a loose rock that moved as soon as he put his weight on it. As his arms went flailing out, the heavy pack he bore threatened to drag him down to the uneven floor of the cave mouth much faster than he would have preferred. Dan ducked under one wildly waving arm and grabbed Nick's coat. Tucking his gloved fingers through the straps of the pack, he pulled the falling man back that vital step. Simone pulled on the rope until it was taut and supported the weight of both men. Dan leaned back into it, bringing Nick with him, both men panting from the suddenness of the slip and how close they'd come to falling. When they'd regained their breath, they stood up and continued the last few feet, more alert now to the easy danger of the rocks.

At the bottom they removed the rope from their harnesses and heaved themselves to a protected area by the cave wall, nearly falling down with relief as they escaped the pounding winds.

"We'd better go help the others past that loose rock," Nick told Dan, removing his backpack and propping it up against the wall.

Dan and Simone followed suit before struggling to the base of the climb in time to warn Elliott as he came down, twisting sideways to assist those behind him. Dan grabbed the end of the rope and whipped it through the air to attract Elliott's attention while Simone and Nick scrabbled back up those last few feet to help out.

Elliott jerked around as the rope tugged on his harness, flicking the carabiner heavily against his upper thigh. He saw Dan hold his hand up, palm outward for him to stop and then noticed the top of Nick's head appear around the rock below him. Nick cupped his hand to his mouth and yelled up at Elliott, but the words could not be heard over the roar of the wind.

Elliott shook his head and mouthed, "What?"

Nick climbed a little higher and leaned on the loose rock, tilting it sideways and almost dislodging it. Elliott's mouth was a wordless "oh" of understanding, and he turned back to warn Eliana of the problem. She gave him the hand signal for okay, not even bothering to attempt speech against the storm and started guiding Finn around the dangerous ground. Nick waved Elliott down and pointed to the protected alcove where the packs had been left, then met Eliana and Finn and helped them down to safety.

When the rope was detached, Eliana gave two hard tugs to let Rose know they were down then moved over to the alcove.

Nick reached for her arm. "Where's Pete and Rose?"

"Gone back for the rope," she replied.

Nick looked out at the worsening weather. "They're risking their lives for a goddamn rope?"

"Can't afford to leave it behind," Eliana said, her eyes focused on Dan's face.

Dan seemed to pale even further under her steady gaze. He shook away the sound of clawing feet in his memory. "Rats are following," he whispered.

Eliana pulled away from Nick's grip. "We don't want to make it easy for anyone that might be following along behind."

"There's been no sign of someone following us. Who're you expecting?" Nick asked.

"No physical signs, no. Just have a feeling and I don't like unnecessary risks."

Nick recalled Dan's outburst at the cabin and his fear of coming into the caves. He'd heard Dan's whisper of rats and could see something was going on between him and Eliana. They knew something. He looked from one to the other, letting his expression demand an answer.

"If you know something, tell us. Don't leave us in the damn dark!"

"All we have to worry about right now is getting our asses out of this blizzard. The rest can wait."

The others had gathered around, stomping feet and rubbing hands to keep warm. Finn and Simone had each pulled the turtle-neck collars of their sweaters up over their noses, so only their protective glasses were visible. Elliott had pushed his hood back to adjust his caving helmet. A gust of wind dusted his hair with snow before he could get the hard hat back on and he shivered as some of it travelled down his neck.

"There's a better place to shelter further in. We'll wait there and get lighted up. One of us should stay behind to warn Rose and Pete about that rock …"

"I will," Simone volunteered, pulling her hood down further over her hard hat she walked back into the wind.

"Good," Eliana said. Pulling a heavy-duty flashlight from her pack she switched it on and aimed it into the darkness. "The path's fairly good just here; we don't need to belay again yet."

The group picked up their gear and followed her in.

Simone watched the rest of the group disappear into the cave, swallowed by the darkness. She turned away and gulped, wondering what on earth had possessed her to actually volunteer to stand out in a blizzard. Peering up the hill, she could see no sign of Rose and Pete. To ease the tension of waiting and attempt to take her mind off the definite possibility of freezing to death, she took a good look around.

Surely they should be down by now. She stared harder and thought she could just make out the roof of the cabin far above. The wind-whipped snow obliterated any view past the large rocks they'd just climbed down, swirling around in mini-twisters that flattened out against the immoveable rocks. Two figures were moving down the rocky slide.

She made her way out further and started to make the climb up to the treacherous spot where Nick had slipped. She picked up the rope and tugged once, waited, then tugged again; hoping the people on the other end understood that someone was down below waiting for them.

A quick two tugs came back and she moved to get above the unstable rock. She coiled the loose end of the rope, trying to decide how long she should wait before availing herself of the hip flask of cognac she had stored in her pack.

The group was busy setting up carbide lamps when the remaining three members arrived.

Rose turned her flashlight off and dropped the rope beside Eliana. "Here's the rope, had to cut it."

Eliana briefly stopped working as the rope brushed her leg. It was rimmed with ice and traces of moss where it had scraped across the rocks.

"We'll have to stash it somewhere. It's no use now. Pointless taking it with us," Rose continued.

Eliana ran a hand along the rope and nodded in agreement. It was severely kinked in a few places and no longer safe. "I'll carry it till we reach the pit and leave it there," she assured her friend. "Sit down and I'll fix your lamp."

Rose pulled her helmet off and left it by Eliana's feet then removed her pack to retrieve her water bottle. A few feet away, Elliott sat with Finn's helmet resting on his bent knee. He had already applied the water necessary to prime the carbide and was now in the process of lighting it. His own lamp glowed brightly from his hard hat and wavered slightly as he moved his head.

With a sure movement, he cupped his hand over the reflector of the lamp in his hands and drew it across quickly to strike a spark and ignite the gas that the mix of water and carbide emitted. With a broad smile, he returned the helmet to Finn's head.

"Now, we can't lose you," he chuckled and turned to start work on Pete's lamp.

After a few quick instructions from Eliana and Elliott, Nick had lit both his and Dan's lamps and then took Simone's.

In addition to the lamps attached to their hard hats, they each carried a mini-mag pen light—also attached to the helmets—a back-up heavy duty flashlight, candles and matches, and chemical light sticks. Getting stuck in the dark was one thing none of them wanted.

"What we really need are some maghooks," Elliott said over Pete's helmet.

"Yeah and a couple of light-sabers," Pete threw back.

The lack of wind in their little corner of the cave, the light and the meager warmth of the lamps helped to boost half-frozen spirits. While they finished preparing for their plunge under the mountain range, Nick decided it was time for some straight talking.

Turning the full force of his glare to the women, Eliana in particular, he said in a low voice, "I want to know everything you know about this quest we've all been dragged into, starting with exactly why you think we're being followed."

Eliana frowned as she lit Rose's lamp and passed it to her. "All we know about this is we have to get you and your friends to Elphane. The woman you are looking for is already there … I took her there …"

"But you told us you were out of town when she came up here," Pete interrupted.

"I was waiting for her on the trail. She took a different route to this one—easier. At this time of year though, this is the easiest route. I actually prefer this one," she told him, looking around at the earthen walls.

"Did she go willingly?" Elliott asked suspiciously.

"Of course. She is the Staff Bearer, just as your friend here is also a Bearer. Am I forcing him on this trip? Are we forcing anyone? It is our job to get you there. That's all."

"We can't tell you anything about Elphane or the people that live there. You have to discover that for yourself, but you are in no danger from them," Rose added. "We've been there a few times and always managed to come out unscathed."

"Then where does the danger come from?" Nick demanded. "Because there sure as hell is some or you wouldn't have gone back for the rope."

"Just a precaution, Mr. Som—"

"No, it's not. It was done because of me," Dan spoke at last. He locked eyes with Nick, as if looking for strength he couldn't find inside himself. "I had another dream last night. Eliana knows about it. It was like the ones I had before you found me. Something was chasing me and I couldn't move. It was underground just like before." He looked around nervously, longingly, back to the dim light that was the mouth of the cave. "Like now."

"What was it? Chasing you, I mean," Pete asked.

"Rats, or maybe just one. It was a real big fucker too." The shadows that moved across Dan's face as he talked accentuated the hollows of his cheeks and the recesses of eyes that had seen too much. He looked gaunt and tired. His natural instincts for survival, to keep going at all costs, were strained to the limit. Nick could see the haunting of the nightmare in every flinch and nervous glance—they all could.

"I was scared shitless, again," he scoffed, lightly drawing a hand across his face.

"Did it get you?" Pete asked.

Dan looked at Eliana intently.

"Dan?"

He shook his head a little and turned to face Pete. "Nearly, Pete. Nearly."

Dan felt Eliana staring back at him and was surprised to see the faint trace of a familiar smile on her lips. For a moment he thought he was back on the river's edge with Rose—she'd had the same smile. Her calming presence helped the trails of his night terrors to fade away. He closed his eyes and his memory of the valley filled his mind. It was so vivid he could smell the wildflowers, their scent calling to him from within the cave. Feeling centered again, he opened his eyes and stood, picking up his backpack as he moved.

"Let's get this over with." He held a hand out to Nick to pull him up.

"I want to know the rest," Nick said to him quietly once they were face to face. "About the ring and the staff. This is all sounding too much like a fairytale. I half expect a pack of rogue elves to jump out of the walls and have their way with us."

"What? No dwarves?" Dan's joke fell flat and he played with his helmet to cover how anxious Nick's questions were making him feel. Hell, he wouldn't be surprised by anything right now. "I don't know," he admitted and then, to cut off Nick's protest, "really, I don't." He pulled the chain from beneath his clothes, the Ouroboros circlet still fixed in its length. "All I know is that this is important. I'm guessin' it has somethin' to do with the staff, but I don't know what. None of my dreams … visions, I guess, show anything about the professor or any staff."

"And nothing about elves or dwarves?"

Dan let out a breath at Nick's teasing question. "Nope. Nothin' about any of them, either."

Around them, the rest of the team were following Nick and Dan's lead—adjusting chin straps and backpacks, checking their back up lights, water bottles and food. They would not be making as many stops today as they had on their way up the mountain the day before. Conservation of energy in the cold caves was important, and they would maintain a slow but steady pace for as long and as far as they could. They had all gone over the rudiments of caving before setting out on the journey and Rose had assured them that for the most part, and barring any natural changes, the cave was an easy one to navigate.

"A wise man told me recently that we can't cheat fate," Dan whispered to Nick. "Shit's gonna fall, Nick, but not today and, hopefully, not on us. I'm not gonna lie and tell you I ain't scared." He jerked his head toward the dark part of the cave they were about to enter. "Hell! We're about to walk right into my nightmare. That ain't a place I want to revisit."

Finn moved up behind them, his head cocked as he listened to their hushed voices. "But a man has to face his fears and to reach the light we've got to walk in the dark away."

"Finn's right," Dan agreed. "So, let's just get this over with and worry about the shit when it happens."

Rose and Eliana switched positions for the first day of caving. Eliana moved into the lead and began attaching the belay rope, while Rose approached Finn to help him over any rough spots.

Nick turned to her. "Is it worth it?"

Rose's lamp projected a bobbing light around the cave as she checked the carabiner attachments on each of the men. "They tell me it will be," she answered. Her lips pressed into a straight, thin line before she continued. "How do you want your team strung out?"

"Me and Elliott will take the rear; Finn and you with Simone, Dan and Pete in front."

Rose nodded and went to let Eliana know the order. Dan followed, taking up his position between Simone and Pete without another word. The rope was attached and the group started off. The bright lamps pushed the darkness back, the shadows pulsing on the edge of the light threatening to swallow them all at the first opportunity.

The cave was wide enough to allow Simone and Finn to walk almost side by side, and they followed much the same routine they had through the woods with Simone now warning Finn when to avoid a rock or an outcrop.

Nick and Elliott, in the rear, let the group get as far enough ahead as they dared, and the rope allowed. Nick pensively scanned their back trail. Elliott waited, anxious to follow the rest of the group and not sure what Nick could hope to accomplish if someone really was following them. He scrutinized his old friend's face, trying to read what the man always kept so carefully hidden.

"What's your plan, Nick?"

In such unfamiliar territory, Nick's plan was simple by necessity—keep an eye and ear alerted to the trail behind and cover the signs of their passage as best they could. For the next twenty-four hours, occasionally switching with Simone, Pete and Dan, that is what they did.

The walk was long and hard. They traversed the debris of cave-ins and rockslides, scrambled through passages too low for walking upright and crawled—dragging their packs behind them—when the ceiling became too low for scrambling. Rest stops were infrequent and short. To stop too long only made it harder to keep going.

After one particularly bad passage that had ended in the need to drop twenty feet into a pit, a break was called and the group fell to the ground, weary and strained.

"You sure you know where you're going?" Pete asked as he passed a bag of Trailmix to Finn.

"We've mapped most of this system, at least the parts we'll be using anyway," Rose replied.

"How big is it?"

"Big enough that we'll probably never see it all."

"You know, there's a theory that all the caves around the world are connected," said Pete.

"Where do you get this stuff, Pete?" Elliott taunted the detective. "You've got a conspiracy theory for everything." Everyone laughed at Pete's hobby of collecting outlandish stories.

"Yeah, well some of them have proven out. The one that brought us here, for instance," Pete said defensively. "What do you think, Rose? Is it true?"

"Seriously?"

"Seriously."

"Well, I suppose if you take into consideration all the miles of unexplored cave and figure that they've all got to go some place then I'd have to say … no." She smiled apologetically. "The theory isn't provable, Pete," Rose told him. "The unexplored parts of most caves are fairly inaccessible. No one can get to them to prove it one way or the other."

"But …"

"If it isn't provable, it's a waste of energy," she added, standing. "There's plenty of other things more worthy of your attention than knowing whether all caves are connected."

"Like concentrating on not knocking your head on one of these low hanging rocks," Nick said rapping Pete's hard hat with his knuckles.

"Another theory blown outta the sky." Elliott grinned widely, groaning at the same time as he moved his already stiffening muscles.

They walked until their watches told them it was night-time in the outside world and their stomachs said dinnertime. Flashlights flicked on, tracing a crisscross pattern across the walls of a large cavern. The splashes of light revealed the walls to be artificially made—huge, hand-carved bricks beneath layers of moss and slime glittered with the moisture that trickled over them.

A wild jerking of light around the cavern followed a gasp from Dan.

"You know this place, Dan?" Nick asked.

The panicked man fought to control himself as he searched urgently for any more signs from his dreams. His ears strained to hear the sound of claws scampering across rock. The light flashed back into the passage from which they had just emerged, but nothing was there. As the sounds faded back into his memory, he lowered the light to the floor and kicked lightly at the dirt.

"These are the same walls from my dream," he admitted. His voice was sounding distant even to himself. His boot's toe dug into the soft dirt, kicking up clouds of dust. "There's a tunnel that turns into an alley with these walls on either side. Thought it was the one I ran into after the accident, where I was shot. Guess it wasn't." He got down on his knees and began digging in the shallow his boot had made.

"Anything else, Dan?" said Finn.

Dan shook his head, then, realizing it had been Finn who'd asked, said, "No. Only it was a paved road, the old-fashioned kind." He lifted a handful of dirt and watched it filter through his outstretched fingers, then lifted his face to show a relieved smile. "This is only dirt."

The women had started unpacking gear for a night camp as soon as they'd stopped. Rose had been listening to the conversation and when Dan seemed to be finished, she asked, "You were shot?"

"You didn't know?" Elliott dropped his pack with the others and began to sort through his gear.

"Why would we? We didn't know anything about you before you came to Smiggins' Rest."

"And you're not privy to the Brotherhood?" Simone asked. She, and the rest of the team, had assumed the women knew what had been going on.

"Is that who shot Dan?"

"Yes, it was," Nick told her. "Against orders. The group was split up afterwards and the leader branded a leper."

"Do you know what that means?" Finn shifted the group's attention to the Rose and Eliana, much to Dan's relief.

The women looked at each other and shrugged. "No," Rose answered for them both.

"What about Roger de Laurac, the Templar Knights, the Brotherhood of the Grail? You don't know about them either?"

"Heard of the Knights," said Rose. "Learned about them in school. Don't know any Roger, though there's a de Laurac family in the village."

"What about you?" Nick directed at the question to Eliana, who shrugged humbly.

"I was never into history much."

"Wasn't it you who said that everyone in town was related? Descended from a group of immigrants from southern France?" Simone asked.

"I was simplifying," Eliana replied. "Those immigrants were themselves the descendants of a people who were spread out all over the world. They lived awhile in France and then moved on. Some came here, some returned to their homelands, others stayed where they were."

Simone persisted. "But the Cathars are known to be French. They have been intimately connected to the Templar Knights and other similar Orders and Christian sects. We have found them to be involved on many levels with the Sangreal. How is it that you don't know about them, at least?"

"We are not Catharri. The Templars mean nothing to us," Rose said.

"You are not … But Mr. Smiggins or Gabran and his friends were from Langue d'oc, a Cathar stronghold." It appeared that this was yet another twist to the story behind the Sangreal.

Rose looked at the smooth talking woman. "Aiden Gabran is not Catharri, neither were any of the families that travelled with him."

"If he wasn't a Cathar, what was he?"

"Aiden is an elder of the People. You will meet him when you get to Elphane."

"Are you two part of the People?" Simone asked.

"No, they're not," Pete answered for them. "Eliana told me that the other day. They're part of the Nine, like us."

"But not quite like us. Isn't that right?" Finn asked them. "If the people that came here from France weren't Cathars, weren't even French, and weren't of the same people as Gabran, then who were they?"

"The Elbe—Keepers of the Star Forest, Elphane."

"What about this Isabel woman and Braida?"

"Braida is a Mother of the Elbe. I don't know any Isabel," said Rose.

"I do," Eliana admitted. "I met Isabel before I came to Smiggins' Rest. She helped me out with a few things. She was one of the reasons my sister and I moved here." She smiled at Rose. "Isabel is Arwium."

Rose nodded, recognizing the second name and knowing with its telling that they had said enough. "That's all we can tell you. You'll have to save your questions for them."

She turned back to the packs and pulled out two silver space blankets. Eliana helped her to spread the first one out then lined all the packs around its edges and spread the second one over the top.

"That's it?" Nick said, amazed. "Bullshit! We want to know what happens when we reach this Elphane. What happens after? Do we hand over this ring thing and then just walk home again like good little boys and girls, all happy and glowing 'cause we did the right thing? Does Dan get rid of these headaches and nightmares? Will Finn get to see again?"

Rose stood and faced the angry man, her face calm, shoulders back.

"Mr. Somers, we don't know these things. We've told you everything we can. You are not the only ones to have suffered to reach this point. Just as we didn't know about your lives before you came, you do not know about ours—about what we have given in the past and will give in the future. Now, it's late and we need to get some decent food into ourselves and sleep. I suggest we do exactly that."

Elliott nudged Nick as he walked past. "Let's go check the back trail, maybe lay a few rat traps."

Nick stared at the woman a moment longer. "All right. We'll do it your way, but if there's anything else you can tell us …"

Rose nodded and held a hand out. "We would tell you."

Nick took her hand and clasped it in a brief truce of, if not exactly friendship, then at least a certain kind of trust. He grabbed the rope Elliott was handing out to him and swiveled on his boot heel to head back down the passage.

Eliana turned to the rest of the group and pointed to the blankets. "This is where we'll cook, eat and sleep—between the blankets. We'll need our combined warmth to get through the night."

The carbide lamps were all turned off in favor of a free standing one they could use for cooking, warmth and light all at the same time. Their meal consisted of reheated leftovers from the night in the cabin and fresh-brewed coffee. By the time it was finished, everyone was exhausted. They lay down, huddled together between the silver blankets.

Nick and Elliott had indeed set a trap for anyone trying to sneak up on them, using the rope, a pile of loose rocks and one of the less than glamorous sanitary cans they carried with them. "Dunnekins" Rose had called them, drawling out the "kin" sound to a "can". They'd used some of the chemical light sticks to mark the trail back to the cavern, collecting them as they returned and handing them over to Eliana who wrapped them in clear plastic bags and deposited them around the makeshift tent. The single carbide lamp was turned off, and they were bathed with the soft glow of the pink and green sticks.

Their voices murmured through the cavern as they talked, waiting for sleep.

"Do you think it's de Laurac?" Pete asked anyone who was listening.

"Yes," Nick replied.

"What about Sicarius?" said Elliott.

Eliana lifted her head. "You have a Sicarius after you too?"

Dan, who had been silent most of the night, spoke in his husky voice. "Think he's workin' for Aiden and Isabel. Not exactly sure whose side he's on."

Pete snorted. "It was probably him that nearly blew up Finn and blinded him. You know him?"

"Not personally, but I know the name. It's given to certain members of the Elbe from time to time."

"And what, pray tell, does the name mean?" Simone asked on the edge of a yawn.

Eliana laid her head back down.

"Assassin."

56

They slept in their cocoon for four hours before the first of them began to stir. Eliana lay between Rose and Dan, eyes wide in the dull light, wondering what had woken her. A light sleeper for most of her life, it had served her well in the years before coming to the mountains to live, but now that she lived a relatively peaceful and ordered life it was becoming an annoyance. *Just once, I'd like to get a decent night's sleep.* She rolled over, pressing her back comfortably against her friend's body and relaxing slightly when an arm snaked up to rest over her.

A faint snore broke the silence and then a strange muttering, and Eliana realized it was the voice that had woken her. She looked at the man lying restlessly beside her, his lips moving in dream talk, his voice a rough whisper in her ears. If he hadn't been so close, she wouldn't have heard him. He was in the throes of another bad dream and she wondered if it was the rats again. Her own sleep had been dreamless, though she still carried the exhilaration she'd felt the night before when she'd dreamt of flying—soaring through the night sky, spiraling up then zooming back down to earth to skim its surface. She could still feel the touch of leaves and grass as she whistled through them like the wind before rising up to the clouds and circling the mountains at a more leisurely pace. From that height she'd been able to see where her sister slept, and the red glow that surrounded her. She dived down, a soft whisper in the air, smoothed long hair from the sleeping woman's face, and then she was back in the cave with the Bearer of her future.

Eliana brought her attention to the man in front of her. Her hand caressed his face lightly until he stilled once more, his ravaged face calm. She dropped her arm to his shoulders and lay with him in her embrace. Dan opened sleep-hazed eyes to stare at her until he couldn't keep them open any longer. His eyelids slid shut on a single tear.

Eliana was already fast asleep.

"This is the last cavern," Rose told the others as they paused on the precipice of a huge hole inside the mountain. The cavern was massive. The passage they'd been following since breakfast came out approximately halfway up its uneven walls. The light of the carbides disappeared into the gray void ahead of them and the blackness below.

"Is it my eyes, or can we actually see better here?" Simone asked.

"This part of the cave system is becoming unstable. We're very close to the surface and parts of the roof have caved in further up. It'll get windier too. We'll break here for ten minutes. I want to check everyone's gear." Unhooking herself from the belay rope, Rose doubled back down the passage to tug on carabiner buckles and extinguish all the carbides.

"We'll use the flashlights from here. The natural light will get brighter as we get higher." She moved along the line, smiling grimly at the exhausted travelers, knowing they had the stamina and bullheaded determination to keep going, ignoring the tiredness evident in their unshaven faces and rough voices. Even Simone, not quite as clean as she presented in the shop, was nevertheless as tough and determined as the rest.

"This path will take us all the way to the top, but there will be some rough patches, loose rocks mostly. Watch where you're putting your feet and you should be all right. I'll mark unstable areas as I reach them so you'll know."

Rose approached Nick at the rear of the group. "Bring my markers with you."

"You still think we're being followed?"

She paused, his carabiner still in her hand. "I don't know about that. I do know that we don't leave anything behind. This isn't a public trail. The few people who use it know what to look for." She tugged the buckle and checked its connection.

"Everything here's fine." She turned away from Nick and walked back up the passage. "This is the last part of the underground trail. After this we're back on top in the wind and snow, so enjoy the pleasant weather while you can."

Eliana stopped her as she moved past. "Be careful," she said softly, holding her arm tightly.

Rose looked into her friend's face. "I'm ready. Are you?"

Eliana nodded and leaned in to whisper into the older woman's ear.

The pair clasped hands; Rose squeezed her eyes closed for a moment, not wanting to let go, knowing she had to. She turned a haunted face away and stumbled back to the lead.

Further down the passage, in the cavern where the group had spent their hours of sleep, light splashed across the damp walls once more. It moved up to the ceiling then down to the ground in a searching pattern, until it finally stopped on a clear boot print. The light arched away from the print, searching once more and finding the edge of another print and a faint scuff mark on soft rock. The light stopped completely and a gloved hand came into its beam, gingerly touching the crumbling rock, picking up its pieces and tossing them lightly into the air to land in the open palm.

The fingers closed roughly on the pebbles as a low laugh filled the cavern. The laughter rose on a manic edge and slowly ebbed to a mad, choking mutter. The dirt-stained face beneath the light grimaced with the pain of frost-bitten extremities and a body covered in the bruises from a hundred falls as he'd clawed his way through the blizzard and caves. He stood up, his eyes hard and glittering; he was beyond paying attention to his body's warnings or caring about anything except reaching his quarry. The pebbles fell to the ground, scattering across the floor to land in a section where the years of dirt had been washed away to reveal an ancient brick road, rotten and crumbling in the dark.

The group walked steadily along the path, following the cavern wall up to an opening they still could not see. The dim light and the wavering flashlights cast shadows across the walls and the path, making the way even more treacherous. Loose rocks skittered out from under stumbling feet to disappear into the blackness below them.

"I hate that!" Elliott mumbled as another pile of rocks broke loose from Pete's tread in front of him.

It had been some time since anyone had spoken, the cold air, its brittleness in their throats restricting any conversation to bare necessities and finally, silence.

"Hate what?" Nick rasped out.

"There should be a sound when the damn rocks land. But there's nothing. I haven't heard a single rock hit bottom. How deep is this pit, anyway?"

"Keep your eye on where you're going or you'll be finding out first-hand."

They fell silent again as they concentrated on keeping their footing on the increasingly dangerous stretch.

Ahead of them, Rose paused, sighing deeply in frustration.

"What is it?" Simone asked as she approached. Each person, except for Eliana, Finn and Pete, kept a distance from the other to avoid tumbling over shifting rocks or stumbling onto the others and knocking them over.

"This path is much worse than I thought, much worse. I don't like it at all," Rose replied. She squatted down, keeping her weight carefully on the balls of her feet and pulled a light stick from her pocket. Cracking it to mix the chemicals, she gave it a quick shake and propped it up in a cracked rock.

"Can we turn back?"

"No. The path will be even worse for our passing. It would be just as bad, if not worse, to go down from here." She pulled her gloves from one hand and felt the rocks with her bare skin. Standing, she did the same along the wall. "These rocks are much too soft, too wet. Must have been a lot of water go through here recently."

"Aren't we a little high for a flood?"

"For a flood, possibly, but it wouldn't be unheard of. Happens frequently in other systems. But no, I'm thinking of increased flow from up top. A cave-in last winter perhaps, or a big melt afterward. The whole system is damp, just not usually so wet here and it's a long time since these roads were built," she replied, almost talking to herself as she thought about what to do.

"Roads?" Simone flicked her handheld flashlight on and aimed its beam at the path, amazed to see the faint outline of cobblestones beneath a layer of rubble and dirt. "This is all man-made?"

"Sort of. The path was always here. It's a natural cut in the wall for the most part. It was fortified and extended years ago to provide easier access to the door. It widens out around the next bend. We'll stop there a bit and rest. A little scouting ahead might be worthwhile before we go much further. Pass it back will you?"

Rose moved off again before Simone could ask any more questions, so she turned to Dan who was waiting behind.

"We're stopping around the next bend. Pass it on."

Dan nodded and waited for Eliana to catch him up so he could pass on the message. He was glad they were stopping. He'd heard Rose mention the roadwork, had seen the cobblestones in the beam of Simone's flashlight. All of a sudden it felt hard to breathe. The thrum of fear pounded in his head.

57

Above ground, just outside the same doorway the group of eight struggled toward, three men stood, waiting.

"Do you feel the earth rumbling?" The taller of the three asked loudly enough to be heard over the fading blizzard. He apparently didn't require an answer as he looked worriedly into the cave then back toward the tree line a few feet away. The tree branches were heavy with snow, the ground thick with it. As his eyes raked the forest, a loud cracking sound followed by the thunder of a falling tree rent the air. "Do you hear that? The earth is moving. Something is wrong."

"You know there's nothing we can do until they get here," the second man, only a little shorter than the first, replied in a voice as cold as the wind that swept through the mountain range. He pulled a gun from inside his coat. The sharp click as he released the barrel of the semi-automatic weapon, giving it a cursory check then pushing it back into place, pierced through the roar of the wind.

"There was no forewarning of this. What the hell's going on, Gabran?"

Simone would have known the tallest of the three men in an instant as the stranger with Isabel in the warehouse.

"You spend too much time away from us, Roshen," Gabran replied.

"What's that supposed to mean? I've been doing exactly as I was required since the beginning, but these earthshakes were never mentioned. Isn't this cutting it a little fine?"

"You take offence where none was intended. I only meant that you forget the extent of our power. Our predictions are still affected by the unpredictable. We expected the earth tremors but the timing of them is outside of our vision. It was also known that some event needed to take place while they were down there …"

"Some event? Are we playing with people's lives again? Are we so arrogant that we can put them through all this without a qualm? Do you expect them to thank us for this?" Roshen's temper was easily ignitable.

"We don't know the event, only that it must occur. It is important in the web of things. I am no happier than you at this dangerous turn, but we must wait, for just a little longer."

"This is bullshit! This is all bullshit!" Roshen stormed away, kicking at the snow and spraying it into the air. Hands on hips, he stood a moment, glaring into the trees, seeing not their overburdened boughs but people struggling against the odds, like they always did. "Damn stubborn …!" Roshen cursed loudly into the wind before turning and striding defiantly back to the cave entrance. "I'm going in!"

Deep in the Forest of the Stars, in another cave smooth-floored from regular passage, a low fire burned beneath a cauldron of bubbling liquid. The fire provided the only light in the chamber. The shadowy walls glittered with the red glow of joss sticks stuck firmly into the hard-packed earth. Smoke and steam curled through the air, swirling around the bodies of two women dancing in slow, languorous movements around the fire.

The women moved to the music of their voices rising and dropping in harmonious refrains that told without words of the bounty of spring, the joy of creation, of a life essence that waited to be reborn.

One of the dancers stopped and picked up a wooden ladle to dip into the cauldron. She offered it to the second dancer and together they sipped its contents. The flickering of the flames reflected in dark, shadowed eyes, and the two women stared at each other, waiting for the effect of the herbal concoction.

The older woman, black hair brushing the pale skin of her naked shoulders, leaned forward and gently licked a droplet of the liquid from the other woman's lips, bringing her hands up at the same time to brush long brown hair from her flushed face. The young woman stood still. Her skin was tingling, her blood aflame as warm hands touched her shoulders. She drew her breath in and closed her eyes— warm hands brushed past heavy breasts aching with a longing she had never known before this day. The feather light touch stopped at her hips. It traced the curve of her pelvis, stopping again as bone became tender flesh and pressed gently but firmly in.

The young woman gasped at the pain that seeped through her body from that spot. It curled around her tailbone and spread hot heavy tendrils of sensation across her abdomen. Her body throbbed from front to back. She groaned softly and swayed on her feet.

"Your time has started, yee are rich with fruit. In two days will yee wear the radiance of the moon."

The young woman barely heard, so caught up in sensation—pain and ache, heat and lust. Sweat pearled on her upper lip. She didn't notice her hands being taken or that she was being led away to another chamber deeper under the earth to a bed of overstuffed cushions. She was laid down between the layers of a fine, hand-woven rug, heavily brocaded drapes surrounding her on three sides. More of the hot broth was slowly poured between her lips and she swallowed eagerly. A cloth was dipped into a wooden bowl of cool water and gently wiped across her face and down her body.

"It's time to rest," the other woman told her in a soft whisper. "This is the start. The start of the beginning we've been waiting for."

<h1 style="text-align:center">58</h1>

The group gathered in a spot where the path widened an extra three feet. There was still not enough room for them all to sit comfortably. Nick and Elliott were left to sit on the narrow part of the trail, their legs hanging over the edge. Pete managed to squeeze into the more sheltered area with Finn and Eliana. Dan and Simone were on the far edge where the path began to narrow in again.

Pete rested his head on the damp wall of the cavern. "You know, I don't mind if I never have to go in another cave ever again," he said to Finn.

"Just give me a warm, soft bed and I wouldn't mind never leaving my room," the big man replied.

The walk had been hardest on Finn, who couldn't see where he was putting his feet—he could only feel the urgent tugs on his arms when he got too close to the edge, the softened stones crumbling beneath his weight, knocking him continually off-balance. He had been forced to take every step slowly from the start and had stumbled many times. His legs ached and his knees felt raw from repeated blows and falls. If there was truly a reason for being struck blind, he failed to see it. He smiled wryly at his own pun and lifted his hand to wipe away some of the exhaustion and the silly grin he could feel on his face.

"Adequate bathing facilities would satisfy me," Simone added, rubbing her face. "All this mountain woman stuff doesn't really suit the image I try to project. Now, Dan here is right in his element, being the 'one with nature' type of guy he is."

"I don't know, reckon I'm with Pete on this one. Give me open space anytime," Dan forced the words out as he glanced around at the narrow path that had them pinned to the wall. "An' plenty of sky."

"I'm having a great time," Elliott called out. "Can't wait to try this again without, you know, any pressure. Just for the fun of it!"

"Don't talk so loud. You'll have the mountain down on top of us," Nick admonished with a backhanded slap to Elliott's chest.

"Dammit, Nick! I ain't no …"

"Elliott!" Nick cut in. "Look down there. You see anything?"

Elliott looked to where Nick pointed across the cavern to a lower point of the path they had just trekked. The wall had gradually curved right around and they could see how high they had come. Way below, the mouth of the passage they had left behind was a mere shadow on the wall, darker and larger than the other shadows, but indiscernible if you didn't know it was there.

"Don't see a thing 'cept shadows," Elliott replied.

"Wait a minute, it might come again. By the cave mouth. There, do you see it?" Nick pointed again, more confidently this time.

"Yeah, I see it. Seems there's a rat after all. Only one, I'd say."

Nick nodded. "And he's moving pretty fast. Warn the others, we'll have to move."

"Right!" Elliott stood and unclasped his carabiner to move past Pete and get closer to the two guides. Rose had just returned from her scouting trip. Elliott knew Nick hadn't been joking about loud noises bringing the cave down and he wanted to be close enough to talk without yelling. He clipped the carabiner back onto the rope as he reached Pete and Finn. He saw Eliana leaning over Dan and just about to accept something Pete was passing forward when all hell broke loose. His fears of a cave-in were now becoming a terrifying reality.

"You feeling all right, Dan?" Simone asked.

Dan had clamped his eyes shut as he panted for air. He didn't answer as he fought to control the attack of vertigo that gripped him. *I've got to get out! Can't breathe!* He swallowed against rising bile and pressed his head back against the wall. Fingers fumbled with his jacket, loosening it, pulling the sweater and shirts away from his neck. Simone removed her gloves and felt his skin and throat.

"He's burning up. Heart's racing. He was fine a few minutes ago," she said, patting his cheek.

"Dan, can you hear me? What is it?" Eliana shifted her position, moving closer. They were on separate safety ropes because of the need for Finn to take it much slower. Dan and Simone were hooked up to Rose only.

Dan opened his eyes to see her face a few inches from his own.

She smiled slowly. "What do you need?"

Behind them, Pete called out. "Here, give him this. It's not as strong as his pain meds, but it should see him out of here at least." He pulled a small packet from his coat pocket and stretched out to pass it across.

Eliana, still watching Dan's face, saw horror dawn in his eyes. "What is it?" she whispered.

He opened his mouth to warn her, to tell her it was his nightmare again, but the words wouldn't come. Then he saw understanding wash over her. She knew. Understanding and the fierce determination that had got her through bad times in the past glowed in her eyes. She knew and she did it anyway.

"It's okay, I'm ready," she whispered in his ear and reached for the medication Pete offered.

For that frozen instant in time, the woman's body completely covered that of the incapacitated man on the ledge. The impact of the bullet hit her full in the chest, burying itself deep within her body, a split-second before the crack of the high-powered rifle reached them.

Time seemed to slow as the group watched in horror and confusion. She had been half-crouched, caught in a movement that had brought her right to the soft-edge of the path. Her body slumped backward and down as the path gave way beneath her and she disappeared over the edge.

"Noooo!" Dan yelled, scrabbling forward to snatch at her limp arms.

Simone wrapped her arms around Dan's chest to prevent him following the woman over. "It's okay, Dan! The rope will stop her."

But the weight of a person falling increases significantly in ratio to the distance of the drop and the length of rope, and so Finn, unable to see what had happened, was quickly dragged over the edge. Pete grabbed his harness, but as the woman's fall was brought to an abrupt halt by the static rope, the effect was to jerk Finn right out of his grip. Pete latched onto his jacket, all the while being dragged closer to the edge himself. His grip was slipping and the big man dangled precariously, unable to help himself with the weight of the woman pulling him down.

Eliana swung, barely conscious on the rope. She crashed into the wall, dislodging yet more rocks that battered her body further. Her head was flung back; her arms outstretched awkwardly, limply. Blood gushed from her chest.

The ledge beneath Pete began to crack. Sweat poured from his face and he growled viciously against the seemingly inevitable fall. Elliott held onto Pete's harness and pulled him backward then reached out for Finn, to help take some of the strain off Pete. Together they pulled him up. Another crack in the rocks spread out beneath Elliott and he wobbled on suddenly loose ground. Pete grabbed him and saved him from toppling over.

Nick had his gun out, ready to provide cover against the shooter, but more gunshots would only hasten the coming cave-in. The man below had no such concerns as he brought his rifle to bear again and fired at the group.

"Damn idiot's gonna collapse the whole cave," Elliott swore as chips of rock came flying from the wall just above his head.

Rose had dashed back the last few feet, freezing in place as she saw her friend dangling below.

"Eliana?" she called out. "Wake up, dammit! You're weight's dragging Finn down! Wake up and climb up the rope!"

Rose grabbed hold of Simone and helped her scrabble backward up the trail, fighting all the way with Dan who was trying to get to Finn and the rope. A loud crack echoed through the cave and a shower of rocks fell over them from above.

"We've gotta get out of here!" Rose yelled, on the edge of panic. She was an experienced caver and knew the sound of an imminent cave-in when she heard it.

"Eliana! Wake up! NOW!! We've got a cave-in!"

The ground shook beneath them and Finn started to fall.

Eliana responded to the cries from above. She squinted up at them, flinching as stones and dirt showered over her. Rose's voice barely registered through the shock that numbed her senses.

She felt nothing as she swung on the rope, nothing as the falling rocks cut into her body or when she hit the wall yet again. Shaking her head to clear it, all she could think about was her dream.

Rose's words slowly filtered through the fog in her brain. "Cave-in … pulling them down … climb up!"

She blinked once again and focused her gaze on her friend's frantic face peering over the ledge. The pain began to filter through and she moved her head to look down at herself. The blood had soaked the entire front of her coat. Pain surged from her hips up her back. There was no way she was climbing anywhere today. *No way today.* She returned her gaze to her chest. *No way ever.*

Eliana clenched her teeth as the rope jerked downward—Finn was slipping further down. She could hear them clearly now, their cries for her to move, to climb. She screamed in agony as she forced her leg to bend up, her arm to stretch down to her boot. Cursed everything under the sun as she pushed herself to grasp the hilt of the knife that protruded from the top of her boot and wrapped her bloodied fingers around it to tug it free. Above her, larger rocks and slabs of cave wall began to shift.

"It's going! It's going!" they called out.

Then, almost quietly in comparison, a faint pleading came from above. "Eliana, please?"

She couldn't tell who it was that screamed out a piercing, "Noooo!" as she brought the knife up to the rope, but she thought it was probably Rose.

"S'okay," she whispered in reply. "I'm ready. I always have been." She closed her eyes and thought about flying, about the exhilaration of being so completely uninhibited.

The blade sliced through the rope. At last she was free.

59

Deep in the Star Cave of Elphane, through a haze of sensation and longing, the young woman twisted restlessly in her sleep, finally sitting bolt upright, a scream on her lips. She flung the covering back from her body and doubled over with the pain of a loss that pierced her soul. Her cries carried out into the chamber where the cauldron still bubbled over the small fire. They cut through the woman sitting cross-legged by the ancient vessel, searing her like the flames of the fire that erupted around the black pot and licked at her skin. Tears streamed down the seated woman's face as she raised her head to join her own pain-filled voice with the younger woman in a song of death that echoed through the cave and out into the valley beyond.

Roshen had only taken a few steps into the cave's entrance when the ominous cracks and screams began. The dark-haired Frenchman who had drawn his gun from its holster once more quickly joined him.

"You won't need that," Roshen told him, annoyed at the man's quick readiness to use it.

"Won't I? There were at least two gunshots before the screams started."

Roshen was shocked and turned a pale face back to the old man still standing in the small clearing outside the cave. He was dismayed to see that Gabran was equally shocked.

"The Leper?" he asked, turning back to the armed man beside him. "Who else?"

They rushed down the path, still stable at this point but not for long as the crack in the wall of the cave spread rapidly. The wild cries and desperate curses were just ahead of them; they had been so close to the cave mouth before disaster had struck. Roshen cursed the man who had betrayed everything he and his people had worked toward, who had caused the mad fight for survival below.

60

Simone didn't have time to be shocked at the loss of Eliana as she struggled against Dan and Rose. The rest of the group was dragging Finn back to safety, easy to do now that no extra weight hampered them. Rose had collapsed on the path behind her. Simone had heard her soft plea to Eliana and felt her anguish as her friend had cut the rope and fallen into the dark pit. There had been no sound of her body landing. No screams, just silence; even the earth around them seemed to pause in its protests when the woman had fallen.

The shooter was forgotten as they fought to save themselves from the more immediate danger of the cave-in. A large boulder broke away from the wall with a loud rumble just above Nick. He didn't have time to move out of the way as it hit his arm just above the elbow, snapping the bones and forcing the suddenly nerveless hand to lose its grip on the gun. The weapon clattered on rock and disappeared into the abyss.

"Fuck!" he yelled, holding onto the useless arm with his other hand and forcing himself to keep moving.

The path was becoming narrower by the minute as its edge continued to crumble away.

"Damn! We've gotta get out of here right now, Elliott! Get them moving," Nick yelled through clenched teeth.

Elliott helped Pete to his feet and together they pulled up Finn and steadied him against the wall.

"Finn? You okay?" Pete patted the shocked man's face. "Finn? You with us?"

Finn nodded dumbly before finding his voice. "What in God's name just happened? Was that …?"

"She's gone, Finn, and we have to get out before we follow her."

"My God, my God!" Finn stammered.

"No time for that now. Let's move, don't waste the precious time she gave us." Pete's voice was harsh, but it got the man moving.

Finn stumbled, not knowing where to go. "Dammit!" His voice roared with frustration.

Dan pushed the force ten quake in his head aside far enough to be able to respond to Simone, who'd been urging him to get up. "Okay, okay! I'm fine. Lemme go." His legs felt disconnected from the rest of his body, and he swayed violently before he regained some semblance of control.

He stretched out a hand to Finn, the other clinging to a jagged handhold on the wall, and brushed his fingers against the man's coat. "This way, Finn."

Rose couldn't move, couldn't breathe. Her body felt like ice and she knew she'd never be warm again. *How could she? How could she do this? Leave me. God! Why?* Her mind reeled at the shock; her throat was thick with pain and grief. *This isn't what they meant. This is wrong. It couldn't … it didn't … ohmygod.*

"Rose! Rose! Snap out of it!" Simone yelled right into her face. Rose couldn't bring herself to respond, staring into the cavern below. Simone grabbed the shoulder of her coat to pull her back to her feet. Her legs had no strength and she sank back down.

"Dammit, Rose! MOVE!"

A stinging slap accosted her face. She could hear Eliana's voice telling her to get her butt into gear.

"MOVE!"

Then Simone rushed back to help Dan and Finn, who were still clinging to the wall inside the cave.

Stumbling over falling rocks, hauling each other along the collapsing path, they beat the cave-in by inches. The two men from above reached them just as the cave fell in on itself, and a cloud of dust and dirt engulfed them all.

Gabran's weapon was holstered when it became obvious that the shooter was not with the rag-tag group. Roshen grabbed Rose, who appeared on the point of collapse, and half-carried, half-dragged her to the cave entrance.

Flashlight beams appeared as disconnected shafts of energy through the murky cloud of debris, bouncing around randomly as the group struggled to reach safety.

As the cloud began to settle, Simone appeared with Dan's arm draped over one of her shoulders for support, and Finn gripping her other as she led them outside.

"Who the hell's side are you on?" she hissed as she pushed past the Assassin.

"I serve the Grail. Now, as always," Michel Sicarius replied evenly. He moved out of their way and pointed toward the entrance. "The cave ahead is safe enough. You will be able to rest awhile there before we venture outside."

"You've got a lot of explaining to do," Simone continued.

"Simone, let's just get some place where the ground don't move," Dan gasped.

Simone looked at the struggling man's begrimed face and grimaced. "You know, you look an awful shade of green."

"I feel an awful shade of green," he mumbled.

Sicarius left the pair to continue on their own and grabbed Finn's arm just as he stumbled into an invisible rut. Pete saw him straight-away and fought the urge to lash out at the Frenchman. Instead, he issued a terse order through clenched teeth. "Get him above ground. I've got an injured man to see to back here."

Sicarius merely nodded, fully aware of the animosity in the men. Finn, lost for the moment in a wave of confusion and shock, kept his silence. Pete turned to Elliott and Nick who were just becoming visible in the dark, dusty corridor.

"Elliott? What have we got?"

"Busted arm for sure, maybe some busted ribs too. He took a few knocks to the back, and there's a big dent in his hard-hat. He's con-scious, but groggy."

Pete checked Nick over while Elliott continued to hold him up.

"The helmet's not cracked and there's no blood here. Let's just keep him going to the top and strap him back together in comfort."

"Nick? Can you keep going?" Elliott asked. "Or you want me and Pete to haul you up?"

"I can do it," the injured man ground out.

"All right then, let's go. We're nearly there and it seems we've got some help," said Pete.

"Help? Who?" Sicarius had left with Finn before Elliott had seen him.

"Don't matter who. Let's just get up there so they can."

"YOU!" Elliott roared as soon as he saw Sicarius.

He left Nick with Pete and launched himself at the man who represented everything that had gone wrong in the last few months—Dan, shot and psychologically tortured; Finn, scarred and blinded; and now Eliana, dead. Grabbing a fistful of the man's coat, Elliott dragged him away from Finn and threw him across the small chamber to land with a thud against the far wall.

"Do you know the hell we've been through because of your damned Brotherhood? Don't say a word. I'll tell you—with my fists!"

Elliott reached the dazed man in two giant steps, intent on punishing him in the most satisfying way he could think of: violently. He grabbed the man's collar and dragged him back up to his feet, letting him go long enough to land two punches into his unprotected gut. Sicarius doubled over in pain, a rush of air forcefully expelled from his lungs. Elliott went to reach for him again.

"Now, Elliott. Didn't your sainted mother ever teach you to share?" Simone Lang's friendly manner belied the ice-cold glare in her eyes.

Elliott tore his hate-filled gaze from the Frenchman, an evil grin spreading across his face. "Well, where are my manners today? Ladies first, of course. You go right ahead there, Simone." He grabbed a handful of Sicarius's hair and twisted the man's head upward.

Simone peeled off her gloves and flexed her hands.

"That's enough!" came a forbidding voice from the cave entrance.

As one, the group turned to the newcomer.

Elliott frowned, staring hard, semi-recognition and disbelief crossing his face in equal measure.

Simone stopped flexing. "Curiouser and curiouser."

Dan had dragged himself the few feet that had separated him from Nick's side and now just sat with his head between his knees.

"The Raven," Finn said.

Pete looked up from where he knelt over Nick, his busy hands stilled for the moment in surprise. "Jed?"

<h1 style="text-align:center">61</h1>

The man, known at various times as Jed Smiggins and Aiden Gabran, took in the dirty faces of the Questors and Rose's pale blank expression. He knew them all, knew what they had suffered, understood their pain, but he could not allow Sicarius to suffer for events that were outside of his control. He would not allow him to bear the punishment that belonged to someone else. He ignored the shocked looks from the group and concentrated solely on Elliott Byrd.

"You're hitting the wrong man. Put him down," he said sternly.

Elliott nearly did, but caught a flash of triumphant disdain in the Frenchman's eyes and immediately tensed. "Of course," Elliott said smoothly. He tightened his grip on Sicarius's dark hair and twisted it viciously before turning slightly to Simone. "Sorry, Ms. Lang. You're gonna have to wait your turn after all." Then he pushed the Assassin's head down in a sudden move to connect with his rising knee. "Oops," he said, looking up at the old man with a belligerent expression. "He's down now."

A sharp snigger came from the stranger standing behind Aiden, and Elliott tensed again, ready for a reprisal. "We know these two, who the hell are you?" Elliott demanded.

Simone touched Elliott on the shoulder. "This is Isabel McTavish's friend from the freight company." She looked at the man apologetically. "I'm sorry, I don't recall your name."

"Roshen," he replied, an amused grin on his face.

Aiden shifted uncomfortably. "Roshen, help Sicarius."

"Perhaps you'd care to enlighten us now on what you chose not to share with us earlier?" Simone said to Aiden, stepping away from the fallen man at her feet.

"Yeah," Elliott agreed. "Why didn't you tell us a week or so ago who you really are, Jed? Say, when you and your buddy, Will, first found Dan. Is he in on this too? Is this just some big fucking joke to you people? See how many circles you can make us run in? See how far we'll go before we start fightin' back?"

Roshen pulled Sicarius away and left him lying near Rose, then stood and took stock of the situation. Elliott was obviously at the end of his tether. He approached Aiden, seeming to grow taller: he loomed over the old man with the ferocity of a pissed-off giant. The woman was just as dangerous, Roshen realized, but in a more discreet way. She quietly moved in next to Elliott, intent on hearing why they had been used with such apparent carelessness.

"I didn't know who Dan was until after the shooting," Aiden told them sadly. "I was watching out for Will. I didn't know about the rest and by the time I did it was too late. I couldn't tell you anything."

It was true. Aiden's task had always been to guard Enki's ring, or in a truer sense, guard the one who had the ring. Will had not found it by happenstance. Its previous owner had left it hidden in the wall of the basement. Decaying masonry had caused it to fall to the floor where it had lain covered in dirt and debris until the day Will had come upon it.

Aiden had felt the touch of Will's hand on the ring as a call in his mind and had approached the homeless man the same day with a gift and an unspoken offer of gruff friendship. Will had taken both with an eagerness born from being too much alone and the two had stayed together ever since.

The day Will had dragged an unconscious and bleeding Dan Tenney into their underground hideaway, Aiden had felt a twinge of unease, but pushed it aside as annoyance that Will had become involved in something that would only bring them trouble. As he'd watched Will care for the injured man, Aiden had begun to suspect that the time was fast approaching when the ring would again change hands. There was something uncanny in the way Will had so quickly become devoted to a complete stranger. Aiden had started paying more attention to the mumblings of the feverish man, listening for clues to his identity, looking for some sign that he might be wrong.

Though he suspected it, he didn't know Dan would be the final Bearer of Ouroboros, not until he watched from the alley as Will unclasped the chain from around his neck, the chain that carried the precious circlet, and held it aloft between them. Aiden could see the ring flash with energy as it was passed to its new bearer, a flash that told the old man that his days of being Jed were over. Dan was the true bearer.

After centuries of waiting, the time of the beginning was here at last. Jed, in another life known as Aiden Gabran, had slipped back into the shadows and watched as Enki's ring was accepted and the young man departed the alley for the last time. He had seen Arwium in the street. Her presence was a final proof of what he'd half-dreaded. The time of the new Ky-in approached.

"It's on its way," he'd told her and they'd joined hands. There was a vague tension in the air between them. Things had not gone as the woman had planned.

"It's time for things to be put right," she'd said. It wasn't until later that he'd learned about the traitor de Laurac, after he and Will had left the city behind and headed for the mountain sanctuary of Elphane.

Aiden sighed and looked past Elliott to where Dan sat hunched on the floor. He noticed a disturbance in the air around him and moved closer. Elliott stopped him with a firm hand on his chest.

"I don't think so, Jed, Aiden, whoever you are …" Elliott began.

"Elliott? Work that out later. I need some help here," Pete called out urgently.

Pete was standing with Nick, who was half-reclined against the wall of the cave, his face pale and sweating. He'd smiled grimly at the scene in front of him; a sense of satisfaction overriding any concerns when the Frenchman had dropped to the ground unconscious. He had been curious about the appearance of the not so homeless hobo as well, but had much more important things to worry about for the time being.

"Time to look at that arm," Pete told him.

Nick had grunted as he tried to shift into a better position and nodded quizzically in the direction of the old man.

"I have no idea." Pete shook his head for emphasis.

Seeing Jed and learning his real identity was a shock to them all, except Dan and Finn. The pair both seemed sunken in misery, sitting side by side, Finn taking some small comfort from the close proximity of the ill man. Dan remained as before, his head resting on his knees, arms folded tightly around his legs.

"Help me get his coat off then we'll have to lay him down," Pete said to Elliott. "Simone? Find us one of those space blankets. Nick doesn't need to catch a chill from the cold ground."

Simone walked over to where Rose's pack lay against the wall and started to undo the straps. The blanket was on top of her other gear. She quickly grabbed it and returned to Pete unfolding it as she approached. Elliott took one end and they spread it out before helping Nick to lie down. Nick tried to stifle the grunts of pain the movement caused but everyone heard them just the same.

"Elliott, hold him here and here." Pete pointed to Nick's uninjured shoulder and hip. "Simone, keep his head steady. This is bad," he added. "I'll immobilize it for now, but we'll have to check for infection and frostbite. If he loses his circulation now, if I don't get this right … Basic first aid just isn't going to cut it …" Pete's words faded away. He didn't want to curse the injured man by stating the consequences out loud.

"Just do it," Nick gasped. "I'm ready."

Dan jerked his head up at these words, a breathless "no" on his lips. Pete heard him and saw him press his hands to his head as if to stop it spinning. Dan would have to wait.

Pete nodded once. "Now," he said and started pulling Nick's arm, carefully manipulating it back into position.

Nick bucked against the flame of pain that started in his arm and coursed through his body. His scream bounced off the cave walls and escaped into the snowy sky outside.

The blackness was closing in on him. Nick had pushed it away before, determined he could beat it, but now he craved oblivion and release from the streaks of agony that engulfed him. His head hurt, his ribs hurt, his arm was on fire, he couldn't move. A warm blanket of nothingness dropped over him and it all faded away. The screams and the shouts from his friends all melted together in a low blur of sound until he was left with silence.

Where am I? He strained to see through the darkness surrounding him. *Can't see a damn thing! I don't like this.*

Nick moved forward, feeling his way with his booted feet, arms stretched out in front of him. Something soft brushed past him, a feather light touch on his face and hand.

What's that? There it is again. Shit!

There was no sound. His voice barely registered in the dark void he had entered.

God! What is this?

Darkness faded to gray. A bright light appeared as a pinprick in the distance. He began to walk faster.

A way out! Thank God.

A figure emerged from the grayness and Nick stopped in dread. The figure stared, large dark eyes almost glowing in her pale face.

Am I dead?

Finn was more than exhausted. He'd had enough, wished he'd never heard of any damn ring, wished he hadn't become so involved in Irene's disappearance. He should have gone fishing like he'd been thinking of doing before this all blew up. *What has any of this got to do with me? I didn't ask for this special attention. Why me?*

It was strange how he could feel Dan next to him. They didn't touch, Dan barely moved or made a sound, but Finn knew he was there. Every time he turned his face toward him he could see a blur in the darkness. *He didn't ask for this either, but he's in it—up to his neck.*

Nick's gasp of pain tore through the blind man and he jerked his head up in response, then recoiled as a wave of static electricity flickered over him. *What the hell …?* He reached out and touched Dan.

"Dan, did you feel that?" he asked in a hoarse whisper.

There was no response, but when Finn touched him again, he felt another flicker of electricity.

"Dan?"

The glimmering Finn could see was fractured with a myriad of changing colors that reached toward him and covered his arm as he touched Dan's shoulder.

Nick's strained "I'm ready" registered on the edge of his consciousness. Dan's response, however, pierced him—so much pain and confusion and anger in that one hushed "no". Finn held on to Dan's arm as he felt him shudder, heard his desperate groans, saw the blanket of energy around him contract then, with Nick's scream of pain as a backdrop, explode out in a blazing display of white hot light.

Dan couldn't move; to try was to invite wave upon wave of nausea and dizziness. He wanted it to stop, wanted to ask Nick or Pete for the medication to make it stop, but to speak was to think, to move was to hurt. He was pretty sure there were some pills in his pocket that would ease the pain in his head. They might as well have been on the other side of the cave for all the good they did him right now. His stomach cramped in a tight knot and he gasped for a lost breath.

Oh, God.

Dan had tried to ignore Elliott's fury, tried not to feel it as it filled the cave and battered against his weakening defenses. Elliott's roar washed over him, put his hairs on end and threatened to break his tenuous control.

When Nick groaned in pain beside him, the world shifted. His ears rang. If Dan hadn't already been sitting, he would have fallen, unable to keep his balance, caught in a suspended no-man's land between two realities. A land where lightning flashed in a jagged array across his mind's eye, where sound was distorted. There was a storm coming. He could smell the electricity in the air, taste its metallic charge.

And then he heard the words that had heralded a sacrifice he didn't ask for or want.

"I'm ready." Nick's voice filtered through the noise in his head, echoed till it was a hundred whispers tormenting him with visions of death. He felt warmth spread over his chest, the storm was building, burning into him. Then Nick screamed and the storm exploded.

"Am I dead?" Nick's voice sounded flat in this gray void.

"Why would you think that?" Eliana asked him. Her skin appeared translucent. Strange shadows rippled across her face.

"Because you are."

Eliana shrugged and seemed to swell a moment before returning to normal. *"Am I?"* She didn't seem too concerned.

"I saw you die. Saw you get shot. That was enough to kill you alone. There's no way you could have survived that fall."

She moved closer to him, the shadows on her skin glistening with unreal color.

"I guess that makes me a ghost." Her slow whisper sent shudders recoiling down his spine.

"And me?" Nick folded his arms across his chest, determined not to let his nervousness show.

Eliana sighed, a little sadly, and put a cool hand on his face, gliding in close enough to brush her lips across his. Her touch was light, barely there, but his skin burned wherever they met: lips, cheek, ear.

"No," she whispered in that strange, almost sibilant way. *"You're not the one I'm waiting for."* She drew away from him, back into the grayness that surrounded them both.

"Wait."

"I'm not going anywhere," she replied. *"It's you who must leave."*

A roar filled Nick's ears and the gray grew dark once more. He lay down, feeling nothing, seeing nothing, until he became aware of voices that grew louder, buzzing like disturbed bees around his head until he couldn't ignore them any longer. He opened his eyes to the light.

While Elliott and Simone helped Pete, Aiden swiftly stepped over to where Roshen kneeled beside Sicarius.

"He's okay," Roshen told him. "Should start coming around soon. If not, I'll give him a little something to wake him up."

"May have to do that anyway, Roshen. We need to get Ouroboros into Elphane as soon as possible." Aiden turned back to check on Dan, noting with surprise the red glow beginning to emanate through his clothes. He laid a hand on Roshen's arm, his fingers digging into the muscle through the thick coat.

Roshen looked up, alarmed. "What is it?" He followed the old man's gaze and drew a sharp breath. "That's not supposed to happen, is it?"

The disturbance Aiden had noticed a few minutes ago was growing and seemed to be reaching out to Finn. Judging by the awed expression on his face, the professor was aware of the changes taking place.

"We have to stop him. This isn't the right time, or place."

"How do you know?"

Aiden glared at Roshen, affronted that he should be questioned so. So many things had gone so differently to the original story. Yet he was certain about this more than he'd been about anything else throughout his exceedingly long life. The activation of Enki's ring was premature. Other events had not yet occurred—events that couldn't possibly transpire without the correct participants in place. He was left with only one question—what the hell was going on?

"Believe me, it's not," he answered. "Nothing is right. This isn't what's supposed to happen at all."

"So why is it? Is it him?"

Aiden stared at the hunched man on the other side of the cave. *Is that possible?* He turned back to Roshen. "We may need Arwium. There's no telling what could happen."

Roshen headed outside. At this point Nick's scream rang out. An electric charge through the close atmosphere inside the cave instantly followed. Aiden felt the air crackle with the power that surged from Dan Tenney, which contracted just as quickly. It was dizzyingly still for a fraction of time that stretched out far too long. Pete, Elliott and Simone didn't appear to notice any changes, so intent were they on helping Nick. Finn looked shocked—bewilderment and understanding warring on his face.

Nick screamed again, and Aiden flew across the cave, caught in the explosion of raw energy that erupted from Dan. Shouted curses and frenzied activity filled the cave as he brought himself to his feet. Aiden stumbled as the ground beneath him shook. Finn was desperately holding onto a struggling Dan, and Pete was shielding Nick from a shower of falling debris. The ground moved again, this time followed by a familiar rumble in the earth beneath them.

Elliott was first to react. "Let's get the hell outta here before we get buried alive after all!" He knelt down beside Nick to help him up. "Come on, Nick, old buddy. We're on the move again."

Once again, the group rushed to escape a cave-in. Elliott hooked Nick's good arm around his neck and half-dragged him outside. Nick's head lolled awkwardly back as he tried to find Dan.

"Don't let him …" he gasped, trying to pull his pain-scattered thoughts together.

"It's okay," Elliott assured him. "Pete and Simone'll bring him out. He'll be fine."

"No … don't understand … she's waiting …"

"She's just gonna have to wait a little longer," Elliott replied.

Elliott took Nick to the tree line and propped him up behind a huge oak. Pete followed right behind with the packs and first aid kit. He dropped his load on the ground and took a moment to put a pack along either side of Nick top prop him up and wedge a coat between his back and the tree. Taking off his own coat, he spread it out over Nick for extra protection from the cold and whispered that he'd be right back.

Simone fought with Dan to get him to safety. Finn wasn't cooperating either.

"Finn! Come on!" Pete gripped his arm, but Finn shook his head, adamant that he stay with Dan, astounded by the outpouring of power coming from the young man.

Dan's body was racked with the force of the energy that consumed him. His eyes were open wide but not seeing; his mouth stretched tight in an agonized grimace. Spasms rippled through him as he bucked and kicked. The energy that had exploded from him in a brilliant sheet of colored light coalesced into streams that shot into the earth like an ancient sword into solid rock. The rumbling of the earth grew stronger and more ominous with every passing moment.

Elliott returned, moving to Dan's head and shoulders. "Grab a leg each," he told Pete and Simone. "We'll cart him out."

Finn followed them out, Dan's brilliance lighting a path through his blindness. They laid him at the edge of the clearing, a few feet away from the tree that protected Nick. Finn dropped to Dan's side. Roshen had dragged Sicarius out and the Frenchman sat propped against another tree—still unconscious. Aiden brought out an uncommunicative Rose, and Roshen helped get her settled beside Sicarius before returning to the cave with Elliott to collect all the gear.

"This whole hilltop is probably unstable," said Elliott.

Roshen hefted Rose's pack to his shoulder as he nodded his agreement. "It might be a good idea if we got as far away from here as possible." He grabbed the light packs his group had brought up the mountain. "That's not going to be easy."

Elliott collected the rope and threw a final cursory glance around the cave. The threatened cave-in had seemed to slow down now that Dan was outside. Whatever strange thing that was happening was centered on him. Elliott looked at Roshen and shrugged, a coil of the rope slithering down his arm with the movement.

"What's new?"

62

Dan's breath came in strained, raspy grunts. Pete pulled apart Dan's clothes in an effort to make it easier for him. The flashes of energy, still emitting in full force and now visible to all those gathered, pierced nearby tree trunks, sunk into the ground and disappeared into snow-thick sky. A patch of snow had already melted to slush around them. Pete inadvertently got in the way of one beam and jumped with a shocked yelp as his body was energized. His hair stood on end, and he turned a white face to Simone, his mouth a perfect "O" of surprise.

"We've got to stop this now," she said. The strange circlet lay on Dan's bare chest glowing with a brilliance that was painful to behold. She didn't know what to do, but surely this was hurting Dan. Tentatively, she started to reach for the ring.

"I'll get someone to meet us, but we'll have to get started on our own," Roshen told Elliott as they brought the last of the gear from the cave.

"How're you going to do that?" Elliott asked. "On second thought, I don't want to know. Just tell them to hurry up. We're gonna start feeling this weather real fast."

The wind began to roar around them as they moved away from the protection of the cave. "Wait! What about Dan?" Elliott shouted.

Roshen looked at where Dan was expending vast amounts of energy. Outside the cave was no safer than inside had been. The earth rumbled beneath his feet as if to remind him just how dangerous inside was. His gaze fell on Finn, and he saw for the first time what lay hidden within the blind man.

"Aiden will take care of your friend, with a little help. I'll see to Sicarius as soon as I get back."

Elliott put his hands up in innocence. "He's all yours."

"Stop!" Aiden warned, shuffling through the thick snow toward Simone.

She snatched her hand away from the ring as if stung. Impossible as it seemed, the circlet grew brighter. Dan was rapidly reaching exhaustion, the violent spasms reduced to quivers that coursed through his body.

"We have no choice," Simone said. "This thing is killing him."

"No, it's not, but removing it definitely will." Aiden knelt down beside them, a hand up to protect his eyes from the dazzling glare of the ring.

"We have to do something. He can't take much more of this."

"Get your gear and get ready to move out," Aiden instructed.

"What? We can't …" Simone started to stay.

"We must," Aiden cut them off gruffly. "We're too close to the cave. We have to get off this mountain. The quicker we get down to Elphane the better for all of us."

Pete solemnly started to load his arms with the packs and equipment that Elliott and Roshen had rescued. Simone hesitated a moment longer.

"See to Somers. We'll take care of Dan," Aiden reassured her.

We? Simone thought.

Aiden leaned over Dan, placing a hand on the tortured man's forehead. "She's right," he whispered as he felt the waves of power that rolled off Dan's body. "It's time to do something."

"There's a lot you don't know. Isn't there?" Finn's deep voice sliced through the wind as if it was a still day.

Aiden didn't look up. "Too much," he agreed.

"Can he hear us?"

"I don't know."

Finn's hands explored Dan's face for any reactions he couldn't see. He leaned in toward the younger man's ear and spoke in a low, barely audible voice. "Dan. It's Finn. Can you hear me?"

A burst of energy bridged the narrow gap between Dan and Finn. Aiden turned away, no longer able to bear the sight of Enki's ring, so bright now that even Finn could see the circle on Dan's chest.

"He has to control it," Aiden said, not sure if that would be possible.

"Dan, you can control it. Concentrate."

Dan's jaw clenched tightly, a low growl vibrated deep in his throat. The light flickered and dulled. The beams of shooting energy came together to form a single ball hovering above the clearing. Dan's chest heaved, his back arched and his hands formed rigid fists as he fought to gain control.

Finn dropped his hand to Dan's shoulder. Aiden could feel the changes in the air. "You're doing it, Dan."

Dan's growl turned to a harsh snarl and the now pulsating ball of energy began to drop.

"He needs help!" Aiden yelled.

Finn lifted Dan easily and pulled him close to his chest. The energy crackled around them.

"Push through it, Finn. Look into it and guide him through."

Finn heard the Aiden's voice through a thick wall of buzzing energy. Every hair was on end, every nerve tingled, muscles started to cramp. The light was everywhere. He could feel rather than hear the howl that started all around him and was surprised that the sound came from the man in his arms, vibrating in the very air he breathed. He looked down at the shadow in his arms. Dan was haloed by the light and, as Finn watched, the light increased to such intensity that he could discern finer details. The image became clearer as the energy descended over them. Inside the light, the Ouroboros glowed dully and Finn looked directly into it. He slowly moved his free hand toward it and took hold. It was hot in his hand. The heat travelled through his body. He absorbed the excess energy, feeling vitalized. His blood heated, the cold becoming a dim memory. Dan gave an anguished howl of pain and loss and became limp, his head protectively held in the crook of Finn's arm. All traces of the power dissipated as quickly as it had come.

The ball of light exploded with a blast that sent Simone, Pete and Aiden reeling from its force. They got up slowly, shaking their heads and dusting themselves off.

A cloud of dust and debris burst from the cave as it finally collapsed. Rocks, loosened by the continual rumbling and shaking of the mountain, rolled down from above to half-bury in the icy slush of the clearing. The group took their gear and helped the injured out from under the trees as heavy, ice-covered branches started to snap like twigs.

When it was over, Finn stood, Dan held firmly in his arms, and looked at the rest of the group. "Time to continue the journey." He walked toward them, avoiding the rocks that now littered the clearing with unerring accuracy.

Simone watched him, looking for injury, frowning and then realizing what it was that had changed. "Finn, you can see!"

Dan's skin tingled, sending tendrils of sensation snaking through him. His mouth went dry as raw memories of the Eliana's death mixed with remnants of his dreams bombarded him.

Then a new image came to him. She stood before him, her eyes flashing with anger and hate, blood gushing from the wound in her chest, streaming down her face. Her torn hands lifted to her head, holding it on either side and for a horrible moment he thought it would fall off. He was frozen with pure terror as her hands came down and stretched out to him, palms up. Blood and flesh dripped from her fingers.

"*You did this to me,*" her strangled voice accused him. "*Because of you, I lay broken and forgotten. Because of you, I will never again see the light of day; never smell the wildflowers in the mountain breeze.*" She stumbled forward, and he held his breath in horror and disgust. "*Because of you,*" she hissed, "*I will never lie in my lover's arms again. Because of you ...*"

He could hear a scream welling in her throat, but couldn't move to block his ears. The sound gurgled as he stood transfixed. Her eyes were yellow slits of hate in her blood-streaked face. She hissed at him and a familiar fetid stench rolled over him. The sharp tapping of clawed feet echoed through his mind. Something tugged on his jeans, cut through them with sharp precision, piercing his skin. Agony ripped through his body and he fell to his knees. The gurgling scream changed to a full-bodied roar of pain, and he felt himself screaming along with it. He struggled as his clothes were torn from his body, as sharp teeth bit into his muscles.

Her bloodied hands touched his face, and he was filled with disgust and horror and anger. "*Because of you!*" she screeched.

"*Because of me,*" he whispered and the ball of abomination inside him grew and grew.

"*Dan? It's Finn, can you hear me?*"

"*Finn? Thank God! It's my fault. Oh, God! I did this. I can't stop.*"

"Dan, you can control it."

"No, I can't. It's too much. It's because of me. Oh, God! Oh, God!"

"Concentrate."

"Damn you to fucking hell! I killed them. It's because of me they're dead! All because of fucking me!"

A brilliant ring of light pulsed in front of him. It drew him closer, away from the rotting corpse and the screeching rats. He felt stronger. The bile in his gut faded. The burning pain in his arms and legs receded. The mind-numbing terror that travelled through his nervous system dissolved into a sensual awareness of being alive. A shadow formed in the center of the ring and a familiar figure came through.

"You're here," he said.

"It took me awhile, but yes, I'm here." The smooth voice ran like balm across his shattered nerves.

"Welcome to my nightmare," Dan said, his voice tinged with sarcasm. The figure nodded and moved closer.

"That's all it is."

Dan shook his head. *"It's because of me that she died."*

"No. It isn't."

"She knew the whole time."

"Didn't you?"

The silence stretched out between them.

"Yes," Dan finally answered, feeling the guilt begin to churn once more.

"What she did was very important. More than your life was at stake in that cave today. One life was extinguished, but another saved and yet another given a chance."

"Don't think she sees it that way," Dan said sadly.

A soft touch brushed his face. *"That's not her."*

Dan looked up sharply, searching the face before him for the truth. The face remained expressionless. The eyes held his gaze.

"Look."

The nightmare image began to fade away. The horrible corpse disappeared to be replaced by a new image. He knew at once that this one was real. She glowed with supernatural light, her skin rippled with mottled shadow.

Eliana didn't say a word, her expression as solemn in death as it had been in life. Finally, she nodded and gave him the same slow smile that was always ready to be given.

"*Let go*," he heard her say, even though she was now just one more shadow. He felt the same soft touch brush by him, the lift of gentle wings.

"*Let go,*" the voice behind him repeated.

Dan saw the light reflecting brightly off soft, white feathers as the dove flew back through the ring. Then he closed his eyes and let go.

63

When Dan awoke, it was to hushed voices chatting. Some sounded close, others far away. A few he didn't know and Dan wondered who the newcomers were. He could feel the heat from a nearby fire, the heaviness of coarse blankets over his body. He squirmed between the thick layers and sank lower beneath the blankets. He was so comfortable and warm he decided to lay there and savor it all in.

He wished he was in New Mexico. At the ranch, with his grandmother in the kitchen fixing some breakfast, grandfather out front cursing the dog and Meg turning the mess he'd made of his shoelaces into a work of art. Funny that his strongest memory of his mother was connected to his stupid shoelaces …

"How much longer do you think they'll sleep?" Elliott asked Pete, gesturing to where Dan and Nick lay beneath a hastily erected lean-to close enough to the fire to feel its warmth.

"Dan's already stirring. Nick'll be a bit longer. Those painkillers I gave him are strong."

"We'll have to get moving again at first light. We're still too close to that damn mountain for comfort and we don't know what happened to de Laurac."

Pete frowned. "You don't think he could have survived that cave-in?"

"I hope not," Elliott replied, rubbing the back of his neck. "Might go have a word with the others. Maybe Roshen and his friends have some ideas."

Elliott strolled over to where Finn and Simone sat squeezed together by the fire. "Well, old man, isn't it way past your bed time?" he said, clapping Finn on the back.

"Just imbibing in a little of Simone's magic sleeping potion," Finn replied as Elliott sat down next to him. He put the rim of a silver flask to his lips and took another appreciative sip.

Elliott held out his hand for the flask and Finn passed it to him. "What kind of rotgut you got in this, Simone?" He took a generous mouthful of the liquor, savored it in his mouth a moment, then swallowed with an "Aaah" of approval. "Not bad stuff."

Simone looked pained as she accepted the flask back from Elliott. "That stuff that you so derisively label as rotgut, Mr. Byrd, is Golden Viking cognac and worth more than you'll ever be able to afford."

Elliott laughed. "Liquid gold, so smooooth going down."

Simone muttered something about the ignorant, uneducated masses and returned the flask to Finn, flicking a smile at Pete as he joined them.

Elliott stopped laughing. "That was sure some weird stuff with Dan today, Finn. You gonna let us in on what happened?"

"Yes, Finn. How is it that a light so blindingly bright was able to restore your vision?" Simone asked, tightening of her hand over his.

Finn sipped the cognac, thinking about how he could describe what had happened when he'd touched the ring. He remembered everything in fine detail, knew those memories would stay with him forever, but how could he put into words something that was all feelings? The effects of the liquor seeped through his body with renewed warmth as he looked into the fire. Blackened sticks filled with the embers of the fire crumbled into a puff of ash. Flames licked against each other in a mesmerizing dance of destruction.

"You know," he began, "I think I can actually see better now than before the accident."

Simone, Elliott and Pete waited patiently for him to continue. He looked down at his blurred reflection in the flask.

"Something was returned to me today, other than my sight, that I didn't know I'd lost." He shrugged his shoulders with a soft grunt. "*Something lost, now found* means more than just this ring. The ring is a symbol." A frown of concentration appeared on his face. *An enduring symbol so strong in the human psyche as to insert itself in countless stories … A firm fixture, in one form or another, in the traditional hero's journey for millennia, modern stories and ancient legends, and yet still not understood.* "A powerful symbol apparently. Jed, I mean, Aiden, told me he'd never seen the ring do what it did today, thinks maybe they were looking for something too."

"They?" Simone queried.

The day and the liquor finally began to tell on him as Finn fought off the desire for sleep. "Dan and this Ring of Unity."

"You talk as if the ring had a mind of its own," said Pete.

"Not a mind, but purpose. It's not just an old ring after all. It's Ouroboros. Dan triggered the band somehow and it became a focus for what he was experiencing."

"Which was?" Simone asked.

"He was having a kind of waking nightmare. When I touched the ring ..."

"Wait a minute," Simone interrupted. "Jed told me not to touch the ring, it was too dangerous. How were you able to?"

Finn continued to stare at his reflection. The flask caught flashes of orange light from the fire, distorting his image even further. "I was meant to. Remember, Simone, you were told to find the Dove, that the Dove would guide you to the door?"

"As I recall, the message was 'The Bearer of Ouroboros knows the Raven, now you must find the door. The Dove will be your guide.'"

"That's right, but it was a message meant mainly for Dan, I think, unless there's something else I'm missing."

"What do you mean, Finn?" Elliott asked.

Finn handed the flask back to Simone and fumbled in his pocket. "When I touched the ring, I entered the place where Dan was and found the Dove." He pulled his hand from his pocket. It held a white feather. "I found the Dove," he said softly, twirling the feather around. He was still astounded by his discovery. "The Dove is me."

"You?" Pete said. "You don't look much like a dove to me."

"Symbology's a funny thing. Like Ouroboros, it is embedded in our history, yet in such a way that its meaning is unclear or mixed.

"I was blinded so I could look into the light and guide Dan to that which was lost. In the end it wasn't hard at all. No special knowledge needed or daring feat of bravery. Just a few simple words that needed to be said at the right time to halt despair." Finn stood then, his tiredness a palpable force in his body. He needed to sleep.

"Just a minute," Simone began, standing with him and grabbing his arms. "What was it?"

"Hope." Finn looked back into the fire and then beyond to where Dan lay. "Pure, simple hope."

64

It was a legend among the People of the Web, the Elbe, that Ouroboros was a powerful weapon effectively able to split the world in two if used by the wrong person. A key to enlightenment for those chosen to use it. Since its forging, millennia ago, no Sidhe had ever touched it. It was a gift from its creators, a shaman and a warrior of great standing among the people.

The man and the woman had created the ring in a bonding ceremony lasting nine days. Nine days that changed the course of humanity and heralded the end of the power of their people. Nine days that would eventually result in a bloodline of descent that would track its way through history with a determination born from hardship and inherent knowledge.

During those nine days, the man and woman foresaw a day when humanity would overtake their own race and the People of the Web would be forced to retreat into hiding from their own creations, the children of Earth. Yet, they felt humanity, a sometimes troublesome and precocious child, would still need the guidance of their "parents", and so the man and woman met deep beneath the fertile earth. It was there that the Ouroboros was born—a potent combination of steel, earth and the power of gods. It took eight days to create. On the ninth day, the man and woman came together a final time, and the future of a now ancient bloodline was conceived.

Aiden Gabran finished the story as the group reached the last climb that would lead them to the Door of Elphane. They had walked a little over six hours since departing their camp at dawn, and he expected to reach the summit by sunset. He started telling the legends of his people not long after they'd stopped for a break. The wounded men and a grief stricken Rose needed time to rest; those supporting them did too.

Elliott had broached the subject of the Leper with Aiden the night before. They all feared de Laurac had survived the cave-in. "After all," Elliott said, "Dan's still dreamin' about rats."

Aiden and his people had joined the private investigators not long after Finn had turned in for the night.

Dan had awoken again to the sound of voices and the rich aroma of coffee brewing over the fire. The smell was enough to make his stomach grumble. He watched the newcomers from the corner of his eye as he shifted position, groaning as stiffened muscles complained bitterly at his decision to move.

Those around the fire were so intent on their plans for the next day that they hadn't noticed Dan was awake until he was standing behind them.

"Dan!" Elliott stood and moved to help him find a place to sit.

The others made room, Simone pouring him some coffee while Pete filled a plate with the stew they'd been keeping for when he eventually woke up. Simone asked him how he was and he answered with a shrug.

"I'm fine." He sipped at the coffee and grimaced. "Well, until I drank this stuff anyways. I think that when this is all over, I might never drink coffee again. Sure smells better than it tastes." He bravely took another sip and looked at each of the faces, familiar and not so, staring back at him. "What'd I miss and how'd I get here?" he asked them.

"What was the last thing you remember?" said Elliott.

Dan had to think about it a minute before finally answering. "Being inside a mountain with it about to come down on top of us."

"Which time?" Pete blurted.

Dan blinked, confused and uncomfortable that he'd lost at least one day, judging by the night sky, and possibly longer. He put the mug down on the ground and stared at the plate of stew in his lap. Picking up the fork that was resting on the side of the plate, he pushed the steaming chunks of meat and vegetables around in a loose circle, all the while trying to focus on what exactly his last memory was. He looked up, concerned. "Nick okay?"

"Nick's fine," Elliott assured him. "He's sleeping right now." He pointed a finger to the other side of the fire where two bundles of blankets lay still, protected from the night air by a canvas tarpaulin stretched between sturdy bushes. The men beneath the blankets occasionally moved a restless foot but otherwise appeared to be sleeping better than babies.

"An' Finn? He did it, didn't he?" Dan had a sharp memory of the professor's deep voice and the soft scrape of feathers on his skin. He'd known since his first night in Smiggins' Rest who the Dove was but, as with the Raven, was unable to share that knowledge.

"Yeah, he sure did," Elliott told him. "You remember much about that?"

"Bits and pieces. Nothin' concrete. Why don't you fill me in? Startin' with who all these extra people are?"

"You know Jed, or Aiden," Elliott began, fairly sure that seeing the old man up here was no surprise to Dan. When Dan nodded that he did, Elliott continued. "This here's Roshen and Sicarius, formerly of the Brotherhood. The three of them met us in the cave and helped pull us out of that deathtrap of a cavern. Then you and that ring-thing went a little crazy on us and we had to get off the mountain completely."

Dan looked at the other men, his eyes narrowing at the Frenchman, and continued eating. As he finished off his first and then second helping of the stew, he listened to the conversation continuing around him and felt a cold shiver of presentiment when he realized they thought de Laurac might still be alive. He looked up sharply when the voices stilled and discovered the others watching him, apparently waiting for something. In a far corner of his mind, the scatter of claws on rock taunted him and he found himself nodding, confirming their suspicions of the dangers of the morrow. De Laurac was alive and still following.

The next day Sicarius ranged out from the trail the group had been following but found no sign of danger. Simone and Elliott stayed on the back trail, doubling back to lay false trails and set booby traps. They saw no sign of the killer behind them. Roshen hovered in between watching both parties warily.

Dan stopped beside Aiden, white-faced and exhausted, leaning heavily on the staff the older man had given him.

"It won't be long and this'll all be over," Aiden told him.

"I never felt so crappy for so long my entire life," said Dan.

Aiden smiled warmly, and a little sadly. "Won't always be so hard …" he began to say when he was interrupted by the arrival of Pete and Nick.

"We going up there?"

Nick followed Pete's gaze up and groaned. "How the hell're we going to manage this?"

Finn arrived next and dropped his pack on the ground to rest against.the boulders that were scattered around the base of the cliff. Dan and Rose brought up the rear.

"What I don't understand, Aiden, is how your people and Ouroboros are connected to the Holy Grail. You obviously aren't Christians. Why do you protect and serve its concepts?" Finn asked. The unraveling of the mysteries surrounding the People of the Web had fascinated him, but he still felt there was a lot the man wasn't saying.

"We follow the original concept of service and compassion that the Ring of Unity symbolizes. Your faith once followed it as well, still does in its own way, of course. We are different peoples after all."

Pete turned away from his contemplation of the climb ahead and spoke directly to Aiden for the first time. "What I want to know is, what does Cain have to do with it? How come he was so important that he was made to look bad?"

"You know about Qayin?" Aiden asked surprised. His pronunciation of the name was slightly different to Pete's.

"Sure. The ring is a version of the Mark of Cain. Eliana showed me hers, said it was a blessing."

"And so it is."

"But he was a murderer," Pete said bluntly.

Everyone present turned their attention to Aiden, but it was Finn who spoke next. "That Cain was the son of Adam and Eve. Didn't you say the Ring of Unity was given to the son of Hawah? There must have been two of them."

Pete opened his mouth then closed it. "Yeah, I did say that." He walked back the few steps that separated him from the others. "But there wasn't two of them, was there?" he asked Aiden. "They're the same guy."

"They are one and the same. He didn't kill his brother. That was a misunderstanding of the texts by those who were translating them at the time. Eve and Hawah are also one and the same."

"Qayin was the son of Adam and Eve," Pete confirmed.

Nick and Dan had found themselves almost comfortable positions on the ground, resting against the boulders near Finn. Nick groaned audibly at the conversation and leaned his head closer to Dan. "I think I'm getting a headache," he muttered.

Dan gave him a small smile. "How's the arm holding up?"

"Fine. The herbal remedy they gave me tastes ten times worse than anything I've ever drunk before, but once you get over gagging on the stuff, it works like a dream. You should try it," Nick said. "I'm just one dull ache instead of a hundred or so really painful ones."

Dan grinned, but stayed quiet as Pete asked, "And who the hell is Enki?"

"Enki is an ancient Sumerian god. One of the Elohim, I believe," Finn said.

"You know your history, Finn," Aiden said. "Enki, Enlil and Tiamet were the uppermost of the Elohim at the time. It was Enki and Tiamet who created the ring."

"Are you implying what I think you're implying?" Finn asked suspiciously.

Before Aiden could answer, Roshen returned to the group.

"The Leper has been spotted cornered in a narrow ravine southeast of here about two miles. We should continue on and let them handle it."

"Very well," Aiden said with a curt nod. He turned to Nick, still sitting against the rock, one arm in a sling, the other wrapped protectively around his ribs. Eyeing him carefully, he seemed to come to some decision before turning to Pete. "You'll need to give Nick some more of the remedy. Just enough to make it easier for him to move."

"No problem. What about Dan?"

"I'm fine," Dan said shortly.

"Compared to what?" Pete asked just as abruptly.

Dan flashed him a dangerous look that quickly lightened. "Compared to someone who's had his arm broken and ribs dented in a cave-in."

Nick snorted. "Very funny, Tenney."

65

"Putain de merde!" The lone, bleeding man cursed steadily under his breath as he ducked out of sight and made his way into the ravine. He stumbled on exhausted legs, not noticing or caring about the cut on his head or the bright red blood flowing down one side of his face. All he needed to do was stay still just a moment longer and he wouldn't have been seen.

De Laurac had thrown himself back down the path as the cave roof above him tumbled down. He'd watched the woman be hit by his bullet and fall, observed the confusion that followed and had calmly took aim to fire again. Then the roof came down and he had no choice but to stop and escape before he was buried alive. A cloud of dirty and damp, cold air pushed him forcefully into the long tunnel he'd followed his quarry through, and he'd landed in a tangle of arms and legs upside down, dazed and bruised. His flashlight had been dropped sometime mid-flight and still lay buried under a ton or two of rock and ice. The lamp on his helmet was smashed, the hard hat itself seriously dented.

When he'd come to enough to sort himself into an upright position, he pulled a chemical light-stick from a pocket on the leg of his torn pants, cracked and shook it, then waited for its red glow to fill the tunnel. It bathed the wall of debris that had been the tunnel mouth with its dull light, and he limped over to push at the rocks. Dirt trickled down to form a small pile on the toe of his boots. He stared at it a moment and lifted his hand to wipe his face before kicking the dirt away and pounding the rocks with his fist.

The understanding that he was trapped sank slowly into his muddled head and he turned away from the impenetrable wall, not seeing the bloody handprint he'd left behind.

He found freedom, as determined as any half-crazed animal caught in a trap, through a narrow crack in the tunnel wall. If it weren't for the frigid breeze that swirled around him as he limped through the tunnel, he would have missed it completely.

He removed his pack and his coat, hooking them to his gear, and squeezed through the gap, still determined to catch his prey. It was a close call when the mountain rumbled again and the second cave-in collapsed the tunnel and closed the narrow slit through which he was escaping. He dragged his pack behind him and rolled back into the outside world under a shower of rubble and ice.

Pure instinct kept him moving. From his perch halfway up a tall tree he watched his former friend and the rest of the group trudge through the snow. Occasionally they disappeared behind trees or blended in with the rocks that also dotted the mountainside, but he always found them again, his cracked binoculars picking them out one by one. He sat there for hours, watching their slow march, right up until they disappeared through a pass in the mountain.

Bringing his binoculars up, he twisted the focus rings until the rocks above the pass became a sharp image, then slowly lifted the glass higher. The view filled with the granite surface of a jagged arch, almost a keyhole in the mountain through which he could see clear blue sky—a stark contrast to the dull gray directly above him.

He stared through the battered binoculars until hot tears welled in his eyes and overflowed, tracking a path through the bloody grime that coated his face. Then he climbed down the tree to follow them, scuffling down the slope through the trees until he reached a spot where the mountain cut away into a ravine. The ravine was the only thing that separated him from the trail the others followed.

He would stop them and he would show them. They had defiled the sanctified treasure he had given his life to protect. Betrayed the trust of all who had gone before. Soon, through the hand of Roger de Laurac, they would discover God's retribution. Michel Sicarius would go first.

In the end, it wasn't hard at all.

Elliott and Simone had finished checking the back trail and were about to head further up the mountain. Simone casually scanned the snow covered rocks on the other side of what was the start of a ravine that followed the curve of the mountain. Rocks, mostly small, were rolling down the steep slope opposite, loosening chunks of ice and snow as they went. She followed the path they had taken, finally land-ing on a bare patch of earth just before the lip of the ravine.

Simone watched the spot a moment, wondering what it was about it that was sending alarm bells ringing in her head. She sniffed the air and went still as one of the rocks seemed to unfold itself. Arms and legs appeared and the rock became Roger de Laurac.

"Elliott!" Simone whispered. "We've got him."

As she spoke, de Laurac limped to the edge of the ravine, clearly visible against the slate sky, and then disappeared over the other side.

Elliott cursed heavily. "We'll go in after him." He pulled his gun from its holster underneath his jacket, a dark and dangerous gleam in his eyes.

Simone unholstered her gun, a slightly smaller weapon than Elliott's Glock.

"New toy?" asked Elliott.

Simone smiled mischievously. "This is a Ruger P97. Not the latest model by far, but I like it. Reasonably lightweight though a little chunky, takes eight rounds, has an ergonomically designed grip and is guaranteed to blow the proverbial shit out of whatever I fire it at."

"Nice. Real nice," Elliott grinned. "Let's go."

They had barely taken two steps each when a shadow parted itself from the trees nearby with a soft crunch of boots on broken ground. Simone and Elliott swung around, guns up. It was Sicarius.

"You may as well put them away," the Frenchman said in a rough, nasally voice. "I have been here some time. You would already be dead if I had wanted it." He showed them the weapon he held in his hands. A gleaming black hunter's bow, with its arrow, a sharpened rod of stainless steel, loaded and primed to fire.

"What do you want?" Simone asked, holding her gun steady.

Sicarius shrugged and unprimed his bow, tucking the steel rod into a slim leather bag full of such arrows that hung from his hip.

"You will need help. I know the area and I know de Laurac. Neither are soft."

"How's the head?" Elliott asked with fake concern.

The side of Sicarius's face was mottled with ugly bruises. One cheek was swollen so badly the eye on that side was hardly more than a slit in the puffy flesh. "I will live to exact recompense at another time," he replied.

Elliott lowered his gun and stepped forward. "Recompense? You deserve every damn thing you get."

Simone interrupted the tirade. "And we look forward to continuing the conversation at a later date," she said to Sicarius and waved the Ruger to indicate the man should start moving. "In the meantime, let's go stamp out some vermin."

Sicarius started walking in the direction Simone pointed. He had also seen his former partner and now climbed toward the rocks and exposed earth.

Once they'd reached the peak there was no need to worry about losing the man's trail. Blood showed his passage clearly from the rocks where he'd been hiding into the ravine below.

De Laurac's mouth hung open to suck as much oxygen into his body as he could. It was no use. The thin cold mountain air and damage to his body were taking their toll. He bit back cries with every step and thought, in a detached way, that perhaps his foot might be broken. His head had stopped aching, but his eyes felt like a hundred icicles were stabbing them mercilessly. The more he rubbed them to clear his vision the more the pain increased.

He tripped over the roots of an old tree and fell heavily to his knees, an animal-like cry escaping through cracked lips. Numb hands splayed out automatically to stop his fall. His gloves still hung from a branch in the tree, his binoculars lay smashed at its base, both forgotten in a cloud of pain when he'd landed awkwardly on his throbbing foot. He didn't feel the wrenching of the ligaments in his left hand or the lacerations from the rocks he landed on. Blackness played at the edge of his vision, teasing him with release from his existence. He curled up in a ball and rolled toward the tree trunk, sinking back against the hard wood, and simply waited.

Judging by the irregular pattern of blood, small droplets followed by splashes of red, and the failure of de Laurac to hide any of his tracks, the man was seriously hurt. The three hunters following noted every fall and stumble.

"He's gonna die before we get to kill him," Elliott said disgustedly.

"De Laurac has survived many setbacks," Sicarius disagreed. "Do not count him dead until you see his lifeless body." His voice was tight and grim. He brushed past Elliott and knelt down for a closer look at the blood soaked ice and churned up earth. Dabbing a finger in the blood, he stood up and held his hand out for the other two to see. "Still warm."

"Let's spread out. Simone take the high ground to the right, I'll keep on this trail. You can play mountain goat, Sicarius."

Sicarius stared forcefully at the tall man.

"Better sight for that pretty bow of yours," Elliott added, not liking the deadly look he was getting.

The dour Frenchman turned on his heel and started climbing the rough track up the side of the ravine. Further in, the track would all but disappear, as the sloping wall became a sheer cliff. Sicarius aimed for a rock shelf ahead that might give him the sight he needed.

Simone followed a path that would circle behind, and slightly above, a stand of six trees near the end of the ravine where they suspected the injured man might be holed up. The blood trail led straight to it.

A scraping in the rocks above him brought Roger de Laurac from his state of near unconsciousness. The noise was just enough to remind him that he needed to keep moving. Even still, it took a second noise behind to rouse him completely. He forced himself to his knees; one numb hand remained clenched in a strangely clawed fist. His bloodshot eyes skimmed over the contorted hand and searched frantically for the gun he knew he had somewhere. His other hand patted the pockets of his jacket and his empty holster.

"Merde," he whispered hoarsely. His eyes fell on the outline of his gun through the dappled covering of a small bush. He had no idea how it got there, no memory of it falling from his now clenched fist, and he didn't care. He grabbed for it, his fingers wrapping around its fine wood-grain grip.

A branch snapped on the ground and he twisted on his knees, firing as he brought the gun to bear on whatever was approaching. The boom of the gunfire bounced off the rock walls almost smothering the sound of the second crack. If it wasn't for the sudden flame of pain in his side, he might not have realized that his shot had been returned. He clutched his useless hand to the wound, warm blood bringing back feeling to the deathly cold limb, and muttered curses under his breath, forcing himself to focus as he fired again at the dark shadow looming at the edge of the trees. The figure grunted and faltered, dropping to one knee, and de Laurac, using the tree for support, slowly stood. An insane leer crossed his face as he steadied his gun to fire again.

Elliott had seen de Laurac roll away from the tree and move to reach for something under a bush. He recognized the outline of a gun as the man pulled his hand back. Elliott didn't have time to curse his own carelessness as his foot came down on dead wood. The snap of the brittle wood caused an instantaneous reaction from the Frenchman, who whipped his gun up and around and fired all in the same motion.

The shot went wild and Elliott pressed down on the trigger of his Glock milliseconds later. His shot hit the other man low in the side but did not stop him, and as Elliott ducked for cover, he felt the burn of a bullet in his leg. He dropped to one knee, his gun momentarily dropping while he fought to regain control of the pain in his thigh.

He heard Simone's voice yelling some filthy curse about the Frenchman's heritage and took a mental note to ask her about it later, then flinched as guns boomed once again. His own fired almost by itself, so little did he think about his reaction, and he smiled in grim satisfaction at the jerky movements of de Laurac's body as every bullet found its target.

De Laurac's head burst like an overripe melon as the first of two bullets pierced his skull just above his ear. The second caught him in the base of his skull. The third bullet, heralded by the deeper sound of the Glock, burst through his throat. De Laurac collapsed to his knees once more, arms hanging lifelessly by his sides, seemingly pinned in this position for a frozen moment before slowly falling forward.

It had begun to snow, lightly at first but within seconds became quite heavy. De Laurac was already coated in white by the time Simone rushed to help Elliott to his feet and over to the body.

"He look kinda funny to you?" Elliott asked, wincing with every step.

De Laurac had not fallen to the ground. His body had stopped mid-way. He looked as if he was bowed in prayer. His head, what was left of it, hung limply from his torn neck.

Elliott eased himself down to the ground, carefully avoiding the puddle of bloody snow, for a closer look. "I'll be damned! Simone, look at this!"

Simone squatted down and pulled aside the loose flap of the dead man's coat. She took a sharp breath in, then turned and looked up the slope opposite where the second Frenchman stood on a finger of rock that jutted sharply out from the ravine wall—a silent sentinel of ancient justice.

The arrow had completely penetrated de Laurac's body. A sharp protrusion held the cloth of his jacket out like some dreadful tent.

"Well, I reckon he's dead now," Elliott commented mildly. He put his hand on the body's shoulder and pushed it over.

The new snow beneath the ruined head turned bright red. The two stared at it, remembering the pain the man had caused for a brief moment, before turning and walking away. Sicarius met them at the end of the ravine, offered Elliott the bow to use as a cane and led them back to rejoin their friends.

No more words were spoken.

66

Serena sat alone and silent in the cave. The small fire had been stoked, more wood added, until its flames licked the low ceiling. Warm air sat heavily, no fresh currents stirred the cloying atmosphere. Her long hair hung down her back in a single braid. A light, filmy material was draped around her body, fashioned into an ancient style of dress that sat in elegant folds across her still limbs. A brass clip in the design of a raven, its wings outstretched on either side of her shoulder, held the two ends of the cloth together. A snake-like torque circled her head. Its two ends met in the center of her forehead. Her skin was pale but shone with a warm luster in the dim light. Her feet were tattooed with an intricate design that circled around but never crossed or overlapped, the lines appearing to ripple across her skin. A small black snake lay wrapped around her left wrist, its head resting on the back of her hand.

She stared into the flames at the twisting, twirling shapes that waited, as did she, for the coming of Ouroboros and its Bearer.

67

Professor Irene Flemming was a small woman. Her quiet demeanor and the perpetually distracted air that clung to her hid a passionate nature. A nature that required constant challenges and thrived on solving puzzles; striving to reach a single goal.

The professor was a seeker of the truth: that gray, somewhat blurred ideal that explained life and God and everything in between. She'd thought she'd found it on many occasions. Or at least had been close, but it had continually evaded her, slipping through her fingers like the dry dust that coated the mountains of text and old manuscripts she buried herself in. The trail often led to distant archaeological sites and remote villages where she'd spend hours listening to the stories, or on her hands and knees sifting through yet more dust. Again and again, the doors that she was certain led to the ultimate truth would slam shut in her head. The clear path would fade away and her goal would elude her once more.

Then it occurred to her that the path always skirted the same group of legends, each of the closed doors was amazingly similar when looked at in the right light. She collected her notes and thoughts and began to retrace the path she'd been following, going back over the years and concentrating on the minor details she'd skimmed on previous excursions. She traveled along every side alley her notes led her to and eventually came up with a picture that, though sketchy and entirely unprovable at best, was astoundingly obvious once she let go of the academic ropes that tied down her imagination. And it all centered on the myth of the Holy Grail.

Irene had investigated the Grail many years ago only to find her strong leads turning, like everything else, to dust in her hands. Her basement was full of artifacts: numerous cups and chalices, plaques and holy relics, an unusual spear that was said to belong to the mysterious Mordred, bastard son of King Arthur. They were packed away in crates awaiting eventual shipment to a museum. The side alleys in her current research all led back to the Grail in ways so minor, she would have missed them again if they were not the very things she was look-ing for. A word here and there, and then popping up again somewhere entirely different. Irene went back to the Grail to study the dust and found the light.

Her trip to France was to track down the story of Montsegur where hundreds of Cathars were burnt to death, their leaders stoned for her-esy in a power struggle that drove the Cathars and many others under-ground. Stories abounded about the treasures they had hidden, the secrets they guarded; among them was a vague reference to the Holy Vine and Cup—the Grail. She wasn't interested in the treasures, only in the stories that went with them. In the stories, she knew, were the keys to unlocking some of those doors in her head.

She spent her first month in Tolosa listening to the usual legends offered up to the public and then found a guide whose family had always been guides in the region to take her to the caves of the Sabar-thes where the Cathars had allegedly buried their treasures. She found no traces of treasures that day, not even much in the way of stories from her taciturn guide.

What she did find was a drawing on a rock wall depicting a tree, its branches heavily laden with what looked like stars. The tree stood in the middle of nine concentric circles. A snake was entwined around the trunk and branches, its body adorned with unusual markings. She copied the picture into her notebook and made an extra note of the wedge-shaped marks on the snake.

"What is this picture?" she asked the guide.

"It is the Elbe," the man had answered. "A myth the old people tell the young and foolish."

The professor had been called foolish many times. That night she visited the old storytellers and took one more step closer to the truth.

In the village of the Elbe, hidden beneath the eternal Forest of the Stars, Irene waited to take another step toward her goal. She looked over to where the staff she'd brought to the village stood with three others. She remembered the day she'd discovered it, an old gift from her sister, leaning in a forgotten corner of her basement. It had stood guard over a box of yellowed manuscripts for three years, until the day she'd read the *Desposyni* in New Orleans and rushed home to go through the old book.

She'd been reading a description of an ancient papyrus, the text itself now worn with age. The papyrus, found discarded and forgotten among the papers of a dead village scribe in the foothills of the Zagros Mountains of Iran, told of the sacred objects of the Messeh—the Sacred Dragon of the Annunaki—from the land between the rivers. It listed them all, describing them in perfect detail. Professor Flemming had read it all before, the Ring of Unity, the Orb of Knowing and the Staffs of Kiskanu, the Tree of Life.

Her whole body stilled as she reread the description of the Staffs of Kiskanu and then her eyes travelled to the object that she'd just propped against one of the many crates.

The Spear of Mordred was not a spear at all. She picked up the staff and wiped it clean with a handkerchief. Her hands tingled with a raw energy that faded as soon as she hastily put it back down. She contemplated the staff before retrieving it once more and finished cleaning it, polishing it with the cloth until it gleamed. The top end of the staff was carved with the body of a snake tightly coiled around the rod, its skin covered in the same wedge-shaped marks as the Elbe snake in the Sabarthes's cave.

Irene had recognized the marks as cuneiform, one of the first known methods of writing and Sumerian in origin. An acquaintance had translated the marks, telling her that it was an endless repetition of one term—Shimti. It meant breath/wind/life. She flipped through her notebook to the page that explained the meaning and held a diagram of each cuneiform mark, then examined the snake more closely. Its body was a mass of circles rippling outward. On its head was a single wedge-shaped mark—the symbol that meant "ti" or "life". Protruding from the snake's mouth was what the professor had previously thought of as a rather unusual spearhead. Now, looking at it afresh, she realized it was a nine-pointed star of clear crystal, its longest point elongated to resemble a spear.

The dreams started that night, of serpents and dragons, crows and glowing orbs of light, a vague and distant threat, valleys of wildflowers, a young man lost. Less than a week later she was on her way to a mythical hidden land to meet a race of people that had been lost in history.

Whichever name they were given, they were the Sidhe. The Watchers descended from Above, the People of the Web—and their people were the Elbe.

She'd arrived in Elphane, guided through the mountains by Eliana, to find she wasn't the only Staff Bearer. The Staffs of Kinkasu numbered four. Sh/breath, Im/wind, Ti/life were three. The fourth was "Ayin", a triangle with a round orb in its center. Ayin represented the Eye of Illumination, the doorway to the light.

The four staffs stood, stars pointing to the sky on either side of a large gleaming onyx circle. Its sides were smooth except for four holes opposite each other. The base of the circle sat on a granite block sunk into the ground and large enough to accommodate a small gathering of people. The professor didn't know the purpose of the circle or the staffs, only that the villagers were tight-lipped about some things and all too eager to talk about others. They, as well as she, were waiting.

She'd thought they were waiting for the arrival of the last staff, and they were, but afterward the waiting game continued. Then an old man everyone called Aiden arrived with a friend. They too waited.

Irene remembered Arwium from her dreams and greeted her enthusiastically when she showed up one evening, walking into the village center as if she'd only been out strolling. She thought that if she was home then surely the wait was over, but she had ensconced herself in the Cave of the Stars with one of the Elbe, a strangely quiet woman that talked in whispers and only to Arwium or Eliana. When the latter had left, the woman had fallen completely silent.

But the wait was not over and the days passed.

A vigil began. Nine villagers, sitting evenly spaced around the large circle and the four staffs, repeated a litany of ancient words that spoke of life and renewal, blood and sacrifice. Words the professor often found surprisingly familiar and bringing to mind many of the books, songs and poetry of modern literature.

Irene listened, mesmerized, not noticing the passing of time, until the chanting stopped. The nine villagers stood and turned toward the path that cut through the forest. Arwium had appeared and now stood behind the stone circle. A dark cloak covered her from head to foot, a hood hanging low over her face. Only the nape of her neck and the feathery edges of the loose hair that framed her face were visible. She too stared toward the path. Irene followed her steady gaze, standing beside the staff she had brought home, and waited.

And as the light began to dim at the end of another day, she saw movement where the trail disappeared amid the trees. The movement became shadows and then the dark outline of people. One in particular seemed to stand out more than the others, bathed in a faint aura of shimmering light. *The Bearer of Ouroboros* ... even her thoughts were hushed.

As the group approached, the professor knew that the long wait was over.

68

Of all the people Dan Tenney had known throughout his life, he didn't count himself as among those select few that were special, people who made a difference in the grand scheme of things. He strove to live up to the standards of a long dead mother, fought hard to fit in with the people he knew and worked with, whether as part of the Byrd & Somers team, or in the more lonely profession of photographer. He endeavored to meet the grade at every turn in his friendship with Nick Somers. Most of the time, he did this without conscious thought, never once realizing that he was as much a touchstone in the lives of others as they were to him. Dan never thought of himself as special in any way and he didn't want to be.

Even as he approached the village, his walk slowing until he'd stopped before the gathered people, he didn't think they were there for him. It was the damn ring they were waiting for. But the ring wasn't all there was.

His mother had known. From the day of his conception, all through her pregnancy and the first five years of his life, until her death and beyond. She had known. She had met the man who would be the father he never knew while hiking through the Mogollans on a search for Indian artifacts. He'd shown her secret caves, explained mysterious paintings on the walls, offered her water from clear springs, and in the deepest part where it was cool and dark, he had given her a gift. Stars painted on the cave ceiling were their night sky, the heavy branches of a tree etched into the wall their guardian, and a coiled snake carved into the floor their bed. Their clothes dropped to the ground, their bodies twisted and entwined around each other as they'd made love. Her hand reached out and caressed the unseen head of the snake, her fingers brushing over its carved brow.

Shimti, her unknowing fingers traced as she called out her passion. Her back arched and her eyes closed as a silver mist curled around her, shimmered against her body and evaporated into her skin. She felt cold and hot at the same time as the Starfire mist traveled to her center and filled her with a love so complete she would need no other to replace it, a love she would share with her precious son even after her own death. When she awoke, the man was gone but she was not alone and never would be again.

Dan stood at the edge of the village not knowing any of this. He was just relieved it was all coming to an end. He fumbled with the collar of his coat and shirt, searching for the chain around his neck. Aiden stepped up beside him to guide him through the thin crowd of people.

"What's going on?" Dan asked the old man, twisting back to see the rest of the group right behind him.

Aiden looked at the darkening sky. It had taken a full day to hike through the forest after spending the night camped on the banks of the river. He grunted in a half-laugh. "Even in Elphane, time runs short eventually. See that moon?" He nodded to where the silver light of the moon was just beginning to highlight the mountain range. "You have to put the ring in place at exactly the right moment."

"Then what?" Dan asked suspiciously, pulling back on the man's tight grip.

Aiden sighed. "We don't ask for any more than you are prepared to give, any more than you are capable of."

"Isn't that Professor Flemming over there?" Pete said behind them.

They all turned to where the gathering of people had parted to reveal the center of the village. The professor came forward, a tentative smile on her face, and greeted them.

"Gentlemen, Madam, I heard you've been looking for me."

"Yeah, right. Leave a note next time," Elliott muttered.

"Can we get this over with?" said Nick.

Dan's face tightened with concern; handing over the circlet he'd carried so far was not his only task. He was expected to do something else. Confidence eased through his mind and body, and it occurred to him that whatever was left, he could and would see this quest to the end.

"Just a minute," Simone interrupted. "I think we should find out just what Dan is required to do. I, for one, am heartily sick of surprises."

"It's okay, Simone," Dan assured her. "I'm ready."

His words resonated with the memory of others that had uttered the same phrase before facing their fate head on. Finn's fists tightened as he heard Eliana's voice whispering in the night air, repeating her willingness to give everything for the quest.

Rose sobbed. She'd barely spoken a word since the cave-in. "Be careful what you say, Dan. They take 'service and sacrifice' very seriously here." She held his hand a moment before letting him go on.

Dan walked, unaided this time, to the huge stone circle and the cloaked woman who waited for him.

"I welcome yee back."

"Back?" he asked, stepping up to the circle.

Arwium nodded and raised her hands. A ball of light appeared in her palms. In it, Dan could see those who had come before him as the Bearer of Ouroboros, the Ring of Unity. *Not that many*, he thought and hoped that wasn't a reflection of the success rate of his current position. Had so few made it to the end?

"This isn't the end," Arwium said. "It's the beginning."

"A new ripple in the pond," Dan added.

Arwium lifted her hands to the hood still covering her face and pushed it back. The sleeves of the cloak slipped back to reveal two snakes encircling her arms. Around her wrists were bronze bands, each set with a large nine-pointed crystal. A similar band circled her head. Where it crossed her brow, another crystal was set, but instead of the clear star, it was the blood red body of a spider. Dan stared at it, fascinated. The spider was modeled in the action of spinning a web. Fine silver strands came from its body and spread over the woman's head, weaving through her dark hair in a gossamer web that continued down her neck and disappeared under the heavy cloak.

Behind them, the moon crept higher.

"Who are you?" Dan asked.

"Arwium, daughter of Tiamet."

"Who am I?"

She looked at him quizzically for a moment before answering. "The Bearer of Ouroboros, the Ring of Unity and Blessing of Creation. The Father of Faith and son of Sidhe."

"Am I s'posed to know what that means?"

Her shrug was artless and he decided not to push the point, sure that it would only lead to more questions.

"Step up to the doorway."

Dan pulled off his hat and gloves and handed them to whoever stood beside him. It was Pete who, without a word, took Dan's things and held them tightly as he watched the strange proceedings. He'd snuck up close enough to hear every word the pair had spoken.

"Pete, get back!" Elliott growled from somewhere behind him.

Pete ignored him, moving closer instead.

The four Staff Bearers stepped up to the circle as well, waiting until Dan was standing opposite Arwium, only the black stone coming between them. The Bearers pulled the staffs from the ground and raised them higher to the sky. Moonlight caught in the crystal stars and formed a soft pattern of light over those below.

Pete wanted to touch the light, but the weight of Elliott's hand on his shoulder held him back. It just as suddenly lifted and Elliott was standing beside him as the light began to flicker and grow in an ever-widening circle. Without looking, Pete knew that Nick too had drawn closer, and that Finn and Simone were also lining up beside him.

The Staff Bearers approached the stone circle. The first, a tall woman of athletic build, her hair cropped short, dark skin glowing in the brightening moonlight, came right up to the onyx circle and inserted the base of her staff into one of the small holes cut into the stone. She pushed the staff straight through until the end protruded from the outer edge then stepped back to stand beside Finn. The second Bearer repeated the first's actions followed by the third and fourth.

The moon had breached the mountain range by the time the Staffs of Kinkasu were in place, their crystal heads glittering with reflected light. A low murmur came from the gathered people and Pete saw Aiden and Roshen move forward, the practical hiking gear they'd been wearing now gone, replaced by the same heavy style of cloak that Arwium wore. They pushed their hoods back as they reached the circle. Bronze bands encircled their heads. The silver strands of the web shone in their dark hair. Seeing them altogether, Pete noticed how close in likeness the three were.

"They are the children of Tiamet."

Pete jumped to hear Irene's voice in his ear; he hadn't known she was standing so close.

"You were wondering about them?"

"Yes," Pete whispered.

"Once there were nine."

"Where are the others?"

"The eldest joined with Enki to create the Kiskanu Tree of Life and Wisdom. The four staffs come from that tree. They hold the spirit of both Lilith and Enki."

"Was Enki one of Tiamet's children?"

"No, he was her brother. The next child, Lulawa, joined with the son of Enki to create the Sangreal. On her passing her spirit became one with Ouroboros. Thereafter, on each subsequent presentation of the ring, one of the children has joined with the spirit of their sister."

The remaining three children of Tiamet unclasped their cloaks, letting them fall to the ground. The silver webs stretched from their hair to the breastplates they wore. Each breastplate was made in the shape of a raven, its head and beak reaching to the left shoulder. The web met the glossy beaks, wrapping around them to continue down and entwine through the black feathers. The wings stretched around their torsos, the tips joining in the middle of their backs. The body of the birds hung down in front, the tail feathers reaching to the knees. The silver web wrapped around their bodies, gathering at the wing tips and hanging free in delicate folds to brush the ground.

Roshen had taken a place beside Arwium and Aiden. The three raised their arms and the four staffs slid into their proper place, their ends flush with the stone surface, their sharp points almost meeting in the center of the giant circle. Dan unclasped the chain around his neck and removed the circlet: Enki's gift to humanity. He could feel it humming with expectancy. He raised it and placed it between the four points. As soon as the key was in place, the crystal stars flashed with the brilliance of the moon and shot four beams of light through the ring.

"The Mark of Cain," Pete whispered hoarsely.

"And so the union of Qayin and Lulawa was blessed," Irene intoned, her voice now carrying across the clearing. "At one with the land. From the breath of life and the waters of sacred Starfire, the chosen ones will save us all."

"Ati Me Peta Babka!"

A brilliant white light burst from the ring and engulfed the four Staff Bearers on either side. Everyone else threw their arms up to protect their eyes from the glare.

"Peta Babkama Luruba Anaku!"

Pete took another step closer.

Dan collapsed to the ground in pain as every muscle contracted in. His vision blurred to nothing but the light, his stomach knotted, his toes and fingers curled, his heart raced. His mouth was wide open to scream a sound that never came, then he heard someone call his name, hands pulling at his arms and head. He stared transfixed at the light that consumed every fiber of his being.

In Elphane, time moved slower, it followed a different pattern. The shimmering moon had bathed the town of Smiggins' Rest six nights previously. Within that surge of energy from the ring, time was slower still. In that moment, time stopped altogether for Dan Tenney.

When the light flashed through the star crystals, Pete reacted. Seeing the shadowy figure of Dan falling, he ran directly into the ball of pure energy. The light and the power engulfed him as it did the others and threw him into a maelstrom that he was entirely unprepared for. He reached out for Dan, struggling against the roaring around him. He felt nothing of the exquisiteness that Dan had experienced, did not notice the delicate shimmer of light on the edge of his vision, or feel the slow beat of the earth as he became one with the land and fire of creation. Dan knew all of these things. Pete knew only the horror of untimely death.

69

The landscape changed from mountainous to completely flat. Grassland surrounded them on all sides and for as far as the eye could see. The sky glimmered a deep blue. Not a single cloud marred its surreal perfection.

"Where are we?" Dan's voice vibrated in the air, the sound lingering suspended by some unseen force.

"The Plains of Shar-on," Arwium answered. "We have stepped through the Ayin."

Dan looked at her with a frown.

"The Door of Enlightenment," she explained. "We are in the world of the Orb."

"Orb?" Dan moved away and looked around, a sudden vision of a burning orb filling his senses. He'd dreamed about it before and being here now gave him an almost overpowering sense of déjà vu. "I …" he started to say, halted by the sudden realization that his feet were incredibly warm. The earth beneath him was growing uncomfortably hot. He looked back at Aiden and Arwium in alarm, the words dying on his lips. The silver web that covered their bodies seemed to be moving, creeping around their arms and legs. The eyes of their bird-shaped breastplates winked in the changing light.

Dan's feet tingled with the energy rising from the ground. He stole a look down, not knowing what he expected to see but immensely relieved to find his scuffed hiking boots, looking as normal as they should, and a flattened circle of ordinary grass beneath them. He felt a strange calm take hold of him as he looked into the composed face of the mysterious woman. "What do we do now?"

Arwium bowed her head sadly and raised one hand, palm upward to gesture to a spot in the grass behind Dan. He turned and the calm drained away.

"Pete!" He rushed to the fallen man, dropping to his knees to pull him up into his lap. "Pete?"

Pete's face was white, dirt smudged one cheek. His lips were parted but no breath was drawn in. His body was cold as ice.

Dan turned a ravaged face back to the trio who had remained as statues, their heads bowed, their hands joined lightly together. "This is a trick, isn't it? One of my stupid dreams?"

Dan bent over the body of his friend and gently pushed the hair from his face. "Dammit, Pete!"

He squeezed him tightly, then pushed both arms under the dead weight and awkwardly stood. The tingling in his feet spread to his knees and began to flow through his entire body, fuelled by the anger and grief that racked his soul. He clenched his teeth against the faltering strength in his legs, determination and pure stubbornness forcing him around to face the silent Sidhe.

"Answer me, dammit!" he growled but they kept the silence.

Dan lifted his face to the perfect sky and yelled, "Nooo!"

His voice was so loud it echoed across the plains, rippling through the grass in a wave of rage. The sensations in his body grew but where just a few moments ago he'd felt weak, now he felt strong. He yelled again and the air around the trio flinched back, a flash of blackness outlined their figures. The space between them grew heavy with growing darkness.

Dan strode forward, his friend growing lighter in his arms, to push past the still figures and stand in the center of the circle they formed.

"You can fix this. He doesn't need to die. This serves none of your weird fucking purposes!"

Arwium raised her head, her green eyes full of regret and sorrow. "Every death serves a purpose."

"Not this one! You made a mistake! Not this one!"

"We did not cause his death, but it is in within you to change his fate."

"Me? How? Tell me what I have to do. I'll do it!"

The three held each other's hands a little tighter. It was Roshen who spoke next. "A life is forfeited this night, its soul released to be renewed in the Grail."

"Are you ready to meet your destiny?" Aiden asked.

Dan looked at each of them and then down at Pete. "It wasn't meant to be him," he whispered.

The tingling had turned to an urgent stinging. His blood was on fire, every hair on his body quivered with the energy coursing through him. Dan's dark eyes narrowed in a glaring squint and his mouth became a set line. "Damn you all," he hissed.

The energy burst from his hands and into Pete, forcing life back into the limp body. Dan sank to his knees as Pete began to buck and heave in his arms, and laid him carefully on the ground. Dan hurt now, the life flowing from his body to Pete, giving the other man the energy he needed to live again, giving whatever was necessary to make it so.

Pete groaned and a shudder ran through his body. He opened his eyes and looked up to see Dan grinning down at him.

"Hey."

"Is it over?" Pete croaked.

"Sure thing, Pete."

And then everything went black.

All that the villagers and Questors saw was a bright flash of light and Pete falling to the ground.

"What the hell's he doin' over there?" Elliott yelled. "Pete!"

Elliott ran toward him. An explosion of colored light stopped him in his tracks, forcing him back the few steps he'd managed and down to the ground. When he jumped back up, Pete was kneeling in the spot he'd been laying and Dan Tenney had taken his place in death.

The voices of the people hushed, the only sounds now came from the breeze in the trees and the heavy breathing of the shocked group. Elliott grabbed Pete, twisting around to look into his white face and check him over for injury.

Pete's face was horrified and disbelieving. "Elliott?" he muttered almost incoherently. "I wondered … I wondered why I was here … Look what I've done. It … Dan …"

"It's okay, Pete. It'll be okay," Elliott told him, his hands squeezing the man's shoulder. "Oh, God!"

Nick forgot about his broken arm and bruised ribs as he rushed beside them, transfixed by the sight of Dan laying face down on the ground, unmoving. He didn't want to believe the possibility of his friend's death, didn't want to touch him and find that it was true. The familiar jacket was crumpled and dirty. It had seen better days before any of this had happened. *Now it looks as dead as him.*

The upturned collar and fur-lined hood hid Dan's long hair. His moleskin jeans were stained with dirt and grass, legs drawn up beneath him as if he were caught in the process of trying to stand. Nick looked at the mud-encrusted boots; long stems of grass were stuck in the thick ooze. He sank to his knees and reached out to touch Dan's shoulder.

"No …" Pete started to say.

Arwium and Roshen came up to stand behind them, solemnly looking on the scene. Nick took in their grave faces. *Something's not right.*

He looked around. *Where's …* His gaze landed back on Pete.

"It's not Dan, Nick. It's Aiden."

Nick turned the body over and stared dumbfounded at Aiden Gabran. It had looked so much like Dan lying there he could hardly believe that it wasn't after all. He shook his head and looked again: it was clearly Gabran and not Dan Tenney.

"Where's Dan?" Nick stood and faced Arwium and Roshen. "What the fuck is going on here and where's Dan?"

Dan rolled to his side, dazed and confused. *What's new with that?* He blinked, his eyelids scraping down over dry eyes. He continued to blink until tears formed and washed away the hot grittiness and he could distinguish dimly lit shapes in front of him.

Light from a fire threw strange patterns across his vision. He couldn't understand what had happened. One minute he'd felt the life draining out of him and into Pete, his world at that point had been just the other man and himself, joined as one for the briefest moment. Then another had joined them. The intensity increased tenfold, the third presence exploding inside them, all around them, and they were pushed out and away.

Pete? Dan felt a moment of worry before the image of Pete being held in Elliott's arms, alive and well, swam before him. *What happened?*

He flexed his fingers experimentally, stretched his bare feet and straightened his legs. Rolling to his stomach, he placed his hands underneath him and pushed till he was up on shaky knees.

"Are you all right?" a soft voice asked him.

His head whipped around toward the unexpected voice; his eyes widened at seeing a familiar figure seated just a few feet away. "Eliana?"

"No. My name is Serena," the woman corrected. "Her sister. There is a cloak there for you to put on."

Dan realized he was naked, and reached for the coarse cloth that lay folded beside him. He spread it out and flicked it over his shoulders, holding the edges together in front as he stood, walking over to where she sat cross-legged on a rag rug by the fire. "Where are we?"

"The Cave of the Stars," she answered, staring into the fire.

"I don't understand what's happening. How did I get here?" He gathered the cloak up a little higher and sat down beside her. The rug was soft beneath him, comfortable. The tension in his body began to ease away.

"There's no time for questions. You've made it and that is all that matters for now."

Up close, she didn't look quite so much like her sister. Serena was thinner, her face drawn with grief. Perspiration ran down its edges. Her hair, a shade or two lighter than Eliana's and much longer, was damp where it met her skin, wispy tendrils curled around her ears. She was a little younger, Dan noticed and sadder. "You know about her?"

"Yes, I do."

"I'm sorry. We couldn't save her," he said, not knowing what else to say.

A tear escaped her eyes. "So am I," she whispered. "But I will have her with me again soon."

Dan frowned, not understanding and not quite liking her choice of words, but Serena turned aside and said no more. He watched the supple play of the light material that covered her as she moved to reach for something beside her. The cloth hid very little and he felt a warmth that didn't come from the fire growing inside him as the light slid over her bare skin. She turned back to him, holding a wooden goblet and a plate of food.

Serena sipped from the goblet then handed it to him. "Drink," she urged. "It's mead. It will help refresh you." She placed the plate on the mat between them and pushed it gently toward him, then took a small piece of the cheese and bread for herself. "Eat."

Dan lifted the cup to his lips, inhaling deeply of the heady aroma lifting up from its liquid contents. The warmed mead was thick and sweet. It filled his mouth and slid smoothly down his throat.

He took a long draught, offered the cup back for Serena to take another sip herself and watched her tongue come out to lick the sweetness from her lips. The bread and cheese melted in his mouth, the combination of flavors mingling sensually on his tongue. He drank some more and ate the rest of the food, his head buzzing pleasantly by the time he was finished.

Serena watched him eat, her eyes now fixed on the curve of his jaw as he chewed on the food, the line of his cheekbone, the glittering light of his eyes. She pulled the empty goblet from his hands and leaned forward to hover close to his face.

Then she pulled away, put the goblet back in its original place and picked up a small leather bottle. She uncorked and poured a deep red oily substance onto the palm of her hand, pushed the cloak from Dan's shoulders and began rubbing the oil into his skin. Heat spread across his chest as her hands moved softly, almost fluttering at times, against him. Aching muscles eased; pain faded. His mouth went dry as her hands slowly traveled down his body.

"I've been waiting for you." Her voice was warm and soft.

He reached up to touch the band around her head. The metal was surprisingly cool on her hot skin. He lifted it, tracing the indentation it left on her forehead with his thumb. Serena lifted her head level with Dan and his hand slipped down to cup her face, drawing her closer.

"I'm here."

Nick watched the moonlight defract off the ring and crystal stars to shine directly into the mouth of a cave. He wasn't sure if he could believe Arwium and Roshen that Dan was safe.

The beam of light started to break up as the moon rose to its full height in the night sky. The soft tread of boots on hard ground warned him that someone was approaching.

"You should get some rest," Finn said, sitting down beside him.

"I know it."

"How's the arm?"

Nick gave Finn a crooked smile, despite the weariness and worry. "Still flapping."

"After that medicine of Aiden's, I'm surprised you're not flying."

Nick laughed. "That stuff'd make us a fortune on the streets. I was feelin' mighty good there for awhile."

"We know it," Finn replied.

Nick had been exceedingly happy during the climb up to the arch after taking another dose of the herbal painkiller, even greeting Elliott, Simone and Sicarius with a wide smile when they returned from "handling" de Laurac.

"What's he on and where can I get some?" Elliott had said on seeing his old friend as high as a kite. The pair had enjoyed the walk down to the valley immensely, singing old songs as they held each other up and rehashing old jokes and stories all the way.

Finn shook his head as their laughter faded away and their faces grew somber once more.

"Is this it?" Nick asked.

Finn paused before answering to let his thoughts even out into a pattern he could recognize, but they had followed so many twists and turns since starting on this journey the words he wanted to say escaped him.

"It?" he said, struggling to share with Nick what he felt. "No, this isn't it, just part of it. I think there's far more to this than we'll ever know."

"No beginnings, no ends," Nick said morosely. "Isn't that what they keep saying?"

"Their concept of time is somewhat different to ours …"

"Their concept of everything is different to ours."

Finn grinned again. "It certainly is."

"For us though, is this it? Do I get to go back to work in a few days and follow Mr. Leary and his secretary around town again? Do you go back to the university? Maybe make an honest woman of Simone?"

"That's none of your business." Simone said, joining them. "I'm looking forward to a few mundane stake-outs and reports after this. Though I can't think how we're going to write any of this up."

"I don't know," Nick said, giving her a pointed look. "You'll think of something, Simone. How about, Byrd & Somers Inc. helped save the world. On the way we broke, lost or generally damaged nearly every bit of equipment we possess and sustained numerous injuries to others and ourselves. The collapsing mountain was definitely not our fault."

Simone chuckled. "I'll get to work on it as soon as I get back from my trip to the Caribbean." She ignored Nick's derisive snort. "In the meantime, Elliott sent me to drag you two back to the charming little cottages we've been billeted to. He has a pot of some ghastly concoction brewing over the fire though, so I wouldn't rush right back."

"When do we find out what this was all for? Really for?"

"Right now," Finn said standing up. "Irene has filled me in and I'll tell you on the way back."

Nick threw a last look back at the cave and stood as well. The three started slowly walking through the village.

"The ring was created on Cain's birth and presented to him on his joining to the eldest daughter of Tiamet. That joining resulted in the birth of the Sangreal, the holy bloodline. Later, the ring was presented again to Mary and Joseph on their joining. The ring is a gift to the child born of these pre-ordained joinings—the Chosen One, who will lead the people along the path of wisdom and compassion."

"This is the start of the Second Coming?" Simone asked in disbelief.

"More like the seventh. Tiamet had nine children. Every time the ring is passed on one of them joins their spirit to the ring. Arwium and Roshen are the last two."

"The ring is given to the parents to give to the child?" Nick stopped moving as he spoke and stared back in the direction of the cave.

"Exactly. It is both a key and a symbol. The child is conceived in a joining ceremony right after the door or gateway is open, and then passed on to the child."

"You're saying that Dan's in there with a woman?"

"Yes."

Nick shook his head and ran his hand through his hair as he turned back and continued walking. "All this for a quick ..."

"They've been waiting for this for a long time. I don't think it's going to be quick at all."

The three were laughing as they reached the small hut they'd been given for the duration of their stay. Simone pushed the door open and ushered Nick and Finn through. "Hark, the Questors have returned from their vigil. It seems the good Sir Dan doth not require our assistance any further this night, or possibly for a good part of tomorrow either."

The door closed behind them, muffling the sounds of laughter and conversation that continued on late into the night. It was nearly dawn of a new day before sleep came and carried them all into a world where the impossible became possible, the unreal became real and a new Messiah walked the streets to save them all.

70

Dan sat on the low slope of a rising hill, the first of many that led down to the fields of wildflowers where he always seemed to return. Soft breezes sifted through the grass swishing it like silk in ever-changing swirls of green and yellow. This part of the Plains of Shar-on was known as Shinar. The gardens of the long lost city of Eridu, where differing planes of reality met and co-existed in perfectly blended harmony.

A giant serpent of black and silver lay around him. Its body, warm from the sun, pressed up against his back. Its tail lay, almost possessively, over his feet. Dan could feel its ribs move as it breathed, could feel its muscles twitching.

"I like it here," he said. "Peaceful."

"No war has ever stained the Plains of Shar-on or the Gardens of Eridu," the serpent told him.

"Thought this place wasn't real." Dan twisted around to look at the serpent's smooth, glossy head.

Its forked tongue flicked out, tasting the air. "It is like Elphane. Here, but not."

Dan raised one eyebrow. "Yeah, that explains it."

The serpent made a strange, stilted hissing sound. Dan thought it might be laughing.

"Will there be a child?"

"Yes."

He looked away, happy with the thought of impending fatherhood. At the bottom of the slope a river cut through the grasses, twisting and winding like a snake through the gently sloping land. Serena waded along its shallow banks, her long hair loose and falling across her face as she leaned over to splash the water with her hand.

"What happens now?" he asked.

"The baby will be raised in Elphane for awhile. It will run through the grasses of Shinar and play in the sacred river. It will grow in mind, body and spirit until such time as it is ready to begin its own journey."

"And then?"

"Faith will return to the world."

"So this is it for me?"

The serpent raised its head and rubbed its body along Dan's legs. Its tongue brushed his ear. "You are welcome to stay and help guide the child. She will need her father," it hissed.

"I think I'd like that. What about the dreams… nightmares?"

"I do not know."

Dan rose to his feet and walked down to the river. Serena straightened, waiting for him to reach her. Together they followed the river down until they reached the banks of flowers, somewhere along the way their hands clasped. They lay down on a bed of vivid color, disappearing from sight. Their soft voices could be heard mingled with moans of delight as they followed their joined destinies.

"You didn't answer his question truthfully," the spirit of a dead woman said softly beside the serpent.

"Don't you have a rebirth to prepare for?" the serpent asked her. "Your sister misses you terribly."

The spirit laughed. "I'm on my way," she said in her usual low voice. "But still … Is this it?"

Tiamet watched the butterflies flitter above the man and woman, her children. Her sibilant whisper followed the spirit down to the field.

"For now."

ACKNOWLEDGMENTS

There are always a lot of people to thank and acknowledge with the producing of any creative work. This novel has been such a long time coming that the list of people who have been helpful and insightful along the way just might be longer than the story. So let me keep it simple. To my husband, Craig: thank you for your continual support whether you understood my creative urges or not. To Cheyne, Kalin, and Toni, who grew up knowing when not to interrupt mummy and who think just about everything I do is amazing: thank you. To my extended family and friends: thanks for putting up with my daydreaming. To those people who helped mold this story into readability: hearty thanks to you as well.

Vacen Taylor, a great big thanks for putting me on to Odyssey Books. And to Michelle Lovi, my publisher and editor, what can I say? Without your vision my dream might never have become reality. Thank you from the bottom of my heart.

ABOUT THE AUTHOR

A Sydney writer who grew up by the beach, Patricia Leslie spent six months as an exchange student in the Rocky Mountains of Colorado and has been fascinated by mountains, and what they might be hiding, ever since. The idea for *The Ouroboros Key* came from her interest in myths and the connections they have with history and religion as we know it. Every country has their own worldview; every culture their own truths. If you go back far enough, you just might find that many of these views and truths are the same.

Patricia also writes short stories with an historical edge and usually with a dash of the supernatural. She lives with her family south of Sydney where she plots and plans her next novel and the inevitable research trip that will be required. Coincidently, it will be set in France, a country she's always wanted to wander through.

Connect with Patricia:
Facebook: www.facebook.com/pages/Patricia-Leslie/155557924596429
Twitter: @PatriciaLeslieA
Website: patricialeslieauthor.wordpress.com